BEARING WORD

LIU LIANGCHENG

BEARING WORD

Translated from the Chinese by
Jeremy Tiang

BALESTIER PRESS
LONDON · SINGAPORE

Balestier Press
Centurion House, London TW18 4AX
www.balestier.com

Bearing Word
Original title: 捎话
Copyright © Liu Liangcheng, 2013
English translation copyright © Jeremy Tiang, 2023

First published by Balestier Press in 2023
Published by arrangement with Yilin Press Ltd through
Beijing Gliese Culture and Media Co Ltd

A CIP catalogue record for this book is available from the British Library.

ISBN 978 1 913891 33 6

Cover design by Sarah and Schooling

CONTENTS

1

West Kun Temple

Flat

THROUGH A CRACK in the door, a flat pagoda. Behind the pagoda, a flat courtyard wall. Flat Kun devotees sitting around the pagoda. Flat smoke rising from the censers. The hum of chanted scripture, also flat, rising around the pagoda like dust, like fog, up to its glittering point, wrapping the whole structure in holy words. The sound gains a shape as it passes over the tower, forming a second pagoda above its pinnacle. A pagoda of sound erected atop the gilded earthly one. And still the voices rise, creating yet more pagodas. The higher they get, the flatter, the more insubstantial they become.

Each day she stands behind this door that has never been opened and stares through the crack, long and narrow as an eye. She can see the shape of sounds. In the first glimmers of dawn, Kun devotees sweep the fallen leaves below the pagoda, rustling like tree branches gently waving through the air. They know they are sweeping the leaves of noise, and unhurriedly wield their needlegrass brooms so each sound can depart in its fullness. From the village to the east, a cock crows like the fine stitching of a cassock. At dawn each day, its cry casts a sheet of golden gauze over the temple. To the north, the dogs of Pisha City bark in blocks, *wnng wnng*, each a brick flung from afar, only to flatten as it arcs overhead and turn into a leaf, drifting around the pagoda being constructed from chanted scripture, and then over the desert wastes now glimmering in daylight, fading to almost nothing before a dog barks in the village below to receive it. One after another, village dogs bark connections across the land, all the way from the hills in the north to Heile in the west.

The donkey next to her often talks about Heile.

"After changing religion, they stopped eating donkey meat. A donkey can grow old there and not have to worry about getting slaughtered."

These words were borne by a Heile donkey to a country donkey carrying goods into the city, who stood outside the village braying the news to the next village, where another donkey passed it on even farther afield. In a single night, the information was brayed from Heile through Yengisar, Qusha, Siya, Guma, to all the villages big and small around Pisha City. The next morning, the country donkeys hurrying into the city murmured these words to their city cousins. The donkeys knew Heile and Pisha were at war, and news from Heile could only be whispered.

In the past, chanting from West Kun Temple used to reach other Kun temples in the villages and towns and cities, all the way to Sacred Tree Temple in Yengisar and Peach Blossom Temple in Heile. Nowadays, different sounds fill these buildings. With her long donkey ears, she detected right away that the scripture emanating from these temples was different now. The chanting from West Kun Temple is intercepted by other voices on the Pisha border, and must instead rise up into the sky, where it is flattened.

She presses her left eye to the crack for a spell, then switches to the right. People whom one eye has gotten used to appear strange again when viewed with the other. *If I keep waiting behind this door, the crack will grow larger until it's the size of the door, and I'll be able to walk right out. I'll sit quietly among the devotees as they chant, not saying a word, and they won't notice me.* She was already sitting here when she had the thought, she came here when the crack before her opened up. The crack in the rear opened and shut, and she was locked up in the enclosure, where she grew to be a young jenny.

She knows she's young, just a maiden. Her body and fur are growing. In this dark room, taller and broader than the donkey pen, she quietly stares for days on end through the crack in the door, flattening the outside world with her gaze.

Two people walk by. One is the man who takes care of her, Kunmen Virtue, or at least that's what the others call him. The other has a full beard on his long, flat face. At a second glance, he seems familiar. Where has she seen him before? She shuts her eyes to think and decides the second look must have reminded her of the first, as if a year passed while she blinked.

Beard stands at the base of the pagoda, staring up at its pinnacle. She *has* seen this upturned face somewhere.

Kunmen Virtue keeps going for a moment before turning back. When he sees Beard looking up at the pagoda, he tilts his head up too. His gaze is flat. Beard must see the hollow pagodas stacked atop this one. That's what she sees. From behind this long, narrow crack, she has watched the sound pagodas for countless mornings, and now someone else has seen them too. Suddenly stirred, blood rushes through her throat and her voice gallops like a donkey in heat.

Ahnng-jee—

Only half a bray, and her own cry startles her. It booms and swells to fill the whole room, spraying out through the crack in the door and other invisible crevices, echoing thunderously across the temple, confined by the courtyard walls, lofted by the many pagodas, suspended resplendently above. In Beard's vision, an enormous pagoda made from a donkey's bray abruptly manifests in mid-air. He must see it, above the one formed of chanted scripture, a donkey cry pagoda that's taller, brighter, wispier.

The devotees turn their heads mid-chant and see only two tightly closed doors, but not the crack or the eye behind it, nor her mouth snapping shut. Seeing is flat. She watches through the crack as the vast pagoda formed by her cry dissipates like smoke.

Tall

Dawn at West Kun Temple arrives halfway through the morning, and dusk in mid-afternoon. The tall courtyard walls shorten the day and lengthen the night. The sun stands above the rooftops as

Ku hurries from his home to the temple gate, but inside it has not yet risen, and the devotees sit in shadow at their morning lessons. There are five varieties of shadow in the temple: shadows from the walls, the pagoda, the crows, the devotees, and their chanting. The voice shadows rise above the walls, layering another wall atop it, word by word, sentence by sentence, taller and taller.

Ku enjoys early mornings at the temple. The early-rising devotees, the scripture translators and pilgrims from east and west sit in every corner, working at their morning chants in dozens of languages, a single Kun scripture in Pishanese, Kun, Heilenese, Huang, Chiu, each containing a different Kun. This temple has gathered translators from countries across the world, and here they will translate Kun scripture into their countless tongues. One scripture thus becomes many.

Ku is a frequent visitor. He can speak every language represented here, and when one of the languages in his brain gets lonely, he comes to West Kun Temple to find a speaker he can converse with. In the past, outsiders often passed through the city, and they would hire Ku to interpret for them. After Master passed away, no one knew more languages than Ku. Now Pisha and Heile are at war, and fewer merchants come from the west, but more devotees gather at West Kun Temple, and the chanting has grown more cacophonous, more avid.

Kunmen Virtue, who sent word summoning him here, waits by the gate, squinting, unwilling to expose his head to the sun. Yesterday evening, a man on donkeyback looked over the garden wall and shouted Ku's name, and his wife Sha opened the gate. Instead of dismounting, the man craned his neck and said quietly, "I bear word from West Kun Temple. The Great Kunmen requests your presence at dawn."

A message from the Great Kunmen meant something big was afoot. Ku departed the city at first light, and reached his destination when the sun was above the branches.

Kunmen Virtue looks half asleep, his gait and expression still lost in dreams. Ku follows him around the great hall and to the uneven paving stones that run between the pagodas. The whole compound is shrouded in thick shadows, and only the very tip of the tallest pagoda reaches the sunlight. Ku eyes its gleaming point. At thirty-six storeys, it's the tallest pagoda in Pisha. The other seventy-eight are overshadowed by the walls, this one alone surpasses them and thrusts into the morning sun.

The devotees must sit around the pagodas each morning reciting scripture. Their voices incanting in different languages are like three layers of gauze around each pagoda, rousing them. Ku thinks they look much taller than usual, as if the chanting is lifting them from below and up into the daylight.

"The Great Kunmen awaits you."

Virtue sounds as if he is talking in his sleep. He tilts his head up and stares in the direction as Ku.

Ahhnng . . . jee . . . A sudden bray.

The Kun devotees' heads swivel to look at the closed door, and Virtue runs towards the donkey. Ku remains with his face upturned. He sees the pagodas stretching up into the clouds from the commotion of the donkey's cry, before steadily falling back down to earth.

This is the first time Ku has heard a donkey in the temple. There shouldn't be donkeys here. There are rumours about a jenny and a Kun devotee. The Pisha worship Kun, and so placed all the blame on the donkey. Thus, donkeys gained a bad reputation. Even so, Kun devotees need donkeys for travel. Each of the Kunmen and the other leaders have their own animals and carts, while the other devotees share. On the hillside north of the temple, there are more than a hundred carts and several hundred donkeys for their exclusive use. The donkey yard used to be right by the rear gate, but it was moved downhill after the devotees complained about the noise.

Kun devotees hate their scripture chanting being interrupted by donkey cries. Braying covers the sound in the air, preventing their voices from reaching Kun. The high walls around the temple are intended to keep out the donkey cries. Decades ago, the Kunmen two before the present one began the extension, from two zhang to five. When the donkey cries persisted, they raised them again to seven, and when that didn't work, to nine. Finally, the donkeys could no longer be heard. Apparently they had been intimidated into silence. During the original expansion, the donkeys already knew the temple was trying to keep their voices out. The bricks for this project came from the brickworks thirty li away, and it was the donkeys who carried them to the temple, many dying from exhaustion along the way. No matter how tired they were, though, they kept braying. It took seven years to raise the wall from five to seven zhang, and the donkeys cried out the whole time. Then, as nine zhang approached, they grew fearful. They stood at a distance when transporting bricks, not daring to come too close. The high wall terrified them. They stopped braying. If their cries had reached the clouds, the wall would have been extended there too. Human stubbornness scared them. Even though the donkeys had fallen silent, the wall continued rising and didn't stop until the old Kunmen died.

This is also when the Pisha-Heile War began. The autumn after they finished building, Pisha received an official communication from the Heile imperial court, alleging that West Kun Temple's high wall was blocking Heile's sunlight. Pisha lies to the east of Heile, and each morning the temple's walls cast a shadow that reached across the vast desert, past the Ta and Chiang rivers, to land squarely on the Heile palace, darkening the gilded roof of the Heile Tian Temple. This was seen as a serious challenge to Heile authority, and they demanded that Pisha tear down the walls within ten days.

Instead, the Pisha army and Kun devotees went straight to Heile on the tenth day. First thing in the morning, the soldiers set off from West Kun Temple, and in the shadow of the walls they crossed the Gobi Desert, heading west all the way to Heile City. There they met the Kun devotees who lived within that city, and soon managed to break down the city gates. Once inside, they tore down the Heile Sky Temple and returned it to the Kun devotees. This had been built on the ruins of a Kun temple to start with, and on the walls you could still see traces of previous engravings showing the legends of Kun miracles. Ku was still a child at this time; Master served as an interpreter during this war.

"Did the walls of West Kun Temple really block the sun from Heile?" Ku once asked Master.

"Pisha and Heile were two opposing high walls in the east and west, and each believed they were being blocked by the other—and so each vowed to topple the other."

Back then, Master had already realised this war would never end. He taught Ku every language he knew, and Ku spoke to Master in these far-off tongues that no one around them could understand. In the twenty-seventh year of the war, Master died of old age.

Let Rip

Kunmen Virtue sprints towards her, his flat body growing rounder as he approaches the crack, finally eclipsing the courtyard wall, the pagoda, and the other man.

She knows her mouth has gotten her in trouble, and Kunmen Virtue is coming to punish her. She's been locked up in the temple for two months without uttering a sound, a muzzle over her mouth so she can't open it. During the day, the Kunmen never leaves her side as she is fed and watered. Donkeys must clear their throats, lift their heads and take a deep breath before they can bray. This gives Kunmen Virtue ample time to stop her. Whenever she clears her throat, a tamarisk switch smacks her across the jaw before she can go any further. Today she was unable to stand it any longer, and Kunmen Virtue wasn't around. Her own cry startled her, an enormous pagoda of sound rising in the air over the temple.

In the past, she saw each bray as a rainbow, particularly at night, when she stood by the city walls calling into the wilderness, so the rainbow of her voice rose over the walls. Then beyond the city would come the cries of other donkeys, and soon countless rainbows decorated the night sky.

This cry was different. Half a bray seemed to puncture the temple courtyard. The other half lodged in her throat, reverberating through her whole body. It was difficult swallowing this cry that had almost reached her mouth. She felt it doing somersaults in her stomach, causing it to swell, and then escaping in a fart. Of course, farts can't be carelessly dispensed either. She held it in, made sure no one was around before quietly releasing it.

She couldn't fart in front of people, and she had to keep her mouth shut in the temple. The donkey knew this—humans had taught her. They often disciplined other donkeys for not knowing the rules, right in front of her. An owner would hold the reins in his left hand, and a whip in his right. One lash, one lesson.

"I'll teach you to cry out like that."

"I'll teach you to fart so much."

She'd seen with her own eyes a male donkey getting whipped to death in the marketplace. He'd let out a sudden cry while the king was speaking, which prompted a chorus of brays from the other donkeys. They eclipsed the king's words, and all that entered the crowd's ears were *ahnng-jee*.

Who knows how many donkeys had been slaughtered or sold for speaking or farting out of turn.

Nothing is more taboo than a donkey farting in front of a human. The Pisha are superstitious about farting: children can't fart before adults, nor young before their elders. The Pisha have the ability to fart without making a sound. From the palace to the marketplace, you never hear a single fart. As for Kun devotees, their lower bodies have to be silent while reciting scripture. The Kun fear the odour of farts. If you let out a resonant fart during Kun worship, you could spend the next ten years chanting scripture and that wouldn't be enough to make up for it.

The year before last, Heile troops invaded as far as Qusha. They destroyed seven Kun temples, and massacred hundreds of Kun devotees. The king had a magnificent ceremony of transcendence carried out for the deceased at West Kun Temple in Pisha. All the Kun devotees from all the temples in the city gathered, tens of thousands of believers on donkeys and donkey carts, heading to West Kun Temple. Humans and donkeys surrounded the courtyard walls, three deep and then another three. After the ceremony, the Great Kunmen of West Kun Temple thought up a cunning plan to seek revenge against the Heile using farts, promptly gaining the approval of both the king and the Kun devotees.

The plot for vengeance was set in motion immediately. The assembled Kun devotees and donkeys turned their rumps to face west towards Heile. The king stood at the rear of the crowd, so his ass could lead the way.

"Let rip," commanded the Great Kunmen.

The king went first, followed by an explosive succession in and out of the courtyard, human and donkey farts mingling. The Kun continued chanting their curses, while their rear ends popped off.

"I, the king of Pisha, and tens of thousands of Kun devotees, send these foul farts on the eastern wind to Heile. As the wind extends, so shall the farts. First may they spread their stench on the wheat that grows along the Heile border. May they pollute the green apples on the trees. May they foul the river water. May their reek touch every bit of food in every pot and bowl. And finally, may the murderers whose hands are stained with Pisha blood breathe them in and suffocate, leaving behind a body filled with farts. May the reputation of the Heile stink forevermore."

This was the happiest day in the lives of both the Pisha people and their donkeys. The Pisha had held in their farts for centuries, and now they seized the opportunity to let rip. The donkeys sprayed vigorously too. Donkey eyes can see the shape and colour of sounds. The flatulent parps first formed a square Kun temple overhead, then the wind stretched the sound into a shoe, a stinking black shoe that shuffled over rooftops and the crowns of trees, its point facing west, treading darkly toward Heile territory.

When the Pisha were done gleefully farting, they turned and watched the east wind blowing west, and seemed to see in it their smelly farts drifting across the desert, the poplar forests, the villages and towns, all the way to the Heile capitol of their imagining.

Later, as they ate their evening meal, the Pisha smelled something familiar in the air, and so did the donkeys. They watched as the smoke rising from the cooking fires drifted east. A west wind was blowing. The farts they'd expelled at noon hadn't made it across the desert. The wind had switched direction, wafting them back to Pisha City.

Deep

They turn down a dingy avenue of strange-looking elm trees. Kun devotees sweep the fallen leaves, their brooms rustling as if they are clearing all other sounds out of the air. In the shade of the trees is a row of earthen houses, and beyond them the mighty temple. Ku follows Kunmen Virtue through a little door, behind which are a series of ever smaller rooms, each of them containing two Kun devotees, sitting back to back and copying scripture, so silent they might have been sculpted from clay. As Ku walks past, he feels as insignificant as a speck of dust, so insubstantial he can't get them to so much as blink.

Ku has often sat in one of these rooms, back to back with someone else, translating scripture. Every Kun scripture must be worked on in this way, by two or more people facing away from each other, after which they will proofread together. Ku might not be a professional translator, but he knows more languages than anyone else, and so every completed manuscript is read out for his approval.

Murky light seeps through a skylight in each room. As Kunmen Virtue passes through, there is a moment of brightness from the gleam of his head, before the gloom returns.

Two years ago, Ku was guided through a similar series of low earthen rooms in Heile. No skylights there, and the windows were covered with sackcloth. Leading the way, Maisheng's head was covered in sackcloth too, with only his cavernous dark eyes showing. Ku followed timorously behind him. A month ago, the Great Kunmen of West Kun Temple had recited a poem to Ku in the Huang language, four metrical lines he was to translate into Heilenese and bear to Kunmen Maisheng of Heile's Peach Blossom Temple. By the time Ku got to Heile, Peach Blossom Temple had already been destroyed, and foreign troops speaking all kinds of languages were camped out across Heile City. With his fluent Heilenese and knowledge of other tongues, Ku was quickly able to track down Maisheng. The lofty Kunmen was now working as a barber in the remote Jenny Lane, and what's more he'd changed his religion.

Ku sat in the creaking barbershop chair, gazing up at the mighty Kunmen whom Master had often described to him in those early years. Peach Blossom Temple had been a regular stop for Master on his westward journeys. Here he'd rest and pick up the news from far-off places, before setting off again amid the cries of Heile donkeys, proceeding west until the Tai language ran out, to the Kang and Tian language regions. He'd return from each expedition with a couple of new languages which he'd speak alone at home, passing them on only to Ku. With these unfamiliar tongues from distant lands, they'd discuss the people and livestock around them, waiting for the day when a merchant with one of these languages arrived in Pisha.

"Your face is being engulfed by your beard. Would you like me to free it?"

Maisheng's razor blade looked brand new, and Ku was dubious about his skills.

"My brain is full of a poem I've been asked to bear to you. May I pass it on?"

"Leave it in your brain and bring it back with you."

"It's from the Great Kunmen of West Kun Temple in Pisha."

Maisheng's razor, at Ku's throat, suddenly stopped moving. His neck stiffened at the touch of the icy blade. Maisheng must have noticed every bristle standing to attention.

"Just make sure you don't take off my whole head as well," said Ku between his teeth.

In two or three swift gestures, Maisheng disposed of Ku's beard. Moving quickly, he led Ku through a small dirt room, and then another one, until they came to a room with a skylight. Maisheng removed his sackcloth shroud.

"Too many people have been beheaded for refusing to convert. I kept my head, waiting to receive this message from Kun."

A month after that, Ku finally made his way back to Pisha, where he informed the Great Kunmen that the Kun devotees of Heile City had been massacred, their temples destroyed and their scriptures burned. He also bore a message from Maisheng: "At your convenience, please have a set of Kun scriptures translated into Heilenese and bear them back to us."

*

A door opens into a long corridor. The concave ceiling atop the pillars, bright with oil paint, dizzies Ku. The Great Kunmen stands by a window at the far end of the corridor, half of him blending into the mural behind him, the other half regarding Ku as he approaches.

Ku has been acquainted for many years now with the Great Kunmen, who is from Shachow and still speaks Pishanese with the thick word endings of Shachow's Huang language. Ku also speaks Huang with a Shachow accent, and the first time they met, it was like a reunion between two old neighbours.

"We meet again."

The Great Kunmen bows formally to Ku and leads him through a hall to the side entrance of the rear courtyard. Through a crack in the door, Ku sees a small female donkey. Was she the one who cried out earlier? How could a little jenny produce such a big noise, he wondered.

"I must trouble you to bear her to Heile, into the care of Kunmen Maisheng at Peach Blossom Temple," says the Great Kunmen. He has noticed that Ku's eyes are fixed on the donkey.

"I bear messages, not donkeys," Ku replies, befuddled.

"Treat this donkey like you would a message. No need to store her in your brain, she has legs. Ride her or walk with her as you wish, as long as she gets to Maisheng."

Kunmen Virtue hands Ku two silver ingots.

"As usual, you'll get the rest of your payment upon your return."

Ku hesitates a moment, then accepts the silver.

"The day after tomorrow is the procession, and each major temple will send a contingent to the city with Kun statues. After the parade this year, West Kun Temple will lead a thousand-person march to Guma, promenading Kun statues along the western edge of Pisha Kingdom, passing through every temple and village, so as to encourage the Kun faithful in the borderlands. We'll set off from this temple, and you can accompany us."

The Great Kunmen speaks slowly, enumerating these mundane instructions as if they are Kun scripture.

Kunmen Virtue leans closer to deliver a few more orders. Ku holds his breath. Kunmen Virtue's mouth reeks of musty old cornmeal.

Thin

She hears people talking on the other side of the door and knows she's in big trouble. Donkeys aren't even allowed to bray outside the compound gates, and she's done it in the sanctum. Earlier today, Kunmen Virtue ran up to the closed door and lectured her vehemently through the crack.

"Are you tired of living, you reprobate? How dare you raise a ruckus in the temple! You'll be meeting your maker today."

Kunmen Virtue knows about the crack in the door. He's in this gloomy room every day caring for her. When he noticed she had an eye fixed to the crack, he came over for a look. Did the pagoda and people look flat to him too? He stood with his face pressed to hers, stroking her neck in the direction of her mane. He had a good touch. His hand passed along her body to her rump.

The door springs open and two slaughterers burst in, one with a knife and the other a rope. They lunge at her. She recognises them for who they are. Slaughterers carry about them a dark miasma of the lives they've taken. Rope man binds her hooves together criss-cross and heaves with his shoulders. She rises into the air and tumbles to the ground. Knife man glares at her, his blade flashing before her eyes. This is a cow-slaughtering knife, she can tell, it's larger than one for sheep slaughter. Besides, the look on his face indicates cow slaughter. Not a whipping this time, then, but a slit throat. She twists her head, so her reins make the ring on the door rattle. Someone outside will surely hear.

The slaughterer runs a hand along her throat, in the direction of her fur. In his other hand, the blade gleams coldly. She's witnessed butchery. Cows struggle, sheep don't. After wrestling it to the ground, the slaughterer strokes the sheep's neck, at which it quietens and willingly bares its throat to the knife. And now, the hand is on her own neck. Her eyes stare in panic. She doesn't know what to do—she's never seen a donkey being slaughtered. How does a donkey die? Agitated as a cow, or docile as a lamb? Donkeys are dragged behind a wall before getting killed, so the other donkeys don't see. That's the rule.

"It would be bad for the donkeys to witness this."

She's heard the humans say this. Bad for the donkeys, or bad for the humans?

Out of instinct, her hooves scrabble at the ground as she tries to stand, but the hand on her neck is soothing. Her eyes drift shut and she extends her throat, ready for the knife.

"Don't kill that donkey. I'll buy her."

A loud voice echoes around the room.

This is a hallucination, she knows. All livestock have this hallucination before being slaughtered: a person they don't recognise walks up to them with a thin black woollen rope, which they tie around the condemned animal's neck. "I'll take this creature with me," they hear a voice say. Before death, every beast of burden sees themself being led away by a stranger.

She turns to see who will take her away, and it's the flat-faced bearded man who was gazing up at the pagoda. Behind him is Kunmen Virtue.

"I'll buy this donkey."

Again, the echoing voice.

"No sale. Her hide is mine."

The slaughterer is just as loud.

"I'll pay you extra."

He reaches into the pouch that hangs from his shoulder, and bronze coins clink in his hand. She's heard this sound many times at the market. A few months ago, Kunmen Virtue bought her from the donkey vendor with such a jingle of coins. Her eyes roll back as she tries to get a better look at the bearded man, knowing her soul will depart with him. Then she looks back at the slaughterer, but he is nowhere to be seen. Knackers stay out of sight before the fatal blow, for fear of the animal's gaze clinging to them.

The blade is no longer visible, and the stroking has stopped. Soon, she knows, her fur will be parted and the knife will bite into her skin, severing the windpipe that produced her fatal bray. Everyone around her will jump aside, so as not to get sprayed with blood. Only she will know what happens in the time remaining to her. Time will abruptly flatten, and her body will splay over a great distance. With her throat sliced open, her head will grow still and lose contact with her body, the light retreating from her eyes into unspeakable depths, where a spot will glow. Her body won't know what's happening inside her head. Her torso will twist and her legs will writhe, as if trying to reconnect with the head. Every part of her body will grow so remote, she no longer knows what's happening to them. The message of death will be delivered to every part of her body, to her back, her forelegs, her belly, her rump. Her rear legs don't believe in death. They'll kick back, trying to communicate with her head and neck, and when her head doesn't respond, those legs will keep moving, twitching even as the butcher wipes the blood off his knife, as he peels the skin off her belly and limbs. When they get in his way, he'll slam the back of his knife down, and they'll finally be still.

That's how she will die. Just as she's seen other livestock meeting their ends in the marketplace. Once, she was tied to one side, unblinking as a calf was killed in front of her. A protracted death. Even after the carcass was cut in half and hung from a metal hook, the bright red flesh still throbbed with life. The head had been tossed aside, and its eyes still gleamed murkily. At the time, she hadn't known this slow death would one day be hers.

Suddenly, tears are pouring from her eyes. She has never wept before. She struggles to look up, and sees the slaughterer reach out to take the bearded man's money. Coins jingle in his hand. The sale is complete. A thin black rope will be tied around her neck, leading her down a dark and unknown path.

Hsieh

"Hsieh," says Ku. She turns slowly back to stare at him in puzzlement.

"Hsieh will be your name."

He asked Kunmen Virtue before leaving the temple.

"She's just a donkey from Chieh Hsieh Alley, she has no name. Feel free to give her one."

Kunmen Virtue opens a thick door of elm wood. Behind it is an ink-black passageway, and a few paces away, another door. Past a third door, blazing sunlight pours down on Ku's head. The chanted scripture that encircled his ears just moments ago is now firmly sealed on the other side of these walls. He's been released from a bucket of sound, and his ears feel empty.

The slope outside the temple is overgrown with bitter beans, all the way down to the donkey yard. Ku never knew there was a secret exit here.

"Hsieh," Ku calls again. Her ears perk up alertly.

"Her ears are full of fur, so human words don't go in easily. Say her name a few more times and she'll remember it."

As Kunmen Virtue speaks, she turns her head to squint at him—not his face, but his belly and crotch. Ku follows her gaze. Donkeys have naughty eyes, they never look anywhere proper. Kunmen Virtue has noticed too, and swats her on the back.

"Remember, Ku, don't let her get hurt, not one scrap of hide nor hair. Also, she's a virgin jenny, and you're to deliver her to Maisheng intact. Make sure no males mount her."

The Kunmen goes back inside, and through the thick walls they hear as he locks the three doors behind him.

Following instructions, Ku says "Hsieh" a few times. As if awakened by this name, she tosses her head and stamps her hooves, though her eyes remain bemused as they stare at him.

Ku feels uneasy, being scrutinised like this. Back in the temple, Kunmen Virtue had leaned close and whispered, "The slaughterer's been called. When he's about to bring the knife down, go in and rescue her. She'll be so grateful, you'll have her full loyalty."

Ku did as he was told, but now he feels embarrassed to have been part of this charade. He's deceived many people in his life, but never before a donkey. If this beast were to see through his lie, he'd die of shame. The little minx. She may look like an innocent young thing, but there's something shifty in the corner of her eyes, and he can't tell what she's thinking.

Taking the reins, Ku's eyes are drawn to the donkey's body. When the Great Kunmen pointed her out earlier, he could tell at a glance that she was special. Every inch of her gleamed with purity, as if her hide was newly grown and had never touched a speck of dirt. An immaculate spine that no human had ever been astride, nor had the front hooves of any male donkey clambered onto it. Ku can't help stroking her neck, and then her back, unable to take his hand away. This reminds him of the very first time he touched Sha, ages ago. When Ku brought Sha home from a Kang merchant, she was ten, or maybe nine. Ku had just done a week's interpreting, but the merchant's business was going badly and he didn't have enough money for Ku's fee. Instead, he offered him a maiden. Ku could father her for three years, then marry her. Ku remembers a shiver going through his heart when he touched Sha. Now he strokes the little donkey's fresh, velvety fur and feels her tremble, all the way down to her hooves. Perhaps no one has ever caressed her like this.

"Hsieh," he can't help saying again. She turns obediently, nuzzling against his arm. She recognises her name now.

Ku pats her gently to signal it's time to go, but she just stands there. When he tugs on the reins, she retreats. A stubborn ass. He reaches for a tamarisk switch and is about to swat her when he recalls Kunmen Virtue's words, and pauses with his arm in mid-air. He can't hit her. Instead, he tries the soft approach, stroking Hsieh's mane.

"We're going home, all right? Good girl. You can have some alfalfa when we get back. Alfalfa is a type of grass grown specially for livestock, and donkeys love munching on it just as much as humans do meat."

Hsieh's ears prick up at the word. She rears her neck back, shoots Ku a haughty, sidelong look, and ambles ahead.

A patchy track winds between the bitter bean plants to the donkey yard, which contains more than a hundred of them, for the use of the Kun devotees. When Ku helped out with translating scripture here, he was always ferried back and forth by one of these donkeys. This yard contains Pisha's finest donkeys, and Ku sees them all looking in his direction, eyeing the young jenny trailing behind him.

Grown

"Hsieh."

She only realises he's addressing her the second time he says her name. She stares at him in confusion, ears twitching. Again and again, the word "Hsieh" enters her body, where it awakens some deep part of her, filling her with agitation. Hsieh is the name of her hometown. Her family lived in an alleyway called Jie Hsieh, though only the second part of that name reaches donkey ears.

Every strand of her hair is standing on end, and her legs are trembling. She emerges from the dark doorway into the brilliant sunlight and knows that all is well—she really has been bought by this man with the long beard. Her brain knows this, anyway, though the rest of her is still in shock, as if the blade actually had passed through her throat, severing her head and preventing the news from reaching her body.

The man's name is Ku. That's what Kunmen Virtue called him, on the hillside behind the temple. He said the word "Ku" as he stroked her neck, making sure the sound reached her ears. He wanted her to hear.

The bearded man called Ku walks around her, taking her in from head to rump. Seeming to notice something, his eyes narrow and he strokes her coat. His hand is much more gentle than Kunmen Virtue's. He's looking closely. Has he spotted the words?

Two months ago, Kunmen Virtue bought her at the donkey market. She was led to a wooden rack, where they tied her hooves together, passed two leather straps under her belly and hoisted her up into the air. A couple of barbers rubbed hot, wet rags over her body. She could tell who they were because all barbers in Pisha City look the same: shaved heads, a leather pouch containing razors, pumice stones, soap and towels slung across one shoulder. Itinerant barbers go from village to village with these pouches slung over their donkey's backs.

Swaddled in steaming cotton towels, she had no idea what they were doing. After a while, the rags were removed, and one barber stood on either side, shaving her. She twisted her head from side to side, watching as swathes of her hair were removed, leaving her skin refreshingly cool.

They untied her when they were done, and Kunmen Virtue led her a couple of times around the courtyard. She didn't dare to look back at her bareness, like she was inhabiting a different body altogether. He tied her to a post and brought out a basket of hay, chopped up and mixed with bran. When she'd eaten it all, he came back with a bucket of water for her to drink.

It got dark, and she was hoisted up onto the rack again. This time a couple of Kun devotees came to her. One held a lantern as the other leaned against her body. A sharp pain. Her heart clenched—was her skin being cut off? She turned her head sharply, and saw a needle piercing her skin. The devotee with the lantern was also holding up a scroll. Stab after stab of pain, like being bitten by gadflies. She struggled for a while, but finally quietened. In the second half of the night, the lantern moved round to her other side, and she saw that her belly was covered with a dense mass of something she recognised as human writing, the sort of writing she saw everywhere: in the Kun devotees' books, on wooden tablets, on shop signs in the marketplace.

Why had they put these words on her skin? She kept turning to look, and one by one the words imprinted themselves in her brain, dark clusters burrowing painfully like worms into her skin. She endured two nights of this, until it felt as if every inch of her had been pricked with needles. When they wrote on her rump, the devotee's hands passed back and forth across her down there, causing liquid to seep out.

Flies swarmed around her. They kept her covered with cloth by day, when Kunmen Virtue would take her for walks in the sun, then unwrapped her at night.

Many days later, her coat had finally grown back. Kunmen

Virtue groomed her carefully each day. She'd never before felt this pleasurable sensation of her itches being combed away. She could no longer see the words on herself, but whenever she shut her eyes, her mind brought up a donkey whose body was crawling with dark writing. When the devotees chanted scripture at dawn, she saw the words on her body stirring and glowing, as if they'd been awakened to life. She didn't like early mornings, all that buzzing around her. A whole courtyard full of chanting, all that sound surging unbearably into her ears. She wanted to cry out, but before she could make a sound, they'd hit her mouth with a stick.

The bearded man prodded her back, her belly, her rump. She shifted anxiously, afraid he would see the words, but also afraid he would be like Kunmen Virtue, who would sneak into the donkey pen late at night, trying to have his way with her. Just last night, he dragged her over to the trough and climbed up onto its rim, only to fall onto empty air when she shunted her rear end aside.

All day long, Kunmen Virtue hovered around her, feeding her hay, watering her, brushing her fur. She owes the roundness of her rump to his careful feeding. The stroking was nice, but she didn't allow him to get any closer. She still isn't grown, after all. When her eyes drift shut and she lets herself daydream, the image in her mind is a male donkey as big and tall as her father, not a human.

At this thought, she gives Ku a sidelong glance. When the bearded man smacked her back to get her to move, she refused. He yanked on the reins, and she pulled back. She would be stubborn as a donkey, let him feel her donkey temper. She sensed his anger too. Yet he softened first, and tried to coax her. Donkeys can't allow themselves to become too reliant on people, that's where problems lie. Her mother taught her this when she was little. Now they walk side by side, a length of rope connecting them. Her on one end, him on the other. A pleasant fizzing in her heart. From now on, this bearded man is going to hover around her.

2

The Great Donkey Pen

Donkeys Know

As soon as she pokes her head through the city gates, Hsieh is enraptured by a thick donkey scent. After weeks in the temple smelling only humans, it is ambrosial. Not that humans stink, especially Kunmen Virtue when he would caress her neck. She enjoyed the sweet stench of rotting corn on his breath. That was the first scent she remembered—the ground her mother birthed her on was covered with corn cobs. As she staggered to her feet, her mother licked her neck and head, clearing the mucus from her mouth and nostrils. She smelled maize, which she would one day sample for herself when her teeth had grown in. Their owner showed up every day and produced a small handful of kernels from his pocket, which he held out in his palm for her mother to crunch on. In time, Hsieh sprouted teeth, and she too could partake.

There are donkeys all around her: pulling carts, carrying people, hauling goods. Donkeys tied to roadside trees and wooden posts. Many people and donkeys have fled the countryside for the city, and when they ran out of places to stay, they built rooms on top of existing ones. The whole of Pisha City is now two storeys taller than it used to be. Roads are narrower from the extensions. Temples of all sizes are crammed full of people and donkeys. The king has started charging a toll to restrict donkeys from entering the city. Pisha used to have more people than donkeys per head, but more donkey than human legs. Now there are as many donkeys as people, but a donkey takes up as much room as three humans, so they predominate. Peasants who can't afford the toll leave their donkeys outside the city walls, creating a makeshift donkey sanctuary, a wall of donkeys beyond the wall of brick. At night, they bray at the city, laying yet another wall: a wall of sound. Inside, the owners can stop worrying, as they make out the cries of their own beast. The guards must keep up their vigilance, though. A few days ago, Heile soldiers hid among the livestock outside the city, then clambered onto the donkeys and tried to scale the walls in the middle of the night. It was a starless night, and the entire herd held its breath, not daring to call out as they stared at the men swarming up the walls. The gleam from the donkeys' eyes helped the sentries, who were able to slash each Heile soldier's hand as it closed around the ramparts. They plummeted back down to earth like stones, and now the donkeys brayed like crazy. The Pisha troops rushed out, and amid the squalling donkeys, they caught more than a hundred Heile soldiers, writhing on the ground and clutching their severed hands.

*

Hsieh doesn't look behind her at her belly and rump. She doesn't dare glance at the other donkeys, but she knows their eyes are on her. They are not able to detect the words densely written across her body—these have now submerged in her fur, her flesh, her brain. Perhaps they're only interested in her gleaming black hide.

Ku is more concerned. He moves to lead Hsieh from the front, then he walks behind her, trying to keep her in the middle. When he moves her to the side of the road, the other donkeys crowd to the side; when he pulls her towards the centre, that's where they go too. He urges her to move faster, to break free of these lusty males. But how is that possible? A young jenny like her, whose rump is just blossoming, is the centre of attention in the donkey world. The ones ahead turn back to stare at her, the ones behind lean forward to sniff her. Even the humans gawk. Ku keeps yelling at her. Leaving the temple, he only knows that he's going back home to the city, but he doesn't realise this is also a return to donkey society for Hsieh.

The Great Donkey Pen

In donkey circles, Pisha City is known as the Great Donkey Pen. Donkeys from all around call it that. Back in the day, when the donkeys were made to carry bricks and soil to build Pisha's city walls, the idea of the Great Donkey Pen began circulating among them. The Pisha donkeys brayed vigorously, and the news travelled from one village to another, one city to another, spreading farther and farther afield. All places were connected by donkey cries, all roads united by their hoofbeats. A donkey's bray could reach the ends of the earth and back, just as a donkey could cover all that lay under heaven before turning around. Pisha's donkeys always knew they were at the centre of the world, that humans and donkeys would gather in this city before dispersing in all directions. The world revolves around donkeys. Donkeys in Pisha are born knowing that every sound they utter will be heard by humans and donkeys across the land. When they scream into the distance, their necks extend rigidly.

Donkeys perceive sounds as shapes and colours, and so they see their cries stacking up above Pisha City in the shape of a red castle, from which red roads extend towards the east and west. Each donkey knows which small strip of castle wall came from their voice. The structure rises with each bray. A donkey cries out, and the castle grows an inch taller. If they went quiet, the castle would collapse. In order to keep it standing, the donkeys bray without pause.

People have no idea why donkeys keep braying, whereas donkeys understand why humans keep chanting scripture. Every household in Pisha City is at it morning and night, while in the temples, the droning continues all day long without a break. Listening to the Kun devotees chanting at the temple, Hsieh realised that both humans and donkeys use sound to build castles in the sky. People can't see the shapes their voices make, but are certain that they're going up to heaven, that they'll manifest a celestial palace in the clouds. Why doesn't this human structure collapse? Because it's held up from below by donkey cries—each bray is a pillar. If the donkeys fell silent, the sky would crumble.

Is this true? Would the heavens actually come crashing down if the donkeys fall silent? Hsieh doesn't know. What she does know is that donkeys must call out or they will die. Besides, she wants to bray. Her voice itches to be released, her throat swells with sound. She's back in the Great Donkey Pen, and she has to call out—but she holds back. She glances at Ku, the bearded man who saved her life. Does he know that Pisha City, his home, is known to her as the Great Donkey Pen?

Early Days

In the early days, all of Pisha's donkeys were involved in building the Great Donkey Pen. Before dawn each morning, while the humans were still in bed, they called out to each other that the work day was starting. Arriving at the construction site first thing, they formed long lines. Humans tied their cargo—bricks, clods of soil, wooden planks—to their backs, and the donkeys would trot to their destination, deposit their load, and return. No need for instructions. The donkeys said the humans were helping to build the Great Donkey Pen, and so would gallop ahead.

God knows how many years it took to construct the Great Donkey Pen, exhausting generations of humans and driving hundreds of donkeys to death. Finally, it was completed in the year of the donkey. The donkeys joyfully flocked here, and because humans were needed to care for them, they lived here too. There were many more humans than donkeys, so each donkey had several servers. Lacking hands, donkeys require someone to cut their hay, shovel their dung, water them, groom them, nail shoes to their hooves and nurse their foals. Donkeys just move their mouths and legs, that's all.

"What an excellent beast of burden a man is," say the donkeys, eyeing the humans sideways.

After some time, the more intelligent donkeys realised that the purpose of the great pen was to gather labour for construction work. Apart from pulling carts and carrying people, the donkeys were also expected to bear endless bricks for the building of Kun temples and pagodas. After a thousand years of this work, the donkeys were exhausted, and so were the humans. Spent, the humans climbed onto the donkeys' backs, tiring them even more. After Hsieh's mother was used up by their owner, he led them both to the marketplace. They stood for hours by the side of the road, but everyone ignored the older jenny and only showed interest in her fine young daughter. Eventually, an old man with a yellowing beard bought her mother for a low price. Hsieh watched her mother walk down the street, the weariness of the entire world in her ageing body, and in the eyes that kept turning back to look at her.

Even today, half the donkeys stubbornly insist that Pisha was built for them, that the world belongs to donkeys, that humans are merely their servants, that people may ride donkeys, but donkey voices ride atop human ones, and therefore donkeys occupy a higher position than humans in the heavens. The other half accepted long ago that they are livestock to be ordered around, that those with four legs must obey those with two. Each donkey must think this through and decide how to lead its life: willingly serving humans or seeking to command them.

Hsieh's mother was one of the stubborn ones. As a foal, Hsieh heard many tales of the Great Donkey Pen, of the building of West Kun Temple's high walls, of how donkeys bring every mirror a Pisha person looks at, every stick of incense they burn, every letter they receive. When she spoke of such things, her mother's eyes would shine with donkey pride, even though she was just a draft animal carrying firewood day after day, which had rubbed bare a patch on her back. Hanging to her sides were neat bundles of tamarisk, saksaul and fruit tree branches, and in the middle a bale of hay from which she was fed. Her mother said people were born to serve donkeys. To cut them grass, draw them well water, feed them corn and carrots, build pens for them to live in, sweep up their dung. As long as the donkeys squinted their eyes shut and walked behind their humans, all would be well.

The donkeys know that they just have to keep walking, and eventually the humans will end up following them.

Looking around the streets, that's how it is. Young people hurry along in a frenzy, clutching their reins ahead of their donkeys, believing there's some bright future they must rush towards. Middle-aged people walk alongside, one arm across the donkey's back, like a married couple or two brothers eking out their days together. Old people shuffle along slowly, behind their donkeys as they lead them home. A man spends his life orbiting his donkey. By the time he's drifted round to her rump, death can't be far behind.

Hsieh was born a proud little jenny. She inherited the haughtiness and obstinacy a donkey ought to have from her mother, and knows how to look sidelong at humans, how to squint at them imperiously.

Half a Person

In Hsieh's eyes, most people on donkeyback are half dead, and so are the donkeys, heads lowered, eyes asquint.

The streets of Pisha are full of sad, tired people. Those with vigour head out to war and return mangled and broken, relegated to spending the rest of their lives on a donkey's back. Hsieh's mother told her that twenty years ago, there was a war and the Heile captured one thousand Pisha prisoners. Rather than killing them, the Han King said they should be destroyed and tossed back like rubbish. All one thousand men had their arms and legs chopped off, the severed limbs strewn across the Gobi Desert. The Heile had intended for these amputees to be a burden, but the Pisha donkeys took up the slack. Their legs became the legs of these men, who now lived on donkeyback. For decades after this battle, more than a thousand donkeys carried riders who couldn't walk or even feed themselves.

Every war led to mutilated people returning to Pisha to live the rest of their lives on donkeyback. The elderly, too, did the same when they ran out of energy. Every old donkey in Pisha carried an old person. Donkeys lived half as long as humans, so each person had to rear two donkeys in their lifetime. When a donkey got used up, it faced the knife. Word got round that the Heile had changed religion and no longer ate donkey meat, so donkeys could go on living into old age, and when they died they were buried beneath a fruit tree. Soon all the Pisha donkeys knew the Heile had stopped eating their kind. Their conversion also meant no more Kun pagodas were being built, and Heile donkeys didn't have to spend their days hauling heavy bricks.

Hsieh's great-great-grandfather died of exhaustion from carrying building materials. That year, the newly-converted Heile defeated the Pisha twice in battle. Licking their wounds, the Pisha took the bricks meant for the city walls and built a thirty-six storey pagoda instead, praying to Kun for protection. The following year, the Pisha invaded Heile City, and when they were victorious, they erected even more pagodas to give thanks to Kun. The Heile launched a counter-attack the year after, while the Pisha were busy with their pagoda-building. All this work had worn out every man, woman and donkey in the city, and Pisha suffered the greatest defeat of all.

Pagoda

Turning right from the main road, Hsieh follows Ku down a shady avenue by the city wall. She recognises this as the way home. By the side of the road, donkeys stand tied to the poplar trees. As Hsieh walks past, their brays are even taller and sturdier than the trees, reaching up to pierce the clouds. Is Ku bringing her to her former home? In the distance, Hsieh can see the three pagodas belonging to her former owner, a tall one in the centre and two shorter ones to the side. Blackbirds were always perching on their peaks, and her owner would shoot at them—not to hit them, just to scare them away. These pagodas crawled with ghosts at night, layer after layer, lying in wait. Donkeys can see ghosts, though humans can't.

Last year, Hsieh's former owner and his son were conscripted to fight in Guma. This war sent ripples through donkey society— more than a thousand Pisha were killed, so more than a thousand donkeys had to go and bring the corpses back. Her former owner's son managed to survive by outrunning the enemy on his horse, though he fainted and had to be carried home by a donkey. Hsieh was only six months old when she saw the son being carried limply into the house. A doctor was summoned, and when he arrived said the boy still had a pulse. He was alive, but his soul was gone.

Next they asked a witch, and she said the donkey had galloped so fast that while his body was brought home, his soul was left behind on the road between Guma and Pisha.

"What can we do?"

"Wait."

It was just as well he was ill—illness is good, it makes us pause.

But his family was impatient and went to the Guma road to guide his soul home. One person was stationed at each fork in the road, calling out the son's name, fearful he'd take a wrong turn.

The road was full of people searching for souls. Some families wandered around clutching a head, the only body part they'd managed to salvage, calling for their loved one's soul. Some only had half a carcass, and still they carried bloody garments screaming for the missing head. Hsieh's owner's son was lucky to have returned with his body intact.

Around this time, the ghosts slid off the pagodas. They vanished at noon when the sun was directly overhead, but as soon as there was any shade, they'd be there—in the shadows of walls and donkeys and people and trees—waiting to lure away soulless bodies. At night they swarmed so every corner, every rooftop, every pot, every drying rack was full of ghosts. Some of the bolder ones climbed up onto the sill and reached through the window, until Hsieh cried out to scare them off. They'd behave themselves while she was around. Ghosts are frightened of donkeys.

One day, the soul returned. Scrabbling at the door, it saw its emaciated, deformed physical frame. Hsieh held her breath. The witch, who had been waiting by the bed, sensed its presence. Flinging the door open, she gently urged it to re-enter its body.

What had been a corpse for half a month abruptly sat up, its eyes staring at the people around it, as well as the little donkey looking in sideways from the shed outside. Hsieh raised her head and coughed lightly by way of greeting.

The next morning, while the sky was still dim, Hsieh watched as the resuscitated man saddled his horse, filled a waterskin, slung a bag of food over his shoulder, grabbed his scimitar and rode off. Behind him, his dad screamed, his mum ran from the house, and his little sister sprinted like a lunatic calling her brother's name, following him down one street after another. But he didn't turn around as he galloped back to the Guma battlefield.

That very night, the little sister was stricken with a high fever and wouldn't stop shrieking. They sent for the witch again, but she said there was no cure. They had to bring the girl with great haste to West Kun Temple, where the Great Kunmen was able to raise the dead.

The father put the girl on one of the big donkeys, but she refused. She wanted the little jenny. Every one of her quiet sobs was a stab through the heart. Hsieh carried the girl out through the city's southern gate and towards the temple, where crows cawed overhead. As soon as the girl slumped onto her back, Hsieh could feel the heat emanating from her. When she started cooling along the way, Hsieh knew something was wrong. She turned back to look at the father, who had also realised his daughter was gone. Tears poured down his face as he spurred the donkey on. Hsieh didn't know if she ought to speed up or stop. As she hesitated, she saw the daughter's soul rise through the top of her head, and settle onto Hsieh's back facing the opposite direction, watching her own body growing cold and stiff.

The girl was buried three days after that, in the large graveyard to the west of West Kun Temple. Her soul refused to leave and kept riding Hsieh's back for seven days after that. Hsieh had no idea why. Several times, the gates of heaven opened a crack, only to close again. Hsieh recognised the distinctive creak of heaven's old mulberry wood gates—Pisha people don't make gates of mulberry wood, a custom from the central plains. "Mulberry" sounds like "mourn" in the Huang language, and is considered inauspicious. Instead they use elm, poplar and wild olive. Her owner's family had a courtyard gate of poplar, and it shut with a satisfying clack. Hsieh spent the night beneath a thatched shelter against the wall, watching the household dream. She didn't sleep, but stood lost in thought.

The morning came when Hsieh heard the mulberry gates of heaven open a crack, and she knew the girl would be departing. She looked up. *Ahng-jee ahng-jee . . . ahng . . .* She let out seven brays, each louder than the last. Hsieh saw her voice turning into a seven-storey pagoda rising up above the earth, a red one whose peak touched the heavens, awakening the sentry. A donkey's cry from the mortal realm passed between the sturdy mulberry gates and filled the air, startling everyone within from their slumbers. They listened attentively to this beautiful sound from another world. They had forgotten what a donkey's bray sounded like, and that exceedingly mundane noise became the most holy tone in the heavens.

The girl's soul ascended into the sky on the donkey's escalating cries. As soon as she arrived, everything flipped over. The mortal world that she'd been unbearably reluctant to leave suddenly grew as insubstantial as a cloud drifting listlessly overhead. She could no longer recall what donkeys looked like, and a donkey's cry became an unfamiliar noise she didn't understand. Hsieh shut her eyes and heard her cry fall back to earth. The pagoda of sound crumbled brick by brick, tile by tile, taking quite a while for it all to collapse.

To the child, the sound seemed to retreat upwards. This noise was her only memory from her human existence, and many years later, she would follow it back to the village where she heard donkeys bray, saw their hoofprints, found the pastures where they grazed, and even spotted a little donkey who looked like Hsieh: black belly fur, dark circles around her eyes, watching her asquint.

Soon after the girl was buried, Hsieh's owner sold her at the market. To the Pisha, a donkey who has carried a dead person is unclean. Her buyer was Kunmen Virtue.

Use

Hsieh stops by the Kun pagoda at the entrance of her former home and stares at the closed door with narrowed eyes. Her mother is no longer in this courtyard, the little girl who was nice to her is dead, and the man who carried bundles of straw to her and her mother each night is probably gone too. As for the young man who set forth on his horse that morning, he never returned. Something surges through Hsieh's heart and she wants to cry out, but bites it back. This household is no longer hers. She was sold to Kunmen Virtue, and then passed on to this bearded man.

Without meaning to, Hsieh's hooves bring her towards the house, until the man tugs the reins to keep her moving forward. She turns to look as she passes. Where is Ku taking her? By rights, she should already have had her throat slit and her skin flayed. Instead, this man has bought her. Is he going to sell her? Donkeys have no fear of being traded, they're taken care of wherever they end up. Ku has only just got her and still hasn't made use of her, so how could he bear to relinquish her this soon? Donkey fanciers like to have their way with the animals they acquire before letting them go. Is Ku that sort of person?

When she was little, Hsieh's mother told her men divide donkeys into good or bad, while donkeys themselves can be split between those who let humans treat them well, and those that didn't. If you accept human favours and allow yourself to be adored, the other donkeys will resent you. There are so many female donkeys in Pisha, and the males are exhausted. At the end of the day, donkeys must live with other donkeys. If you aren't liked by your own kind, what can you do?

Expression

A team of drovers comes towards them, their donkeys' backs piled high with goods. On the lead donkey is a blue-eyed man who hastily dismounts to pay Ku obeisance. They have a gurgling conversation. When Ku speaks a language from a distant place, his face takes on a faraway expression and he looks like a different person. Different languages make you move your mouth differently, which changes your expression—not to mention the way you see things. Your whole brain changes depending on the language you are speaking. Hsieh has met donkeys from hundreds of rivers and thousands of hills away, whose brays and faces are exactly the same as their Pisha brethren. Donkeys all over the world make the same sound, and so they look alike too.

As Ku talks to the man, the other humans and donkeys look at Hsieh. A rod protrudes from the lower belly of a randy male, and he would have launched himself at her if his drover had not caught hold of him. The drover stares at Hsieh's rump too, and she clamps her tail against it. An itch is starting down there.

A gaggle of Kun devotees pass by. Their leader greets Ku, and the others glance with one eye at him, and the other at Hsieh. She knows what they are looking at. Kun devotees have cunning eyes, and wherever they look is sure to itch.

Hsieh has two itches. One is from Kunmen Virtue, who came to her pen each night at the temple. Where he stroked her, an itch blossomed where she had never itched before, starting deep within her body. That's what a human hand does to a jenny's rump. At the time, Hsieh wondered how a jenny who'd encountered such a gentle hand could ever bring herself to spend her days with a rough male donkey. Her other itch comes from the words etched into her skin like insects, the ones growing into her fur, into her flesh, itching deep beneath. Hsieh is afraid they'll see what is written on her body. When the words were first written, she could look back at herself and see them. Now her fur has grown back, but they are still imprinted in her brain. When she shuts her eyes, she can see her bare self, skin crawling with words. The self in her mind remains bald, the words standing out clearly on her skin, every one of them familiar to her.

Itch

At this moment, both itches surface. The root of her tail and her neck flare up. She moves towards the wall, but Ku yanks her reins. Rebelliously, she shuffles so her rear is pressed against the corner. In a rage, Ku yells at her. Hsieh glares at him as she begins rubbing her rump against the wall.

This corner has been scraped smooth by donkeys. The earth bricks are matted with fur, and the wall reeks of donkey pee. Hsieh scratches her rear itch, but that leaves her neck. Only another donkey could help. Biting a donkey's neck is how the humans refer to fake work—because two donkeys might nibble on each other's necks to relieve an itch, but donkeys mostly deal with their own discomfort. In the early days, Pisha donkeys would scratch against trees and walls. Almost every tree in the vicinity leaned to one side or had been pushed over. These days they only have walls. When two donkeys meet, the first thing they'll ask is:

"Where have you been scratching?"

"Oh, over at the western city wall, how about you?"

"At East Kun Temple."

The temple pillars are a very effective scratching post, as is the octagonal pagoda, and donkeys love heading over there when their backs itch. Old buildings get pushed over all the time in Pisha.

When getting acquainted, donkeys don't ask how old you are, they'll say, "How many walls have you knocked over?"

When a donkey is rubbing itself like this, a wall will begin to wobble, and then to sway, and then it collapses. Thirty walls fall each day in the old city of Pisha, but the humans don't know the donkeys are responsible. Donkeys often talk about going to West Kun Temple to scratch an itch. Every Pisha donkey has a West Kun Temple itch on their body, but when they get there, the high walls frighten them off. On either side of the city walls, donkeys talk about bringing them down. The ones outside push inwards, the ones inside push outwards, but generations of donkeys have grown old and died here, and the wall hasn't moved an inch.

Home

The sun has set behind the city walls. Ku's home, standing against the western wall, is in shadow. Two pagodas stand by the entrance, neither particularly tall. Hsieh looks up at their peaks, and Ku does the same. Then he turns his gaze to Hsieh, unable to determine what she's staring at.

Seven or eight donkeys are tied up in the garden, all of them refugees from the countryside, bedding down here alongside their owners. One of the visitors comes over to take Hsieh's reins, but when Ku sees how agitated the male donkeys are getting, he quickly shakes his head and declines.

A small woman emerges from the house. She looks at them both strangely.

Ku ties Hsieh to the window frame, apart from the others. On the other side of the window is their bedroom. Hsieh looks around the courtyard. Apart from Ku's room, the rest of the space is taken up by one donkey pen after another, all of which are full of humans and animals. The rank stench of donkey dung and male donkey urine fills her nostrils.

It's completely dark out here, and even darker in there. Hsieh cranes her neck to peep through the window. After a while, she makes out two people in the bed murmuring to each other, mouth to mouth. She doesn't want to hear human words. In the gloom, the other donkeys try to get her attention, stamping their hooves, clearing their throats, eyes gleaming as they stare at her. They're all tied up and can't get any closer. Hsieh lowers her head and looks at them bashfully. Her ears perk in their direction, but instead she hears the humans in the house talking about her.

"Ku, you'll be on the road astride a sultry jenny. I'll be jealous of her."

"Don't be like that. The Kunmen of West Kun Temple ordered me to bring her to Heile."

"Didn't you wonder what it meant for the Kunmen to send you to Heile with a jenny?"

"The Kunmen said to treat the donkey as a message. Not held in the mind, but ridden or led to the Kunmen of Peach Blossom Temple. Her hymen must remain intact, he said."

"Well then, you'd better not break her hymen."

"What kind of person do you think I am?"

"I've heard of people hiding gold or jewels in donkey vaginas. Jennies who haven't done it are tight enough down there to hold valuables. Stick your hand in, Ku, see if you can find anything."

"You stick your hand in. I'm a grown man, I can't do that sort of thing."

"Oh, now you're pretending to be all respectable?"

"It's not what you think. We'll be going on a long journey together, that's all. Travel companions. Like they say, you can't be lonely with six legs on the move."

"And even less lonely with a pretty young jenny to keep you company."

The couple abruptly stop speaking, and only rustling noises come from the house. Hsieh turns to look at the other donkeys in the gloom, who are staring back at her. Who knows what these males are thinking about when they look at her? Hsieh pretends not to notice. Raising her head, she sees the dark city walls standing tall beyond the courtyard and stars twinkling overhead—unless those are the lights of patrolling troops. Hsieh's old home was also against the western wall. Each night she would watch the lanterns move atop the wall, listening to her mother talk about building the city fortifications, about the affairs of humans and donkeys inside the city and out.

Door Opening

All of a sudden, there is a banging at the door. Ku is slow to appear, and the door bursts open before he can get to it. Brandishing knives, the city guard charge in like a battering ram, their voices just as unyielding. Loud enough to rouse both residents and donkeys, who huddle in the yard. The soldiers search all the rooms, including the donkey pen. They claim they're looking for Heile spies. They caught three of them a few days ago, who'd slipped into the city amid the swarms of Pisha refugees. One of them inscribed the Pisha intelligence he'd gathered onto a sheepskin, which he then stuffed up a jenny's rump. They caught him trying to leave the city. This spy then gave up the names of two others, and now their three heads hang upside down from the rack over the main gateway, tethered with a leather cord and dangling just above the ground for passers-by to kick.

A soldier walks up to Hsieh, clutching his knife, and eyes her beadily.

"There wouldn't be anything up this jenny, would there?"

He strokes her back, hand sliding towards her rump.

"She's a virgin," Ku says hastily.

The soldiers depart, and they hear knocking at the neighbour's door, and then a while later, the next one along. Sometime after this, the knocking moves to the next street.

The owners and their guests go back to bed, while the donkeys' eyes gleam in the murk. Hsieh squints at the blackness of the window, listening to the rustling within, imagining how the man and woman are groping each other in the dark, face seeking face, mouth seeking mouth, legs seeking legs, every motion of their bodies vividly described by the sounds they make, their embracing bodies futilely attempting to fly, taking off and landing again, then lifting off once more, endlessly.

Finally, there is silence. Then, the woman speaks.

"You haven't gone west for many years now, Ku. When I pledged to spend my days with a message bearer, I had in my mind that this day would come: you'll pass by my home village, and you can bear a message to my mother. Perhaps the old woman is still in this world. In order to raise my brothers and sisters, she sold me to a Kang merchant. I was first sent to a Heilenese-speaking region, then sold on to an area that spoke Pishanese and Huang. I've only ever known my own language, and never tried to learn any of these others. I was afraid that if I became fluent, I wouldn't be able to return to my hometown—that if I was able to live in another tongue, I'd no longer want to go back. While crawling atop me you learned Kang—I only allowed you to speak my hometown tongue while you were in me. You're like my father. He was always off fighting wars in foreign parts, and one year he came home converted. He made us smash the Kun idol we had in the house, but my mum refused. 'While you were away,' she said, 'I prayed to this statue every day for your safe return. This clay figure is a member of our family. When I offer him incense, he's Kun; when I pray to him, he's Kun. The rest of the time, he's just a man standing there. When I get scared at night, I only have to remember that he's there, and my heart eases. When you're away for a long time, he becomes the husband I can rely on, the father who's there for our children. You can't smash him.' But my father smashed the Kun statue anyway. While he was away, he'd placed his faith in Tian, which left no room for any other deity. He left us some money and was hired by someone else to go into battle. I heard he was fighting in a Heile area. Perhaps he's a Heile mercenary now. While you're there, please keep an eye out for him. Maybe he's dead. After he left, my mother swept up the fragments of our Kun and piled them up where the statue had stood. 'Even a shattered Kun statue is still a Kun,' she said."

Only the woman's voice could be heard. Even after the man started snoring, she kept talking.

Donkeys Know

Again and again, brays waft over the city walls, agitating the donkeys in the courtyard so they snort and stamp their hooves. Hsieh's ears perk up. Last year, she was in this yard with her mother, listening to similar cries. Her mother said, "Every bray is a message from a distant donkey."

Donkeys pass on information for humans about far-off events— when people do battle against other humans, donkeys in nearby villages see what's going on, and immediately cry this out for donkeys in the next village to relay. Within an hour, the message reaches the perimeter of Pisha. The city walls are as tall as five or six donkeys standing one atop the other, but if the donkeys outside raise their heads and shout to the clouds and stars, their bright red brays will arc across the wall like a rainbow, reaching the donkeys in the yard, who then take up the call until the whole of Pisha is alive with donkey cries. Hsieh remained silent, eyes fixed to the window. Donkeys bray for people to hear, and if the humans were in trouble, she'd have to wake them first. Ku pushed the door open and came out, placing one hand on Hsieh's neck and the other on her lips. He must be perplexed by this sudden outcry.

The pitch-black city walls are now lit up by many lanterns as the sentries are awoken by the dense thicket of braying. *To be atop the walls and hear the donkey cries is akin to watching a sky full of rising stars.* Hsieh's mother was once on the city walls with a load of rock when she heard one donkey call after another soaring from the ground. In this city there are dedicated donkey wranglers, people who understand donkeys and are in charge of deciphering their cries from afar. All of them were born in the year of the donkey, and therefore have donkey eyes and a donkey heart, making them instantly recognisable to donkeys.

The guests have all come out to stand alongside the donkeys, whispering to each other beneath the resonant braying. After a while, the bell on the palace tower abruptly strikes, *dong dong dong, dong dong dong,* an urgent tolling swiftly followed by the pealing of the temple knell. At these sounds, the donkeys fall silent—they know the humans have received the message.

3

Procession

Crows

THE FIRST HALF of the road between Pisha City and West Kun Temple is paved with donkey cries, and the second half is shrouded by the wings of crows. Ku and Hsieh pass through the city gates and depart with braying resounding behind them—the donkeys tethered outside the wall are sending them off with a volley of cries, so loud that Hsieh can't stop herself looking back. As soon as she turns her head, Ku does the same, nervous that some randy male donkey is launching an attack. Not long ago, while he wasn't looking, one of them almost managed to mount Hsieh.

The idol procession stretches ahead of them. Ku didn't arrive in time for the ritual at the gates, but isn't too fussed about missing what he was told afterwards was somewhat of a letdown. Apparently a much grander ceremony had been planned, only to be cancelled after the recent defeat in battle. The king and his ministers watched from atop the city walls, while throngs of concubines and palace ladies scattered flowers in many hues as the parade passed before them. Ku has seen many such sights. Ever since the Pisha-Heile war began, each year's idol procession has become a major event for Kun devotees.

The previous night's braying kept interrupting Ku's sleep, and he woke up late as a result. Besides, his wife roused him before dawn by nibbling on his ear—she knew he'd be gone for at least a year, and wanted to squeeze him dry of all his energy.

"I'll make sure you're too feeble to mount that little jenny," she proclaimed, loud enough that you'd have thought she wanted Hsieh to hear.

The procession has now reached the stretch of road where crows fill the skies.

West Kun Temple is also known as Crow Temple. From a distance, you see a thick mass of black above its walls, which, as you draw closer, you realise is made up entirely of crows. As a little boy, Ku often followed Master to this temple, and along the way everyone gazed at the birds filling the air—hence its nickname. People only switched to the correct title when they were right in front of it. Half of West Kun Temple's crows fill the skies, and the other half perch on its roof, its tall old trees, its thrusting Kun tower. If they were to all take flight at once, there would be too many for the sky to contain; nor are there enough surfaces for them all to settle at once. And so they must take turns to rise and fall. They caw in the air and remain silent on earth, standing there black and mute, listening to the Kun devotees chanting scripture.

Slant

Today the chanting of scripture and sobbing outside the temple are loud enough to drown out the caws. Outside the gate is a cluster of people and donkeys. Corpses, more than a hundred of them, are being bundled off the donkeys' backs and laid out on linen sheets, some beheaded with only a square of white cloth laid across their necks. The idol procession quietly comes to a halt. With worship objects in their hands, devotees circle the dead bodies chanting Kun scripture. The parade follows after them, as do the donkeys, and even the clouds of crows swirl in sympathy. The buzz of scripture rises into the air, and the crows overhead caw for lost souls, dizzying Ku and making him feel as if his spirit is also ascending.

After the crossing ceremony, the corpses are placed into desert poplar coffins. These will rest under an unadorned canopy for three days, during which time mourners can burn offerings according to the custom of the Central Plains. During this time, all roads beneath the sky will be laid open to the dead, and the scattered breaths of the deceased converge here just as their bereaved families gather in mourning. Wisps and strands come together to form a complete soul which will shroud the corpse, wafting away three days later, while the bodies are buried near the temple.

For centuries now, the dead of Pisha City have been entombed beyond the walls of West Kun Temple, the legs of the deceased uniformly pointing towards the towers in accordance with the folk saying: feet towards Kun tower for an easy ascent. West Kun Temple has a hundred and eight towers, the tallest of which developed an eastward slant two decades ago. Rumours circulated that too many people had been buried west of the temple and their feet had kicked the tower out of alignment. The Kun devotees believe this too, and so after the passing ceremony they pick out favourable feng shui spots east of the temple, in the hopes that burying fresh corpses here will right the tower.

Master lies beneath the hilly ground west of the temple, in the largest Pisha cemetery. In the thousand years that the temple has existed, Pisha's royal family have all been interred here (it was once an imperial mausoleum, but regular folk are now allowed here too, so subjects can accompany their king in death). Among the many feet kicking the Kun tower aslant are those of Master, whose feet walked the furthest of any in the kingdom, reaching the realms of virtually all regions that spoke the languages of Tai, Huang, Kun, Kang or Tian. Fifteen years ago, Master died during a Pisha-Heile battle—he'd accompanied the troops into Heile territory as an interpreter, breaching Heile City only to be forced into retreat. During this protracted war, he died of old age. War broke out when he was a child, and hadn't reached a conclusion by the time of his demise. Ku chose Master's final resting place on the slope outside his temple, with his feet facing the tallest Kun tower. Ku's eyes were the only plumb line he needed. Eyelids hooded, he had pointed his nose at the tip of the tower, absolutely level. Carpenters habitually shut one eye to draw a straight line, and go awry when both are open. If you're buried even a little bit off centre, your feet step onto empty air and you'll never reach the heavens. Fortunately there are many towers in West Kun Temple, and even if you miss your footing on one, you can still gain purchase on another. Or at least you would be able to, except the temple's high walls block all the shorter towers, so the feet of the dead only reach the tallest tower or the wall itself.

Ku leads Hsieh along the high wall, seeking Master's grave among the tightly-packed tombstones. Hsieh grows fearful as they approach, her eyes turning furtive—donkeys can see ghosts. Ku perceives nothing. He burns offerings for Master and kneels to kowtow, a ritual he enacts without fail before each long journey. Every distant road he walks down, Master has been there before him, and Ku believes Master's spirit will protect him.

Master's grave faces the tallest Kun tower. Ku squints and draws a plumb line with his eyes, and realises the tower has once again tilted a little to the east. His heart thuds, and a nasty premonition percolates in his heart. This feeling has been lurking deep within for a dozen years now, growing stronger with each trip to Heile, with each time he bears witness to the Heile-Pisha War. He refuses to believe that it is real, though.

When he arrived at the temple gate, Ku saw the donkeys bearing corpses and heard one of their drovers say, "The Heile have breached Guma and Pisha troops are gathered there too."

Ku's sense of foreboding surges once again.

Kun Legs

The idol procession follows the Kun worship road that leaves Pisha City and connects West Kun Temple, Janmo Temple, Oxhead Hill Temple and numerous others. Dozens of large temples and countless smaller ones—so many that a donkey, running non-stop, wouldn't be able to reach all of them in a year. The pilgrims must offer incense at every temple and pray to every Kun statue. At the start of the year they begin with West Kun and Janmo; one temple a day to start with then two or three later on, but by year end they'll still be less than halfway through. Wealthy families are able to hire Kun legs, hirelings who go in different directions on donkeyback or in donkey carts. After a year of travel, their wages go into their purses, while spiritual rewards accrue to their employers. The donkeys of Pisha do two things: carry bricks to build towers and ferry humans to pray at them. As a result, the roads beyond Pisha City are trampled flat by the Kun worshippers and their donkeys who roam them in all seasons.

Eye Colour

Stretching westward is the vast Gobi Desert. Murky grey sky reaches down to the earth, the far side out of view. You'd only know from the donkey cries, front and back, how long the procession of Kun devotees is. Getting to Guma means passing through dozens of villages, each of them a day apart. Whether near or far they require a day's walking, with nowhere to rest along the way. This is the route Ku takes each time he goes to Heile. First with Master, and later on his own.

Donkey riders keep coming over to speak with Ku, the humans exchanging greetings, the donkeys making eye contact. Hsieh feels a stirring in her heart, but lowers her eyelids and refuses to pay these other donkeys any attention. Ku can tell she's a haughty little jenny, but also that she respects her owner's dignity and won't allow herself to be seduced by any of these males while he's present.

After walking for a while, Ku vaults onto Hsieh's back, his bum in close contact with her fur, his legs pressed tight against her loins. *How light he is*, thinks Hsieh, relieved that she hasn't been saddled with some obese deadweight. When she was a foal, Hsieh's only rider was her owner's little daughter. After his daughter died astride Hsieh, the owner brought Hsieh to the donkey market and sold her. She'd never been mounted by an adult. When she was little, Hsieh's mother told her that people and donkeys were originally a single being, with a human top half and a donkey undercarriage. This man named Ku is her top half now. They are one body, him the brains and her the hooves. People have two fewer legs than donkeys, so when they think of far-off things, they need a donkey to take them there. Without donkeys, they'd never get anywhere.

Right now, Ku is looking down at Hsieh's neck and belly. Perhaps he's never been on such a young and beautiful jenny. He's paying such close attention that she worries he'll see the words beneath her fur. Hsieh launches into a gallop, tossing Ku back before he regains his balance and settles into his seat as if he's growing out of her torso.

Kun Destiny

At the very front of the idol procession is the delegation from West Kun Temple, led by Kunmen Virtue himself, followed by fourteen donkeys bearing a five-yard-tall Kun statue made of wood and inlaid with gold, vividly-painted, and flanked on either side by a hundred Kun devotees blowing horns. The other Kun delegations follow behind, spanning many li.

Hsieh and Ku are far in the distance—she doesn't want to get too close to the statue bearers, all of them male, as she fears they might distract her. These donkeys were specially bred to carry Kun statues, a task the average donkey is incapable of—most donkeys are ghost-stricken, and are fearful of Kun. These elite donkeys were raised in a pen with a Kun statue which they had to look at day and night. Only when the Kun statue is seated firmly in these donkeys' minds will it be placed on their backs too.

Hsieh's father was one of Kun's legs for many years. He bore West Kun Temple's great Kun statue, twice as tall as any human, balanced atop fourteen donkeys serving as fourteen pillars, the statue's wooden base lashed to their backs. The donkeys moved in unison as the statue sat serenely above them, their bodies draped with gold and silver, bridles adorned with scarlet tassels, tails wrapped in red silk, fetlocks embellished with bronze bells whose tinkling let the drovers know if their steps were out of rhythm. The donkeys used those bells to fall in sync with each other. Hsieh's father was the first donkey on the left, and his fetlock bells were the loudest. Before setting forth, the drover would crack his whip. Hsieh's father would raise his left fore hoof, and the other thirteen would follow suit, smaller bells tinkling. That was the most glorious time of Hsieh's father's life. With the glow of gold on his back, every young jenny hoped to be mounted by him.

"You have Kun destiny," Hsieh's mother said to her when she was just a little foal. "Your father carried the great Kun statue of West Kun Temple with an even keel, all the way to the viewing gallery outside the Pisha city gates. He was dripping with sweat by the time he arrived, and when his owner led him to the river to be watered, so many young jennies swarmed after him, but his training held firm, and no matter how beautiful they were, he just kept on walking. Then the moment he lowered his head to drink, he caught sight of my reflection in the water—I was on the opposite shore staring at him—and his head jerked up to meet my eyes. Now his steps were no longer steady, and he raised his head to let loose a bellow. He lurched forward, tossing his rear hooves to wrest the reins from his owner's hand, and lunged right across the river so he could scramble up onto my back. And that, my darling, is how we came to have you."

Hsieh's final sight of her father was a few months ago. He was an elderly moke tethered to a ramshackle cart. Her mother had said, "That's your father. He's old now, and can't carry Kun statues any longer. It only takes a couple of years for a donkey to be over the hill. His coat may be threadbare now, but he was very dashing when he was young, and lissom jennies followed him around in all seasons, ready for the taking, though he didn't give most of them the time of day. I was drawn to his rampant arrogance. I think you have to be a libertine to be a real donkey. In this world, us donkeys and humans are the only creatures who are in heat all year round, though people are even lustier—they aren't only attracted to their own kind, but to us as well."

Her mother was elderly too, when she spoke these words. Hsieh would probably be her final foal.

Hsieh's eyes glistened as she stared at her father where he stood by the cart. When he'd noticed them, a donkey smile flickered across his weary face. He tried to turn his head towards them, but his reins got in the way.

Entry

Each village seems farther away than the last. Some are surrounded by thickets of trees, while others are completely barren, lurking desolately on an arid plateau.

Each time the procession passes by, the village donkeys kick up a riot of celebration and charge over. Donkeys are always overjoyed to see large numbers of their kind. With their steeds running in the direction of the Kun devotees, their owners can't be far behind. Bringing up the rear, after the humans and donkeys, come the goats. Each village household offers one up to follow the procession. The goats know their fate is to be slaughtered and eaten during the course of the journey, so they throw their heads back and bleat a lengthy Kun scripture that transcends life and death. The village dogs show up too. Now is the time when plants are putting forth seeds and animals are going into heat. The air reeks thickly of animal musk, and the humans are also invigorated when they breathe it in.

The pathways of the wilderness have been trodden into wider roads, and their bends have been straightened out. This was all done by donkey hooves. Atop the donkey backs are a dark, dense layer of human mass, clouds of dirt above them, some falling back to earth and some soaring. Nothing is visible beyond the dirt shroud, nothing echoes there but the cries of donkeys. Even the chanting of Kun scripture is absorbed by the cloud.

The next village is within range of a bray. Just how far can a donkey's cry travel? As every rider knows, from the moment you first hear the donkeys of the next village, you still have half a day on donkeyback ahead of you. All the roads in the world are measured out by donkey's braying. Donkey cries, interspersed faintly with dog barks, are what connects two villages that otherwise have nothing to do with each other.

Almost every village is half empty. Half the houses are deserted, with no sign of human habitation, and even some of the occupied ones contain only half a family—the men have gone off to war, leaving old people and children. The women are in hiding and don't dare to venture outdoors.

Arousal

A burst of braying erupts behind them. Hsieh and Ku turn to see a man being dragged along by a large male donkey, who is crying out and trying to shake off his reins, making a beeline for Hsieh. Ku quickly picks up a tamarisk switch and hurls it at the rampaging stud, thwacking him on the nose so he stops, blood trickling from a nostril. His owner catches up and grabs hold of the reins. The jack stares at Hsieh with reddening eyes, stamping his hooves, neck craned and head raised, a string of groans escaping his lips. To Hsieh, who sees sounds as shapes and colours, these manifest as a dark donkey phallus ten li long and thrusting into the air. Drawn by the commotion, the other males turn and start braying at Hsieh too. In an instant, the sky is full of engorged donkey erections, some horizontal, some reaching straight up, some quivering at an angle. Hsieh squints bashfully at them. She now knows what happens between male and female donkeys—unlike last year, when she was still living with her previous owner and her mother was around to protect her from randy males. The strapping jack next door knew she was young and kept coming over to sniff at her rump, his eyes lecherous, flirting with her mother while waiting for Hsieh to be grown. There are two markers of adulthood: the maturation of the brain and the blossoming of the rump. Hsieh knows the second has happened for her, and her behind is sending out an aroma discernible to males for dozens of li around. Every male donkey is yowling, intoxicated by her scent.

That evening, the owner of the male who first brayed at her comes over to Ku.

"I have something to discuss with you."

Ku dislikes the man and his impetuous donkey and decides to ignore him, already knowing what he has in mind.

"It's like this, you see. My donkey has been drawn to your little jenny this whole journey, and I haven't been able to drag him away. He can't stop thinking about mounting her. If you don't help me out, he's not going to give me a good ride the rest of the way."

Without saying a word, Ku puts his arm around Hsieh's neck.

"I can see that you like her, but at the end of the day, a jenny is going to prefer a jack."

Ku is silent.

"I'll give you two flatbreads if you let them do it. If this stud of mine doesn't sow his wild oats, he'll get stroppy and throw me off. Besides, he's carried me all this way, I owe him this. I find him a jenny every year, and once he's had his way with her, he gives me no trouble the rest of the time."

Ku abruptly explodes at the man.

"Get the hell away from me, you donkeyfucker! Neither man nor beast is going to touch her. I'm going to Heile, a long way from here, and she's my only companion. I spent decades alongside my old master, and I've been with my little wife Sha for five years, but for the next year, I'll be with this jenny. No one else is allowed to have designs on her."

Ku says all this in Huang, which the man clearly doesn't understand, but he can see that Ku has lost his temper. Shaking his head, he leads the donkey away. Understanding that his owner has failed, the jack gives a couple of backward kicks in Ku's direction before leaving.

Night

The head of the procession stops, and those behind follow suit. The dust kicked up by donkey hooves can't settle so quickly, and so it billows out behind them, a yellow-brown pennant fluttering across the sky.

The humans at the rear come forward, leaving their donkeys behind. Once it is removed from the donkeys' backs, the Kun statue requires over a hundred people to carry it, and everyone wants the chance to be a bearer. One person is left holding dozens of donkey reins, and the beasts roll in the dirt, watching humans do the heavy lifting. Ku stays put. He doesn't dare relinquish Hsieh's reins. Kunmen Virtue's words swirl around his brain: "She's a virgin jenny, and you're to deliver her to Maisheng intact. Make sure no males mount her."

Kunmen Virtue's eyes bored into Ku as he said these words, as if he didn't trust Ku.

And Ku doesn't trust any of the donkeys or men here. These males look at jennies with covetous red eyes.

There's a spring in this part of the desert with a lone tree growing beside it. The humans queue up for water. The last time he passed through, Ku also rested his feet here. The geyser is so narrow that each jet is barely able to fill a bowl. Holding onto Hsieh, he stands there a very long time before it is finally his turn.

Night in the desert is like a giant blanket suddenly sweeping in from the east, shrouding humans and donkeys in darkness within moments.

Ku takes the saddlebags off Hsieh's back and spreads them across the sand to use as bedding. One of the pockets holds flatbreads, with bronze coins hidden beneath them, and the other contains hollow gourds filled with water. He uses the flatbread side as his pillow, because flatbreads beneath your head induce sleep. Then he pulls out the gourds so they can rest by his head too. The reins are tied to his arm.

Now recumbent, he looks at Hsieh and twitches the reins so she obediently settles next to him. He snuggles against her, and his hand reaches for her flank. Not knowing what he has in mind, she quickly stands back up, eyeing him suspiciously while he tugs futilely at her reins.

Soon all the humans are asleep, and only the donkeys remain on their feet. Donkeys sleep standing up, and dream like that too.

The sky grows a smidgen darker, and the jacks' eyes gleam as they stare at Hsieh. They stamp their hooves and snort lustily. Hsieh demurely lowers her head and huddles close to Ku, pretending not to notice.

Ku soon drops off and dreams that he is cosy next to Sha. As if for the first time, he strokes her pale down—it hasn't darkened yet, and though he wants to wait, he's too impatient. As his hands run over her, thick fur sprouts over her entire body, and he wakes abruptly to find himself clutching Hsieh tightly. She nestled next to him at some point without him realising, and now his entire front is sweaty from her warmth. He awkwardly moves his legs, which are pressed against her belly, and sees her move her head to look shiftily at him.

Hsieh stands for a moment, then settles back down, face to face with Ku. He pulls back a little so he can rest his head on her neck, avoiding her breath.

Resting with one arm across her back, Ku absorbs Hsieh's heat. He can feel her young heart beating tremulously under her skin. She's just a filly, maiden-aged, even younger than his wife. Thinking of Sha, Ku's heart melts. She was only ten when he brought her home, and he raised her for three years before marrying her. Sunk in recollection, his hands roam across Hsieh. If Hsieh were a girl, she'd only be ten, but she's already a mature jenny, as all these jacks can tell from her scent. Ku smells it too, a sort of grassy musk that sends waves of excitement through him.

Hsieh twists her head to watch Ku's hand moving gently along her belly, itching her entire body. She's seen human men touching women with such tenderness, but this doesn't work with donkeys—their fur makes such caresses too ticklish. It's making her tremble all over.

Ku can tell he's making her itchy, and gives her a good scratch when he gets to her rump, which makes it even worse. He's scratching out itches that weren't there before. Unlike Kunmen Virtue, he doesn't reach a finger in to tackle the tingling inside. Ku's fingers glide across her as lightly as the wind, and beneath her fur, the words etched into her skin come alive. Even as he plunges his fingers into her thick coat, he has no idea that if he were to keep going, he would feel the words, then his eyes would follow. What would happen if he discovered them? Would their journey continue? Hsieh isn't sure. All she knows is that he mustn't find out.

Thousands of people snore and mumble in their sleep, these sounds drifting above the desert. The moon rises. All night long, the expressionless face of the moon shines down on expressionless human faces attached to bodies that slump or curl on the ground.

A short distance away, seven Kun statues of varying height rest on the sand dunes in a neat row. The moonlight clearly picks out their features. They all face west, eyes obscured, as if Kun has fallen asleep sitting up, as if he's dreaming, as if these donkeys and humans merely exist within his dream.

Before the statues, Kun devotees sit meditating, smaller figures facing Kun in silence through the night. Breathing Kun devotees facing seven unbreathing Kuns. Ku gets up and meditates for a while. He has spent many nights all alone in the desolation of the desert, and meditation is the best way of avoiding the terror of the dark. He enters the silence and goes somewhere else altogether, far from this night, so the ghostly shrieks and lupine howls no longer concern him.

Raising Kun Statues

The ceremony to raise the Kun statues begins in the murky light of dawn. Fresh from sleep, the Kun devotees sit cross-legged facing the statues, each with a donkey by his side, reins tied to the owner's arm. Before the seven statues, the team of jacks that will bear them stand assembled. The wooden frames are lifted and placed on their backs, then securely tied in place.

Once the Kun statues are settled, the Great Kunmen begins reciting scripture, and the devotees repeat after him. In a moment, even the sand gusting between earth and sky has been stilled by the chanting.

Hsieh stands next to Ku as he sits in prayer, her eyes fixed on the tall statue from West Kun Temple. Her father once bore this figure, so much more magnificent than the others, gilded body gleaming in the dim light. In the left-hand position that was once her father's, a strapping jack stands proudly. Hsieh never had the chance to see her father in his full glory, with the statue on his back—all she has are the recollections her mother passed on to her. Whenever she spoke of Hsieh's father, her mother's head would lift with pride, straightening the back that was normally bowed and piebald from the weight of the firewood she carried. Her mother said any jack who'd borne a Kun statue would have a soul larger than his body. Any human who rode him would seem superior to the rest, and jennies would throw themselves at him. Hsieh gazes with meaning at the leading jack who resembles her father, but he seems unaware that a jenny is staring wistfully at him. Naturally, though, he is aware that many jennies are fixing their blazing eyes on him, which is why he doesn't look at any of them, but keeps his head held high.

Desert

The procession begins. From a distance, it looks as if the Kun statues are striding above the donkeys and humans, as if donkey and human legs alike belong to the Kuns. As they rise into the heavens, the creatures left behind in the dust seem to shrink.

All day long they move through the desert. The sun is a fireball overhead, and the sand begins to scorch their feet. Most of the pilgrims are farming folk and do not wear shoes. The next village is still behind countless dunes—they can't even see the smoke of cooking fires—but neither humans nor donkeys can take another step, so they stagger to a halt. The riders dismount and take refuge in the shade beneath their mounts.

Ku scoops away the scorching sand beneath Hsieh's belly, creating a shallow trench just large enough for him to recline in her shadow and cool down.

The barefoot peasants thrust their legs past the surface to reach the moist sand beneath, while the donkeys remain standing, their hooves unbothered by the heat. Hsieh notices the other donkeys tucking their heads beneath their flanks to avoid the sun and does the same. Donkeys and humans alike are afraid that their brains will get addled from the heat. They'll be in trouble if they can no longer think clearly.

As the sun begins dipping towards the west, the procession arrives at a village in a gully, a swathe of collapsed houses, withered trees, dead crops and grass. Only the Kun tower remains upright, a solitary structure thrusting into the sky. Ku passed this place on his last trip to Heile, in the company of three donkey drovers. Their hair had stood on end, and they hurried past, not daring to stop. A dead village is far more terrifying than a dead person.

Everyone slows down as they head towards the tower. The donkeys don't need to be herded—Pisha donkeys automatically know to circle any tower they see. It's part of their training from a young age, to make sure they don't get lost. Circling towers is the only thing they need to be taught; they're born knowing how to pull carts and get ridden. It ensures that no matter how far they go to the east or west, they will eventually circle back.

The best way to teach them this is to have them pull a millstone. Hsieh was just six months old when she first accompanied her mother to the millhouse, a windowless building with a sliver of light spilling around the door. Her mother was made to trudge blindfolded in a deep circular channel. Eyes wide, Hsieh tottered along beside her, followed by the hunchbacked man who was minding them. After a couple of revolutions, a piece of felt was wrapped around her eyes, and instantly the millhouse was plunged into darkness. Hsieh knew the invisible figure by her side was her mother, and continued following her footsteps, one circle after another. The clip clop of their hooves was round too, and so was the crunching of the millstone as it ground the wheat. The hunchback didn't make a sound and she no longer knew where he was.

After who knows how many rounds, Hsieh was back outside, so dizzy the sky and earth were spinning, getting flatter the more they went round. Eventually they stopped moving, and Hsieh learned how to weave her own circles around hitching posts, around donkey pens, and especially around Kun towers, which her legs automatically lead her towards whenever she sees one. Every Kun tower in Pisha City, large or small, has a ring of donkeys encircling it, some led by humans, others pulling carts holding their sleeping owners, who will soon wake up to realise they've made countless rounds of the tower and the sky has grown dark.

Like the others, Ku looks up at the tip of the tower as they circle it. The donkeys are looking up too, though they don't know why, this is just behaviour they learned from humans. Hsieh doesn't know what Ku sees, but in her eyes the tower is crawling with all manner of ghosts, row after row of them, waiting to ascend into the heavens. They need assistance to do this, and jump with joy to see so many donkeys approaching. Ghosts leap with their arms clamped to their sides and legs held together, going straight up and down, a towerful of bobbing spirits. Hsieh understands that humans can't see ghosts, otherwise they'd have fled in terror.

Ahng-jee ahng-jee ahng-jee! The jack behind her begins to bray.

At almost the same instant, the rest of the donkeys join in.

In droves, the ghosts rise from the tower, riding the donkey cries. No donkey cart could make it to the heavenly court, but braying paves the road upwards, and each call lifts at least one spirit. Many of them only get halfway up before swooshing back to earth like a dust storm. Ghosts are dry, and there are more of them in a drought, which makes life difficult for the living. With every crop of humans that die and turn into ghosts, the survivors walk the roads they've deserted, live in the houses they've left empty, eat the grain they've left behind, the ranks of ghosts watching them the entire time. Every family courtyard is jostling with spirits that people can't see, all of them departed, but lingering to watch humans living their lives. Human existence is a show put on for ghosts. They don't have facial expressions, but look on with blank faces, occasionally moving around in the night so the humans know that ghosts are stirring. People feel uneasy with ghosts around, and try to think of ways to drive them away, to dispatch them to the heavens, clearing more space for a peaceful life on earth. Each new crop of people wants to send the previous one away, hence the temples, Kun towers, scripture chanting, gongs at dawn and drums at dusk. All of this is in aid of this work. Donkey cries too. Keeping a donkey at home is a form of celestial protection. When braying fills the sky, people know. We ride donkeys while alive, and our souls cling to them after death too.

An endless stream of humans and donkeys join the whirl, so the eddying mass grows bigger and bigger, tighter and tighter, until they've coalesced into an enormous millstone. Those at the heart grow dizzy, but are unable to stop or barge their way out. Those behind push those in front, and Ku feels himself getting squished in the huge maelstrom.

Ascending

Dozens of donkeys, surrounded by clouds of sand, are approaching. As they get closer, it becomes clear that each is carrying a corpse, lashed in place by leather ropes. The drovers are behind their animals, not holding the reins but allowing the donkeys to move at their own pace.

Hsieh sees a ghost astride each donkey, facing the rear, lifeless eyes staring into the distance. She steps back in alarm, every hair on her body standing. She once bore the dead body of her owner's little daughter, and the tiny ghost mounted her backwards in the same way. She isn't willing to take on any more spirits.

The night Hsieh was born, her owner waited outside the donkey pen for her to appear, and a horde of ghosts stood next to him, watching. Spirits enjoy clustering around both living and dead humans. The first thing Hsieh ever saw was these ghosts, groups of them passing in front of her. More ghosts than humans lived in that courtyard. It took her half a night and half a day before she was able to tell them apart. The ghosts had once been people, and were now left-behind shadows. They were cold to the touch and smelled of nothing. They appeared at night, but then sometimes humans did too.

One evening before the owner's daughter died, a little ghost clambered onto the window sill and beckoned. Hsieh gave it a sidelong glance, which it returned. She stamped her hooves to chase it away, but it simply vaulted onto the roof and dangled down so it could keep looking in through the window.

All ghosts know that a donkey's back is their first step to ascending, and every donkey's cry carries a ghost into the heavens, though they may never reach paradise. When donkeys call out, dogs follow quickly behind, *wnng wnng*, dragging the spirits back to earth. Dogs want ghosts to stick around, to accompany them through the night, eyes wide open as the dogs sleep.

Most ghosts fail to ascend, and so they climb the towers, scrambling up storey after storey towards the sky. At the pinnacle, they jump and bob enthusiastically, shouting up at the heavens. Those behind them shove past. Whenever anyone builds a tower, a ring of ghosts immediately gathers around it, forming a new layer as each floor is put into place. But they are invisible to humans, and so many ghosts get bricked into place, which makes the walls unstable. Whenever the ghosts move, the tower shakes. Humans build by day, and the spirits take over at night. Big ghosts fold the little ones in three and stack them up to climb, moving ever upwards until the cock crows and they come crashing down.

Now the statue bearers get out of the way, and the Kun devotees and other believers silently chant scripture as the corpse bearers walk past.

"What war was this?" Ku asks one of the drovers as he passes by.

"Guma," the man replies, face full of sorrow. The dead body on his donkey's back must have been someone close to him.

*

The procession suddenly halts. They've heard there's fighting up ahead, so their route must change. Ku watches the column turn across the grey sand. First the statue bearers at the front double back on themselves, then the humans and donkeys behind them follow suit. Ku and Hsieh stand to one side, watching the vast loop of the grand procession. Right in front is the lofty statue of West Kun Temple, with the other temples' statues close behind. Ku must go to Guma, so he can't return with them. Soon the two of them have fallen behind, and dust rises like a wall, cutting them off. Ku tugs at Hsieh's neck to say it's time to go. She tosses her head a couple of times and follows him. When they turn back to look, the procession has vanished into the low clouds of dirt in the distance.

4

Guma

Battlefield

DIRT DRIZZLES MURKILY from the heavens, floating all around. There is no path across the sandy waste, and ahead of them they can only see the squat, blurry outline of some trees. Ku leads Hsieh towards the grove. Where there are trees, there may be a dwelling.

To their left and right, walls of sand abruptly spring up, connecting the earth to the sky and blocking out every sliver of daylight. The walls gradually draw closer, with Ku and Hsieh in the middle.

Hsieh keeps twisting her head, her ears twitching. She can hear hostile movements in all directions, and jerks her neck to pull Ku back.

By the time Ku realises they are caught between two clashing armies, it is too late to get away. Almost at the same instant, bloodthirsty cries in Pishanese and Heilenese erupt on either side. They can't see how many people and horses there are, all they hear is the murderous yelling that is approaching with alarming speed, as the two walls of dirt press together and become one.

Ku quickly jumps onto Hsieh's back and spurs her towards the Pisha side, but then fears they will mistake him for an advancing Heile, hastily comes to a halt, and jumps back to the ground. No horse rider would kill a donkey rider, because donkey riders don't fight in wars—that's the rule. Ku clutches the donkey's reins tightly, and all but hides himself under her belly.

The screech of metal against metal is spliced with battle cries and shrieks of agony. Ku wraps his arms around Hsieh's neck and tries to shut them out. Sure enough, the soldiers show no interest in a donkey drover.

In just a short while, the battlefield grows still again. Ku looks around and sees that practically the entire first wave of troops are now lying on the ground.

Playing Dead

Knowing the second wave of battle will soon begin, Ku swiftly leads Hsieh away, though he doesn't know which direction to go in. The sight of all this killing has left Hsieh faint with terror, and she keeps burying her face in Ku's chest. Once again, two walls of dust are rising on either side, and they hear galloping hooves. Panicking, Ku drops the reins and stumbles over to a Pisha soldier who's been stabbed in the back after his armour was hacked off— although he still seems to be alive, and his twitching leg has carved out a little trench in the sand. Ku crawls over to his puddled blood and rolls around until he is bloody too, smearing some on his neck and face for good measure.

Ku has abandoned Hsieh to play dead, but Hsieh doesn't know how to pretend. She remains standing, glancing sidelong at Ku, inching closer. Ku flaps his hand, telling her not to come any closer, but she ignores him.

The soldier's leg is still moving. His face is half buried; only one of his eyes can be seen, gazing dully at Ku. Ku buries half his face too, leaving one eye uncovered to stare back.

Only now does Ku see that he is a Pisha general. Has he seen him somewhere before? No, best not to acknowledge it.

The eye across from him is unmoving, as if fixed on some object. Ku's hairs stand on end when he realises his bloodstained face is that object. He wishes the other man would look away, but his eye remains skewered by that other one.

With a flapping of wings, a flock of white doves swirls overhead. Perhaps they were roosting in that low grove of wild olive trees nearby until the horses startled them.

The next round of killing begins. Ku's ear, which is pressed to the ground, fills with the steady thrumming of hooves. The sand trembles. Ku's uncovered eye sees two men on horseback heading in his direction, one of them pursuing the other who appears to be injured, one of his arms dangling limply as he frantically spurs his horse on.

And still the leg twitches, scrabbling at the ground, like the general is trying to dig a hole to bury himself in. Worried he'll attract attention, Ku stomps on the leg, which grows still, though the eye keeps staring blearily at him.

When a line of soldiers comes rampaging over, Hsieh ducks to one side, shooting a look at the bloody Ku. The horsemen don't get very far before they are driven back by Pisha troops. One of the horses is dashing straight at Hsieh. Just as she's about to get trampled, she lets out a bellow.

Ahnng-jee ahnng-jee . . . ahnng—

The horse stops so abruptly that the rider is almost thrown off, and the pursuers halt too. Hsieh is startled by her own cry, just as she was at the temple not so long ago. A bray in the wilderness has no form, like an eddying wind carrying grains of sand, rising into mid-air then riotously plummeting again.

The blazing battle has been brought to a sudden halt by a donkey's cry, and now all eyes are on Hsieh—human and horse alike. Even the single eye of the man across from Ku widens and lights up for a second, though it quickly dulls again.

Another spate of braying finds its way into Ku's ears—by now, the human voices have completely disappeared. A Heile donkey with saddlebags sprints by, with more following close behind. A stiff rod thrusts bluntly from the front donkey's undercarriage. Heile donkeys are grey, Chiu donkeys black, and Pisha donkeys have white bellies. And no jackass on earth doesn't want to fuck these pale-bellied jennies of Pisha City. Hsieh knows all about this sort of thing. The male donkeys of Chiu and Heile love nothing better than to be sent on an errand to Pisha City, where they can have their fill of the local lady donkeys.

The front donkey reaches Hsieh and, without a word, begins to mount her. She shakes her rump this way and that, fending him off. After several attempts, he still can't get in. Seeing that he won't get his way by force, he nuzzles and nibbles at her neck. This is something donkeys do to relieve each other, but she has no desire to scratch his itches. He murmurs sweet nothings as he works away, and meanwhile the next donkey has begun trying to clamber atop her. Agitated, the first donkey bucks his rear hooves into the other's belly. The two Heile donkeys begin kicking at each other, and Ku watches their entanglement anxiously, afraid Hsieh will run off with them, but not daring to dash over and grab her reins. Then he realises that Hsieh's eyes have remained on him the whole time and relaxes a little.

Human Heads

The sudden donkey cries have cleared the commanders' heads. The generals on both sides shout orders to get in formation, and the space in front of Ku's open eye is overwhelmed by a flurry of hooves. All around him are the screams of Pisha men, while threats in Heile and Tian pour in from the other side. The two armies charge at each other, and after a burst of wild neighing and the clashing of blades, the ground is littered with bodies. Those who haven't died are groaning with pain. A Heile horseman has three arrows in his back, but doesn't know yet that he's dead and raises his sword for another thrust, only to freeze in mid-air as he realises, and his body tumbles off his steed. Riderless horses charge in all directions, some blundering in panic, others searching for their owners. Hsieh remains where she is, jerking her head from side to side, turning back so her eyes rest on the recumbent Ku. Human battles have nothing to do with donkeys, and she knows she just has to stay put. The two Heile donkeys are still circling Hsieh and throwing kicks at each other, while she keeps looking steadfastly at Ku. He blushes furiously. How mortifying, to be playing dead like this.

What happens next horrifies Hsieh: a horseman falls to the ground after getting stabbed, and his killer jumps off his own horse to lift the fallen man's head by its hair so he can slice through the neck with his sword. Back on his horse, he gallops towards the frontline with the grisly head, which he lobs at the enemy. Before long, they are flinging severed heads back in the other direction.

One of these thuds into the sand not far from Ku, and several soldiers cluster round hollering, "Doumu! Doumu!"

This must be a Pisha general's name.

The screams of "Doumu!" arouse another spate of battle cries in Pishanese.

The Pisha troops kill a Heile general and toss his head back at his countrymen. Human heads fill the sky, and the soldiers have to dodge the cannonballs of their comrades' skulls that litter the ground. Almost every corpse has been decapitated, their heads turned into projectile weapons.

The enemy cries—Heilenese sprinkled with Tian dialect— suddenly rise in volume, and the Pisha troops are unable to hold the line. They swiftly retreat, ceding ground. Now a sword-wielding Heile soldier strides towards Ku, making Hsieh stamp her hooves in fear. The soldier grabs the head of the fallen man next to Ku. Opening his eyes a crack, Ku sees the soldier bring his sword down on the corpse's neck. One blow isn't enough, and with the second, the man's legs jerk violently, as if he's been awakened from a dream of death to live a moment more. Ku rolls over and jumps to his feet. Startled, the Heile soldier takes a couple of steps back and prepares to strike, but Ku hastily shouts something in Heilenese, then adds in Tian, "Tian above all!"

The soldier's sword freezes in mid-air.

Out of nowhere, an east wind rises, filling the air with sand. The Pisha troops charge with the wind, and the Heile quickly jump on their horses to flee. Ku drops back to the ground and huddles against the now headless corpse, trying to see where Hsieh is but unable to open his eyes. A severed head drops out of the sky and lands on Ku's face, almost knocking him out. He risks a quick look and sees a nose, a beard dyed red with blood. Shutting his eyes in terror, the thought comes to him that he's seen this head somewhere before. Another glimpse, but he can't recall. The head's eyes are half open, and seem to stare hazily at Ku, or perhaps at the headless body beside him.

The battle cries sound further away, and once again Ku hears the flapping of wings overhead—the large flock of doves has returned. Three spiral down out of the sky, each landing beside a body. Hearing them coo, Ku's heart quietens.

Pisha voices draw close, and a spate of galloping passes by. Ku thinks it's about time he stood again. As he raises his head, a hand catches hold of it.

"I'm Ku the Pisha translator," he shouts in Pishanese, followed by a burst of scripture in Kun.

The Heile have retreated to the far side of a dry riverbed, leaving the Pisha unable to press their wind-assisted attack. After a battle stretching from noon to evening, both humans and horses are exhausted. Ku has been playing dead for so many hours, his head spins and his ears echo when he stands. Hundreds of horsemen have been fighting and their chaotic hoofbeats still sound in his right ear, which was pressed to the ground the whole time.

"Hsieh!" he calls. The soldier who is still holding him asks who Hsieh is, and Ku points. Another soldier has his hands on her, but she shakes him off with a toss of her head and runs over to Ku.

"She's mine."

Ku takes hold of the reins, and only now that he has his donkey back does he feel safe again. People with donkeys don't fight wars. *The horseman doesn't bully the donkey drover, the donkey drover doesn't bully the shepherd, and the shepherd doesn't bully the chicken farmer.* That's the rule of the marketplace, and it applies to the battlefield too.

Chokanurkan

Even though Ku's face is covered in blood, General Chokanurkan recognises him at a glance.

"My soldiers reported that they'd caught a Pisha man playing dead. Everyone was fighting for their lives, and you were just lying there on the ground—do translators have special rights?"

"Kun scriptures in a few dozen languages live in my head. You don't want it chopped off and turned into a chamber pot, do you?"

General Chokanurkan grins, though there are two expressions at war within his smile. Ku sensed this too, when he first saw Chokanurkan thirty years ago at Pisha Palace, then again at Qusha two years ago. His smile conceals an unsmiling man. At other times, a smile flickers behind his unsmiling face.

The general orders his men to find Ku a good horse.

"How could we allow our great translator to roam the battlefield on the back of a little donkey?"

"I'd rather stick to my donkey. If I mounted a horse, I'd be a soldier."

Ku puts his arm around Hsieh's neck. She can tell they're talking about her, and presses close to his chest.

Someone calls for the general and he bids Ku goodbye, disappearing into the sandstorm.

The sun is on the brink of setting. After being obscured by flying dirt all day long, it can finally show its face now. The crimson twilit clouds look like a reflection of the bloodstained earth. From this distance, all the shouting blurs together—battle cries, horses neighing, screams of pain. The horsemen slowly assemble and set up camp. The bright red Pisha flag goes up in the distance, and beneath it stands General Chokanurkan on his chestnut horse, looking uncommonly splendid.

An armed rider draws close and says, "The general summons you."

All around them are men on horses, heading for higher ground.

Ku leaps onto Hsieh's back. He can faintly hear the general shouting something, and everyone around him quieting down. Ku's ears are still ringing and he can't make out Chokanurkan's words, but he can tell that another voice is floating within them. He had sensed, many years ago, that the general has two voices just as he has two faces.

Although Ku and Chokanurkan have known each other for three decades, they've only met a handful of times. Once ten years ago, when the general successfully led a charge to occupy Heile and the Pisha king threw him a banquet, which Ku attended in his role as interpreter. Chokanurkan arrived with representatives from the surrendered Heile and other regions, each speaking their own language, and Ku accurately translated their praise for the king. This war began when the Heile Han King Abu led his troops west to attack Pisha's Saman court. When the Pisha learned of this, they sent an army out to attack them from behind. The Heile were forced to retreat to Yengisar, where they had a decisive battle with the Pisha. Abu was killed, and the Pisha occupied Heile. Another occasion was thirty years ago, at a banquet the king gave for Chokanurkan's father, who had led the Pisha forces to bring down Heile in concert with the Kun devotees within Heile City. Ku attended this celebration with Master, and there he met Chokanurkan, the great Pisha general's fifteen-year-old son who had already accompanied his father in countless battles and had ridden at the head of the army during this last assault on Heile City. They'd slept in peasant villages during the day, and gone on the move by night. At the time, virtually every town and village on the road from Pisha to Heile was full of Kun devotees, so they were able to conceal this vast army in farmlands, sheep pens, haystacks and vineyards. Unfortunately their triumph was short-lived—the fleeing Heile forces managed to quickly regroup and mount a counter-offensive, taking back their city. From then on, the two nations were enmeshed in war like lumberjacks sawing back and forth. Both Master and Chokanurkan's father grew old and died amid this endless conflict.

After Master's death, Ku became the most famous translator in

Pisha. Likewise, his father's passing left Chokanurkan to take on the mantle of legendary general, leading his sleepless soldiers through battles day and night, attaining glorious victories as they went.

Roll Call

The desert twilight reddens half the sky. Under guard, Ku and Hsieh walk to the top of the dune. The general has finished speaking and greets Ku with a glance, which of course has another look lurking behind it.

The Pisha army begins a roll call. The officer in charge is seated atop a huge black horse holding a thick register with a sheepskin cover in his arms, from which he reads out one name after another, to which the soldiers call out, "Here!"

If no one responds, the name is called out twice more, then crossed out. They come to a long stretch of names without a single reply, and the attendance officer looks uneasily in all directions. Ku glances around too. It sends a chill prickling along his scalp, hearing all these names shouted three times without an answer.

"Jue."

Silence. The officer's voice trembles.

"Jue!"

The final repetition is almost a scream.

There is silence all round—not even the wind stirs. After a very long pause, a hoarse voice comes from the distant wilderness, where bodies are piled in rows: "Here."

Almost a sigh, the word arrives close to the ground. All the humans turn to look where it came from, and so does Hsieh.

A soldier spurs his horse in that direction, and then another, and a third. Only two come back to report that Jue is indeed over there, but only his body—they can't find his head. The frontline troops he was leading were all sacrificed there and are headless too. Ku notices the place they're indicating happens to be the spot where he played dead.

Quiet sobbing begins to emanate from the army, spreading from one platoon to the next. When a relative's name receives no reply, it is answered by weeping instead.

General Chokanurkan remains expressionless.

"Jue is the elder brother of the attendance officer. Four brothers joined the army, and the two youngest died in a skirmish half a month ago, killed by the same man. The youngest was lying on the ground with a sword wound, and just as the enemy was preparing to behead him, his brother charged in to rescue him, only to get stabbed too. Both their heads were lopped off. The Heile horseman flung these heads at their big brother—the frontline general thought he'd slaughtered the most Heile soldiers, and he became the target of all Heile troops in each battle. That's why they always sent their strongest forces against Jue's division, allowing the others to get massacred by the Pisha. They were happy to lose the battle in exchange for gaining the small victory of exterminating the glorious Pisha frontline," whispered the soldier next to Ku.

Now Ku was certain it was Jue who'd lain beside him and got his head cut off. He committed the name to memory.

The attendance officer's words grew wispy, as if the wind were tugging them apart. Still, his steadfast arms held the thick vellum book aloft, reciting the names one by one, his voice hoarse and dispassionate. Perhaps he didn't have a single family member left in the book, and so these responses—or lack of responses—stirred nothing within him.

Ku can't look away from the officer's dirt-covered face, the two streaks of tears running from his eyes to his nose, where his grief also stops. Ku strokes Hsieh's neck, worried that she'll let out an inappropriate cry. Hsieh's long ears take in one name after another, the living and the dead, as if the wind itself is snatching these names from the book and hurling them into the air.

"Haji."

As soon as the name has left the officer's lips, a soldier falls off his horse, and the Kun devotee who is serving as their medic hurries over to take his pulse and examine his wounds. The man named Haji is lying right in front of Ku, who can see a blade sticking from between his ribs. He must have died some time ago, but stayed on his horse's back because he didn't realise until the sound of his own name snapped him back.

Another three soldiers fall down dead as soon as they hear their names.

"What's happening?" says General Chokanurkan, walking over.

"He didn't know he was dead. Look at his injury—it hit his vital organs. If his name hadn't been called, he would have gone on thinking he was alive."

Chokanurkan looks dubiously at the Kun devotee, then down at himself, and at the soldiers around him. Finally, he turns to Ku, who nods. Hsieh nods too. She knows the purpose of the roll call is to separate the living from the dead. Some of these people are dead, like the spear carrier lying at her feet, who answers with a corpse's voice.

"Stop the roll call. Dismissed," shouts the general.

All around them, the lingering sounds of hoofbeats, of manes fluttering in the wind, of armour clanking resounds in the desert air.

A few more soldiers fall from their horses. Perhaps the wind roused them, or perhaps it was the neighing that called their spirits away.

Ku rides Hsieh in the wake of the departing horsemen. Again Chokanurkan offers him a horse, which would be faster, but Ku refuses.

Two soldiers escort Ku and Hsieh, one with a sword, the other with a pike.

Hsieh's right eye takes in the pike bearer, who is dead—he's not breathing. He hasn't realised, and nor has anyone around him

The general instructs him to keep Ku safe.

"This head of his must be protected—it contains all the languages of the entire world."

"Yes, sir."

The pike bearer nudges his horse over and stands next to Ku like a brick wall. As the troops begin moving, he remains on Ku's right, looking up ahead and behind them, glancing at Ku's head every now and then. The general said to keep Ku's head safe. Hsieh notices that Ku is looking back at him. When their eyes meet, can Ku tell that there isn't a shred of warmth in his hollow gaze? Best if he can't, or he'd be terrified. On the battlefield that day, Hsieh saw many dead people charging on horseback, their eyes cloudy, shouting and brandishing their swords, unaware they were deceased. Many corpses were killed a second time but still didn't realise, and continued fighting as if they were alive. Hsieh almost brayed from anxiety, but stopped herself at the last second—it wouldn't do her any good to speak out of turn.

Every donkey's cry is a roll call for the dead. Those no longer living depart when a donkey brays or a horse neighs, or with the whooshing of the wind, or a human voice. Hsieh can tell if someone is living or dead. So can the bald Kun devotee. Ku can't, though—he understands many profound theories about life and death, but he doesn't have the sight. Riding his little donkey in the midst of these strapping horses, he feels safe in his lack of height. It's different from Hsieh's point of view. In her narrowed eyes, half the horde of soldiers jostling behind them are dead, yet they keep moving ahead unthinkingly. For them there is no tiredness, neither day nor night, neither fear nor sleep.

Sleepless

The galloping horses stop without a sound. The wind is still too. All around them are the tramping of hooves. The horsemen in front turn around, as do the ones behind, as do the guards to Ku's left and right. He doesn't understand what's happening, but tugs the reins anyway so Hsieh will turn too.

No command was given, yet the army turns around in the dark so the front becomes the rear. The North Dipper, which was behind them, is now up ahead. There are more stars after the wind has blown away the clouds, leaving the sky brighter, but the earth seems to have darkened.

A thick mass of soldiers on horseback still surrounds them, only their direction has changed. Ku and Hsieh are sandwiched among them as they head back to the place from whence they began at dusk. A few hundred men and horses retracing their steps, kicking up dust they've already stirred once.

Ku glances sidelong at the pike bearer on his left and thinks of asking what's going on, but doesn't in the end. Not a single person is speaking. The commotion of a moment ago has quietened, and even the hoofbeats are softer. It's like a different army is now marching in this new direction.

Don't beat a retreat by night. Ku knows of this taboo, and so does Hsieh. Particularly when passing through the wilderness. Your footsteps are liable to waken sleeping spirits. When people double back on themselves, ghosts lie in wait along the path. They recognise footprints, which ghosts themselves don't leave. Awakened by the sound of steps, they can follow these tracks. When Pisha people return home from the countryside, they'll turn around every so often and walk a couple of paces backwards. Confused by these reversed footprints, the pursuing ghosts will stop to ponder them and eventually drift back to sleep. Meanwhile, long before the traveller reaches his destination, he'll stamp his feet and pat down his clothes, so dust from the journey doesn't lure far-flung ghosts into his home.

And now, a few hundred soldiers and their horses startle awake ghosts who've lain dormant in the wilderness for thousands of years.

Spectral

A spectral glow lights up the entire wilderness, the gleam of waking ghosts. The humans and horses can't see this, but Hsieh can. When they clattered past at dusk, they rattled the spirits from their slumber. Ghosts are slow to rise from sleep. The first to waken saw clouds of dust as the army faded into the distance, while the later ones had no idea what was going on, but knelt to study the tracks, each ghost choosing one trail to follow. No footprints, only the round marks of hooves. Ghosts fear circles. Human footprints are elongated, easier to identify. When a person walks alone across the wilderness, a long trail of ghosts follow his footsteps. Ghosts following ghosts through the void, all knowing the frontmost spirit is following a human, trying to jostle their way ahead.

Coming back the same way, the horseback riders startle the ghosts, who scatter to either side of the trail. Their vast spectral luminescence converges around the Pisha troops, who are a shade darker than the night, their hoofbeats a shade darker still. The gathering ghosts are watching a show being played out in the gloom. Asleep for centuries, these spirits of humans and horses and donkeys, of trees and grass and rocks, of extinguished stars, have all been startled into wakefulness, and are opening their eyes for the first time in years. The entire landscape lights up, and only the retreating Pisha army is dark.

Night Battle

The pike bearer tells Ku to halt, and Ku pulls on the reins. There is loose shale underfoot. They left the sandy waste a few li back and are now on a dry riverbed. The soldiers quickly overtake them, and soon there is nothing but silence behind them.

The hoofbeats ahead grow frenzied, then battle cries fill the earth and air. The low night sky squashes the voices flat and hurtles them forward. Murderous yells cover the clouds and stars, which grow dimmer as the voices get more resonant.

"The night battle of the sleepless general has begun," comes the pike bearer's voice from somewhere overhead. His horse is half as tall again as a donkey, making him half as tall again as Ku.

This is Ku's first sight of such a night battle. The sleepless warriors are legendary among the Pisha people, while in the lands where Heile, Tian and more far-flung languages are spoken, they are the stuff of nightmares. Anyone who has clashed with the Pisha army, spent from a day's combat and collapsing wounded into sleep, will have heard the howling Pisha troops descending upon them in their dreams, the very same humans and horses who fought them all day unleashing the same vicious Pisha battle cries. So many people have been hacked to pieces while slumbering. Whether they defeated or were defeated by the Pisha forces by day, they'd still face the wrath of the sleepless warriors in the night.

Now a swathe of murderous yells surges through the dark. The spot where Ku, Hsieh and their guards are standing slowly lights up. Hsieh stamps her hooves uneasily. Thousands of ghosts are stood alongside them, also watching the fighting up ahead. On the heads, backs and shoulders of the two soldiers flanking Ku and Hsieh, faintly gleaming spirits are perched. The others leap upwards, treading air for a moment to peer into the distance before falling back to earth. Thanks to them, the night sky is glowing with a dull blue hue, full of ghosts bobbing up and down, while white spirit feathers drift across it.

5

Goatman

Tanner

THE SUN HAS ASCENDED to horsehead-height by the time the Pisha army arrives back at yesterday's battlefield. Last night's fighting hangs there like a dream, or perhaps it really was a dream—Ku can't be sure it actually happened. He hasn't slept a wink, and his brain is fuzzy.

The Pisha army puts its horseback soldiers in front, its infantry in the middle, and its donkey riders in the rear. This last group are volunteers from Guma, whose job is to carry the bodies of the dead. When the fighting is over, the donkeys and surviving humans carry out the work that needs to be done. Donkey riders don't take part in battle, that's the rule. Some livestock must be left so people can go on living. Donkeys can't fight, anyway; they retreat when horses advance, and jacks only charge when they have a jenny in their sights, never at the behest of humans. Everyone knows this, so they do not allow donkeys to take part in wars.

Generation after generation of donkeys have been born, grown old and died during this interminable war. This group of donkeys clearly aren't bothered by being on a battlefield. They nuzzle and nibble at each other, bucking their rear legs, the males taking the opportunity to mount the females. A tall, black jack brays as he tries to climb atop Hsieh. When Ku intervenes, he unleashes his hooves and almost kicks Ku in the face. The pike bearer rushes over with his weapon, startling the black donkey into taking a few paces back, only to fix his eyes on Hsieh and prepare to lunge forward again.

Ku tries to work out where last night's battle took place, but there isn't a trace to be seen. It must have been on a riverbed in the heart of the desert, or else somewhere in dreamland. He and the two guards are stood a good distance away, and though he looks as hard as he can, he isn't able to see the great battle. After who knows how long, a west wind rises and the shouting grows softer. The pike bearer urges Ku to retreat, and he makes Hsieh turn back. When she hesitates, the soldier bangs his pike on the ground and she begins running. Behind her, the sound of horses galloping at her heels.

The army retreated dozens of li through the sandstorm before setting up camp, and only now, at dawn, does Ku see they are next to a dilapidated, abandoned village. Horses stand around the murky wasteland, and the two guards loom over him from either side. A little further off, someone has built a bonfire, with more camps beyond that. Human and horse shadows flicker in the light of the flames. Ku shakes the sand off himself, and so does Hsieh, sneaking a glance at the pike bearer, whom she suspects might not have slept at all, but remained all night on his horse.

All across the ground are headless ghosts bent over like wheat gleaners, searching for their missing heads. Worried that they'll possess her, Hsieh weaves gingerly between them, ducking around so much that Ku thinks she must have trodden on a hedgehog.

The Heile army is bivouacked on the other side of a dry river gully, a great mass of humans only hazily visible. They don't look as if they're about to attack. Last night's battle must have completely sapped their strength, and they won't have recovered yet.

Leading Hsieh along, Ku goes in search of the person who fell next to him yesterday. When he dozed off for a moment before dawn, that man's twitching leg flashed into his mind: the jerking foot that dug out a little trench, a receptacle for his own blood. Ku recalls them lying across from each other, his cold nose touching Ku's, wind gusting between them, Ku not daring to open his eyes, afraid of the man's stare. Ku felt guilty—it was his foot that stamped this man to death. Hsieh had crouched down next to him. Ku's back was pressed to her belly, and soon it was sweating while his chest grew cold. He had wished he could roll over and warm his other side, but didn't dare move. Hsieh remained perfectly still. All Ku's thoughts were in her heart, and she felt it had always been this way. She stood up when the first glimmers appeared in the sky and stamped her hooves. Ku opened one eye (the other was buried in the sand). The wind had stopped.

The terrain is littered with corpses that the wind has half buried in sand. With a start, Ku realises all the Pisha dead have been beheaded. He finds the place where he played possum yesterday. The man's body is still there, facing the sky. Ku recognises his legs and leather boots right away. The trench under him has been filled in with the sand, and his head is gone. Someone else's head is nearby, though, face down. Ku picks it up to look at it, then sets it down again.

All around them people search for severed heads to reunite with their bodies.

A scrawny tanner comes over, picks up the head Ku just put down and attempts to fix it onto the man's body.

"That's not his head," says Ku.

"Go fetch his head, then."

"Where would I find it? The wind was blowing all night. Heads are round—it would have rolled far away."

"He needs to have a head, never mind whose. I'm going to put this one on him for now."

The tanner opens his leather bag and produces his tools: a needle, a leather strip to serve as thread, an awl to poke the holes for the needle, just as he'd sew together any two pieces of hide. Ku takes one look and has to turn away. Hsieh keeps an eye on him as she watches the tanner work. Back in the marketplace, Hsieh saw many sheep and cows with their heads cut off, but she's never seen a human head being fixed onto a neck. The tanner doesn't seem to have done this before. He keeps his face turned away and his eyes shut. After a few stitches, he gets into the swing of it and begins working in earnest. This head clearly does not belong to this body: their skins are a different colour, and the neck stumps are different sizes. Still, the tanner is skilful enough to make them fit with a shove here and a tug there. He calls Ku over, who looks at this reassembled corpse and thinks actually, this head does look right on this body.

Fighting Commences

Seeing the Heile troops get in formation on the far side of the gully, the Pisha donkey squad hastily abandons their work gathering corpses and beats a retreat. Hsieh feels uneasy carrying a dead man whose head and body have just been stitched together. Ku shouts at her to move faster, while the two guards hurry Ku. The fighting is about to start but Hsieh refuses to move, instead turning in circles, looking all around her. Frantic, Ku kicks her, making her jolt ahead, only to slow down again. The dead man grows heavier with every step she takes. Donkeys are reluctant to carry the dead. Death weighs heavy; living people have breath, dreams, thoughts—these things keep them light. When the air goes out of a person, they sink to the ground. Ku holds a sheep's bladder full of water and a pouch of rations, and is tiring faster than Hsieh as they walk. She was carrying the food before, but he thought it would go rock hard sitting next to a corpse. Hsieh agrees. The head belongs to a hungry ghost who probably died with an empty stomach. His eyes are fixed on Ku's rations, though now he's been sewn onto someone else's body, someone with a full belly.

The donkey squad curves around the back of the neatly ranked Pisha soldiers, but Ku doesn't see General Chokanurkan anywhere. He ought to be in the midst of his troops, commanding them. First thing this morning, one of the guards delivered some dried meat and fried noodles from the general.

"The general said you can take a look at this battle," said the pike bearer. He then bent closer and murmured into Ku's ear, "And also, he said if he's killed in battle, he hopes you will bear word to his family."

The donkey squad abruptly begins braying when they catch sight of the peasant soldiers. All these donkeys have been press-ganged into the army, and now that they've seen their owners, they want to say hello. When the peasants see their donkeys, they make shooing noises and flap their hands, but the donkeys stay put and begin braying louder than before. The horseback troops turn back to see what's going on, and even the Heile forces across the riverbed must surely also be able to hear the chorus of *ahnng-jee ahnng-jee.* The braying of a few hundred donkeys is more blood-curdling than the battle cries of a few thousand men.

Hsieh is silent because she doesn't recognise anyone amid the mob armed with spears, axes, hoes, rakes and pitchforks. Ku tries to spur her on, but she only glares at him. Where is she supposed to go with all these other donkeys crowding her?

A couple of the donkeys break free of their reins and run towards the peasant soldiers, from whose number someone runs out to intercept them. It is inauspicious, Ku thinks, for the Pisha army to show signs of disarray before the fighting has even started. A few horsemen chase the donkey squad away, but every few steps, they look back and let out a bray. The peasant soldiers can't stop turning to look too. Hsieh narrows her eyes. She is anxious for these donkeys, who can see their owners are in trouble and are telling them to flee. Donkeys can tell a few days in advance when humans are going to die. Half the humans of the ragtag peasant army as well as the neat rows of horseback troops are already dead—they just don't know it yet.

*

Hearing murderous yells behind them, Ku and Hsieh come to a halt. The donkey squad, riders and mounts, look back. Not five li from where they are, the Pisha peasants and soldiers are charging with clashing blades and screams of rage and agony. A great cloud of dust rises into the air.

"The battle's begun. Quick, get moving," say the drovers, urging the donkeys on.

When they pass by the site of yesterday's battle, Ku feels no fear. Here is where he played dead a day ago, and now the slaughter is starting again. He knows this will go on for a while. There are thousands of people and horses, thousands of heads, and the exchanging of blows—now you strike, now I do—will go on for ages.

Head Body

The sun is bearing directly down on them, and the heat is making Ku dizzy. His scalp is scorched so dry it isn't even sweating. Hsieh's belly perspires freely, and so does the dead man on her back. The body is bound to her torso with leather ropes. Now and then, Ku glances at the dangling leg and imagines he sees the toes twitching, digging away at an invisible trench. Hsieh worries he'll be scared if he sees the ghost. Even as they were tying the corpse to Hsieh's back, the spirit was already leaving it to mount her, his dark visage turned towards her tail. The ghost of the head doesn't know the ghost of the body, and now they're quarrelling.

"Hurry up! One more day and this carcass will really start to stink," says the head. And indeed, Ku and Hsieh have begun to notice the stench of the body.

"It's a two-day journey to Pisha City."

"Pisha? I want to go back to Heile!"

"Tell it to the donkey."

"Shut up, you headless fool. What are you thinking with, your ankles?"

"Aren't you my head?"

"You dimwit, imagine losing your head and not even realising. Reach up and touch me—do I feel like your head?"

The ghost of the body runs his hands over the head's nose and eyes, his hair and beard and ears, and falls silent.

"Where's my head, then? And your body?"

"You're my body now. I'm Tuo, by the way, a Heile man, so that's your name too."

"I don't want you as my stinking head. I have my own name. I'm a Pisha man. I'm Jue, and that's what you'll call me."

"People recognise each other by their faces, not their legs and torsos. Bodies don't have names, you putrid Pisha."

"Why don't we call ourselves JueTuo?"

The Pisha body softens his tone.

"No, we'll be TuoJue. Head first, then body," says the Heile head firmly.

Hsieh listens as the ghosts of head and body bicker. In the end, the head gets the upper hand. The body is silent for a while. Lacking a brain, he has to borrow the Heile head to think this through.

"Fine, we'll be TuoJue. You're right, you're the head, so you can come first. But the legs are mine, so I'll be the one who decides where we walk. And I want to go back to Pisha."

"A pox on Pisha. I'm the head, I say where we go."

Hsieh twists around, but the ghost named TuoJue doesn't see her roll her eyes at them. They are facing the other way, looking at the past.

Dust

They reach a desert poplar grove and the donkey squad stops for a rest. Ku takes out half a flatbread and sets it atop his bag, then drinks a mouthful of water. There isn't much left in the waterskin. He glances at Hsieh, who is twisting around to graze on the poplar leaves. TuoJue jumps off her back and goes to sit next to Ku. When Ku reaches for the flatbread, Hsieh sees the ghost's arm stretch out too, brushing against Ku's hand. His fingers spasm. One flatbread becomes two, and the ghost takes the shadow one, splitting it in half to share between head and body. The head eats his half, and the body has to put his into the same mouth—it is only now sinking in that he doesn't have one of his own.

"So my arms will have to work for someone else's head," grumbles the body, "but when is this head ever going to think of me?"

Ku gnaws at the flatbread, which is dry and hard to choke down. The sound of fighting has faded to nothing. Someone climbs a poplar tree to have a look.

"Can you see anything?"

"Nothing but dust. It's coming this way."

A stir goes through the donkey squad. Ku hastily puts everything back into his bag and nudges Hsieh to start moving. She glances at the corpse, which is slowly growing longer as it stretches out along her back. Soon it will touch the ground.

My Knife

Past the desert poplar grove is a stretch of flat land, and next to the trees is a burnt out village. This isn't where they camped last night. The donkey squad sprawls over several li, and Ku and Hsieh have fallen behind. Hsieh hasn't done much heavy lifting, and is shaking after carrying a corpse for several hours. Behind them is a large jack with three dead bodies—one slung on either side and one across his back—still full of beans. He keeps leaning forward to sniff Hsieh's rump. When Ku thwacks him on the nose, he dashes ahead and tries to mount another young jenny, braying enthusiastically all the while. All of a sudden, the corpse that the jenny is carrying lets out a shriek. The drover quickly makes her stop and unties the rope. The dead body tumbles to the ground and stands up.

"My knife, my knife."

His eyes stare vacantly into the distance. Terrified out of his wits, the drover quickly hands him a bent wooden club.

"Charge!"

The man raises the club high and sprints back the way they came. In an instant he has disappeared into the dust.

*

They've been walking less than an hour when the dark dust cloud threatens to overtake them. Hsieh thinks this can't be good and keeps looking back. Ku agrees, and tries to make her run. She gallops a few paces. Ku can't keep up and falls back, breathing hard. The dust cloud gets closer, as do the battle cries. The rest of the donkey squad is running now, leaving Ku and Hsieh further behind.

A short while later, the defeated Pisha army surges over like a herd of donkeys set loose into the wild. Hsieh stands still, and Ku is stunned to see all these men and horses rushing past. Only when the enemy arrives in hot pursuit does he come to his senses. With a few slashes of his knife, he cuts through the leather ropes so the corpse falls to the ground. Jumping onto Hsieh's back, he digs his heels into her belly to make her run hell for leather, though she stops abruptly after a short distance and turns to see TuoJue is still with them, riding backwards behind Ku. She wonders if Ku realises. They're stuck with this ghost.

Smoke

Ku wakes to find himself slumped on Hsieh's back. They are under a lone, short desert poplar. Up ahead is a taller tree with a fenced courtyard beneath it. *What place is this?* Ku dismounts and looks at Hsieh, while she stares at the rising smoke from the courtyard. The sun has set but the sky is still light. This family has tucked their home beneath a poplar tree, but Hsieh managed to find it. Ku doesn't know how far she ran while he slept, but she's covered in sweat.

They walk halfway round the tree before finding a gate which, like the courtyard wall, is woven from red willow branches. Ku listens but can't hear anyone stirring. He rattles the gate and calls out. Footsteps. Someone peers through a crack, then opens the gate.

"Could you spare a mouthful of rice for this traveller?" says Ku in Pishanese.

The man eyes Ku, then the shrivelled bag on Hsieh's back. Ku holds out a bronze coin. The man steps aside to let them in, but doesn't take the money.

Inside, Ku sees a series of little rooms built around the thick tree trunk, like the endless strings of rooms in West Kun Temple, joined together like a bottomless pit. High amid the leaves are a couple of cage-like rooms. The man looks up and yells. Two boys and a girl, all around ten, leap down from among the branches. There's no sign of their mother, but Ku feels he can't say anything. Instead, he asks where they are.

"You came here on your own legs, don't you know?" the man says. Glancing at Hsieh, Ku explains he was asleep on the back of his donkey.

The man gets him a scoop of water, which he drains in a single draught. The boy fetches Hsieh a wooden basin of water, and she does the same.

The man then pours another scoop of water into the pot, and Ku knows that's for his benefit. Another mouth to feed means the stew must be diluted. Pisha people make stew by tossing whatever they have into a pot; Ku can smell dried fruit, čamǧur turnips, wheat, meat jerky and poplar mushrooms.

Hsieh is vigorously chewing some straw, shooting sidelong glances at Ku and at the steaming pot. Without them realising, it has gotten dark.

The man pokes some willow branches into the stove, causing a puff of bluish smoke and some sparks to shoot out, lifting the dome of night.

Hsieh sees TuoJue the ghost slowly ascending. The head and body, stitched together with leather string, come apart. First the head rises on the most energetic plume of cooking smoke, while the body remains behind, shocked. Then the body goes up too. Drifting on the smoke and cooking aromas, on the wheaten scent of toasting flatbread, on the fragrance of hay being crushed between a donkey's teeth. They say a ghost who is wafted aloft by good, rich cooking smells will be warmly welcomed at the gates of the celestial court, for such delicious scents are rare in the world above. And so Pisha families send off their dead in a waft of grease. None of that today, though. These ghosts will have to rise smelling only of plain stew.

The rising smoke is trapped by the crown of the tree, with the greater crown of night above it, shrouding the earth. Hsieh recalls how, back among the tightly packed houses of Pisha City, smoke would rise between the various Kun towers, forming dark towers of their own that would fall apart just as quickly as they'd come together, day after day, year after year. In Pisha City, where there are as many towers as there are chimneys, Hsieh raised her head and gazed at the towers, and as she looked she felt a tickle in her throat.

"Cooking smoke will not reach the heavens," that's what donkeys say. Donkeys who have been to the heavens report that the smoke from Chieh Hsieh Alley, from Guma, from Qira, from Qusha, has never crossed the threshold of the celestial court.

"People rise to the heavens with smoke guiding the way," and "Chimneys are a pointing finger, leading us into the darkness." That's what humans say.

Hsieh keeps her eyes fixed on the chimney above the stove. After quite a while, the headless body slides down it, followed by the severed head. Reunited, they climb back onto Hsieh's back.

"The celestial court didn't want a head without a body," Hsieh hears Tuo mumble. He had gotten there first, and was turned away by the gatekeeper. Jue arrived shortly after that, which surprised Tuo—wasn't Jue a Kun devotee? Why was he at the celestial court? That's for Tian devotees.

"You ought to be in hell," Tuo seethed, glaring at Jue.

"There's no such place as hell, you imbecile. Look, everyone's here," Jue pointed with his ankle.

Tuo turned and, sure enough, walking hand in hand along the white jade terraces were all the dead of Heile and Pisha, laughing and chatting. Doumu, whom he loathed, was there too. That bastard had killed seventy of Tuo's brothers-in-arms during a battle by the Yarkand River and flung their bodies into the water. One of them was from Tuo's village, and his corpse floated downstream all the way home. *Who killed Doumu?* Tuo wished he'd been able to do it with his own hands. The Pisha man who'd killed Tuo was there on the heavenly terraces too, as was another Pisha man whom Tuo had killed—this one had been raising his blade, ready to bring it down on one of Tuo's subordinates, when Tuo got him from behind. The man screamed, turned to stare numbly at his right arm where it lay on the ground, unable to believe it was his. One of his fingers, still wrapped around his sword handle, kept moving. It didn't know what had happened to its body, so there it was, twitching away. Tuo froze too, one eye on the severed limb, the other on the man, who likewise had one eye on the ground, and the other on his killer, though he didn't know yet that he wasn't long for the world. It's only when a person is about to die that his eyes look in separate directions.

All Tuo could see was that face. As life ebbed away, fear, pain and shock quickly faded from it, and his body stilled. The black horse he was riding stopped too. The chaos occurring around them no longer had anything to do with him, the terror vanishing from the face that wasn't his any longer, and even time was stopping, though the battle continued. Horses were still galloping, men were still attacking, but he and this man had come to a halt, just for a moment, then a blade went through the back of the man's neck, and the head Tuo had been staring at tumbled to the ground, horrifying the horse, who sped off with his owner's headless corpse. Tuo stared blankly at the wide eyes of the fallen head, then he heard someone yell his name, and the word arrived at the same moment as an icy blade through his neck.

Now it was his eyes that were open wide as his horse's hooves pummelled the sandy ground rushing up to meet them, then a second later he was looking at the emptiness, at the borderless sky, and his own headless corpse still sitting upright in the saddle, neck stump spurting blood. And next to him a man on a white horse, the one who'd killed him, high nose bridge and deep-set eyes, reaching down to pick up Tuo's head. And now Tuo quietened, his gaze calming and broadening so he could see the entire sky and land, his past and future lives, his whole world unfurling in all directions like a blossoming flower. By observing the Pisha man whose right arm he hacked off, he learnt how to have a good death. This moment filled him with gratitude. And now the man who'd taught him to die had arrived at the heavenly court before him.

Seeing Tuo hesitate, Jue stepped in front of him, but the gatekeeper blocked his way.

"You have to leave. Go find your head."

Jue picked Tuo up, put him atop his neck stump, and tried again. The gatekeeper snapped, "You dolt! How could you put someone else's head on your body?"

And so this Heile head on a Pisha body could only gaze haplessly at the people frolicking on the infinite white jade terraces of the heavenly court. The war was over for them. Tuo's war had ended too, but he wasn't in their midst. His head was on a Pisha man's body, his body was probably being used by someone else's head. Perhaps it didn't matter any more.

*

The three children go to sleep in the tree branches. The man offers Ku a room, but Ku says he's happy to sleep outside. Hsieh watches as he gathers a mattress of straw and lays the saddlebags over it, tucking himself into the fabric, looping the reins around his wrist.

Ku dozes off, but is soon awakened by the stamping of hooves. He opens his eyes to see the pike bearer on his horse in the courtyard, both their heads higher than the roof. Ku climbs to his feet and wraps his arms around Hsieh's neck. She looks grimly at him, sensing the dark energy that has arrived.

"The general sent me to find you—he's worried for your safety."

His tone is ice cold, leaving no room for question.

"I want to spend the night here. I'll see the general tomorrow."

"My companion was slaughtered while looking for you. There are enemies everywhere in these parts. Please come back to the camp with me immediately."

Their host pokes his head out in alarm, unable to work out how this massive horse and its rider made their way into his locked compound.

Defeat

The guard leads Ku and Hsieh along a dry riverbed. After walking all night, a village appears in the distance. As they draw closer, they see the Heile troops in the midst of ransacking it. They hide in a grove nearby, but can still hear the piercing screams of women and children. By mid-morning, there is silence and thick black smoke is rising from the village. They venture in and find dead bodies everywhere, some decapitated, some sliced in half. The houses have all been burnt to the ground. Only one family remains alive, and they prostrate themselves before the pike bearer, grateful that a Pisha soldier is finally here.

Ku and the guard ignore them, rushing through the smouldering village as quickly as they can. Some distance away, they turn back to see the family still standing in the road, hands clasped in a Kun bow.

It is evening by the time they get back to the Pisha camp. Ku and Hsieh are exhausted, while the pike bearer doesn't seem the least bit tired. The camp is in chaos. Weary soldiers are lying any which way across the ground, and it seems clear they've suffered another defeat. Yet General Chokanurkan is beaming, completely unbowed. Summoning Ku to his hastily-erected tent, he regales him with tales of their past acquaintance and doesn't mention a word about the war. Ku is uneasy—Hsieh remains outside the tent, held by the pike bearer, and a good many soldiers have gathered around the opening. He hurriedly says farewell and, as he leaves, turns back to say, "Does the general have a message I should bear to Pisha?"

"It can wait till you're on your way home—I don't need you to bear my words all the way to Heile and back. Your head must already be crammed full of other people's talk. Not that I'm going to pry your brain open for a look, I doubt anything in there is a threat to Pisha security."

Ku has no idea how Chokanurkan knows he is on his way to Heile. Eyes wide, he stares at the general, and thinks about mentioning that he is bearing word from the Great Kunmen of Pisha's West Kun Temple to Kunmen Maisheng at Peach Blossom Temple. Then again, he decides, the general doesn't need an explanation from him.

Goatman

A soldier arrives to report that they've captured a talking goat. The troops requisitioned a nearby field of grazing goats, a reward for the men after all their hard work. They began to slaughter them, but when they got to a black goat, the goatherd—a man named Mazaghan—leapt forward and hugged his neck, begging them to spare this one. They pushed him aside and shoved the goat's head to the ground, but before they could bring down the blade, the goat suddenly spoke. Now both the black goat and Mazaghan are being detained in the little grove behind the tent.

Ku takes Hsieh's reins and goes to see what's happening. Chokanurkan stares at the goat's front hooves, which look like human hands.

"A goatman," Ku and the general pronounce at the same moment.

Ku has known for a while that the Tai were making such creatures, so naturally Chokanurkan is aware of this too.

"What orders did your owner give you? Speak!"

The general holds the tip of his sword against the black goat, who fixes the blade with a frosty stare and shakes his head.

"What did you ask this thing to do? Speak!"

The sword swivels to face Mazaghan, who shakes his head exactly as the goat just did.

Two soldiers lunge over and tie Mazaghan to a tree branch by his feet. Ku has seen Pisha dealing with their enemies this way before. It is apparently a tactic they learnt from the Kang. Anyone from petty thieves to traitors gets strung up upside down and interrogated. No matter how stubborn, people usually give in after half a day of this treatment, the words tumbling out of their mouths.

Mazaghan has had four fingers chopped off before he begins to talk. He is of Kang descent, but his family has lived in Pisha for several generations now, and they're all Tian believers. There are Tian temples amid the Kun towers in Pisha City, and there didn't use to be any discrimination until the war with Heile began, the Heile being Tian converts. Mazaghan admits that he has been in contact with Tian devotees from Heile for twenty years now, collecting and passing on information. The rest of the time, he herds and trades livestock. His goats travel with him wherever there is fighting. Local officials have praised him for supporting the troops in this way, but actually he has been using his proximity to the front line to gather intelligence.

This is the first time Ku has heard a person speaking from this position, and his words feel upside down too. Sometimes a clump of them get stuck in his throat, which is uncomfortable to hear.

"Let him down," says Chokanurkan.

As soon as Mazaghan is back on the ground, he clutches his hand and howls, "My fingers!"

The soldiers tie his arms behind his back. He stops screaming, now he can no longer see the bleeding stumps.

The black goat bleats to see his owner the right way up again. Mazaghan glances at the goat, whom a soldier is clutching by the neck.

"I bought him more than ten years ago in the marketplace. He was two years old, a special little boy. I put him in the goat pen to live with the goats for the next three years. He learnt to walk on all fours and bleat, just like them. When he was five, I skinned a yearling and pulled the pelt over the child, sewing his mouth shut, covering him head to toe so the goat skin would become the boy's skin. It hurt at first, and he tried to struggle free, but after enduring two years, the two skins grafted together, and his human skin melted into his flesh. He's accepted his lot—he's a goatman. I've made three of his kind, but the other two died after less than six months."

The black goat listens, head tilted to one side. This is the first time he's hearing his own history.

"He helps me gather intelligence from the Heile army. When I let my flock graze in the wilderness, he edges over enemy lines and brings back everything he learns."

"I've been fighting for five years now between Guma and Siya. Is that where you've been operating?"

"Yes."

"Because something's been puzzling me. I'd noticed that before each battle, I'd see a herd of goats grazing nearby. I asked a local official who told me they made sure there were always goats near the battlefield, so the men could feast afterwards. The only thing is, whenever I saw these goats, I knew we were about to be defeated. And now I know. Those were your goats."

"Yes, general. My herd and I have been following you."

"Do you have anything to say for yourself?"

Chokanurkan turns to the black goat, who ignores him and keeps staring at his owner.

"I may have bought him, but after rearing him for so many years, he's like my own son. Please spare him. The guilt is mine. He's just a dumb animal—"

Before Mazaghan can finish his sentence, a blade slashes across his throat. His eyes were on the black goat as he spoke his last words—they were said for the goat's benefit. Like any other animal that doesn't understand human speech, the goat watches indifferently as his owner's head is lopped off. Ku shuts his eyes and Hsieh begins backing away, only stopping when she sees Mazaghan's ghost leaping easily onto a tree.

"Take charge of the animal," Chokanurkan says, as goes back into his tent. The pike bearer puts one hand on the creature's head, the other on his side, pushing it to the ground and resting a knee on it.

"I'll help you get rid of the goat skin."

With his knife, he slits the goat's belly, his throat, his chin, his mouth, his nose, his forehead, splitting apart the pelt with its thick dark wool. The goatman stamps his hooves and shrieks, half human cries and half bleating. The pike bearer works slowly, deliberately, so Ku can see the whole thing. The goat skin has fused with the human one, and hairs from the human body grow through the animal pelt. The soldier's blade slips nimbly between the two skins, and as the goat one peels off, a human face reveals itself, deformed after being compressed for so long, twisted in human agony and issuing cries of pain through its human lips. Both man and goat are hurting, but it is the human screams that pierce Ku's heart. He can't look any more, and shuts his eyes as he clings to Hsieh's side.

The half-flayed goatman dies of pain. His final cries sound purely human, as if his goat self has already died and only human torment is left. Hsieh's ears twitch and Ku strokes her neck. After a long while, Ku turns around to see human arms, chest, stomach and legs revealed. Hsieh sees TuoJue staring at the goatman, and she stares too, worried about what goat-skinned soul will emerge from the body. She already has one monster on her back and can't afford to attract another one.

North Dipper

The sky suddenly darkens.

The scattered Pisha soldiers silently assemble, all the horses facing north, General Chokanurkan on his great white steed. He rides a black horse by day and a white one at night.

The troops set forth, the same men who were fighting during the day, the same horses. Ku follows behind on his donkey, feeling as if he's entering a dream he has had before: the same starry night sky, the same mounted troops boldly advancing in darkness over the ground they retreated from that afternoon, soldiers who'd fallen by the wayside during the day now rising to their feet as the horses clatter by, dead horses reviving too, so the army grows larger and larger. The Heile camp appears beneath the distant starlight, the snores of the Heile army wafting on the night breeze. The Heile were victorious by day, and now the snores of a thousand people are drifting across many li to the advancing Pisha army. Ku and Hsieh hear it too.

"People are snoring in five languages," Ku murmurs to himself.

General Chokanurkan must have heard this some time ago. His sleepless warriors have been tracing the Heile army's thunderous snores, their vast dreamscape, ready to pounce.

The pike bearer holds Ku back.

"This is as far as we'll take you. Head west for three days, and you'll be at the Pisha border. The general says he hopes to meet you again in the future."

The horseback troops hurtle past noiselessly, just as they did the night before, then all is silent. The dark Pisha army seems to press down on the ground ahead, and their flag with the seven stars of the North Dipper unfurls across a cloudless sky.

6

Fence Village

Village

THE VILLAGE GRADUALLY reveals itself. First, sounds: dogs, chickens, humans, donkeys. Then the smoke of cooking fires, and finally the houses, low to the ground.

This road through the wilderness is marked with donkey hoofprints, some shallower than others, scattered between sparse stalks of southern wormwood and tamarisk. Footprints vanish as soon as the wind blows, and the only traces humans leave are the deeper hoofprints caused by their weight on a donkey's back.

Half a day passes between spotting the village and actually arriving at its entrance.

Seeing a lone person by the side of the road, Ku and Hsieh peer until they can make out his face through his beard and long hair. Only one ear is visible, pressed to the road listening for movement.

"I'm blind. Please tell me the way to Pisha."

Ku recognises the blind man. Two years ago, he was standing here too, when Ku passed through Fence Village on a different jenny. As he drew near, the blind man suddenly looked up and stared with the dark holes of his eyes, speaking a language Ku had never heard before. Agape with confusion, Ku didn't know how to respond. He'd thought he'd learnt every single language of this region.

This time round, Ku understands him. The blind man is speaking the language of a small village in western Tian, and he's asking for directions. Ku is about to tell him the way to Pisha, but he hesitates and falls silent. Ku is a man of words—he knows all the languages of the world, but they are all for the sighted. How should he describe the way to a man who can't see?

An old lady arrives holding a stick. She puts one end in the blind man's hand and leads him towards the village. Ku calls a greeting to her, and she smiles faintly. Ku and Hsieh follow her to a small Kun temple beneath a large mulberry tree.

Two years ago, Ku also followed the blind man and the woman leading him to this temple and asked for lodging at the old lady's home next door. She was a woman of few words, and even her fleeting smile vanished the next moment.

The little temple shows signs of having been burnt down and rebuilt. Ku can imagine what happened here.

The courtyard is full of Kun devotees, mostly women and old men. When the blind man enters, they suddenly begin chanting scripture in Pishanese. The blind Kunmen lets go of the wooden stick and walks along the path laid out by the chanting. These voices illuminate the entire courtyard for him. Only when he has stepped up onto the Kun dais and is sitting cross-legged do they fall silent. Now the blind Kunmen's voice soars. To the donkeys, who can see the shape and colour of sounds, a resplendent Kun statue erupts from the ground, sculpted by the Kunmen's voice. Hsieh and the donkeys outside the courtyard crane their necks to watch as it rises into the sky, while Ku and the Kun devotees shut their eyes and listen.

Only Ku understands what the blind Kunmen is chanting, and even then only roughly. Having proofread Kun scripture at West Kun Temple, he can rely on what he remembers of these manuscripts in Pishanese and other languages to guess the contents of the blind man's chanting. Meanwhile, the devotees sit in meditation across the courtyard as if intoxicated. Despite not understanding the language, they seem to directly grasp the meaning of the blind Kunmen's words.

Wind

Two years ago, Ku had to linger in this little temple because there was fighting up ahead. That night, he groped his way through the dark to the blind Kunmen's room and found him meditating in a particularly dark spot, which somehow made his silhouette more prominent. Ku sat across from him. That afternoon, they'd spoken in the shade of the tree. Ku had tried the dozens of languages he was fluent in, but wasn't able to communicate with the blind man in any of them. The Kunmen spoke as if his mouth was full of gusting wind, just a stream of *whoo whoo*, as if air was blowing past the things and ideas he was talking about before emerging from his lips.

Ku understood the wind—it helped the silent things of the earth and sky produce sounds, and he could tell which object, near or far, made each of these noises.

Yet he couldn't identify the source of the wind spewing from the blind Kunmen's mouth.

Wind billowed through the courtyard, and the rustling of poplar leaves mingled with the many sounds from every nook and cranny of the temple buildings. Sound poured from the eaves into the courtyard, from the tip of the tower into the air. The little temple and Fence Village were crisply described by the wind.

"Wind," Ku said in Pishanese, trying to untangle his windswept beard. Then he tried again in Heilenese, Kun, Chiu and Huang.

The blind Kunmen kept one ear turned towards Ku, who flapped air towards it, to no avail. The bright wind whooshing through the sky at the moment was nothing but darkness in the Kunmen's heart.

Ku and the blind Kunmen sat across from each other. In the dark, Ku was blind too, and they grew a little closer. He could hear the blind man's slow breathing, and thought the Kunmen must hear his too. Ku wanted to say the word for "breath" in Pishanese, hoping the Kunmen would respond in his language, but instead he reached out to touch the Kunmen's hand. The Kunmen started and pulled away, then immediately groped his way back, five fingers seeking Ku's, clasping their palms firmly together.

"Hand," Ku said in Pishanese.

The Kunmen reciprocated in his own language.

Then they were joyfully shaking hands, each saying "hand" in the other's language.

Next, they touched feet and said the words for "leg". Knee to knee, they said "walk", followed by verbs for every bendable part of the body. Hand in hand, they groped their way around the dark room and named each object they came across until they ran out. When the first rooster crowed, the blind Kunmen mimicked the sound, *gogg gogg gogg*, in exchange for the Pisha word for "dawn". And the skies of both languages lit up at the same moment.

City Gate

Through his interactions with the blind Kunmen, Ku learnt about his mysterious past: the Kun temple in his hometown was destroyed, leaving the Kun devotees without a home. He decided to seek out the legendary Kun kingdom of Pisha and climbed across the snowy peaks until he arrived at Heile. At the eastern city gate, he asked how to get to Pisha, and in response the Tian devotees gouged out his eyes. The blind Kunmen remained outside the eastern gate asking for directions. Over the years, everyone came to know the blind Kunmen. When he stood by the eastern gate and called out, "Pisha, Pisha!" the clandestine Kun devotees, of whom there were many, would lead him eastwards and tell him to keep walking, but the Tian devotees would just as quickly turn him around and tell him to go west instead.

The blind Kunmen trusted he would be able to find his way east to Pisha using only his nose and ears, listening and sniffing his way from one village to the next through the wilderness. Some reeked of donkeys, others of goat dung, and yet others of women's lower bodies, as if every female flower had bloomed at the same time. There were villages perfumed by the first shoots sprouting on the white poplar trees, and when the almond trees flowered, no other fragrance could make its presence felt. Then the blossoms fell, and it was as if the trees no longer existed—at least, not until the nuts ripened and the aroma of bitter almonds filled the village. Almonds were the first crop of this region. When stockpiles were low and even the bitter leaves were running out, poor families no longer had anything to put in the stew pot. Then the almonds would ripen and blanket the ground beneath each tree. Soon the air would be filled with the sound of cracking shells and the scent of bitter kernels being chewed. The blind Kunmen paid close attention to the smells of every place in every season. Each village had a route to Pisha, but those were meant for people who could see. The Kunmen had to make his own way, guided only by his nose, ears and soul.

Whenever he went the wrong way or got lost, the Kunmen would return to the eastern gate of Heile. He made note of a protruding knot on the gate frame, harder than steel. As they brushed past on their way in, camels and donkeys would leave a few strands of hair on this knot, and women awaiting the return of family members would tie red ribbons here. This knot is all the Kunmen remembers of Heile City. When the Pisha army fought their way here and rammed the city gate, it seemed nothing else resisted them but this knot. It tore at Pisha sleeves, ripped their clothes, tangled the manes of Pisha horses. Then one day it was chipped away, and the blind kunmen could no longer feel Heile.

"A very long time ago, a blind man could walk from Heile to Pisha, but that's no longer possible. The land is filled with people whose souls face opposite directions, and there's no way to ask for directions," the blind Kunmen said to Ku, using the Pishanese he'd just learnt.

Kunmen

No one knows how the blind Kunmen found his way to Fence Village, but everyone remembers the early morning he walked into the temple as the bells were ringing, eyes shut tight, as if walking into his own home. He had confidently strode up the stone steps with the groove worn into them, through the front door and straight to the central dais where he sat cross-legged and began reciting scripture.

The Kun statue at the centre of the temple had been smashed by marauding Heile troops three years ago. They chopped off its head with a hoe, then tied its body to thirty donkeys who pulled it to the ground, after which they poured three hundred buckets of water over it and got the donkeys to trample it into sludge. The villagers were forced to change their religion, to fetch the water, to pull the donkey reins so they'd stamp on the fallen statue. As soon as the Heile army left, they knelt in front of the muddy mess that had once been their Kun statue and kowtowed for mercy, smacking their mouths and hitting their heads till they bled, pleading that Kun would forgive them, proclaiming that their conversion had only been in words, that their hearts had never wavered from Kun. The only reason they hadn't held firm, they said, was so they could hold on to their heads, the same heads now kowtowing to Kun, with the mouths chanting Kun scripture. Fence villagers had done this many times: obediently converting to Tian for a couple of days, only to resume their Kun worship as soon as the soldiers moved on.

Master passed through Fence Village on many occasions. He once told Ku about a man who was forced to convert to Tian at knifepoint, but when the other villagers converted back after the Heile departed, he wasn't able to—he'd accidentally become a true believer. He gave away everything he had, including his wife and children, and left to join the Heile, walking backwards all the way so he could keep facing Fence Village where they spoke Pishanese, and the Kun land of Pisha, and the Kun religion that had been his and his ancestors' for a thousand years.

"He walked backwards all the way to Heile, where he intended to turn around, face west and worship Tian."

This man never actually got to Heile. Walking backwards, he failed to see the canyon between the two kingdoms. He fell in and died.

*

The Kun statue had been irrevocably destroyed. The villagers weren't able to build another one, so they cleaned up the dais where the statue had sat and waited for the day they could replace it. It was then that this living Kun arrived instead. That morning, the blind Kunmen walked through the temple door in the bright morning light, as if this place had always been his, his features exactly the same as the Kun statue that had gotten smashed. With no one to guide him, he made his way up to the dais and sat cross-legged, holding his hands exactly the same as the statue, and when he opened his mouth to recite scripture, his voice was the voice of Kun. No one who beheld this could resist immediately kneeling in worship before him.

No one could understand the language he was chanting, but every single person could tell it was Kun scripture, and soon they were bewitched, lost in his voice as they prayed or sat in meditation. Not only were the villagers rapt, passers-by were also drawn here by the sound of his chanting. Soon, he'd become the Kun of this little temple, the living embodiment of the destroyed statue. When he sat motionless on the dais, everyone felt compelled to pray to him.

Return

The blind Kunmen has been at the little temple in Fence Village for three years now. The wilderness beyond is covered in his footprints. He sets off for Pisha first thing each morning, and by afternoon has returned to the village. The villagers treat him as a Kun, unwilling to let him go, but scared to disobey him. At dawn each day, he walks out the temple door calling, "Pisha, Pisha!" Knowing where he wants to go, the good-hearted villagers lead him to the east end of the village, point him straight ahead, and tell him to keep walking.

Eventually, though, his steps begin to curve, and he makes a loop through the wilderness back towards the village. By afternoon, when he's too exhausted to take another step, a villager will be waiting along the way. Delighted to hear a human voice, the blind Kunmen will call out, "Pisha, Pisha!"

"You've already been to Pisha, and now you're back at Fence Village," will come the reply.

Naturally, the Kunmen will have no idea what these words mean, but he'll recognise the speaker and sit heavily on the ground, uncertain where he went wrong in the interminable darkness.

The villager will lead him back to the temple, though he needs no guidance here. The temple bells guide him straight there, paving a pathway of sound.

Each day he wakes before cockcrow, before birdsong, ears pricked for the bells of Pisha ringing in the east. All he hears, though, are the little temple's chimes.

When he sits on the dais chanting scripture, not a word is heard from the speakers of Pishanese, Heilenese and Huang in the temple—they can all tell that what he's reading is true Kun scripture.

"One time, I got all the way to the outskirts of Pisha City, then a child gave me directions, and I ended up back here," says the blind Kunmen, in the Pishanese taught to him by Ku.

The blind Kunmen had been tricked by old men, middle-aged men, and women of all ages. Finally he trusted a child. On that occasion, he'd been walking east for half a month, and could hear the great bell of West Kun Temple, whose high walls scoop up the sound and disseminate it in all directions. Kun devotees in distant parts talk about bells sounding in the heavens. Relying only on his nose and ears, the blind kunmen found his way into Pisha City. Then he heard a child chanting, "Turn around, turn away, night is gone, then it's day. First walk north, then go south."

The Kunmen called out, "Pisha, Pisha?"

The child led him to the middle of the street, spun him around several times, then pointed his arms straight ahead, indicating the direction he should walk in.

"And half a month after that, I found myself back in Fence Village."

Drawn-Out

Once again, Ku seeks shelter in the old lady's house right next to the temple. Chanting seeps through gaps in the wall, which consists of a wooden frame with earth smeared over it. The sound invades the little room Ku is staying in, as well as the one next door where the woman and her daughter-in-law sleep, out into the donkey pen and fodder shed, and finally drifts out into the wilderness. The old lady doesn't light any lamps, and when it gets dark, the courtyard falls completely silent. Ku goes to the shed for some wheat chaff, which he tips into the trough in the donkey pen. When the chanting has faded away, he goes to the temple and pushes open the Kunmen's door. It is darker in here than outside, and Ku can't see anything at all, though he can hear the Kunmen's drawn-out breathing, just like the last time. He gropes his way in, knowing the Kunmen is sitting in meditation, his body darker than the rest of the room and the night outside. Ku stops in front of him, kneels, and reaches out a hand, which the blind Kunmen takes, just like the last time, their hands clasping tightly in the dark.

"Wait here for me. I'll bring you back to Pisha with me, on my way back from Heile. You won't get lost anymore—my eyes will be your eyes," says Ku in the blind Kunmen's mother tongue.

Ku already made him this promise when they met that afternoon.

The blind Kunmen shakes his hand vigorously, and slowly lets go. Hearing him raise his head, Ku looks up too, and finds the Kunmen staring straight at him, which sends a shiver down his spine. The Kunmen's lightless eyes are darker than night, darker even than his body, a darkness that no illumination will ever pierce, where dawn will never break.

"Your road is a dark one too," the blind Kunmen says in Pishanese, and when he says the word "dark", all the darkness in Ku's heart suddenly swamps him. The word "dark" appears in his mind, in the dozens of languages he knows, as if a few weeks' worth of nights are pressing down on him at once, and darkest of all is Heilenese. He is about to enter the region where this language is spoken, but he has no idea what will happen there; it's just a wash of black.

Breast-Tassel

"With each new language, you gain another night."

Master was well aware of the darkness that deep knowledge of languages brings. He was old, and had learnt all the languages on earth. The way he saw it, some things might seem to be illuminated by different languages, but those were actually the darkest of all. You couldn't describe a Heile dawn in Pishanese. Kun scripture was meant to shine a light for the world, but when translated into Heilenese, Pishanese, Huang or Chiu, it was, without exception, cast into the darkness of these tongues.

Ku learnt Pishanese on the dark nights after Master brought him from Heile to Pisha. All day he was left in the courtyard with only donkeys for company, while Master interpreted for merchants and ambassadors from other kingdoms. He'd return home late at night and would never light a lamp, but lay down next to Ku in the darkness and spoke Pishanese to him while half-asleep. With each sentence Master uttered, Ku's face would light up. It was from these words, spoken as Master was drifting off, that Ku learnt the Pisha language.

Master said Pishanese was a language created in dreams, and was therefore suited for night. The earliest people spoke it in their sleep, then their dream talk was learnt by the waking. People began speaking it during the day, and everything they said was like a dream.

Ku was five when Master bought him on Jenny Lane in Heile. All the way back to Pisha, Ku rode backwards on the donkey, learning

Heile during the month it took them to traverse Heile territory until finally they reached a village where Pisha was spoken, and it felt like moving from one dream to another. All languages from distant places felt like dream talk—at least to Ku.

Ku learnt Bod under the lash. At the age of thirteen, he was captured by the Bod people and imprisoned in a stone goat pen high in the Kunlun hills. His interrogator knew about three lines of Pishanese and two of Huang, and with these five sentences, while being whipped, Ku mastered fifty lines of Bod. With this Bod, interspersed with Pishanese and Huang words, he was able to explain himself. By the time he was set free, he'd been tortured so badly he was barely skin and bones. Coming back down the mountain, he spoke nothing but Bod, which many Pisha people understood, because the Bod had ruled Pisha for eighty years.

Even more people in Pisha knew Huang, because almost everyone in the imperial palace spoke and wrote it, so Ku picked it up along the way. He only had to look at a Huang character to remember it forever. Every Huang word was an open window, a bottomless pit. When you knew it, you'd be trapped. Master refused to let Ku learn its writing.

"Become literate," he said, "and you'll be tempted to write, which will fix the language in your mind. The words we bear are living ones."

Even so, Ku mastered Huang writing.

It seemed that many things in Pisha could be resolved by speaking Huang. Whenever anything happened, big or small, a delegation would be sent to the Huang region, and they'd return with a Huang message. Every third sentence spoken in Pisha was in Huang, their backbone, their pillar.

One time, Ku accompanied a Pisha delegation, passing through five language regions before reaching their destination, Shachow, the northernmost point where Huang was spoken. Ku spoke Huang with the local Kun devotees, and they told him that eastward was an ocean of Huang. You could ride a donkey for two lifetimes and not come to the end of the Huang territory.

Master had been several times to the capital of the Central Plains, and five years ago when the Pisha army was victorious, he was sent to deliver an official document to the Central Plains court along with an elephant that had been a war trophy. The first time he sat on the elephant's back, he felt the same way he had in his youth, riding a donkey cart piled high with bundles of wheat. From Hetian he went to Shachow, Soochow, Liangchow, then Singan and Chengchow, staying at staging posts and Kun temples along the way, noticing the word "Kunmen" everywhere he passed. In these parts, all Kun devotees were known as Kunmen.

"No one can outrun words," he said. "Kun scripture has been translated, and now it's reached places where there are no Pisha people."

Many years later, Ku tailed another word to the Central Plains court, one he'd learnt from the Kang language of his wife Sha: breast-tassel. Of all the tongues he'd picked up, only Kang had been learnt with his eyes shut, all from Sha when she was sent to him to repay a debt. Wherever he put his mouth, she would say the name of that body part in Kang, and so her figure was sketched out in Kang, lit up as he kissed her over and over, the sweetest possible way of learning a language.

Each word had its own flavour. The first time the tip of Ku's tongue touched Sha's, he knew Kang was salty, a saltiness that had nothing to do with salt. This was the language he spent the most time immersed in, and Sha's wondrous body was his textbook. The Kang language was created by men lying atop women, he thought. Looking at Sha's wheat-coloured nipples, hearing her say the word "breast-tassel", a hunger he'd never felt before suddenly came over him.

Kang merchants often passed through Pisha City, and now Ku imagined the land covered in stalks of wheat, and women's nipples the same golden colour, the same wheaty fragrance. The ring around the nipple was known as the "field", and when the wheat was ripe, it would lay itself bare.

Ku kissed Sha all the way from her breast-tassels to her toes, and discovered that the Kang language distinguishes between legs: the right is called "go", the left "come". They believe we walk away with our right feet, and return with the left. Whenever Ku set out on a long journey, Sha would keep a close eye on his legs to see which took the first step. As long as it wasn't the left, she could stop worrying.

On another occasion, Ku accompanied a delegation to an audience with the emperor of the Central Plains. As they headed east along the long Gansu Corridor, Ku heard Huang being spoken everywhere, and once again encountered the word "breast-tassel". This was what people called nipples, it turned out, in all regions where wheat was grown. He only stopped hearing the word when they'd gone far enough south that the main crop around them was rice.

Smile

Ku returns to the old lady's house and finds her sitting by a lantern, awaiting his return. When he steps inside, a faint smile flickers briefly across her placid face, before vanishing again into the stillness.

He looks at her in silence. He'd like to give her a smile, but can't summon one.

That afternoon, he heard in the temple that the woman's four sons were all in the Pisha army. Two of them died a couple of months ago—the elder was struck, and when the younger ran to his rescue, he got hit too. They lay on the ground next to each other. When the news came, their father hurried there with a donkey, only to find two headless corpses. He tied these to his donkey, handed the reins to a drover, and set off to wander the wilderness and seek out their heads. He hasn't returned yet.

"The other two sons are still alive. The eldest is on the frontline at Pisha; his name is Jue."

Ku shudders to hear the name of the Pisha general beheaded a few days ago, the name he heard on the dunes that twilight from the lips of the roll call officer, after which he learnt that this was the man who'd lain dead beside him. News of his death hasn't reached the village yet, or perhaps he comes back to life night after night of fighting, fastening his head back on his shoulders, the blood he shed pumping back through his heart. Pisha's nighttime army requires an endlessly advancing frontline general, and his life or death must be hidden deep within day and night, so even when the news of all other deaths has arrived on donkeyback, there are no such reports of General Jue, for he is not dead, but is leading the Pisha night army in their charge on the enemy camp each night.

Ku lowers his eyes, afraid to look at the old woman. He saw with his own eyes that Jue was on the brink of death. He smeared Jue's blood on his face to play dead. He watched as Jue's head was cut off, lying perfectly still next to Jue's corpse for so long it seemed to take more time than his own eventual death. When the fighting finally stopped, the tanner sewed a Heile head onto Jue's body and put the mismatched corpse on Hsieh's back, making Ku responsible for transporting it. During their chaotic escape, he abandoned the body by the roadside, something he still regrets. But he and Hsieh were fleeing for their lives. Jue no longer had anything to run from.

He can't tell the old lady any of this, of course. Some news should never arrive.

The woman's husband was still here on Ku's last visit, a droll, chatty old codger who regaled Ku with all kinds of stories about Fence Village, though he didn't breathe one word about his four sons in the Pisha army. Now all Ku sees are the old woman and a daughter-in-law clutching a little girl, and two boys of about ten who say nothing, but hang their heads when they see Ku.

Ku gives the old lady three bronze coins. She says that's too much and tries to give one back, but he insists he wants to pay for the donkey's feed too. She smiles faintly and accepts the money.

Bearing Word

Ku can't sleep, so he goes out to the donkey shed, where he sees Hsieh and another jenny standing quietly, like two women who have nothing to say to each other. Worried about Hsieh, Ku decides to sleep on a pile of hay. Hsieh inches over and settles with her flank pressed against him. The other jenny watches suspiciously. Ku was riding a different female donkey on his last visit, and he slept next to her too. This jenny must remember.

The roof and walls of the shed are riddled with holes through which the murky sky is visible and the sound of dirt falling can be heard. The moon and stars have been swallowed by swirling dust.

A faint donkey cry echoes in the distance. Hsieh angles her ear. Another bray, at the very limits of its range, petering out.

Behind the pen is scrubland covered with low southern wormwood shrubs, and beyond that is Qusha, which was once Pisha territory, but has since been taken by the Heile. The bray must have come from the village by the dry gully, a message for this village.

In a short while, the donkeys at the west end of the village begin braying, and so do these two jennys. Ku walks out and sees three wooden poles, each with a donkey tied to it, facing east and crying out. Almost immediately, more braying starts in the east. To the donkeys, their voices look like stars shooting up into the sky. Word spreads to more villages. In less than four hours, the message will have made its way to Pisha City.

Now the dogs in the east of the village begin to bark. Whenever a word bearer rides his donkey from the village, their *wnng wnng* sees him out. In the same way, whenever a visitor arrives, he is greeted by a crescendo of barking.

Many people in Fence Village make a living bearing words. Most of them speak Heilenese and have secret dealings with the Heile village across the way. The goat drovers in the wilderness often send word this way, until all the Heile news is gathered in

Fence Village, at which point a word bearer on donkeyback will ride through the night to the next village, and the information will be relayed to Pisha City before dawn.

Darkness

The darkness of Fence Village can only be described in Pishanese. First thing tomorrow morning, Ku will set off through Heile, passing ten Heilenese-speaking villages, as well as Aoba, where prayers in Heilenese and Tian can be heard all day long, where the magnificent palace of Lanshihan used to stand—and is now his mausoleum. In this season, Pisha is resplendent with the loud pomp of idol processions, while Heile quietly enacts the grave spiral ritual, a pilgrimage in which people visit tomb after tomb, circling towards the largest cemetery in Aoba.

Ku gazes at the westward gloom and feels an unease he can't explain. He seems to remember being in a similar state the night before his previous departure from Fence Village. He is about to cross the Pisha border. Now he can no longer be a Pisha man, but must appear to be Heile. If he carelessly lets a few words of Pishanese pass his lips, he may be in danger of losing his head. The Pisha language is incapable of expressing the darkness of Heile. Every object in Fence Village is called by its Pisha name. Tomorrow, on the other side of the dry gully, everything will be called something else. And once he's climbed out of that deep opening, Ku will renounce Pishanese for the safety of Heilenese or Tian.

The Pisha sky over Fence Village grows light as the temple bell sounds *dong dong dong*. In this moment, the sky in each of Ku's languages is bright—but these words for daybreak, and all other words, must now go dark for him.

Stroking

Ku leads the blind Kunmen out of the temple and over to Hsieh, who gives him a sidelong look as he touches her belly, sending a fearful shudder through her. When his hand makes contact with her pelt, she feels the words wriggle towards it. The blind Kunmen seems to sense something too. His fingers probe deeper, as if they have eyes that see these scriptures, four fingers along four lines of text, thumb pointing towards the sky, like he is broadcasting the words to the heavens. Hsieh lowers her head in fear, every one of her hairs atremble, the hidden words coming to life like insects, itching her as they float on her nervous sweat, along the lines that were carved into her skin. Donkeys see itches as colours, and now she squints at the red glow enveloping her body. The blind Kunmen must feel this illumination too.

Hsieh glances at Ku, who is fortunately looking away, otherwise he'd surely notice the words wriggling like black beetles where the Kunmen's hand has parted her hair.

His hand continues along her spine, then jerks suddenly when he reaches her rump. Hsieh sees the ghost TuoJue tumbling from her back, drifting slowly back into place, only to get knocked off by the Kunmen again.

So the blind Kunmen can see ghosts. TuoJue has distracted him.

The Kunmen vaults backwards onto Hsieh's back, startling both Ku and Hsieh. Ku thinks he must have gotten muddled about which way Hsieh is facing, but doesn't bother correcting him—front and back are equally dark to a blind man.

At the east side of the village, the Kunmen dismounts and TuoJue returns.

The blind Kunmen lifts his face to the newly risen sun, which Ku knows he does every morning. The sun is invariably hidden behind swirling clouds of dust, and those with sight cannot see it, but by the heat on his face, the Kunmen knows it's there.

He walks east till noon, but with the sun directly overhead, he is lost again. The people of Fence Village seldom realise the sun is right above them, as a thick layer of dust hides the sky.

As the blind Kunmen stands lost in the wilderness, the bell of the little temple chimes, and noises come from every corner. Fence Village uses all sorts of sounds to lead him by the ear, so he thinks he's following his ears to a distant place but is actually wandering in a circle around the village.

Ku sends the Kunmen off on his way, and watches as the blind man marches directly ahead, his path even straighter than most sighted people. Beneath his feet are sand dunes, southern wormwood, tamarisk and camelthorns, all giving way to him. Ku knows the Kunmen will never get to Pisha. Now Ku leads Hsieh westwards. They still have a few days' journey before they reach the dry gully that marks the border between these two kingdoms. Ku will wait on this side till nightfall, when the darkness will obscure the gulf. When that happens, he'll lead Hsieh along a small trackway only donkey drovers know about down to the bottom of the gully, through thickets of tamarisk and salt trees, to the path that will bring him up the other side.

Once he's there, he'll be in the land of Tian devotees. With his fluent, accentless Heilenese and Tian, he'll immediately turn into a local.

Spirit

Hsieh can't stop looking behind her. Ku turns, assuming she's watching the blind Kunmen.

In fact, Hsieh is staring at TuoJue. The Kunmen's hand seems to have roused the ghost, who is now riding her backwards, speaking in their ghostly tongue.

Jue says, "Help me look around, Tuo, the wind on my body feels so familiar. I'm listening to village noises through your ears, and it feels like a dream I've had before."

Tuo says, "I didn't tell you, Jue, but we've already passed all the way through your hometown. Without your head, you didn't even realise you were back home. We stayed in your house last night, and in the donkey pen, I listened to your family's old jenny telling Hsieh all about you. She could see that you'd returned with someone else's head on your shoulders, and when your mother came in with fresh straw, the donkey's eyes were fixed on her, but your mother couldn't see you now that you've become a spirit, so she doesn't know you're dead. I watched the old lady feeding Hsieh straw, then she stroked Hsieh's back, almost touching her son's ghostly leg then abruptly stopping, and in that moment I thought to myself, lucky these are my eyes and not yours, I don't think you could bear seeing this."

Jue listens in silence. All of a sudden, tears stream from Tuo's eyes and down his face, flowing across the seam in their neck and onto Jue's chest. Finally, the head has felt the body's suffering.

Barking

"Dirt's been falling all day. Damn this spooky weather," grumbles Ku. They've gone from a gloomy day into pitch black night, and Ku casually says the word "spooky" without realising there's an actual ghost riding his donkey. The word rouses the ghost—first Jue, who hears the word through Tuo's ears and moves his hand up to tap the head, making Tuo open his eyes. Through Tuo's eyes, Jue can see that the sky is dark, meaning the time has come for ghosts to be active.

Ku has to stop every now and then to brush dirt off himself, while Hsieh tosses her head and shimmies her body to do the same, otherwise she'll get weighed down. Dirt doesn't bother ghosts. It passes straight through their brainless heads and organless bodies, right down onto Hsieh's new growth of donkey hair. Hsieh turns back to look, hoping she's jolted the ghost off her back. Donkeys can be spookier than spooks, that's something both people and ghosts say about them. When Hsieh shakes herself, Jue rises slowly into the air, and Tuo goes higher still—he seeks a higher vantage whenever he can. Jue knows what he's looking for. Aoba is within sight.

7

Aoba, Part I

EVEN BEFORE CATCHING SIGHT of it, Jue knows they've reached Aoba when he hears the dogs barking. A whole pack of them, enough to make you shudder. Ku feels the same too. When Ku turns things over in his mind, a ghost stirs in his heart. Hsieh can see this happening, though Ku himself is unaware. This poor man, he doesn't know a single thing.

Now Ku leads Hsieh through the burnt-out village, and barking comes from beneath fallen roofs and collapsed earth walls, from the road that's been buried in sand. Through Tuo's eyes, Jue sees the ruined walls of Aoba Palace, taller and darker than when he saw it with his own eyes last year. Thickets of barking are reflected back by the high walls, and the dogs quarrel with their own echoes.

He heard the same dogs barking last year, in the same voices. Ghosts face backwards, so everything they see and hear is from last year. Hsieh tilts her head, one ear and one eye facing behind her. She can see ghosts' thoughts. They appear to her as a white glow, dimly illuminating events from their living pasts. Now Jue is speaking with Tuo's mouth, telling the head about the battle that took place a year ago at Aoba Palace.

Hsieh slows down so she can listen better, and Ku's steps slow too. He seems to have fallen asleep, still holding the reins. The ghostly chatter doesn't bother him, because he can't hear ghosts.

Night Watch

The evening we set out from Guma, I had a bizarre feeling: that we were moving the night towards Heile. The goatherd bore word to say we had to march through the night, staying away from settlements so not a single person or dog would detect our presence. There were night watchmen and guard dogs in every village. If a single dog discovered us, its barking would alert the next village, sparking a chain leading all the way to Heile within an hour. At the same time, a word bearer would be sent out on a donkey, carrying a message for the next village, then another word bearer would take up the relay, and within a single day and night the word would reach Heile, matching the intelligence sent by the dogs, at which point the king would muster his troops and declare a state of war. Barking alone, without the confirmation of a human word bearer, wouldn't lead to action. Similarly, a word bearer's report without canine corroboration would be harmless. This is the double-reporting system Heile established during its protracted war with Pisha.

The goatherd word bearer said the most dangerous point would be the three villages next to Aoba, which functioned as three vigilant ears for the palace. Each of these villages had a hundred dogs and three hundred peasant soldiers on night watch. Not even a ghost could get by undetected. The goatherd must have known when he said this that among the Heile, the Pisha night army was already known as a ghost squad.

Daylight

Day no longer existed for us. Darkness was a black shield fastened to our backs, and the army huddled underneath, all of us beasts of burden, shouldering the hefty bulk of night. Only night walkers understand this weight. After a week of this, I'd forgotten daylight and didn't even know if day had broken in this time, or what happened during it. I was on the frontline of General Chokanurkan's night army, his valiant vanguard, and we fought from the Pisha River to the Yarkand River, all the way to Heile, while my own battle was from day to night, moving my entire life into the darkness. After that, all my memories were black, and daylight no longer played any role in my life.

Our Guide Luo

On every stretch of the journey, our guide Luo would let out a few barks—an uncanny impression of the *wnng wnng* of male dogs, followed by female cries. He'd get a response before long, sometimes a lone voice from nearby, probably a sheepdog in a desert drover's home. Other times there'd be a whole chorus, which would mean a village was up ahead.

Luo could tell from this barking whether the village had been abandoned, and so could I. Dogs from empty villages sounded desolate—they knew their owners were gone, and there was a hollowness to their howls. Most of the villages we passed were uninhabited. The humans here had once been Kun devotees, and the dogs shared their beliefs. Then half of them converted to Tian, and the dogs went along with that too. The Pisha army purged the Tian believers when they passed through, and the Heile did the same to the Kun. After a few rounds of this, only the dogs were left alive, guarding empty homes and waiting for their owners to return. Years passed and the dilapidated settlements became dog villages. Dogs nested in their owners' homes, spawning future generations. Luo once took refuge in such a village. Each building was tenanted by a pack of vicious dogs who, after many years of eating human flesh, had developed reddened eyes and elongated fangs. With nowhere to shelter, Luo had to spend the night perched atop a crumbling wall, trying to look like a chimney, watching his pursuers pass by amid a chorus of barks.

Luo had fallen in with my troop five years earlier, after the Pisha army broke through the Heile line. He was the first to rush up the gate tower, where he chopped off the Heile guard's head and flung it to the ground below. He was a sincere Kun devotee, and though his family had been forced to convert to Tian, he'd refused and gone on the run instead. Some time later, he crept back home under cover of night. Clambering atop the fence of the donkey pen, he saw that the Kun tower at their courtyard entrance had been pushed over and the Kun statue had been smashed, its head thrown into a filthy puddle. After the second cockcrow, the family emerged and pushed open the courtyard gate, then they all knelt facing west and prayed as the call to prayer from the Tian temple sounded. Luo watched unblinkingly as his parents, brothers, sisters and eighty-year-old granny prostrated themselves, and just like that, they were no longer related to him. He couldn't make himself jump the fence to be reunited with his family. A patrol going door to door dragged Luo's granny to her feet and kicked his little sister, shouting that women shouldn't pray together with men.

The next-door neighbours got into trouble. Although the family was facing west and saying Tian prayers, in front of them was a cracked Kun statue they'd retrieved from wherever it had been thrown. The man of the house was beheaded right there and then, and the rest of the family was ordered to pick up his severed head and bang it against the head of the Kun statue. Luo couldn't bear to watch any more. He slipped away and lingered in a nearby alleyway. When the patrol departed, he tiptoed up behind them, and one by one, beginning with the hindmost, he slit their throats. He managed to get four of them before the final one, the one right in front, noticed and ran away with a shriek. After this, nights in Heile became a terrifying affair, with Luo prowling around killing people. During the day, he sat atop a dilapidated wall after smearing his body with ink, impersonating a chimney, watching strangers and past acquaintances pass in front of him, while soldiers tried fruitlessly to track him down. Eventually, he fled Heile City. The whole place was crawling with people out for his blood, but he managed to creep from one broken wall to another under cover of night—Heile was full of ramshackle structures, thanks to the first invasion by the Pisha army twenty years before—getting closer and closer to the city limits. On the final day, he was camouflaged as the chimney of a family home right next to the city wall, and all day long patrols passed overhead. As soon as it got dark, he climbed up onto the wall, killed two sentries, slipped down the other side, and ran. Luo was now a wanted criminal and grew used to life on the run. This left him familiar with how every village and every pathway looked in the dark. He mostly avoided the main roads, choosing instead to flee into the wilderness.

Cockcrow

The army keeps going, giving the villages and goatherds' huts a wide berth. Luo's impressive barking fooled all the dogs: it sounded like one dog greeting another across the distance, tearing a hole in the night and immediately sewing it up again, leaving nothing but silence.

The night before reaching Aoba, we got lost in the desert. The North Dipper was hidden behind dirt and clouds and couldn't point us in the right direction. We dizzied ourselves wandering in circles through the endless sand dunes. Luo and I kept barking, but not a single dog replied, and all around us was quiet.

Luo said he'd never travelled to Aoba from Pisha. He'd only ever approached from the west and south and had no idea what Aoba looked like coming from the east.

The army groped its way through a sandthorn patch. Passing his hands over the ground, Luo found hoofprints and dung from donkeys and goats, and a wet patch of sand which he sniffed at and held up to my nose: donkey piss. There must be a village nearby. I barked like Luo had earlier, but he said that wouldn't work, we ought to mimic a cock's crow instead.

Gogg gogg gogg. Luo let out a string of cries, each more vigorous than the last. Soon enough, we heard clucking to our left, then a couple of roosters up ahead. Thus the location of the three villages was revealed.

"We're near the imperial court," said Luo, "and the darkest spot between these three is Lanshihan's palace."

General Chokanurkan caught up with us and stayed behind

me till dawn. On starry nights, I'd see his eyes glinting. That night, flying sand darkened the entire sky. One of my ears heard movements up ahead, and the other picked up the general's hoofbeats. I was his most dedicated, valiant vanguard, and I could pick out the sound of his horse among a thousand others on the battlefield.

We climbed another sand dune in the dark, the throngs of chicken noises like three bonfires lighting up the night. Further away, bursts of clucking stretched westwards, growing louder as they approached what must have been Heile City.

Chokanurkan and I stood in silence atop a dune. I'd never been this close to him. All around us were chicken sounds. The three villages in Aoba, the great mass of Heile, yet farther west where chickens were squawking in Osh and Kabul, where I'd followed the general seven years ago to ward off the Heile, and westward still to strange places I didn't even know the names of—the familiar crowing spread across the vast and unfamiliar land, slowly calling the sky into brightness.

Behind me, one village after another filled with cockcrows, reaching all the way to Pisha, which was fuller and louder with chickens than anywhere else. I'd grown up amid these cries, and from a young age I understood that the cockcrow began in my hometown. At dawn each day, the roosters of Pisha would set the lead, after which the ones in villages and towns for miles around would follow suit. We all believed the chickens of Pisha brought us daylight.

At that moment, however, it was the three villages of Aoba who began the dawn crowing.

Scripture

General Chokanurkan silently pointed the way with his sword, and our horses began to move. Luo the guide had tricked the roosters into crowing an hour before they should have, while the Heile soldiers were still lost in dreams, unaware of the ruckus.

The cacophonous cockcrow covered the swish of hoofbeats on loose sand, and swiftly our army sped through the narrow gaps between the three curtains of sound. We were approaching the danger zone, the three vigilant villages our word-bearing goatherd had pointed out to us. Only this shroud of crowing could stopper their ears and give us a chance to get close.

The outlines of the imperial buildings came into focus, a looming mass darker than the surrounding night. We couldn't make out doors or windows in the high walls. The Tian tower was a giant astride us. Soon it would be the hour for Tian prayers, and the palace doors would open. We lay in ambush behind a sand ridge east of the palace, awaiting this moment.

General Chokanurkan led his men around to the other side of the palace in the west. I heard his horse come to a halt. Heile stood around a day's journey away in that direction, and the general was lying in wait there to cut off Lanshihan's retreat. Once we had Aoba in hand, the main force could swoop in and take Heile City.

As the cockcrows petered out, the sky dimmed, and the palace grew even blacker and loomed even larger. All around us was absolute silence. When I turned, the soldiers and horses behind me had completely melted into the night, a sheet of black steel lurking on the horizon.

A short while later, the roosters began crowing again, and Aoba was once again surrounded by a dense wall of sound.

Luo the guide said the fowl had realised they'd been tricked, and were back on schedule now.

*

A cry abruptly cut through the night—an unseen Tian devotee atop the tower was sounding the call to prayer. I worried that he'd spot us; if he happened to look in our direction, he'd surely notice the army that was concealed within this darkness, so black and dense.

Following the call to prayer came noises of wakefulness: yawning, getting dressed, coughing, bronze washbowls being set down on stone terraces. With a start, I saw the ground outside the palace come to life. Between low houses and even lower mounds of earth, so close to the ground they were barely visible, groups of people slowly emerged, still half asleep. The great doors of the palace creaked open and more people walked out, quietly assembling at the base of the Tian tower.

The crowd looked like a piece of night solidified in place, not making a sound. We all held our breath. Luo said they were waiting for the roosters to stop crowing—the Tianmen couldn't speak a word of Tian scripture before then. They would have to hurry to get their chanting done in the gap between the second and third rounds of cockcrow, or risk being interrupted.

This morning's prayers were actually an hour early. We waited anxiously for the chickens to fall silent, at which point we might be exposed. Their crowing was a dense forest shielding us, as was the dirt swirling through the air, blocking out the daylight. The coating of dirt on my head and torso grew thicker and thicker, and the same was happening to my horse's mane. I wrapped both arms around his head so he wouldn't shake it or snort. The soldiers behind me did the same.

Layer after layer of night faded away. The palace, the Tian tower and the people on the ground grew clearer. Fortunately for us, the clouds of dirt drifting through the air didn't fade, but grew even denser.

And still the roosters kept up their endless crowing, perhaps annoyed at having been mistaken before. My horses and men could barely restrain themselves from charging, yet the worshippers were motionless, standing before the door of the Tian tower, listening quietly to the chaotic cockcrows.

Then came the Tianmen's soaring voice cutting through the dirt-filled air, way up high where the crowing couldn't reach, as if his words were raining down from the heavens themselves.

The crowd bowed in prayer as the Tianmen chanted. From behind them, we watched the black mass of bodies dip, rise, then dip again.

After these orisons, the Tianmen's chanting mellowed and the devotees stood still, so silent you could hear the grains of dirt bumping into each other in mid-air, like the sound of scripture and the upheld arms were raising them aloft. You could hear dirt landing on the edge of a blade, on a horse's mane. Every Heile soldier had a thick layer of sand on his hair, eyebrows and beard, and the Tianmen's chanting poured down likewise, filling the worshippers' ears too—otherwise how could they have missed the sound of mounted troops drawing closer? The dirt and prayers thickly covered the sky and earth like a felt blanket. Even I was half-asleep, brain dulled although my eyes remained wide open. Our target of many months, Aoba Palace, was right before us, and so was Lanshihan. Seven days ago, a man on donkeyback had borne word that Lanshihan was currently at home in the palace, and that the best time to attack would be during Tian prayers, when the soldiers would have set down their weapons.

We expected the chanting to be over quickly, but each passage of scripture led to the next, droning on endlessly.

Amid this lengthy recitation, we stealthily rose to our feet, held our breaths, and crept those final yards towards the backs facing us like the night itself. I kept my eyes fixed on the Tianmen atop the Tian tower, the only person facing us. His gaze was raised to the heavens, although surely he must have seen our dark mass drawing closer, yet his chanting never wavered. The rear row of Heile soldiers must have sensed hoofbeats and footsteps behind them, yet not a single head turned around. As the word bearer told us, at this moment their hearts and ears contained nothing but Tian, and no other noises could be permitted to enter their senses.

We didn't howl as we usually did, but as we came within reach of the now clearly visible human silhouettes, the frontline quietly drew their daggers and slashed through the back row of devotees.

The Tian scripture continued as we hacked our way through the middle row, slicing them down like stalks of corn. Soon the core of our army had reached the Tian tower. Even as the incantation rumbled on, our right flank charged the great doors of the palace, and still the chanting would not cease.

Lanshihan

The soldiers who burst into the palace failed to find Lanshihan. Then his harem rushed out screaming and weeping, helping us to locate him among the many dead bodies littering the ground. At dawn, as dirt rained from the sky, Lanshihan had been praying in the midst of his troops and our men had cut him down without recognising him. This poor king had been slashed three times by our cracked, chipped blades, and still his head remained attached to his body. The final blow was mine. I'd lifted his head by its yellow beard, and with a single stroke, severed it. What happened next was beyond my control. The horses thundered by, Lanshihan's corpse merely a bump in the road for grizzled veterans of the long wars, and foals who hadn't yet grown a full set of teeth trampled past, hooves stained with his blood.

I held up Lanshihan's head, so he could watch through narrowed eyes as countless horses trampled him into the ground. He'd been responsible for the deaths of too many Kun devotees, and this was his retribution.

My soldiers cut down a white poplar tree and mounted the head on its trunk. Holding it high, we marched on Heile City. Only one of his eyes remained open and his beard, now red with blood, billowed behind him. The Heile men fled at this sight, and it took no time at all to break open the gates.

8

Aoba, Part II

Tuo

TUO HAS BEEN LISTENING QUIETLY to Jue's story, but this is the part that involves him. He wrests control of his mouth from Jue, and once Tuo speaks, Jue must fall silent, because they only have one mouth between them, and it's on Tuo's face. Jue can do nothing but listen with Tuo's ears.

Tuo takes over the story, which Jue never imagined he had a part in.

*

Oh my beloved King Lanshihan, they cut your head off and planted it on a tree trunk as they invaded. I was standing on the city walls when I saw them advancing with your head held high, tens of thousands of Pisha men and horses, and your head aloft on a white poplar staff. I recognised you at once and so did everyone else; you'd been turned into the Pisha figurehead, leading their invasion, boldly forging a way forward. You are invincible, even in death, so the sturdy city gates burst open, and the walls were taken. Now our vast Heile army was defeated.

We didn't fire a single arrow or hurl a single spear, because your head was right in front, held up high for all to see. We couldn't defend ourselves against your head. With tears in our eyes, we retreated before your gory visage, off the walls and into the centre, fleeing all the way past city limits. Your head chased us out of the city, and we could only keep retreating.

All the way to Yengisar we ran, and then there was nowhere else to go—we were caught between the flood of sword-wielding soldiers behind us, and the farmers armed with hoes and scythes who blocked our path. News of your demise had spread through the entire kingdom the instant your head left your body, and everyone had witnessed your head bobbing across the sky, no body below it, just your head in mid-air howling for its body, which had been trampled into the mud. But still your head cried out, and all living bodies heard it and came to your summons, farmers abandoning their crops, drovers abandoning their flocks, blacksmiths and tanners and carpenters, all wielding the tools of their trade, hammers and axes and clubs, even the bakers and cooks with their tongs and cleavers. Every single person was there.

No one was issuing commands, but they all knew what they had to do. Stampeding through the west gate we'd so recently abandoned, they broke open the tightly sealed doors, trampling the sentries to death. The cityful of Pisha soldiers were in a panic, eyes wide, unable to believe that we were already mounting a counterattack.

Undone

A hundred thousand Pisha soldiers were scattered like sesame seeds across the criss-crossing alleyways of Heile City, fighting in every lane. They'd burst past our walls and invaded the city, only to be confronted with thousands of enclosed courtyards, each household in its own little fortress. And in this spiderweb of streets, a hundred thousand soldiers were separated. Ten years ago, the situation had been very different: when the Pisha army invaded, many families were still Kun devotees, and although they said their Tian prayers by day under supervision of the patrols, each night they dug up the Kun statues they'd buried and knelt before them. My mother was the most pious of Kun devotees, and when she heard the Pisha troops arrive, she began making flatbreads with all the wheat and corn flour in the house. The battle raged for three days, and she spent that entire time baking. The day they entered the city, she piled high her mountain of flatbreads on a donkey cart by the side of the road and handed them out to the hungry Pisha soldiers. Almost everyone threw open their doors and welcomed the invaders like family, offering a hundred thousand Pisha soldiers food and drink. This victory exposed the city's clandestine Kun worshippers, and when the Pisha troops retreated, the most vicious purge yet took place. Soon there were mounds of human heads and shattered Kun statues outside the city walls.

A mere decade on, everything was completely different. The Pisha had been welcomed with open arms, but this time round, they found closed doors everywhere. Even the windows facing the street were shut tight, and every courtyard gate was locked to them. They may have broken through the city gates, but couldn't do the same to every front door. And so the mighty Pisha army was undone by these little courtyards. The city filled with the sound of stones chipping at doors, crowbars smashing windows. The Pisha soldiers used all their energy getting through these wooden doors and windows. When we came surging back through the west gate, we didn't find a battle-ready army waiting for us, because the Pisha soldiers were dispersed throughout Heile City, trying to break into houses.

Head

Your head was gone, and the white poplar tree holding it up had vanished too. We shouted your name, calling out to the heavens and across the earth, screaming at the white poplar groves as they swayed in the wind, all of them now cursed to lose their own heads. From then on, heading east from Heile to Pisha, every poplar along the way would be decapitated.

We roared as we burst through the western gate, throats rigid with the sound, crows cawing as they scattered overhead, stirring up dirt that had only just fallen to earth, burying the sun once more behind dust clouds. We chopped off every head we saw, until the streets were full of headless people. Machetes, scythes, hoes, cleavers—their blades only knew human heads, and in just half a day we had reclaimed fallen Heile.

We scoured the city for your head. Everyone knew your face. Nothing could be worth more, the very expression of our dignity. Every other head—whether on a neck or littering the ground—recognised yours, and all the other heads knew we were seeking yours so they turned to face upwards, both Heile and Pisha heads, all facing the sky. We searched among thousands of closed eyes for your gaze, thousands of stifled noses for your breath, thousands of silent mouths for one word of yours, thousands of blank faces for your features, but your head was simply gone.

The Pisha must have hidden your head. We demanded it from the retreating army, we captured Pisha soldiers and asked if they'd seen it, after which we beheaded them. We pressed on with blood streaming from our eyes, and in our reddening gaze, no head had anything below the neck; we saw only heads bobbing through the air. We cared about nothing but heads—yours, and the heads of Pisha soldiers that we were lopping off.

*

Every battle after that became an exercise in harvesting heads. We gathered Pisha heads, and they did the same to us. After each skirmish, both sides had the same task: retrieving heads. Sometimes the Pisha would win, and the long line of the donkey squad would hurry onto the battlefield, seeking the heads of headless Pisha men, though those careless Pisha frequently jammed Heile heads onto Pisha bodies. The Pisha custom was to carry the corpses off to be buried in their hometown, but it was different for us—we were being martyred on our land, and all earth that was touched by blood was sacred ground.

At other times, we were victorious and would go out to find the Heile heads of our troops, but many bodies had to be buried headless—we'd search for their heads later. The Pisha donkey squad moved slowly, and we'd catch up with them in half a day. The donkey drovers were peasants who dumped their cargo and fled when they saw us coming. Ignoring them, we would search among the abandoned Pisha corpses, looking for Heile heads sewn onto Pisha torsos, which we cut off and buried on the spot.

Everywhere we found a head became a head cemetery, and likewise there were torso cemeteries, arm cemeteries, leg cemeteries. Twenty years earlier, a man named Maahong lost an ear in battle at Yengisar and started an ear cemetery. He lost all ten fingers to the west of Heile City, and so there was a finger cemetery there. Then an eye cemetery to the east of the city, a nose cemetery at Siya, and a genital cemetery by Heile River. This wounded Heile man, whose valour had only increased the more he fought, was eventually beheaded at Yarkand River, by which time his body parts rested in seven different places. The genital cemetery has become the most famous of these. Each May, when the wild olives blossom, men and women hoping to have children flock to that side of Heile River, cavorting around bonfires as dusk falls, and when the flames go out late in the night, they find one another in the dark, taking pleasure from each other without ever knowing the other person's face or name. Many women find themselves pregnant after this festival, and the children they give birth to are invariably called Moon or Star. Maahong's other resting places have become pilgrimage sites for the deaf, for the arthritic, for those who have lost their sense of smell or sight. The afflicted visit these spots and pray to be made whole again.

Avenging Army

We charged into your palace and found the retreating Pisha army taking a stand—they hoped to gain victory here, but they were wrong. The endless sand dunes didn't help them, nor did the dirt that filled the air, or the village dogs and roosters.

No one had ever seen such an avenging army. Dogs stood before the mounted troops, behind whom were peasants armed with axes and rakes, followed by ranks of donkeys and goats, then chickens and ducks. As the Heile forces rampaged past, peasants in the fields and villages grabbed whatever came to hand and ran after them. The donkeys followed their owners, the goats followed the donkeys, the poultry followed the goats, the women followed the men, the children followed the adults, and our ranks swelled and swelled. By the time we reached Aoba, our army filled the earth and heavens.

A Vast Sand Dune

Terrified out of their wits, the Pisha army took to its heels.

Right behind them were the dogs of Fence Village who knew they'd committed a grave error, and pursued the Pisha troops to make sure they'd never dare to come back. Two nights ago, their barking had helped the Pisha storm Aoba Palace. It is Heile law that any dog who fails to bark when an outsider enters its village will be clubbed to death. Heile animal regulations are strict. If a donkey kicks someone, its leg will be broken. If it brays during Tianmen prayers, its throat is slit. A horse that throws a soldier will be whipped. Roosters who crow at the wrong time have their necks wrung. Cats who refuse to chase mice have their fur singed. All these punishments are carried out before an assembly of fellow animals.

According to dog law, the entire canine population of Fence Village ought to have been put to death, but we didn't have time for that.

All around the palace were heads and bodies separated from each other, and around the Tian tower were ranks of headless corpses like stalks of corn. The morning before, we'd slashed our way through them like harvesters, bringing down row after row with great efficiency.

By now the wind had brought enough dirt to cover your torso and limbs. A group of women in black veils were kneeling on the spot, holding hands in vigil. The morning before, they'd been prostrating themselves when they saw your head being removed and carried off on a poplar trunk. Then your body was trampled into the ground, and they knelt on the spot to shield you from hawks and crows, from wild dogs and wolves. They didn't dare go any closer, not to clean the bloody mess of your flesh, not to straighten your shredded clothes. Your loyal slaves and worshippers watched as the gusting sand and falling dirt buried you. In just two days, a vast sand dune swallowed up your corpse.

Retreat

Jue can't resist interjecting here. He can make Tuo stop talking— the body's hands are his, after all, and Jue's hands can go up to shut the mouth. When the mouth speaks again, the words that come out are Jue's.

*

I'd never experienced a retreat like that one. A tidal wave of people poured out behind us—mounted Heile troops, villagers they'd picked up on the way, along with their donkeys and goats, mules and dogs, every long-legged creature chasing after us. I'd been at the front, and now I was the rearguard, but there was no way I could have stopped this huge, unruly mob. All I could do was watch those who fell behind—the wounded and those who lost their horses—get trampled to death, their bodies torn apart.

We'd thought Aoba Palace might be a refuge, but the enemy pushed open the doors and swarmed in. We retreated to the inner courtyard and barricaded the gates, but they simply pushed over the walls.

We were forced into the desert behind the palace, where we'd lain in ambush just two mornings ago. Now this would be our graveyard—there was nowhere to run.

From behind us came an earth-shattering burst of sobbing— our pursuers seemed to have suddenly awoken from a nightmare. Coming to a halt, they turned to the sandy ground northwards. It must be Lanshihan's body.

We couldn't stop, not with a huge pack of mad dogs snapping at our heels. As we'd pulled back to Aoba, dogs from the three surrounding villages charged at us, staying in front of the pursuing troops, taking bites out of human and horse legs, ripping wounded soldiers apart. They'd helped us once, closing one eye as we passed through their villages on our way to attack Aoba. Now they were attacking us in a frenzy. This was a performance for the army behind them. The dogs knew they had been derelict in their duty and were frantically trying to make amends.

Chickens and Dogs

Later on, I learnt that the night we lay in wait outside Aoba, the dogs from the three surrounding villages barked non-stop, and the Aoba guards hadn't dared to sleep a wink. The dogs had sniffed us out right away and sounded the alarm—only to stop just before dawn. Just as the longsuffering guards were finally drifting off, cockcrow began. The time shortly before sunrise was reserved for the roosters, and the dogs would never interfere. During the night, while humans sleep, villages belong to dogs and chickens. This is a secret known only to ghosts. I know this, now I've become a ghost myself. Chickens and dogs discussed many nocturnal village matters and settled between them how things would be run. The dogs decide when the moon should appear. That's why they howl at the moon, which sends a shiver through any ghosts around. The chickens determine when day breaks. Once this was agreed upon, no one could change it. Donkeys feign ignorance during the night—if anything goes wrong, the dogs are held responsible.

Cows, horses and goats follow the orders of dogs and chickens, as do ghosts. Ghosts crouch by the pillows of sleeping humans, whispering ghostly words as they sleep, leading the most peculiar lives in their dreams all night long, till cockcrow.

The ghosts depart at the first cockcrow, and the second cockcrow awakens the humans. People and ghosts are both guided by roosters.

That morning, the dogs heard the *dok dok* of hooves, and the thick reek of strangers enveloped the village. But the roosters were already crowing, and the dogs thought this should be enough to wake the humans. It wouldn't do for dogs to interrupt chickens. Besides, the dense wall of cockcrows wouldn't admit so much as half a bark. They groaned in agitation and spun in circles, waiting anxiously for the crowing to end.

As soon as cockcrow ended, the Tianmen began reciting scripture. It would have been even more taboo to cry out then—roosters, dogs, donkeys, horses and goats know to listen in silence during prayer. Ghosts don't make mischief at this time either. All the old ghosts around these parts were oppressed by the Kun back in their day, then watched as Kun statues were smashed and Kun temples burnt, replaced by Tian ones. Tian devotees prayed to the celestial court in the heavens, and sometimes ghosts wedged themselves in there; the Kun sat in meditation all the same, and no one could see—humans prayed to a god that ghosts couldn't see either.

Only when the dogs sniffed the choking stench of blood did they begin to bark. It was daylight by then, and they knew it was too late. Now there was big trouble, and they howled for all they were worth.

The yapping annoyed us. Three villagefuls of dogs were helping the Heile, but only with their mouths—not a single dog ran over. The bristling thicket of barking was enough to make anyone sprout fur. When the fighting at the palace ended, we followed the barking, which led us to the villages. The chickens were slaughtered for a feast for the officers, and the dogs ran and hid some distance away, not daring to let out a sound, watching from afar as their dwellings went up in flames. Amid the three burning villages was the even greater fire of Aoba Palace shooting up into the sky, singeing the gates of the celestial court.

The dogs only returned when the villages were no longer smouldering. Seeing the people and chickens gone, they howled at the broken walls, then ran off in the direction of human scent, calling for the figures they remembered, irritating even the ghosts. They wanted to rouse the people from that morning, to summon back the people and chickens who'd vanished.

The dogs have no idea that one of the Pisha soldiers who invaded Aoba all those years ago has now returned in the form of a headless ghost.

9

Aoba, Part III

Familiar

Ku has drifted off—his body sways from side to side like a sleepwalker. Hsieh nudges him with her muzzle, trying to tell him he's walking into the cemetery, but then she thinks it might be best for him to remain in dreamland. Hsieh often dreams too, mostly of war. It's been quite a few days since they fled the battlefield at Guma, but as soon as she shuts her eyes, she's back among the charging mounted troops, looking everywhere for the new owner who saved her life. She knows this version of him so well through this repeated dream that when she awakens and sees the actual Ku walking next to her, he seems less familiar than the one she sees in her sleep.

Hsieh matches Ku's pace, following behind him neither too fast nor too slow. Ku treats her well, and only climbs onto her back when he truly can't walk another step. Hsieh wishes he would ride her more often, maybe sitting backwards to push the ghost away.

TuoJue look at the cemetery in silence, then turn back to glance at Ku. Hsieh doesn't understand why. This hybrid ghost has been telling stories along the way, which have found their way into Hsieh's donkey ears.

*

Ku stumbles and rouses himself. They're some distance from the village, and a burst of barking has abruptly risen behind them— another group of donkey drovers. There will be several more groups behind this one. They began trailing him at dusk. The closest group is a couple of li behind and he can hear their voices and make out their brows and beards. Behind them is a pack of merchants with their families, and beyond that all he can see is plumes of dust. Ku is deliberately keeping his distance. A few days ago, he fell in with a group from Siya, but both the men and their donkeys couldn't take their eyes off Hsieh, and a burly bearded fellow came over to ask what he wanted for the jenny. Ku said she wasn't for sale. The man replied, "I don't want to buy her, just to use her for a while." Pretending not to understand, Ku shook his head. While they were speaking, a randy jack tried to mount Hsieh. The bearded man reacted faster than Ku, and tossed a clod of earth at the jack so he brayed and ran off. He then held out a bronze coin, but Ku kept shaking his head. The man remarked, "You don't seem to be saving her for yourself either. If a jack happens to take her first, she won't be worth more than a handful of straw."

Ku knew what he meant, and so did Hsieh. When a man wants to make use of a donkey, he first stuffs a handful of straw into her mouth to stop her from crying out.

*

Gravestones stand in the gloom around them, marking the victims of last year's Aoba battle. Ku heard the news from a donkey drover in the Pisha marketplace: the Pisha army had decapitated Lanshihan and over a thousand Heile soldiers, and were now attacking Heile City. Half a day later, Ku received an invitation to a victory banquet thrown by the king. The news in the marketplace was brought by donkeys, but the king had word bearers on horses who surely moved faster. Yet after every battle, win or lose, it was the marketplace that heard it first. At the banquet, Ku learned that their army had held Lanshihan's head high as they invaded Heile. Halfway through the meal, news arrived that Heile City had fallen, and the hall erupted in celebration. Their small cups were replaced with goblets, and everyone got thoroughly drunk. As the sky darkened, another report arrived to plunge them into sorrow: the Pisha army had suffered a defeat, and was retreating from Heile.

*

Hsieh sees a headless ghost squatting on every grave, the emptiness above its neck stump gazing in her direction. Some run angrily into the road, small groups of them trying to block her way, forcing her to stop and stamp her hooves. When Ku sees her come to a halt, he knows there must be something up ahead. Donkey ears are sharp enough to hear ghosts breathe. He puts his right hand on her neck and holds her close. Ku knows donkeys can see ghosts. Humans may do headcounts, but ghosts count legs. When you encounter a ghost, stand with the many-legged. Ku knows to do this.

The cemetery extends from the side of the village all the way to the blackened palace wall, where figures can be seen moving, though it isn't clear if they're people or ghosts. Ku decides to wait for the people behind to catch up so they can traverse the cemetery together, but after a while there's no sign of them, and the barking has stopped too. The village they passed through feels like a dream he can't return to.

Hsieh stirs a hoof, urging Ku to start walking again. They can't just stand here. Startled, Ku jumps onto Hsieh's back. A ghostly chill comes over him.

*

The moon rises. It looks like a scythe after the harvest, hanging there with its blade facing west. Ku glances at his donkeyback shadow, flickering against the palace wall that still stands tall despite the defeat, and Hsieh looks that way too. At the foot of the wall are the blurry outlines of humans and donkeys at rest. Follow the wall northward and turn a corner, and you'll see the Tian tower like a giant against the night sky. Five years ago, Ku spent a night in Aoba and was awakened at dawn by the call to prayer, the Tianmen's voice increasingly urgent, pouring down from the sky and sending a shudder through Ku, who thought something must have happened in the heavens above. He recalled the countless Kunmen he'd heard chanting scripture, voices rising calm and languorous into the sky. At West Kun Temple, Ku recited Kun scripture in the original, as well as translated into Huang, Chiu, Pishanese and Heilenese. Each time, he noticed such disparities had been introduced by the translation process that these were effectively different books.

*

On the north side of the Tian tower is the dark mass of a sand dune, out of which rises a latticework of branches: Lanshihan's grave. A dense crowd of men and donkeys are clustered around the dune. Some have gone to sleep, humans and donkeys leaning back to back, while others chat in groups. New people keep arriving, leading or riding their donkeys, hitching them by the outer edges of the circle. Ku doesn't want to get too close, so he and Hsieh stop by a clump of tamarisk. Spreading his bag to use as a sleeping mat, he takes off his water gourd and pats Hsieh on the flank, hoping she will lie down so he can snuggle against her for warmth. Instead, she stamps her hooves uneasily and turns in circles. He knows she sees something. His hair stands on end, even though by the light of the moon there seems to be nothing unclean on the ground.

*

Ku's eyes blink open in the middle of the night, and he sees Hsieh's eyes gleam as she stares at him. Behind her, a half moon hangs over the great sand dune. Ku's head nestles in the curve of her neck, his spine pressed against her belly. He doesn't know when Hsieh decided to lie down so he could warm himself against her—she was still standing and shuffling nervously when he drifted off. He doesn't know that she drove away quite a few ghosts.

Not far from them, a few donkeys stand close together, perfectly still. A group of people are huddled head to head, having apparently fallen asleep while seated. All of a sudden, someone begins to sing in a raspy voice:

> *On the road to Aoba oh,*
> *There are dunes of sand oh,*
> *I could never finish telling*
> *How much I miss you oh.*
> *By the heavens above,*
> *For you oh, beautiful maiden,*
> *I sing this love song.*
> *It's dark in the courtyard oh,*
> *Don't put out the oil lamp,*
> *Those who walk in the desert,*
> *Will sing this endless song.*

In the moonlight Hsieh can just about make out the forms of humans and donkeys scattered across the ground. There is no wind. The cloudless night sky jostles with these people's dreams. Hsieh hears the *dok dok* of hooves, as if the song, so like braying, has summoned the spirits of donkeys—in the air, amid the dirt, donkeys gathering here from all around. Worried, Hsieh turns to Ku, only to see he is asleep. He can neither hear nor see this ghostly world, but he will dream. With his eyes shut, he will dream a world in which he is once again on the road, on journey after journey. Through dreams he takes himself to distant places, avoiding the peril that is drawing ever closer.

Human Heads

One donkey cart after another passes before Hsieh's eyes. The *dok dok* of hoofbeats rings through the air, and the carts are full of human heads, facing upwards, their eyes empty holes. Curious, Hsieh tilts her head back and sees swirling dirt illuminated by the moon. From the ground to the sky, there is nothing but moving shapes: donkey carts. Donkeys move on three levels: their bodies on the ground, their hoofbeats through the clouds, and their braying even higher up. Donkeys know that they will eventually live above the clouds where their cries go, and so they call out as loudly as they can, storing these sounds amid the clouds like stashing silver away.

The donkeys of Aoba are kept busy, and their days of living amid the clouds are still in the distant future. As soon as it gets dark, carts made of sound rumble down from the clouds and are hitched to their backs—the *guhh tschaa* of earthly axles and *kwung dung* of earthly shafts rise up into the clouds to form carts of sound, running along a pitted road formed from the *dok dok* of donkey hooves. The donkeys at Aoba cemetery are mired in serious events, keeping them busy night after night.

The moon is overhead now, and Lanshihan's headless body sits atop the tall sand dune, while donkey carts come racing from all directions, carrying human heads from nearby villages or from rivers and deserts further afield. Carts full of heads form a line so long that no one can see its end, and headless ghosts parade one by one past Lanshihan, each bearing a head, held facing upwards for headless Lanshihan's inspection.

Unfortunately, the eyes with which he would see are not there, nor are the ears with which he would hear, nor the tongue with which he would speak.

Every head hopes Lanshihan will claim it, so it can rest on his royal shoulders. None of these heads know who they belong to—they have been away from their bodies for too long.

Lanshihan's headless spirit is surrounded by a throng of equally headless ghosts. Each night, human heads from near or far are gathered and brought to his grave for identification. The ghosts doing this ride donkey carts made of sound, scouring an entire catalogue of heads to find Lanshihan's. Every head in the vicinity has been picked up and looked over, and the carts are sent ever farther afield. Everyone in the world would willingly hand over their head and let it be carried away by a cart of sound. All the heads on earth have been transported here, and not one of them belongs to Lanshihan. His head is not among the many thousands of decapitated ones. Where has the king's head gone?

The heads that have already been seen now lie piled up in the wasteland behind the grave, with a dark mass of headless ghosts picking over them, hoping that this will be the night they find their own. Almost every head has been wrongly placed—tracking down noggins has become a major headache after each battle. With so many heads and bodies in separate locations, they frequently get wrongly matched, leading to more mishaps. If half the heads are assigned to the wrong bodies, then the other half will be too.

Before dawn, each ghost hastily clamps a random head onto his neck and scurries back to await the next delivery. Aoba Cemetery has become the busiest head exchange in the world, and everyone arrives willing to surrender their misallocated head, hoping to get back their rightful one. Likewise, every head dreams of finding its body, or, failing that, to be chosen by Lanshihan to serve as his kingly poll. Every night is another opportunity, and more spirits arrive from Pisha, from Heile, along the path of battle, assembling at the graveyard. Every sound ever produced by the donkey carts that passed through here become the carts of sound at dusk, rumbling endlessly on through the night.

The donkeys have no idea when their task will be done—perhaps never. Their hoofbeats pave a road among the clouds they are not yet permitted to walk along, just as cockcrow produces the seven-coloured celestial court that heavy wooden carts cannot reach, nor the planks or firewood that weigh down donkey's backs, nor bricks and mud clods, nor humans. From their vantage point here on earth, donkeys can see their heaven, a little higher than the human one. There are two storeys to the celestial court, one for donkeys and the other for humans. People may ride donkeys, but braying soars atop human voices. In the world of sound, humans are the beasts of burden. From the very beginning, donkeys have used their cries to construct a heavenly court.

Dream

All night long Hsieh lay next to the slumbering Ku, watching donkey carts and headless ghosts shifting more heads, not daring to stand in case the ghosts of humans or donkeys summon her away. It's not a blessing to see ghosts, it's a reminder that after death, she too will have to join this company who work tirelessly through the night.

Perhaps Ku fears waking and having to deal with the night alone, so he has one dream after another. Not that dream-Ku is having an easy time of it. First he sees himself losing his head, his body like a bare tree in the wilderness. The subsequent dream leaves him bodiless, his head like a plucked gourd rolling to and fro across the windy Gobi landscape. Next, a decapitated person leans against his back, but when he turns around he can't quite see who it is. It's TuoJue, but he doesn't know this—the ghost isn't visible to him whether asleep or awake. He also dreams of a woman with long hair, whom he seems to have been sleeping with for many years. Each night he clambers onto her, but can't turn her over to see her face. He tosses and turns until finally he wakes and sees that the body next to him is a young jenny. Looking awkwardly at Hsieh, he strokes her long hair, at which she tenses up, fearing he will feel the words etched underneath, and also that his hand will go farther and farther, reaching for that place.

Likeness

Stunned by the sight unfolding before him, Jue clutches his head with both arms, terrified that the head which does not belong to him will be snatched away by these ghosts.

Tuo, meanwhile, is ecstatic, tugging at the leather stitching, ready to hand himself over to the gathering ghosts—but Jue plants him firmly back on his neck.

"You can't do this," says Tuo. "I need to find my own body."

"Your body is far away in Pisha," Jue replies. "I'm your body now."

"If I have to be on the wrong body, I'd rather it were a Heile man."

"That's not going to happen. The thread that binds us together is made of donkey hide, horses or oxen couldn't rip us apart."

Since there's no escape, Tuo orders Jue to kneel and hold up both arms, which Jue reluctantly does. Tuo then raises his face and fixes his gaze solemnly to the great sand dune, weeping silently as he speaks:

"Oh my King Lanshihan, I have returned with a Pisha carcass, to the place where your body rests. Many more Heile people with heads are searching for yours by day, and those without are doing the same by night. Everyone longs to possess your head. Your lost regal skull is the dream of countless mundane bodies. We willingly go to our deaths for you, we happily part with our heads.

"My body is surely among those seeking your precious head, though who knows what fate he has suffered in this search. Perhaps he has had a Pisha head clapped to him, just as I have been wrongly given a Pisha body. Day and night he is commanded by that head, just as I must take orders from mine. We quarrel day and night, uncertain whose life we are leading.

"Or perhaps not. Perhaps the wind has buried him beneath a tamarisk grove, and each night he rises from the sand to challenge the wind, forgetting the enemy who slaughtered him, remembering only the insult of burial. He chases the wind across the wilderness, pulling its hair, ripping its clothes, spreading his arms to block its way, though of course the wind passes through regardless, right over his headless shoulders. And when he runs, he stumbles, sprawling on the ground where he gropes for his head, finding instead camelthorns, southern wormwood, tamarisk and bones. Here is a skull, but no, it's not his, toss it aside. There's another, no, that's not it either.

"Then one night he finds his own head, runs his hands across the nose and mouth, tweaks the ears. Sadly, so much time has passed that he no longer remembers his own features, and the hands that once washed this face daily, that touched this face for no reason at all, can no longer recognise it. He flings it aside. The head recognises its body but its screams do no good, for the body has no ears to hear them with, and the head lacks legs to run after it.

"My body remembers only you, your noble head and lofty gaze, your nose like a mountain ridge, your pristine beard and the steadfast lips that spoke the words of heaven. Alas, beneath me is another's body, and he no longer remembers what he looks like, nor does he know my likeness, and though he can see, the eyes are mine."

*

Jue hears these words through Tuo's ears. He tries to walk away, but is unable to. His Pisha body is now completely under the control of the Heile head.

Warmth

Hsieh itches all over as the words once again writhe around the roots of her hairs like worms. She twitches, and Ku wakes. He has been leaning against her the entire night. Hsieh knew he was relying on her warmth, and kept perfectly still. For a while one of his legs was thrown across her back, and his arm embraced her neck. Hsieh has seen men holding women in their sleep—her previous owner used to bring the household maids into the donkey pen, and afterwards they would doze off in the straw. For a moment her body softens and she feels like a pampered little miss, but no, she is a jenny. She knows women, and more than that, she knows girls. Before being sold to the temple, she was the favourite of her owner's daughter, and the young daughter-in-law loved her too. Ladies don't like to talk in the vicinity of male donkeys. Jacks are too randy, and as they eavesdrop their dark rods protrude from beneath them, thwacking their bellies in a low drumbeat. Instead, women seek out the company of jennies. From a young age, Hsieh has heard much womanly talk. The ladies notice her donkey ears prick up as she listens, but they don't care.

Leaning against a nearby wall, a drover has fallen asleep between two reclining donkeys, one male and one female. Halfway through the night, he climbs on top of the jenny and wriggles around for a while, before drifting off. The jack keeps his eyes shut and pretends to sleep through the whole thing.

Hsieh glances sidelong at TuoJue. They'd been having ghostly conversation on her back through the night, and now they've finally fallen silent. Tuo's head slumps onto Jue's shoulders. Jue's leg is still twitching. Ku's calf has been pressing down on it—the living can weigh the dead down. Jue stamps his foot and asks Tuo if he feels anything, but Tuo shakes his head. Jue had hoped to transfer the soreness to the head, but the head has no sensation.

Ku gets his thingy out to pee, not bothering to turn aside. He is hard as a rock. Hsieh stares boldly at him. When she was still a foal, jacks would flash their rods at her, and now Ku is doing the same. She felt it against her in the night. His pissing sets her off, and she moves her hindquarters to do the same. Ku wrinkles his nose from the sharp reek of it.

Against the *hwuh luh* of their urination, TuoJue notices all the spirits down below and up above have begun to fade.

The sun is rising over Aoba.

10

City Gates

The City by Night

I SEE THE HEILE city gates, the battlements atop the city walls. A pair of eyes stare at me—look, that's the gaze I left three years ago. From the time I became a soldier, I guarded the city by night, always yearning for the dawn, though actually the dawn was of no concern to me. During those long nights I used up all my vision and wakefulness, and daylight shone only on the endless dreamscape of my drowsiness. Only from dusk till daybreak was I awake. The brightness of day was for soldiers who guarded the daytime city, and those who could sleep till cockcrow.

When I was a little boy, the grown-ups told me daybreak didn't use to come so late for us, but then Pisha's West Kun Temple built an enormous wall that reached the clouds, blocking our early morning sunlight. The people of Pisha were up early, tilling their soil and planting their crops while we were sound asleep. They sharpened their scythes and harvested their wheat, and still we slumbered. They picked up their bowls and devoured everything that was delicious, while we remained in bed. That's how they stole a march on us, getting up an hour earlier each morning, which added up to an entire month over the course of the year, an entire year each decade. You can imagine how much time that was over a century, a millennium. They were leaving us further and further behind.

Because dawn came sooner for them, their spring was earlier too, meaning their crops were planted first, their wheat ripened and was harvested first, and they got to experience the invigorating taste of flatbreads made from new wheat before anyone else. Three years ago, fortified with fresh flatbreads, the Pisha army invaded Heile at a time when our wheat was barely ripe, so we were still gnawing on last year's rations. We were no match for our well-fed enemies and were quickly defeated.

In previous years, the Kun devotees in both nations mingled freely, and when those from Heile travelled to Pisha to get more scriptures or pay their respects to the king, the first words out of their mouths would be: "Our Heile roosters are woken by the ones here in Pisha," or "Pisha sees daylight before Heile does," as a token of respect for Pisha. When the Heile converted to Tian, they no longer mentioned cockcrow, and would only say, "The call of Tian comes earlier than any rooster's cry."

With their swords, the Heile brought the voice of Tian to the borderlands of Yengisar and Qusha, but were never able to get any farther than that. The rumour was that the cries of the Pisha roosters blocked their path eastward, because no matter how early the Heile got up in the morning, the first Pisha cockcrow sounded before the Tian call to prayer. Others said it was Pisha braying that prevented them. The sound of Kun had long taken root within the flourishing cries of donkeys, and after hearing this for a thousand years, their ears had gotten used to it. Donkeys don't like new noises.

*

The city guards were split between day and night camps, and never the twain did meet. The night squad spent many years becoming familiar with the dark hours, while at dusk, their counterparts found their heads filling with dreams from which they could not awaken.

Now there is only night for me, and my days no longer exist. My body, which walked the days and nights of Heile for over forty years, is lost in the Gobi Desert. All I have left is my head, which has been stitched with leather thread onto the body of a Pisha man, who must now look through my eyes, and even though I know it's really me seeing, he is doing the same. My eyes have become his.

Jue, I want to tell you my story, so this body can know about its head. These things that have been in my head were done by a different body, which has nothing to do with you. But you are my body now, and you have to acknowledge these deeds.

And now, I am going to make use of your body to walk through the city gates.

Artisans

With your hands, I touch the gate's sturdy frame, in which there is a fist-sized hole. In my third summer on watch, the Pisha invaded and laid siege to us for two days and two nights. A hundred of them came at the gates with an enormous battering ram, and the *kwong kwong* echoed through the entire city, but the wood held firm. One cart after another arrived full of straw and twigs, burning from below while being doused from above, and still the gates held.

On the morning of the third day, at the moment the night watch handed over to the day, a group of Pisha artisans arrived on donkeyback armed with axes and saws. Their soldiers protected them so our arrows and stones couldn't reach them. They wore wooden boards on their heads and were able to walk right up to the gates, where we heard their tools hacking away. After a day of loud activity, they dispersed, apart from a carpenter who was beheaded. Later, we learnt that the dead man had been the most famous carpenter in Pisha. After hearing about the long Heile siege, he'd petitioned the king for permission to lead a delegation of craftsmen to break through the door. When they failed, he accepted decapitation as his punishment.

The carpenters may have retreated, but it was the turn of the blacksmiths next, also on donkeyback, brandishing awls and hammers. The Heile city gates had a metal frame studded with nails, which the blacksmiths now began to prise out. Their tools clattered *ding ding dang dang* against the frame, sending tremors through the gatehouse and walls. Soon there was a heap of nails and rivets on the ground, yet the gates remained intact. On the inside of the wall, the blacksmiths of Heile had gathered to hammer in more nails, which could not be removed from the outside. Amid the commotion of their clobbering, the craftsmen on either side of the wall screamed at each other, their voices passing through the holes left by the nails.

From inside, the Heile blacksmiths shouted, "Make your soldiers go away, and us blacksmiths can duke it out. We forged the blades they've been fighting this war with, why shouldn't we get to decide who wins and loses?"

The blacksmiths of Pisha and Heile came from the same clan. Centuries ago, two brothers from a dynasty of blacksmiths didn't get along. The younger brother was left-handed, and the pair of them were always clashing as they faced each other across the forge, because their hammers kept colliding. They squabbled relentlessly about this, and went from forging steel to unforging the bonds between them. Eventually, the younger brother moved west to Heile, where people appreciated his left-handed skills. All his sons and grandsons were left-handed too, but the blades they produced were ideal for right-handed warriors.

War gets through a lot of metal, and even more metalworkers. Over the course of this protracted war, half the blacksmiths in this extended clan have died of exhaustion. During each big battle, more blades were destroyed than people. When two soldiers meet in combat, the first thing to make contact is their swords. You slash your blade towards me, I raise mine to parry, and it becomes a contest whose is hardest. The person whose weapon breaks first is the one who gets hacked to pieces. Afterwards, the dead get buried and the ruined blades go back to the smithy. Half the swords in each battle are wrecked and get sent to the blacksmith, jagged and bloodstained, to be smelted and beaten anew. When they go into the forge, the reek of scorched human blood invades the senses. The blacksmiths wield their hammers large and small, and no matter how many of them work themselves to death, they still don't produce enough swords. The war expands as it goes on, and the number of casualties is uncountable.

The Pisha blacksmiths were getting worried that the war would only end when all the blacksmiths had died of exhaustion. They shouted through the nail holes, "Open the city gates! We'll have fisticuffs on Jenny Lane—donkeys and people will see who's stronger."

The blacksmiths didn't manage to reach an agreement. When they'd finally removed the last nail, there was nothing left but the wooden frame and gates, and they could do no more. Now they needed the carpenters to come in—they'd easily be able to rip the boards apart. At this moment, though, the carpenters were trudging back through the desert to Pisha, bearing the body of the Great Carpenter.

Next to step up was a delegation of Pisha farmers, protected by soldiers as they made their way to the wall. They'd gotten anxious at the army's failure to take the city, and had arrived with their shovels. They were experts at digging, and would be able to burrow beneath the wall like mice. Meanwhile, we were agitatedly pressing our ears against the wall, listening to the *tschaa tschaa* of metal slicing through earth.

At this moment of crisis, a thousand Heile farmers arrived and stood in a row against the wall, listening intently to the soil, plunging in their spades wherever they heard a sound. Like their Pisha counterparts, they had been digging all kinds of holes for a thousand years. Now they tunnelled towards the Pisha folk, and the two met in the dark underground, where they hurled their shovels at each other. The donkeys with their sensitive ears could detect the sounds of people slaughtering each other like mice beneath the earth's surface, and not one of them emerged alive.

Next, the Pisha people caught ten thousand hungry mice and set them loose in the holes, then set a thousand cats to chase them. The mice frantically scrabbled their way to freedom, digging a tunnel all the way into the heart of Heile City. The Heile folk, with their ears to the ground, broke the surface to find what was making this noise, and a horde of mice surged out. They tried this elsewhere too, with the same result. Soon, ten thousand rabid mice were darting everywhere, biting anything they could see. In the course of a single night, every bow string had been bitten through, every saddle strap.

Now the underground passages belonged to the mice, and the people who had died in there were mouse food. The shovels rotting down below were wielded by ghosts who continued digging away, dreaming of the day they might once again tunnel their way back to the land of the living.

*

One morning some time later, just after dawn, the day shift came to relieve us, but before we could get back to our quarters to sleep, a swarm of Pisha troops charged the city gates, led by a strapping general wielding a white poplar trunk, on which a large head was impaled. We all recognised Lanshihan right away, and stared in shock. Someone tossed down his sword and ran, shrieking and wailing, and others swiftly followed. In an instant, Heile City was defeated.

Recognition

Now I think of it, I actually do know you. Three years ago, I saw you during the attack on Heile City. I was on the ramparts, and you were leading the charge. Right above you was Lanshihan's head, no longer bleeding, riding high on a poplar pole. During the three-day siege, every inch of Heile City had remained impregnable. On the fourth day, you used your most vicious tactic yet: advancing upon us with the head of Lanshihan, slaughtered at Aoba, so we would see his staring eyes, his beard matted with blood and sand, his gaping mouth in mid-air, as if every soldier's cry was coming from that mouth. We couldn't aim our arrows in his direction, we couldn't wield our swords.

We were frozen, still as corpses on the battlements.

And that's when I saw you, directing the attack. Your noble bearing and gleaming gold helmet caught my attention. All this time I'd been thinking your body was familiar, and now I know why. I felt great envy at that moment, thinking how fine it would be to cut such a dashing figure. The thought made me more commanding and I drew myself up to my full height, raising my sword high, as if to decapitate you, this debonaire general. The battlements were too high to jump down, so I could only stand there, towering above you, roaring at the Pisha army.

You must have seen and heard me, although you paid no attention to the cries of a rank and file soldier. The rest of the Heile army was fleeing in fear, while I alone was on the city wall, shouting at the advancing troops. You were the commander, and your eyes had to take in the entire city.

By the time you entered the city, all our men had escaped through the west gate, and I was the only Heile soldier who'd held my position. With my scimitar aloft, I remained at the highest point of Heile City. You must have noticed. Not that you would have cared about a lunatic standing at a spot no one could reach, screaming incoherently. Yes, the Pisha army must have thought I was a madman, because no one paid me one bit of attention. For all the noise I made, no one thought to attack me.

A short while later, the Heile troops who'd fled had come to their senses, and a few thousand of them got back into formation to mount a counterattack. From my vantage point, I saw you turning tail. From the only part of Heile that hadn't fallen, I ran down and put myself at the forefront of our army. There was nothing in my mind but the noble commander I'd seen. I wanted to hack your head off and be lauded for it. We chased you out of the city, and your army was scattered like a flock of goats, scampering towards the villages. You might as well have been a bunch of farmers.

I saw you in those narrow country lanes, your back still dignified in retreat. There was a moment when I'd almost caught up with you, but you pivoted into a field of corn and vanished without a trace.

Flying

From then on, your body filled my mind. I pursued you by day, and in my dreams also. I no longer felt my own exhaustion. It was as if I already possessed your carcass, like I was chasing you while inhabiting your body. Finally we reached Guma, and the two armies confronted each other on the shifting sands. I was deployed to the second rank, but forced my way to the frontline. At last, I was within reach of you, this familiar figure from my dreams. You were at the head of your army. In my eyes, the soldiers behind you melted away, and you were standing there alone. All I wanted in that moment was to cut off your head.

Unfortunately, I had no right to do that—you were the general, and I was nothing. Our general had his eye on you too.

I was pushed aside during the charge, yet I had no interest in killing anyone else, so I remained still, staring as you spurred your horse in the direction of the slaughter, hoping you would cut a swathe through your enemies, slicing down all the people who stood between us, until there was no one left on the battlefield but you and me. Whether I killed you or you killed me, I only wanted you to watch as I decapitated you, or vice versa.

That's when my head abruptly disappeared.

Through my eyes, not yet completely closed in death, I saw bloody heads flying through the air—hacked from dead soldiers and turned into projectiles.

My head flew through the air too. Through half-shut eyes, I saw headless bodies on the ground and tried to find mine, struggling to remember what it looked like, and suddenly I understood that my head and body would soon enter a long period of forgetfulness, which caused me to shed tears of sorrow.

The instant before I hit the ground, my eyes lit up as they spotted your headless body lying nearby. After that jolt of joy, I remember nothing.

A tanner later sewed my head to the stump of your neck, which had stopped bleeding. I woke up in pain, watching contentedly through barely open eyes as he went about his work. He was a fine craftsman, working with as much practiced skill as if he were making donkey reins. You never saw this, of course—at the time, my eyes were not yet yours. Then followed another long spell of dark forgetting, during which we didn't know each other, and I quarrelled with you even as we tried to remember what had happened. Then I woke again, and it all came back to me.

Finally, Jue, I have possessed your body. My head has brought your body back here. Your anatomy is my captive. All the ghosts on the city tower are watching as I, a Heile head, walk back through the city gates atop your magnificent Pisha body.

Headless

Through your eyes I can see that all headless ghosts are Pisha men. The battle three years ago left countless headless corpses, and the defeated Pisha troops abandoned their fallen comrades, whose decapitated bodies were left in the northern desert for wolves to gnaw at, for the sand to bury. Their heads were tossed in the southern Gobi, where the wind blew them to and fro. Not even a stalk of grass can grow in the barren Gobi, and when the west wind rises, thousands of human heads trundle in the direction of Pisha, flesh wearing away till only bones are left. The clatter of skulls bumping, the whistling of air rushing through eye sockets, as sharp as the blade of a knife, all the way to Guma, to Pisha, to be heard by headless ghosts.

Each time the west wind blew, the headless ghosts of Pisha turned towards the west, their neck stumps straining to hear the rolling of their heads, staring hollowly with the empty space where their eyes should have been. When the wind turned east across the Gobi, the heads rattled back towards Heile.

Through your ears, I hear the rolling heads, and one of them was mine. My head is among the thousands of skulls tumbling this way or that at the whims of the wind, but I can no longer recognise him.

"Why have you come here with a Heile man's head?"

"Why are you staring at us through his eyes?"

"Speak Pishanese to us, through his lips."

I began a conversation with them, then felt I shouldn't make too much use of this head that wasn't mine. You must have your own words to speak. You pathetic, bodiless bastard. You're back home now, and you're still not happy. That's because of me. My sorrow has spilled over into your consciousness.

Back Home

Hsieh keeps twisting her head to stare at her back. Ku senses an invisible figure there. Ku knows her ghostly eyes can see spirits that his can't, and senses a chilling energy that attacks the base of his neck.

The battered city walls are crawling with headless ghosts glaring with the eyes they lack. All the Kun towers in Heile have been destroyed, so these spirits have climbed atop the battlements instead. Hsieh knows they are looking at TuoJue, this hybrid Pisha-Heile ghost mounted backwards on her, chattering about events they've all lived through, and about donkeys. Whenever Hsieh hears people talking about donkeys, she perks up.

A headless ghost drifts over to Hsieh's rump and asks TuoJue where they're going.

"Back home," says Tuo.

"And whose body is that, going home with you?"

"Foolish man, the body beneath my head is mine, of course."

"Don't try to deceive a ghost. This strapping torso belongs to your puny head? Ha! Come stand over here and tell me if that looks like your body."

"I can't stand across from myself."

"You already are. When people die and become ghosts, they stand facing themselves."

Tuo falls silent. He thinks Jue might pipe up, but instead Jue remains silent, only puffing up his chest even more than usual, which makes Tuo's head look absolutely minuscule.

Donkey Marshal

The houses on either side of the street have scorch marks from the Pisha invasion three years ago. Ku was in the marketplace when he heard this news from a donkey drover. First thing in the morning, a wave of braying vaulted the city walls. Every donkey drover in Pisha's alleyways learnt that Aoba had fallen to the Pisha army, and that Lanshihan was dead. Jubilation filled the streets, and long before noon, every restaurant and roadside stall was packed full of carousing folk. Ku's friends led him to a roast meat place where he supped five bowls of wine made from Pisha black grapes.

The same news, travelling on horseback, only reached the palace at dusk. All night long, the king gathered his ministers and prepared to host a banquet, to which Ku was invited in his capacity as a translator. The festivities lasted three days and nights. On the fourth evening, the donkey marshal came in to say something was wrong with the donkey cries, like there were bumps in the road ahead. At dawn the previous day, he'd already told the king about the word that was arriving via braying and drovers, but the king insisted on waiting for horseback confirmation. He didn't heed donkeys, yet whenever their cries turned strange, he summoned the donkey marshal, whose job was to hear donkey voices day and night, in all four seasons, to learn of happenings near or far.

That night, the king sent the marshal off in search of a drover to learn more and told Ku to go with him, reckoning that if he spoke dozens of human languages, surely he must understand donkeys too. The streets were full of drunken drovers, but the donkeys were sober, letting out resounding brays. Ku and the drover made their way to the battlements on the west side of the city, where the starry sky hung low and all around them was darkness. They could clearly hear donkey voices passing from one village to another in the distance, all the way to the Pisha city walls, where they would soar over like a clod of earth, but instead of falling to the ground, would be received by braying from within the city, each utterance louder than the last, shrouding the entire area. The donkeys knew their drovers were intoxicated and would need to bray louder than usual to rouse them.

"Looks like the tide has turned," the marshal said darkly to Ku, who nodded mutely.

Back at the palace, the two men made their report to the king, and the banquet fizzled out. Ku hurried through half the city to his home on the west side, passing clusters of chattering folk. The drunken donkey drovers had sobered up, and beneath the *ahng-jee* that filled the upper air was a layer of their agitated babble. Both donkeys and humans were discussing the Pisha retreat. Ku still recalls how, from then on, each night brought news of further defeat, spread through the streets by donkeys and their drovers, plunging the whole of Pisha into a state of battle readiness.

11

Bearing Word

Peachwood

K U STICKS HIS HEAD through the city gates and is immediately greeted by the pungent reek of donkeys. There are as many donkeys in Heile as humans, and the streets are just as full of dung as Pisha's. These donkeys are prone to dropping black, shiny pellets as they walk, which gets crushed to powder by the hooves and feet passing over them. Both humans and donkeys enjoy the soft surface this gives their streets. Heile doesn't levy a fee for donkeys to enter the city, but there is a marshal stationed at the gates whose job it is to count them, tapping each donkey head with a peachwood rod to keep track. He counts the humans too. When he touches Hsieh's head, she rears up and kicks her back legs into the air, as if trying to shake something off. Ku watches, startled. Peachwood repels ghosts, and perhaps the touch of the rod disturbed whatever was on her back. All this way, Ku had sensed something was riding her. She kept turning back, but he didn't know what she was looking at. She could see something he couldn't, and even if he could, he wouldn't want to. He'd kept his nerve and faced forward, thinking, *As long as I can't see ghosts, there's nothing they can do to me.*

Jenny Market

Enter Heile City through the eastern gate and turn left, pass through the marketplaces for lumber and grain, then the one for male donkeys beneath a row of white poplar trees, and you'll come to Heile's famous jenny market.

Two years ago, after passing through a series of small rooms by the jenny market, Ku encountered the recently-converted Kunmen

Maisheng from Peach Blossom Temple, who asked that Ku bear word to the Great Kunmen of West Kun Temple, requesting a copy of Kun scripture in Heilenese to be sent whenever it was convenient. In fact, Ku knew Kun scripture by heart in Chiu, Kun, Huang, Pishanese and Heilenese, and at a gesture from the Great Kunmen, he could have recited it to Maisheng in any language he desired. Instead, the Great Kunmen asked Ku to bear a small jenny to Maisheng, his words when he handed Hsieh over haunting Ku this whole journey: "Treat this donkey like you would a message."

He has translated this sentence into every language he knows, and each time it means something completely different. With a donkey in tow, he's sauntered through dozens of languages, finally returning to Pisha, and still she remains a jenny named Hsieh, who does indeed seem to have a message in her bray, *ahnng-jee ahnng-jee*, the same words over and over. Can this be the message the Great Kunmen wishes him to bring to Kunmen Maisheng? But all the donkeys in the world sound the same, whether they're from Pisha or Heile, Shachow or Bod, so why this particular Pisha jenny? Has she been trained to sound a particular way?

But no, Ku has been listening closely all the way, and apart from her delightfully girlish tone, she sounds exactly the same as any other donkey, *ahnng-jee* after *ahnng-jee*, just as all bricks are the same but can make a Kun or Tian tower, a palace or a donkey pen when arranged differently. Could it be that these identical brays are creating different things in mid-air, beyond human sight? Perhaps this donkey really is a message. Ku has learnt every language there is in the world, but he's never thought to know what the donkeys around him are saying. Yet now he's beginning to feel as if he does understand. Every single bray he's ever heard is congealing in the air before him, sentence by sentence, a book made of sound. But what do these sounds mean?

Donkey Year

Wave after wave of braying assaults Ku from behind. Separating the jack and jenny markets is an alleyway made of donkey cries, thousands of lusty males calling out towards the females. Inside Ku's ears is line after line of brays, paving a road rising to heaven. He looks up and listens carefully to this braying, more than he ever has. He first went through this alleyway of sound when he was a very little boy riding a jenny through this clamour of jacks.

That was many years ago, when Master spotted a three-year-old jenny at Heile market. On each long journey, he would sell the donkey he'd ridden there and buy a young female for the return trip. The seller wanted a coin and a half, and Master tried to haggle him down to one. Instead, the seller said he would throw in the little boy sitting backwards on the donkey.

"No," said Master, "just the donkey."

As they reached a stalemate, the boy began babbling. Asked what he was saying, the seller replied that the child only spoke some dark tongue no one understood. That's what the Heile call languages they don't speak, dark tongues. No one knew what the boy was saying, so no one wanted him, and that's why he was being offered free with a donkey. Master recognised the words: a dead language from a distant place, which he'd heard a long time ago at West Kun Temple, spoken by a Kun devotee from that region. Since then, other languages had come to dominate that place, but this tongue remained alive in Master's brain. And now, at a bargain price, he had a child he could converse with. He was ecstatic.

He asked the child's name, but the seller shook his head.

So he asked the child instead, and the boy was startled to hear his native tongue.

"Ku."

The boy's voice sent a jolt through the donkey beneath him.

Delighted, Master asked for his age, but Ku shook his head.

"Your zodiac sign, then?"

Another shake.

"Another one born in the year of the donkey."

And that's how Ku learnt, from Master's lips, that he was born in a donkey year. Later, he would get to know many others like himself, just as donkeys seek out other donkeys. In Pisha, they form a mysterious community. When these people of uncertain origin get together—donkey sellers, leather merchants, procurers of women and children—their greatest similarity, apart from their ability to bray, is that they know at least three or four languages, more often a few dozen, meaning they are able to converse with people from all over.

In Pisha, those who can speak seven languages are called seven-tongued. The one-tongued can only wander around their own town or village, the three-tongued can travel a thousand li to interpret for the Heile, the five-tongued can roam the mountains and valleys doing business, and the seven-tongued can go anywhere they want in the world. With seven languages at their command, they'll easily understand every other language that exists.

Each additional language is one more road. Every pathway into Pisha is watched by people born in a donkey year, every one of them holding on to several donkeys, one for each language they speak. Merchants coming from far-off places are completely dependent on them.

Master was also born in the year of the donkey. The twelve actual zodiac animals are: mouse, ox, tiger, rabbit, dragon, snake, horse, goat, monkey, chicken, dog, pig, and back round to mouse. Donkeys aren't included, but there are always going to be people left outside the circle, born in a year not known to them or anyone else: the year of the donkey.

After Master's death, no donkey-year in Pisha knew more languages than Ku. Or as the donkey-years say, every donkey knew Ku.

Goatskin

When Ku was three, a leather trader wrapped him in a goatskin and carried him away from his hometown. This man had just bought forty-two goatskins from Ku's family. Ku had already learnt to count, and the previous evening, as the goats returned to the fold, Ku and his older brother had clambered onto the gate that was open a crack, counting the goats as they squeezed in: ninety-seven in all.

"One extra," said his brother. Perhaps it had snuck in from another family's flock. His brother went into the pen and emerged with a white nanny goat. Ku shouted for his father, but his father told him to hush. Then the next day, Ku saw the white goat's pelt among the ones that had just been sold. His father had been up to no good the day before. Ku looked at his father, and then out through the courtyard gate, where the trader was spreading out each skin to examine it back and front, then tossing it up onto the top of his carriage. Forty-two skins soared through the air. The trader paid Ku's father and began arranging the pelts in the packed interior of his cart. Ku's five older brothers and little sister sprinted around the cart and clambered into it. Ku climbed onto the roof, where he saw the trader rolling up the goatskins one by one. When he got to the last one, he glanced around, gave Ku a strange look, gestured for him to lie on the skin, and quickly rolled him up in it. Ku thought this was a game, like hide and seek, and waited quietly to be found. As the cart gently trundled away, he dozed off. By the time he woke up, the sky was dark, and he began howling to find himself still inside the rolled skin.

Two years later, Ku had been sold to a donkey vendor in Heile. Annoyed that Ku only spoke a language no one understood, the man tossed him onto the back of a donkey. Each time Ku wailed, the donkey brayed, and Ku imitated that bray. The donkey's ears pricked up. Then the day came when a middle-aged man saw Ku on the donkey's back and bought them both. This was Master.

With Ku in tow, Master walked out of Jenny Lane, though the alleyful of braying remained in Ku's ears. Together, they walked to Pisha. The two kingdoms were not yet at war back then, and the people of Heile were still Kun worshippers. Each village they passed through had a Kun temple they could lodge in. During this long journey, Ku rode backwards on the donkey and learnt Heilenese from Master. And in the many nights that followed, he learnt Pishanese too.

Languages

In Ku's recollection, Master was constantly being sent at the king's behest to districts near and far, where all kinds of other languages were spoken. His most frequent destination was Heile, where Ku guessed he might have another home. Master's house in Pisha was merely a large courtyard filled with donkey pens, so Ku felt it was likely he had a wife and children somewhere else, which could only mean Heile. Pisha and Heile had many dealings back then, and Master was the interpreter for the king's delegations. No one in Pisha spoke Heilenese as colloquially as Master, but he could only speak it, not write it. Indeed, he refused to learn to write a single word from any language. This was the fundamental quality of word bearers—they only carry spoken messages.

Whenever they came back from an expedition, the king would listen only to Master's reports of the Heile situation. Any report from the rest of the team, after all, would consist of words that had passed through Master's mouth, so the king preferred to go directly to the source. These interpreting jobs caused Master a lot of anxiety. He was the only person in any delegation who spoke Heilenese, and often found himself between two groups of people who had no common language. Sometimes the other side would have their own interpreter, other times he had to translate in both directions. While the Heile team were speaking in their language, the eyes of the Pisha delegation would go blank, and vice versa.

Master was a solitary lantern in a pitch-black night, now lighting the way for the people on his left, now turning to do the same for those on the other side.

Most terrifying of all, scribes on either side would write down everything he said. He feared the words he'd spoken so lightly being pinned down on paper, lying there dead on the page.

When the war started, Master stopped going to Heile. Instead, he was sent to the Central Plains. Many people in Pisha could speak Huang, so an endless stream of merchants and officials would go in that direction.

*

In the last few months before Master passed, Ku was his only companion. Master spoke on and on in languages no one else could understand, and listening to him became Ku's most important task. Master went through every single language he'd ever learnt, from the ones closest to Pishanese—Chiu and Bod—to Heilenese, with whom they'd been at war for many years, then on to Huang and Tian. Master drew him an expansive map of languages, all these tongues lighting up one distant patch of land after another. Huang took up the most space.

"You could spend your entire life walking," said Master, "and still you'd be in the Huang ocean."

By the time he'd gone through every language he knew, Master was almost out of strength. Right before he died, he gained a burst of energy. As he lay on the heated kang, his neck suddenly stiffened, his head reared, and there was a gurgle in his throat that became a cry: *ahnng-jee ahnng-jee.* His voice ended abruptly, and so did his life—just like that. The donkeys in the courtyard brayed in response, which quickly spread to the ones next door, then to the rest of the city, then the neighbouring villages. Their cries spread across the land, everywhere there were donkeys.

As Master said, every donkey in the world brays the same way, and they have no need of translation. In his final moments, Master let out a donkey cry, untranslated, and blood rushed into Ku's vocal chords, but he restrained himself till Master had stopped breathing, until the braying outside had died down. Finally, he couldn't help it, but reared back his head and bellowed at the sky. *Ahnng-jee ahnng-jee!*

He screamed till his voice was hoarse, till his face was covered in tears.

A Bunch of People

Ku locates the rooms where he met Kunmen Maisheng two years previously, though half of them have now collapsed, and people are living in the intact ones. Beneath the large mulberry tree next to this building, a bunch of old men sit by a bunch of donkeys, all of them staring at Ku and Hsieh as they approach.

"Pardon me, is Maisheng around? He used to be a barber here," says Ku in Heilenese.

"You're from Pisha, are you not?"

"I'm from Kang," says Ku in Kang.

"But you have a little Pisha jenny with you, a virgin by the looks of her. Which lucky beast are you saving her for?"

The humans gather around them, some stroking Hsieh's rump, others prising open her mouth to study her teeth. Hsieh wriggles her behind and stamps her hooves, trying to get away from these groping hands. The other jennies give her sidelong jealous glances. On each of their backs is a headless ghost, facing backwards, its neck stump turned towards Hsieh. The headless corpses carried back from the battlefield, plus those left buried in the wilderness, all became donkeyback ghosts. They've tried riding donkey brays to heaven, only to find the celestial court does not want headless spirits. Hsieh twists around to glance at TuoJue, thinking how lucky it is for a Heile head to have found a Pisha body.

Donkey Fanciers

Hsieh so excites the elderly man that he forgets to answer Ku's question about Kunmen Maisheng.

These donkey fanciers are known in Heilenese slang as "old knives", once-sturdy blades worn dull by constant stropping on a donkey's back. All they talk about are donkeys, and listen as you might, you won't hear them breathe a word about humans.

Back in the day, when Master taught him Heilenese on the long journey back to Pisha, the first word he learnt was "donkey".

Master said there are more donkey legs than human ones anywhere Heilenese is spoken, and you'll see more hoofprints than footprints on the ground, smell more donkey reek than human scent in the cities, and hear donkeys mentioned in one out of every three sentences. He got Ku to lead a donkey and enumerated donkey heads, back, hooves, organs, asses, jacks, jennies, donkey fanciers, donkeyfuckers, son of a donkey . . . all manner of vocabulary and how to use it:

> **Donkey head**. The head of a donkey, and also the leader of a herd. Everyone from village chiefs to city mayors are called donkey heads. The king is a Great Donkey Head.
> **Son of a donkey**. An insult, meaning a brute raised by a donkey, not a human. In Huang and Pisha, the equivalent insult is "donkeyfucker"—they care who you fuck, whereas in Heile the concern is who birthed you.
> **Donkeybeast**. A human as horny as a donkey, in heat four seasons of the year.

Master taught him the entire Heile language from a donkey's body. Whenever Ku spoke Heilenese, he felt as if he were on donkeyback, trotting amid everything he was talking about. Donkey vocabulary permeated every aspect of life. This language began with donkeys, and he couldn't express anything properly without them.

Ku had a vague sense that Master was also a donkey fancier. The old man was always haring off to distant places where different languages were spoken with a donkey as his only companion. He invariably set forth with a Pisha jenny, trading rides several times in the towns and villages he passed through, riding foals till they were grown and mature donkeys till they were old, only getting back to Pisha after who knew how many steeds had been under his rump. When he spoke about donkey fanciers in Heile, his voice and eyes would brighten. From the Heilenese words Master taught him, Ku knew about these people early on.

Donkey fanciers are barter merchants. They buy a donkey in the morning, and after half a day's use, sell her in the afternoon for a tidy profit, which they use to acquire another one before evening, swapping a grey one for a black one, or a foal for a grown donkey, walking along with a different donkey every day, always a jenny. They also exchange donkeys between themselves, and earn their livelihood that way. Seeing this old man can't stop mentioning donkeys, Ku has a sudden impulse to speak Heilenese. He leads Hsieh to the middle of the crowd, and talks about how he bought her in a Pisha marketplace, how he arrived in Heile amid braying, how every jack they encountered along the way wanted to mount her, how he had to fend them off. Why fend them off? Because once a young jenny has been mounted once, she'll want it to be twice, yearning for it every day. They'd never have reached Heile that way.

Ku talks about donkeys in Heilenese with as much assurance as if he were riding a donkey through the market, and everyone is mesmerised by his narration. He successfully opens the conversation with his tale of a young jenny, leading them all to join in, pulling the conversation from Pisha to Heile, to the prolonged war between the kingdoms that has continued for so long that many people have grown elderly in combat, several kings have died in battle, many ministers have passed away from old age, huge numbers of men and horses have been laid to waste. Yet, the number of donkeys has actually increased, and the braying is thicker than ever before, because donkeys do not take part in war, they remain free while humans do battle. Not that they seem to be free—they have a lot to do. Heile is busy building Tian temples, and donkeys are required to carry bricks. Heile donkeys have spent a thousand years bearing bricks for Kun temples, and who knows how long they will do the same for the Tian religion. Perhaps one day the Pisha will conquer this land again, and the destroyed Kun temples will have to be rebuilt. In any case, donkey hooves are never at leisure.

The donkey markets are empty now—donkey traders only work alongside labouring donkeys. The tower of the Great Tian Temple is even taller than the one at Pisha's West Kun Temple, and its walls are higher too. Heile demolished all the Kun temples in the vicinity, and their bricks were brought here for the Great Tian Temple. Halfway through construction, the whole thing was torn down—bricks from Kun temples had been deemed unclean, still permeated with the voices of Kun devotees chanting scripture. Kilns from near and far were tasked with producing new bricks. They started building again, only to stop once more. The same kilns had previously made bricks for Kun temples, meaning the kilns themselves were unclean. New kilns were built, and brand new bricks brought in, but even those were deemed useless— the donkeys that brought the bricks had done the same for Kun temples, and furthermore Kun devotees had ridden them. Ultimately they concluded that the people themselves were sullied, because everyone in this place had once worshipped Kun. The Great Tianmen of the temple had to step forward and say it was precisely because people were unclean that they needed the temple, so everyone could be purified. Uncertain what the humans were doing, the donkeys were, for the first time, confused— previously, of all the animals in Heile, they alone had understood that the humans had changed religions. The chickens and goats had no idea, and nor did the horses, who only knew how to gallop into battle, but not why they were fighting. Horses can't see ghosts.

Humans can't either, but there are ghosts in their minds, which are visible to donkeys. And when donkeys see that the ghosts in people's minds have changed, they understand that the human world has been transformed.

Having said this much, Ku realises donkeys have brought him where he needs to be. Every word that's been said in this crowd has touched on donkeys, making every sentence a cart. Their donkey-led talk contained everything there is to say about Heile, indeed the whole world. They could trundle on till dawn, but Ku has no time for that. Having led the conversation to the Great Tian Temple that donkeys are ferrying bricks from, his tongue swerves to his true subject.

"What about Peach Blossom Temple? I hear it's become a Tian temple now. I wonder what happened to Maisheng, who used to be there?"

"Ah, Maisheng. He's the Great Tianmen of Peach Blossom Tian Temple these days.

"Back in his Kunmen days, he was a donkey expert—he was always going on donkeyback journeys. His favourite trick was to recite scripture while wandering the streets on a donkey. For a while the Heile people copied him, sitting cross-legged on their donkeys. Then a dozen years ago, when Tian devotees barged into Peach Blossom Temple, they found him cross-legged on donkeyback, his mouth spewing Kun scripture. The invaders thought he must be a god, and didn't dare to touch him.

"After that, he led five hundred Kun devotees to convert, and he changed to worshipping Tian too, though he still rides donkeys just as often, sitting cross-legged as he trots through the city—it's just the book in his hands and the scripture on his lips that are different now. Everyone in Heile knows this, even the donkeys, and every donkey in town hopes to be ridden by Maisheng at least once. They knew as soon as it happened that he was no longer a Kunmen, but a Tianmen now."

Pink

Hsieh has been listening with one ear to Ku and the old man, while her other ear points up. Earlier on, she heard the call to worship from the Tian temple at the far end of the alleyway, followed by the doors all down the street opening as everyone answered the summons, and above them the faint creaking of the celestial court's ancient mulberry gates as it open and shut. Someone else has arrived up there. Ku can't hear this, his ears are filled with the old codger's droning. They say only the elderly are able to hear the celestial gates. The dozing old folk by the side of the street have their heads tilted to the side, one ear pricked up. Mostly what fills their ears are hoofbeats and braying that has soared into the air then fallen back to earth. Only individuals here and there make out the quiet creaking of these gates, whereupon they depart, and their place is taken by another old person. Or else they remain among the living, pretending not to have noticed, stealing a few more years on earth.

No one knows that there are dead people mixed in with the human heap, living their lives and not drawing breath.

Only donkeys, dogs and particularly sharp-eyed Kun or Tian devotees can tell the difference between the living and the dead. Dogs detect the sourish smell of death. Donkeys and Kun devotees use their eyes—dead people's faces turn black, their eyes are grey and dull. The Kun worshippers pretend not to notice, but donkeys can't ignore it. When they see a dead person, they let out a bray.

At this moment, all the jennies in the lane abruptly cry out, and Hsieh sees thousands of ghosts glowing blue as they rise into the air, fresh spirits still radiating heat as well as old ones whose heads are thick with dust, a blanket of braying shrouding them. To Hsieh, who sees sounds as colours and shapes, the jenny cries have built countless pink rainbows arcing up to the celestial court. The jacks in the next lane call out in response, and every ghost in Heile City rises on these brays.

Of course, braying alone will not send every ghost to the heavens. The donkeys watch as most of the souls fall back to earth like dirt, their thoughts snapping off, leaving them as inert as the soil. Where they have piled up, no seeds can grow, no mice can dig holes, and the wind produces no sound as it gusts past. Only the stamping of a donkey's hooves will raise ghosts who have lain dormant for many years.

Even more people are deaf, and cannot hear the celestial gates. These old men have been longing for the day they will no longer be able to hear. Then they will go blind, and not see death either. Their legs will go lame, so they can't walk into old age, but will instead dither in the realms of childhood and youth.

12

Peach Blossom Tian Temple

In Heat

PEACH BLOSSOM KUN TEMPLE is now Peach Blossom Tian Temple.

A man in a long robe stops Ku and Hsieh: donkeys are not allowed in the temple. Ku knows this, but a moment ago, they walked past a row of hitching posts beneath a large willow tree where a few hundred donkeys were tied up, and it caused quite a stir. A grey jack broke free and charged over, and though Ku tried to lead Hsieh away, she dragged her rump and refused to move, her eyes glued to the thingy poking out between the jack's legs. Her itch down there is back.

Two drovers emerge from the temple. One strokes Hsieh's flank, the other her neck.

"When a jenny is in heat, she won't listen to the heavens themselves—and you want to tell her what to do?" jokes the man at her neck.

Ku ignores him and keeps trying to drag her away. They follow him.

Ku gives his name and says he wishes to see Tianmen Maisheng, to whom he bore a message two years previously.

The man in the robe goes inside. Quite a long time passes before a tall Tian devotee comes out and says Ku may enter once he's tied up his donkey.

"This donkey has come a long way to be presented to the Great Maisheng. I have to deliver her in person."

The Tian devotee studies Ku and Hsieh with a peculiar expression.

"Have you come from this little jenny's hometown?"

Ku stares back, his face blank.

The tall Tian devotee leads Ku round the back of the temple. As they pass the willow tree, there is another chorus of braying.

"It can't have been easy, coming such a long way with a jenny in heat," says the man rather nastily, looking back at Ku.

Thief Over the Wall

Behind Peach Blossom Temple is a swathe of houses, higgledy piggledy all the way down to the river terrace.

On his last trip, Ku noticed that courtyard walls in Heile are taller than the ones in Pisha—the sign of a city full of thieves.

The walls of Peach Blossom Temple are three times the height of a man, the least you need to keep burglars out. Twice human height and two thieves could get in if one stood on the other's shoulders. Two-and-a-half-times, you'd just need a donkey: one thief on another's shoulders, and the donkey beneath them both. But thrice human height? That's much trickier.

Because there are so many thieves in this town, the locksmiths of Heile are famous everywhere. Rich Pisha people all use Heile locks. Ku himself has a Heile bronze lock on his door. These locks can't be prised or smashed open. If a Pisha household loses their keys, their only option is to get a Heile locksmith to come open it. No Pisha thief would dare tackle a Heile lock—they back away when they see one. It's the same with Heile thieves. They choose instead to go over the garden walls, and so these walls must be built higher and higher.

Donkeys Brayed Along

They reach a lean-to in the lee of a wall thatched with mouldering straw, and next to it is a courtyard full of donkey carts. This used to be Peach Blossom Kun Temple's donkey yard, and although the temple has switched religions, the courtyard remains. It's actually larger than the one at West Kun Temple, but the outer walls here are much lower and can't keep out the braying.

Ku asks the middle-aged man whether the Tian devotees are ever disturbed at their chanting by donkey cries, given how close by the courtyard is.

"Of course they are. After Peach Blossom became a Tian temple, the Tian devotees chanted their prayers at dawn each day, and the donkeys brayed along. Then they learnt to shut up—leather whips taught them that lesson. Our Tianmen Maisheng doesn't mind, though. He says the voice of Tian is not only to be found among human beings, but also manifests in other forms of life. He taught us to listen carefully to the cries of donkeys. As long as your heart is pure, you will hear the true word among dogs barking and chickens clucking too."

Back Courtyard

The gate in the wall beneath the lean-to looks just like the back gate of West Kun Temple. The tall Tian devotee knocks a few times, and they hear a lock turning.

The wooden gate creaks open, and they step into a small courtyard that, again, looks like the one at West Kun Temple. Kun temples all used to have a back courtyard for storage, and whenever it wasn't convenient to enter through the front door, you could just as easily slip in from the rear. The last time Ku came to Peach Blossom Temple, all the Kun statues at the front had been destroyed, and the space that had once been for Kun worship was now used to recite Tian scripture. Unexpectedly, the back courtyard hasn't changed at all: the cooking stoves, tables, pots and ladles are all exactly the same. A large metal cauldron bubbles gently as two workers busy themselves making lunch. The sight reminds Ku how hungry he is, and Hsieh too stares at the boiling liquid.

The tall Tian devotee orders one of the servants to stay with Ku, while he goes through the side door.

After a while, Maisheng appears in a Tianmen's garb. Ku doesn't know how he ought to bow, so instead he hands over the donkey reins.

"The Great Kunmen of Pisha's West Kun Temple instructed me to bear a young jenny to you. He insisted that I had to deliver her to you intact," he says in Pishanese.

Rather than taking the reins, Maisheng walks around Hsieh, studying her.

"Last time you asked me to bear word to the Great Kunmen, and I did as you asked."

"What did I ask you to say?" Maisheng asks in Pishanese.

"You wanted the Great Kunmen to send you a copy of Kun scripture in Heilenese," Ku murmurs.

"Then why did he send me a donkey?"

"The Great Kunmen said this jenny was a message, and I should bring her to you unscathed."

Maisheng strokes Hsieh's fur, and as it parts, he thinks he sees something beneath. Ku notices Maisheng parting the donkey's fur. Maisheng glances up and smiles at Ku, then his face suddenly darkens and he signals for two burly men to come over and tie Ku's arms behind his back. Hsieh watches frantically as they bind him to a pillar. She tosses her head and jerks back. Only when she notices Ku staring silently at her does she begin to calm down.

Butcher

Tianmen Maisheng's hand reaches once again towards Hsieh's belly. Slowly he parts the hairs there, then gently smooths them flat again. The gesture reminds Hsieh of Kunmen Virtue, back at West Kun Temple. Even through a thick layer of hair, she can feel the warmth of his hand, of human touch.

The tall Tian devotee cranes his neck for a closer look, first at the spot where the hair is parted, then at Ku. For his part, Ku regrets not having thought to do this on the long journey here. Now he understands what words the Great Kunmen wanted him to bear: the ones hidden beneath Hsieh's fur.

Tianmen Maisheng whispers an order, and the tall man leaves. Maisheng continues stroking Hsieh, all the way from her spine to her belly, then up the other side, a pleasant sensation that somehow leaves her tense. All the itches in her body are brought to the surface. She wriggles her rump and twists around. Maisheng rubs her neck to calm her down, but she only gets more agitated.

After quite a while, the tall man brings in a butcher with a yellow beard who tosses down his bag in front of Ku and begins removing one tool after another: a long knife, a razor, a scraper, a metal hook, a whetstone, a leather strop. The slaughterer's complete kit. Ku realises what he is about to do.

Yellow Beard grabs Hsieh's reins and looks her over, groping her rump along the way.

"A virgin jenny. What a shame," he says, glancing at Maisheng.

The attendant also looks at Maisheng, who gestures. Yellow Beard gets the message, and takes the reins off Hsieh. He ties her right rear and left fore hooves together, then pulls the rope over his shoulder so she falls to the ground. Her other two hooves are now bound together too, criss-cross. She struggles to stand till she runs out of energy, eyes turning to her tormentor, then back to Ku, whose arms are tied to the hitching post. His eyes meet Hsieh's, full of desolation.

A fire is lit, and a great vat of water set on it. Soon, it is emitting steam. *They aren't planning a feast of donkey flesh, are they?* Hsieh has heard that since changing their religion, the Tian no longer eat donkeys. Will they carve more insect-like words into her skin, as they did at West Kun Temple?

*

The fire is fuelled by red willow branches, and magenta flames leap through the vent. Hsieh remembers the evening in Guma when she saw ghosts rising into the air on the smoke from cooking fires. She twists around to look at TuoJue, and finds Tuo staring back at her, before abruptly leaping into the air. Jue hesitates, then follows suit. The head and body join back together in mid-air, and TuoJue drifts back down to squat by the boiling water, gazing hollowly at Hsieh. Her hair stands on end. She knows she is done for—the knife is coming for her.

The water bubbles, and TuoJue glistens with sweat, looking first at Hsieh, then up at the heavens. *TuoJue is about to leave*, thinks Hsieh. Such a plume of steam, such a burst of red willow flames, perfect for ascending on. She jerks her head towards the sky. Jue waves goodbye, but a second later Tuo shakes his head. This time, though, the head must obey the body, and TuoJue begins to rise, till he is mounted backwards on Ku's bent back, as if Ku were a donkey. Ku jerks violently, feeling something settling on him.

Ahnng-jee ahnng-jee!

Hsieh screams as she struggles. Ku knows this is for his benefit, and looks at her full of tenderness. Hsieh gazes back at him, and TuoJue turns to Hsieh amid the braying.

Four men arrive to hoist Hsieh onto the wooden table by the pot. Her muzzle points towards the boiling water, and she knows what they are about to do. Not wanting to think about it, she turns to Ku, haplessly tied up, who looks back at her. She can read pain in a human face. Knowing he is hurting for her, she feels at peace, and even manages to bat her eyes playfully at him.

Yellow Beard dips the metal hook into the pot to pull out some scraps of cloth, which he drapes over Hsieh's mouth. She tries to rear her head, but they have a firm hold of her ears, and she can't move. Her bound hooves churn, as if she is running. Her whole body twitches hopelessly.

Ku can see that they are smothering Hsieh. His mouth opens wide, and many languages struggle to pour out, but all get stuck in his throat. No words will emerge. After a lot of effort, he finally produces: *Ahnng-jee ahnng-jee ahnng-jee!*

His cry soars towards the sky. Everyone turns to look at him, and even Yellow Beard stops his work for a moment. Hsieh's ears prick up. She's never heard Ku make such a sound before. This is for her, she knows. She tries to answer, but is no longer able to. She struggles to turn her head, so her bulging eyes can see Ku, tied to the hitching post like a donkey. A bray bubbles in her throat, but then it retreats, it retreats, the final speck of light in her eyes fades away, and her head crashes down.

Pain

Ahnng-jee ahnng-jee ahnng-jee.

Hsieh hears it again, the sound Ku just made, arching into the barren sky like a rainbow, then back down to her. Her soul breaks free from her physical form and comes to rest atop the wall. She stares back at her body, lying next to a bubbling pot. She doesn't recognise herself.

Yellow Beard cuts a small incision by her left foreleg, but she feels no pain. A metal rod as thick as a finger plunges in, pokes around inside, and withdraws without a drop of blood on it. He blows into the hole, and Hsieh's front half slowly puffs up, while an attendant beats her with a rod to distribute the air. Still she feels nothing. Where has all her pain gone? The thought suddenly comes that she hasn't been beaten very often, and what she remembers is actually the agony of a whip landing on her mother's back. Yellow Beard ties her aerated front leg with a strip of leather, and moves on to the rear, where he does the same thing: a small cut, the metal rod, filling her with air. Soon he has inflated all four limbs, and Hsieh lies there like a large bucket. He ladles boiling water over her, then gently scrapes her skin with his razor, and her hair falls to the ground. Still not a bit of pain.

Hsieh has seen butchers inflating and shaving goats in this way. Years ago, she watched her mother pull a cart home from the marketplace containing a goat which was slaughtered, blown full of air, and then scalded till its fur came off. Each time they cut a hole in the goat's leg, she felt a jolt of pain on the same part of her body, and all the pain when they were shaving the goat settled on her body, as if she were the one being killed.

Now it's her turn. Boiling water pours over her skin but she feels no pain, because the donkey lying there is no longer herself.

Ku looks up at Hsieh's swollen body lying on its back, legs pointing up. Yellow Beard squats by the side of the bubbling pot, using a hollow gourd to scoop scalding water over her. Ku's own body convulses, as if the water is pouring over him. Hsieh watches his torment and knows that all her pain has been transferred to him.

Words

The butcher shaves Hsieh, revealing a greyish white belly covered in the words she dreamt of on those countless nights. In her dreams, sometimes she was a Kun devotee, sitting in a high-walled courtyard, studiously parsing the words on her own body, chanting them in a human voice. Other times, she stood naked in the courtyard surrounded by Kun devotees, all of them staring at her bare skin and reciting the words inscribed there, every one of them bursting into sound as if she were enveloped in scripture, the voices taking form as they passed across her, creating layers upon layers of donkeys made of sound, stacked atop one another with the topmost one touching the heavens.

*

Everyone gathers around and stares in shock. Tianmen Maisheng bends over for a closer look. Ku cranes his neck. Something strange has happened. They are all huddled over Hsieh's corpse, mumbling something Ku can't quite make out.

When they kneel, Ku finally sees Hsieh's shaved skin and the dense lines of Heilenese script across it. He gets on his knees too, pressing his head to the ground and chanting Kun scripture, and in an instant he feels calmer.

A moment ago, when he saw Maisheng parting Hsieh's hair, Ku immediately understood. All this time he'd never thought of doing that. If he'd only paid a little more attention as he'd sat on her back—but he never noticed. Those nights he lay against her for warmth, face pressed to her belly, eyes open in the bright moonlight, stroking her like a lover . . . he never once considered examining her more closely. Only once, that night at Aoba, did he slip his fingers beneath her fur, hoping to feel soft skin like under a person's clothes, instead finding the coarse roots of her hair. How many times on the way here had he turned over in his mind the Great Kunmen's instruction to treat the donkey as a message, imagining the answer might lie in her voice. *Did Maisheng understand braying?* He would never have guessed the message he was bearing was written on her skin.

Celestial Court

Hsieh's ghost sees Ku prostrating himself, his head to another man's rump, reciting scripture so quietly only a ghost could hear it, soft as insects chirping in the soil, as the celestial court's creaking gate. Hsieh knows it is time for her to go. No sooner does this thought come to her mind as she finds herself at the celestial court, which stands ajar, but as she tries to enter, a whip lashes down across her muzzle.

"Hey, bald donkey, scrub those words off your hide before you come in."

Hsieh turns her head and sees that every shred of fur has been removed from her body. Words are crawling like bugs across her bare skin.

"Humans carved this into me. They said it was Kun scripture, bestowed on them from above. People have been chanting these words for a thousand years, and now I'm bringing them back up to the heavens," she retorts.

The sentry comes closer and looks her over.

"We've never bestowed scripture on anyone. Humans came up with these words themselves. Send them back where they belong."

"I'm a donkey. Someone will have to lead me back."

She is feeling stubborn.

"A human is holding your reins. He used to lead you, now it's your turn. Go back."

She stares at the sentry, but he only waves goodbye. Still confused, she returns to earth.

*

They are peeling her skin off, beginning with an incision on her belly, revealing bloody redness. Hsieh has never seen her own flesh. When the goatman was flayed in Guma, the goat being peeled off had long lost all sensation, and it was the human shrieking in pain. Now she sees them doing it to her, but she feels nothing, no sensation at all. She wishes it hurt, even if it made her scream in agony. But no. This carcass no longer has anything to do with her.

Possessing

Hsieh's spirit sees TuoJue riding on Ku's bent back as if he were a donkey. This brainless body and bodiless brain have abandoned her and are possessing Ku instead. TuoJue waves at Hsieh, who shoots them a sidelong glance, and drifts down onto the wall. TuoJue looks up at her, trying to get her to join them. She ignores the ghost and raises her head to the sky for a while. When she looks back down, TuoJue is still staring at the heavens. From TuoJue's empty gaze, she understands that she is a ghost too. The sentry at the celestial court said she would have to lead Ku now. The force of the words hits her suddenly, and like a child she nestles into Ku's embrace.

Ku shudders, and all the breath in him tries to repel her, but his breath is weak, and she easily breaches it. Just like when the headless bodiless ghost decided to possess her, and try as she might, she couldn't prevent it. Life has unknown cracks, and while Hsieh was able to keep any jacks from invading her body, she wasn't able to ward off spirit possession.

Like entering a donkey pen, Hsieh slips into Ku's body. She rears her head, and Ku's head tilts back. She stretches, and his back arcs. She wriggles her long ears, and his twitch. She doesn't dare kick her legs because his are curled up and his hands tied. Hsieh's heart aches for this man. She tries not to move too much, in case he can feel her. When a human realises they've been possessed, they'll seek out a Kun devotee for an exorcism, or grab a talisman, or begin hitting themselves with peach tree switches, all of which cause the ghost to suffer. Hsieh doesn't want either Ku or herself to be in pain. They have many days to spend together, and she will gradually slip into his every cranny. She no longer has a body of her own, and Ku's will have to be her home. TuoJue has taken up residence here too.

Hsieh mounts Ku backwards, just as ghosts have done to her. TuoJue was already facing backwards, so when she turns they are now facing front, which immediately feels wrong. Ghosts can't afford to face forward—humans might recognise them that way. TuoJue turns around again.

*

Ku is convulsing violently. He feels he may be losing his mind. His eyes are shut so he can't see Hsieh's skin being peeled off, but he can hear the blade slicing through her flesh, as if it's cutting him too. He feels an entire donkey inside him hurting. His feet throb when they slice into Hsieh's hooves, his stomach clenches when they rip open her belly, and every inch of his body stings as they tear off her skin.

Good Scriptures

Hsieh's ghost watches her skin being removed in a single piece and spread across the floor. The men huddle around, and Ku looks too. Tianmen Maisheng's eyes follow the lines of scripture and his lips move. Ku can tell he is silently reciting scripture. Ku does the same, in his mind, in many languages.

"Fold this up and bury it," Maisheng orders his underlings. "We've converted and no longer worship Kun, but these are good scriptures, and we ought to bury them in the ground for people who might believe them in the future. We worshipped Kun for a thousand years, no one knows what our children or grandchildren might believe a hundred, a thousand years from now."

Ku watches as they roll the donkey skin and press it flat, fold the two ends towards each other, and press it into a rectangular bundle, which they tie with leather strings.

Convert

Tianmen Maisheng walks up to Ku, and the tall Tian devotee loosens his bonds. Maisheng orders him to stand, but Ku can't. The tall man hoists him to his feet. Maisheng orders him to straighten his back, but he can't do that either—he feels as though a donkey is holding up his body from the inside. All he can do is stiffen his neck and look directly at the Tianmen.

Maisheng refuses to meet Ku's gaze. His eyes slide sidelong towards the donkey pelt.

"I heard you bray a moment ago. We all have a stubborn donkey inside us, and who doesn't want to cry out like a donkey? But we control ourselves. Could you speak to me in human language?"

Ku's head rears back, and braying wells up in his throat. He clenches his teeth to hold it back.

"Don't blame me for killing her. The instant the Great Kunmen put her reins in your hand, she was already dead. You didn't know it, that's all, and nor did she. Many people in this place don't know they're dead. I spent decades chanting Kun scripture, then years reciting Tian scripture, and I've gained the ability to see death— mine and other people's. I died the moment they burnt Peach Blossom Temple. They didn't know I was dead, and forced me to convert to Tian. I pretended to believe for two years, but now I actually do. And once I had faith again, I came back to life.

"People like us are different from common folk. We know we're dead, but we can toughen our hides and keep going. Many people don't realise they're dead. The reason I changed my religion, the reason I chose not to ascend to paradise after my death, is because I couldn't stop worrying about the living dead. They fear nothing, there's nothing they mightn't do. Each day I call the summons to prayer from the Tian tower, and many corpses clinging to this mortal world are woken by me.

"This world should be for the living. That's just as important as keeping the celestial court for the dead."

Ku can hear the rhythms of Kun scripture in Maisheng's words. He might have changed his religion, but he can't alter his way of speaking. After spending most of his life chanting Kun scripture, he now recites Tian scripture with the same voice, and people probably feel nothing has changed.

Try as he might to respond to Maisheng, all Ku can think of are the Heilenese words carved into Hsieh's skin. In his mind these turn into Chiu, then Huang, then Pisha. He translates them to and fro, and all the way back to Heile, but when he opens his mouth, what comes out is braying, as if the donkey within him has reared her head back. He can't stop her. His face and neck flush bright red, and his body trembles as if he is about to gallop away. The tall Tian devotee restrains him.

"Why not worship Tian, like me?" says Maisheng, having waited with the utmost patience for Ku to calm down. His warm gaze washes over Ku. Sensing in it the benevolence of Kun, Ku's heart unclenches right away.

"I'm a word bearer, and this message that you've just spoken, I will bear truthfully to myself. The journey from my ears to my heart may be as long as the road from Heile to Pisha. Please give me some time. All my life I've carried words to other people, and now I'm doing it for myself. Once the message reaches its destination, if my heart receives it, I will convert to your religion. Otherwise, you may chop my head off."

Ku thrusts his head forward, meaning, *My head has been given unto you.*

"I'm not going to put a knife to your throat and say you have to answer right away. When someone did that to me, years ago, my voice agreed, but I couldn't get rid of the Kun in my heart. Now I have true faith. Tian is merciful, and waited three years for me. I will give you three months. By the time the wheat in the fields ripens, you must give me an answer.

"The power to chop off or leave your head rests entirely with us Tian believers. The Tian devotees and the butcher control the lives of our prisoners and conquered peoples. I am not as patient as them. The butcher comes with me, chopper in hand. I ask everyone once if they will convert, and if they hesitate for even a second, the blade comes down. I loathe those who do not stand fast, and will not give them the chance to destroy their virtue. But with you, I will be patient."

Ku feels a chill against his neck, as if the blade is already touching his skin from three months in the future. His hair stands on end. Yet he feels a sudden jolt of stubbornness. He thrusts his head forward and his neck stiffens obstinately, stretching out long, just like a donkey's.

13

Conversion

Pelt

KU DOESN'T WAIT for the wheat to ripen, but goes early to the Tianmen and sticks out his long neck.

"I will change my religion to yours."

He has no idea that the spirit of a little jenny lurks within him, and he cannot induce Hsieh to change her religion too. Hsieh's skin is carved all over with Kun scripture, and she can't change her skin. Those who have Kun in their hearts can profess Tian beliefs, just to preserve their lives, and no one will be able to see what they actually have or do not have within them. With Hsieh, there's no bluffing. She has Kun on her pelt and can't wipe it away. Humans may change their beliefs, but not her. She only has one hide, and even as a ghost, it is covered in the holy words of Kun.

Maisheng raises both hands high and recites a passage of Tian scripture in a voice coarsened by decades of Kun chanting. As Ku listens, the Kun figures in his heart feel like they're being read aloud, one by one.

When the Tianmen is done speaking, one of his hands comes down to clutch three times at Ku's head. Ku knows this gesture— Kun devotees do it to catch ghosts. Maisheng must see the spectre of Kun in his mind and is trying to claw it out.

"You have a donkey within you. Make sure you keep it tied up."

At Maisheng's words, Ku's neck abruptly stretches and shrinks again. He doesn't realise this is Hsieh, shuddering with fright. Ghosts are even more terrified of being spotted by humans than humans ever are when they see a ghost.

Chanting Scripture

After his conversion, Ku is moved out of the donkey pen—he will still be in the yard by the temple's back door, but no longer with the donkeys. During his three months' grace, Maisheng kept Ku locked up with three jennies. When throwing him in there, the tall attendant said this was the best treatment he'd ever seen a Kun believer getting, three donkeys keeping him company. The two older jennies eye him suspiciously each night, assuming he has designs on them, but the youngest one doesn't seem to mind at all, and keeps coming over to playfully press her face against his. Whenever she gets too close to Ku, the other two give her a nip.

Tianmen Maisheng gives Ku a book of Tian scripture to chant. By the faint light that spills around the edges of the door, Ku reads it from beginning to end. After just three times, he can recite it from memory. When the sounds of Tian prayer waft in, he mimics its cadences, causing the three jennies to swivel their ears in his direction. After a few lines, they join in. Their braying makes Ku's neck stretch out, as though they've awakened the donkey within him, and he begins to *ahng-jee* too. Then he gets himself under control, refusing to sound like a donkey, and takes up his Tian chanting again in a ragged voice. Eventually, he chants himself into the scripture.

Ku spends his days in the temple, translating for Tianmen Maisheng. When he gets bored of that, he arranges the scrolls in the library, something he did at West Kun Temple when he was a little boy—that was Kun scripture, of course, and this is Tian. He doesn't need to read these words, he already knows them all by heart.

Maisheng can also recite Tian scripture from memory—it's not difficult for him. Anyone who has several hundred scrolls of Kun scripture locked up in his mind isn't going to be deterred by one little volume of Tian holy words.

Drive Out the Kun

During this time, Ku's only task is to drive out the Kun that's in his heart. He has learnt various methods of expelling ghosts, all kinds of curses, but none of them will work against Kun. He sits alone in a corner, reading Tian scripture over and over, yet all that appears in his mind is one Kun statue after another.

On one occasion, the Tian devotees overhear him, and mistakenly think he's chanting Kun words. He is almost hauled off to be decapitated. He almost effortlessly finds Tian within its scripture but has no idea how to put it into his heart. The Tian religion has no statues, so he doesn't know what Tian looks like. No matter how hard he works at his chanting, the only image in his mind is a likeness of Kun. *Tian can look like Kun*, he tells himself. Hsieh can see all these thoughts. Whatever goes through his mind causes the ghost in his heart to move.

Ku wants to stay alive. Ever since Hsieh's death, the image of his own passing has swirled around his mind. He has witnessed many people being decapitated for refusing to convert, their heads flung into the sandy wastes to the city's north, their bodies into the Gobi to the south. That's how they deal with Kun believers, ensuring they won't be able to reach the celestial court in the afterlife.

Hsieh's ghost would like to convert along with Ku, but it doesn't feel possible. Ku is converting to Tian, which she can't see, unlike the Kun figures of clay or wood. Can this Tian whom Ku now worships see that Ku's body contains within it a young jenny whose skin is covered in Kun scripture? She frequently tries to take control of his body. As she considers these things, it occurs to her that she's gradually coming to think more and more about human affairs. It's been a while since her mind has been on donkey business, as if being in this man named Ku has taken her away from the donkey world. Any number of jacks would have liked to have their way with her, and she evaded them all. This saddens her. She never really lived as a donkey. She never knew the love of a jack, never had so much as a nibble on her neck. Then to die, just like that. The sting of needles poking into her skin at West Kun Temple, the anxiety and pleasure of Ku stroking her belly, the constant itch of words on her rump and beneath her hair—these now feel like beautiful sensations that have since evaporated. All that's left of her is this shred of a soul, taking refuge within Ku's body.

Older

Ku seems to have gotten older all at once. The first time Hsieh set eyes on him at West Kun Temple, he already looked old with his salt and pepper beard. Their journey together lasted most of a year, and she watched as the white strands multiplied. Now he's elderly, his beard the colour of snow, his back bowed. Hsieh thinks with an ache that this is her fault, her presence is making him stoop like a donkey. At a time in her life when Hsieh ought to have been leading a joyous existence with another donkey, she followed Ku instead, all that long way to Heile, over many terrifying months. Ku was good to her. She now knows this was for the sake of her scripture-inscribed hide, yet he knew nothing about that; he treated Hsieh as a message he was delivering to Heile. He pretended to rescue her from slaughter at West Kun Temple in order to win her gratitude, so she would willingly leave with him. That may have been playacting, but she still feels he treated her well.

Hsieh was at her most alluring during the time she spent accompanying Ku to Heile, and here she has lost her life. Her dripping red flesh was hacked up and fed to the dogs, while her pelt will be preserved, thanks to the scripture written on it. She watched the humans roll it up and bind it with leather straps. Her last specks of consciousness clung to her bloody skin and followed them into the desert. They dug a hole and buried it deep in the arid land, and the sensation lingering in the hide slowly died away, as if her thick coat of hair was being forgotten, strand by strand, until there was nothing left but the words inscribed on her, whereupon her consciousness abruptly came back to life, though now she doesn't know where her old self has gone—all that's left is a spirit who holds not a shred of sorrow or joy. Following the brushstrokes of the words on her skin, she wanders far and wide, all the way to the end and back again, over and over, without beginning or end, no more and no less. She feels a faint connection with the spirit currently possessing Ku, but at the same time they don't seem to know anything about each other, like they exist in completely different worlds.

Inside Ku's body, Hsieh feels herself getting old. She can't help ageing, as Ku is doing. She spends a lot of time frolicking as a young jenny should, but when his legs ache and he can't walk, neither can she. When he pants as he climbs the stairs of the Tian tower, she finds herself breathing hard too. Ghosts don't actually draw breath, and what she's expelling is an old man's air.

Old Age

The aged Ku becomes a well-known figure in Heile City, the old hunchback bent over like a donkey. Every donkey in Heile knows who he is, because riding on his back is the ghost of a small black jenny whom he cannot see, and on her back is a second ghost consisting of a body and a mismatched head. They bray when they see Ku, and he now knows what they're saying—he's the only person in the whole of Heile City who can understand braying. He knows Hsieh's soul is resting within him, and he often detects her scent, the one he breathed in while he was riding her. Now it sometimes feels as if her fragrance is enfolding him, that she has taken control of him. His back bends over more and more, and he feels he has been transformed into a donkey.

Ku doesn't know a single person in Heile City. His wife Sha told him to seek out her father, who is among the troops who arrived from the west, but he hasn't done so. Sha's father must be even older than he is, Ku thinks. Or perhaps he's no longer in the mortal world. What's the point of looking for a father who sold his own daughter? Besides, Ku is now more or less an old donkey, and doesn't see the point of meeting anyone.

Yet he misses Sha, the wife he raised as if she were his daughter. If he dies here in Heile, will she grow old among the donkeys of their courtyard? Her old age is still so far away. When Ku thinks about Sha, she looks very young. Perhaps he will die and be reborn. She will still be young if that happens, though he will be even younger, and someone might come along on a donkey and snatch him to sell, then Sha can buy him, raise him as a son, and when he's grown, marry him.

Hsieh's spirit watches quietly as Ku has these thoughts, imagining she's the female he's fantasising about. A sweet sensation.

TuoJue

Ku buys a young grey jenny at Heile's Jenny Lane and names her Hsieh. The donkey doesn't know her name, and doesn't respond when he calls her. She often brays at Ku's back, where she can see ghosts lurking: a black female donkey, and a man whose head and body have come from different people. Ku frequently turns his head too, a gesture that reminds him of Hsieh, who was always staring at her own back. Ku recognises Hsieh in his own movements. Now that his back is hunched, he is finally able to see what Hsieh saw.

He had already sensed their presence on the way from Pisha to Heile. Over and over in his dreams, he saw a man whose head had been fixed to the wrong body, feet tracking sand across a bloody puddle. Whenever Ku shut his eyes, he saw the hybrid man.

Now Ku realises who this being on his back is. He can sense the weight of a ghost.

TuoJue realises that Ku can see them. The two ghosts are getting quieter and quieter. For all that they share a body, they have their own thoughts. The head thinks of Heile, the legs ponder Pisha. At least they've stopped squabbling.

Mother Tongue

Ku goes to Jenny Lane whenever he has nothing better to do—he finds the scent of female donkeys intoxicating. As soon as his head poked into Heile City, he detected this smell right away amid the tangle of other aromas. Heile people like to keep up appearances, so they've separated the jenny and jack marketplaces, giving those who trade in female donkeys their own space.

Ku has a faint memory of Master acquiring him at Jenny Lane, a free gift with a donkey. When Master was still around, Ku would ask about this famous street, and Master would shoot him a suspicious look, thinking Ku wanted to ogle the donkeys. Only when Ku began asking about the exact spot where he'd been bought did Master relax and start describing the street.

Having already visited this place numerous times through Master's words, actually coming here for the first time feels like walking into a long-forgotten dream, everything just the way it was: him mounted backwards on a donkey, staring at the man who'd sold him—the man now hanging his head with guilt and looking awkwardly away. As soon as he realised he was being kidnapped by the leather trader, Ku insisted on facing backwards so he could remember the way. He knew the trafficker would bring him far from home.

He'd spoken the language of his hometown to every outsider he met, but no one understood what he was saying. After Master died, there was once again no one Ku could speak this language with. Perhaps his hometown was as far away as the edge of the sky, he thought, and there was no other language beyond that.

All he can do now is seek out Jenny Lane, where he was sold. He sells the little grey donkey and buys a black one around Hsieh's age who looks like her, a mix of Heile and Pisha breeds. Once again, he names her Hsieh.

Ku sits amid the flock of old men on Jenny Lane. They know him as a former Kun devotee from Peach Blossom Temple, and keep badgering him to recite Tian scripture. Ku would rather talk about donkeys. With his language skills, he knows how to let donkeys lead the conversation, how to lure them out of Heile and down many roads, all of which the old men have walked down too, in the company of donkeys, so their chat wanders through these remote lanes and byways, and Ku's words gradually probe a particular direction: the village where he was rolled up in a goatskin and taken away at the age of three, the place whose language he still occasionally speaks. Only no one understands him, and now he does so again, asking these men who have roamed so far in their discussion whether they have ever heard anyone talking the way he does.

"Of course I have," says an old codger who doesn't have a single tooth left in his head.

This old man sits by a dirt wall dozing, one ear pointed in their direction. He's been waiting for Ku and the donkey fanciers to finish saying everything there is to say about donkeys, so Ku can finally chant some Tian scripture. Now their donkey conversation has reached the edge of the sky, and soon they'll have nothing to talk about, because even he has not been beyond this point. He is the oldest among these old men, and he's travelled further than any of them, also with a donkey, of course, and they are talking about a place he's all but forgotten when, out of the blue, he hears a language that he came across very long ago.

"There's no one in that place any longer. All the tongues that once spoke this language have rotted into dirt. Those who survived now speak something else."

Ku stares at the old codger in shock, wanting him to say more about his hometown, but in the end he doesn't ask a single question, just bows to the man, gets back on his donkey, and rides away.

Talent

Ku's talent for languages comes in useful at Peach Blossom Temple.

With his uncanny memory, he is soon able to recite Tian scripture in its entirety. Tianmen Maisheng can only handle certain passages, and will only deploy these on important occasions. The Tian devotees from the west also respect Ku's abilities. He is the only person at Peach Blossom Temple who can recite the whole text off the top of his head.

Tianmen Maisheng still sits cross-legged on the back of a donkey, roaming the streets of Heile. He holds up Tian scripture with one hand, and all who see him bow. When he did this before, he was the famous Great Kunmen of Peach Blossom Kun Temple, and everyone gave him Kun reverence. Now he is the Great Tianmen, and they bow to him in the Tian way. Maisheng appears transformed, but Ku knows he is going through the same upheaval that Ku is. The Kun scripture he has chanted for decades must still be in his heart—he won't ever forget it. The Kun statues he served must still appear in his dreams. The people of Heile who were forced to change their religion, and those from other places caught up in this war, must all be in the same situation as Ku and Maisheng, experiencing the greatest spiritual torment it is possible to feel in this world. This may be the most consequential event to happen on this piece of earth: the changing of people's souls, the vanishing of Kun whom they believed in for a thousand years, something else occupying their innermost selves.

Every so often, a Kun devotee gets captured and locked up in the donkey pen, and Maisheng will pay them a visit with Ku in tow to convince them to convert. The Tianmen sits cross-legged on a donkey, a Tian scripture in one hand, making a round of the pen. If the captive lowers his head in obedience, he is set free; if his neck remains stiff in defiance, an attendant's blade will slice through it.

*

Tianmen Maisheng puts Ku in charge of Peach Blossom Temple's daily worship. While chanting scripture, Ku often feels a surge of strong emotion that causes him to let out a violent cry. Infected by his mood, the Tian devotees do the same. Each time this happens, Ku's neck elongates and his head tilts back, and his empty eyes gaze hollowly at the sky. The Tian devotees do the same, and their screams shake the heavens and earth.

No other Tianmen has this effect on the faithful. Only when Ku leads worship are the rooms and courtyard of Peach Blossom Temple crammed completely full, with more spilling out beyond the gates and clambering atop the wall. At the peak of his oration, every donkey in the city calls out in response to the clamour. Their braying sends a shudder through Ku, and his voice returns to normal. The devotees too seem awakened by the donkeys, and begin to calm down.

Ku's uncommon chanting might have some believers in raptures, but it causes envy in other quarters. People constantly complain to Tianmen Maisheng that Ku's *ahhnng ahhnng* cries induce his listeners to echo him, which in turn summons the braying of every donkey in Heile City, a grave insult to Tian. They want Maisheng to punish him.

Maisheng's only response is, "Tian above all."

On one occasion, a dozen Tian devotees band together to complain, bringing it all the way to Han King Karhan himself, which results in the Han King paying a visit to Peach Blossom Temple to hear Ku preach. Karhan finds himself squashed among thousands of Tian devotees as Ku's raspy voice rises in its chant. Ku has no idea that the king is here, and proceeds exactly as usual. When he recites scripture, another voice awakens within him. His body jerks upwards, his throat straightens, his neck elongates, his head soars, and his back is no longer hunched. His whole self ascends and the even tones of scripture give way to agitation. The crowd of worshippers convulse and shake too, letting out frenzied yelps. Karhan cannot control himself, and shrieks along with everyone else.

Tongues

Under Maisheng's orders, Ku begins translating Tian scripture. Tianmen Maisheng settles him in a small courtyard on the east side of the temple, where Ku has his own room and outdoor space.

"We can't have you carrying out holy work in the donkey pen," says Maisheng.

Maisheng reports to the Han King that they have gained the allegiance of a famous Pisha translator who knows all the languages in the world, and this great man will translate a copy of Tian scripture into Heilenese for His Majesty. He further suggests that Ku ought to prepare a Pishanese version too, so when the Han King has subjugated all of Pisha, they will be ready to convert its peoples. The Han King says not to bother, a Heilenese edition will be fine. When he has conquered Pisha, he says, the Pishanese that opposed Heile for a hundred years will be completely eradicated, and all the tongues that once spoke it will have disintegrated away into the earth.

When Tianmen Maisheng passes this message to Ku, Ku's own tongue trembles, like his Pisha tongue is already being severed. His mouth falls open but it is empty inside, no words come out, and his heart is empty too. He has seen many languages die out in his lifetime, including the one from his home village.

Maisheng stares at Ku's gaping mouth, waiting for him to speak. Ku's face goes bright red and the tendons on his neck protrude, but all he can muster is a string of braying.

"The Han King knows of your existence," says Maisheng, "and he heard you reciting scripture during Tian prayers. He very much appreciates your vocal abilities. Your distinctive voice has summoned people from near and far. You could bring the dead back to life. The Han King says Heile is ready to launch another attack on Pisha. He wants you by his side as his personal interpreter and spiritual advisor."

"But as you know," Maisheng continues, "many Tian devotees

have laid complaints against you, they say you go *ahhnng ahhnng* while chanting. To be honest, I know you're calling out the sound that's in my heart. All of us have trapped in our hearts an even greater voice. When you shout, we're finally able to let these cries out. Do not lose this voice, and do not listen to their nonsense. Any sound that can summon this many people must be the voice of Tian."

Tianmen Maisheng instructs Ku to ready himself. King Karhan is gathering a hundred thousand mounted soldiers on the outskirts of the city, and the invasion of Pisha is imminent. This will be the final battle between Heile and Pisha.

14

The Path of Graves

Mule

THE ARMY GATHERS to the east of Heile city, a borderless dark mass of soldiers. Ku rides on donkeyback behind a horse-mounted guard, passing through the confusion, past foreign battalions who speak Tian or Tai, up to Karhan's tent.

Maisheng presents Ku to the Han King.

"Another one on donkeyback," says Karhan, glancing at Ku.

Later, Ku will learn that Maisheng also first arrived at Karhan's tent riding a donkey. Wielding Tian scripture, cross-legged on his mount, almost every soldier bowed as he passed.

Karhan orders his guard to bring Ku a horse.

"I ride donkeys, not horses," Ku says.

Maisheng urges Ku to take the proffered reins.

"Even I have changed to riding a war horse," he says in Pishanese, which the king cannot understand. "You can't ride by the Han King's side on a donkey. No donkey guards its tongue. As the proverb says, a bray from the palace will be taken as the king's command."

Ku's neck stiffens and he stubbornly raises his head.

"If our great translator refuses to ride a horse, let him have a mule," declares Karhan. The soldiers do as he says, and Ku's brow crinkles at the sight of this creature.

"Revered Han King, I will accept this mule you have bestowed upon me, the offspring of a horse and donkey—but please permit me to use only her donkey half."

"Are you asking me to cut her in two?"

The Han King's face purples in rage, and his hand rests on his sword hilt.

"She has both horse and donkey in her—they were never united,"

Ku replies, head lowered.

"An obstinate Pisha ass," says the Han King, tossing his head and returning to his tent.

HeiChiu

Ku now has a mule given to him by the Han King.

"She was bred from a royal Heile stallion and a Chiu jenny, so her name is HeiChiu," Maisheng informs him.

A few years ago, a delegation from the Heile imperial court was sent to Chiu. One of their horses, a date-red specimen, caught the eye of the Chiu monarch, but the delegation said, "We can't leave him behind without the Han King's permission. All we can give you is his seed."

They asked the Chiu king to select a mare to mate with the Heile horse, but instead he chose a jenny. The following year, a Chiu delegation came to Heile with the resulting mule, a symbol of friendship between the two kingdoms.

King Karhan was delighted to accept this gift, and in return he sent the Chiu king a superior mare. Only later did the Han King realise that HeiChiu was actually an insult. The offspring of a horse and donkey, the mule, is unable to reproduce.

TuoJue

HeiChiu's left eye is donkey, her right eye is horse. The donkey eye sees a ghost whose head and body are quarrelling. Tuo, the head, wants to stay in Heile, while Jue, the body, wishes to return to Pisha. Ultimately, the head must follow the body. With her left eye, the mule watches TuoJue mounting her backwards. Her right eye notices nothing. Horses can't see ghosts.

HeiChiu is temperamentally a little more donkey than horse. TuoJue senses this mixed animal's imperfect union, the cracks between her two selves. TuoJue has fissures of his own. During their time in Heile, other ghosts called TuoJue a mule. Tuo had been proud of himself at first, imagining he'd brought a Pisha body back with him like a prisoner of war. Instead, all the other spirits looked down on him.

Two Halves

Ku can also sense instability in HeiChiu. She trots as if two different beasts are moving within her body.

The road to Aoba is crowded with people, horses and donkeys. Ku's mule is a little shorter than a horse but much taller than a donkey, so he can see the crowds a long way up ahead, and can hear the sounds of humans and donkeys even farther ahead. Every road in Heile is packed full, and everyone is heading in the same direction.

It is a day's trek from Heile to Aoba, and throughout the journey, Ku feels himself being shaken into two halves—one riding a donkey, the other a horse. The horse half is galloping ahead, *dok dok dok*, with King Karhan's mounted troops, while the donkey half ambles along slowly, unable to catch up.

Night

The sandy ground around Aoba Square is full of soldiers from other regions, camping around Lanshihan's grave. Karhan's men, meanwhile, are bivouacked by the palace.

Ku and Maisheng settle by the square, and Maisheng gives Ku a large saddle blanket. Up till now, Ku has been using the one he brought from Pisha, in which he can detect the smells of both himself and Hsieh within the thick weave of the wool itself. From these mingled scents, Ku can pick out the unique aroma of a young jenny, and this brings Hsieh's likeness immediately to his mind.

"Yours is too small," says Maisheng, "have this one instead."

Ku takes the proffered blanket and spreads it on the sandy

ground, then places his own smaller one on top. These are used by riders of both horses and donkeys: folded for use as a saddle by day, with pockets at either end for water and rations. At night, they unfurl to become bedrolls.

Maisheng tells Ku to prepare himself for morning prayers first thing the next day. The Han King had asked Maisheng to lead these, but Maisheng recommended Ku instead, and the king agreed.

"It's not just any Tian devotee who can ascend the Tian tower of Aoba," says Maisheng.

Ku is silent for a moment, then asks, "A few years ago, during the battle of Aoba, which Tianmen was leading Tian prayers?"

"He's gone missing. Rumour is he was a Kun devotee who hadn't truly converted, but still managed to be promoted to Tianmen. He was supposed to chant a short passage, but switched to a long one at the last minute. His recitation went on forever, and the Pisha were able to creep in from where they were hiding behind the sand dunes. In the middle of prayer, the Heile soldiers were unprepared, little more than lambs to the slaughter. I heard the Tianmen was still chanting even as the Pisha army reached the tower."

Maisheng looks straight at Ku.

Ku raises his head to the sky but he sees nothing, only the floating dirt that drifts down and lands on his eyelashes.

"It was the same on the night that Lanshihan left us. The air was hazy with falling dirt," Maisheng says quietly, almost as if he's talking to himself. Ku hears him shift to one side as he falls asleep.

Their surroundings gradually grow silent, and the swirling dirt makes the night even darker. A moment ago, the silhouettes of horses and donkeys were still visible across the sand, but now they have been swallowed by the night. Maisheng and his horse have vanished, and HeiChiu is gone too. Ku tugs at the reins tied to his arm, but it feels as if blackness has devoured the mule at the other end, leaving nothing behind, not even a breath.

Dream

Ku doesn't sleep well that night. He keeps hearing two people speaking next to him, but when he opens his eyes and gropes around, no one is there. Maisheng is sleeping beyond his reach, and HeiChiu is lying where he can just touch her if he extends his legs. Neither of them are making a sound, and he can't see them in the darkness. Ku shuts his eyes again, and immediately the voices return, one in his left ear, the other in his right. They sound familiar, as if they've been talking by his side for a very, very long time, and everything they say is something he's heard before. When he opens his eyes, though, it slips completely from his mind, only to return when he closes them again.

As Ku listens to their droning conversation, he sees the ears that he's listening with, long and furry. Startling awake, he touches his ears, one at a time.

Now Ku hears the noise of a hundred thousand men snoring and mumbling in their sleep, transmitted through the surface of the earth. Their snores rumble and tunnel through the ground, while their blurry dream talk rises into the air. The dreams of a hundred thousand humans, their horses and donkeys create a thin glowing layer between the earth and sky, illuminating each soldier where he lies, each animal where it stands. Ku is also bathed in the light of his own dreams. He squints and looks sideways, just the way Hsieh used to glance at him, turning around to see four hooves planted in the sand, a belly gleaming with wispy hairs, long ears picking up all kinds of noises in the dark. Ku watches in silence, unstartled, as he's always known this version of himself.

Cockcrow

Still suspended in his dreams, Tianmen Maisheng's hand finds Ku's leg and tugs at it, and Ku understands that he is being awakened— it is time for Tian prayers. In a haze, Ku hears a rooster: the first cockcrow. Tian worship takes place between the second and third cockcrow, when the heavens and earth are particularly silent.

Ku gropes for the water container in the dark to wash his hands and face. Someone has lit a firebrand at the base of the Tian tower, and Ku follows the Tianmen there. The sleepers are now on their feet, and the ground suddenly feels thicker.

Beneath the torch at the Tian tower's entrance stands a row of Tian devotees, whom Ku makes reverence to one by one. He walks up the spiral staircase alone. Ever since he was a child, Ku has climbed the crowded steps of Kun towers, looking down through the tiny windows at each landing, finally reaching the cramped uppermost room, which has the smallest window of all, where he feels himself pressing against the sky. Looking down from atop a Kun tower, you see houses, people and donkeys, all so minuscule they don't look real.

The passage up the Tian tower is narrow, and the stairs are steep. Ku doesn't know how long he's been walking. His ears fill with cockcrow, a little more resonant with each storey.

When he finally reaches the Tian balcony, the sound seems to invert, and it sounds like roosters high in the sky are calling down to him. Standing in the dark, he straightens his clothes and rubs his hands across his face. He can just make out the crowd on the ground below, filling the square before the Tian tower and the undulating dunes beyond that. A hundred thousand men, all standing in absolute silence as they wait for him to begin chanting. Ku waits too, for the cockcrow to stop.

From his perch, Ku can clearly hear roosters in Pisha begin the crowing, their call taken up by the chickens of one village after another, heading westward. The inhabited areas of the earth are roused, while the Gobi Desert continues to slumber.

Ku's mind wanders. This is the first time he's noticed how long cockcrow lasts, going on and on. When the final wisp of sound passes over his head, he thrusts his chest out and holds his arms aloft.

"Oh, Tian!"

As he utters his first cry, he feels heartened by his own voice. He hears his exhortation soaring as it leaves his body, as if it comes from the heavens above, and his mouth is only opening and closing, his neck stiffening.

Ku's voice grows higher and higher. He feels as if it isn't him who is chanting, but that another being inside him is crying out. A stir goes through the people on the ground, as his voice ignites them, and their blazing lightens the sky.

Only now does it dawn on Ku what a long passage he's reading out, not one he ever chanted at Peach Blossom Temple. In fact, these are the words that were spoken during Tian worship several years ago, just before the battle of Aoba. When he realises this, Ku feels as if his head is blowing apart, and his legs tremble so he can barely hold himself upright. He chose a short reading, as Maisheng repeatedly instructed him too. The excruciatingly long scripture recitation back at Aoba Palace is still vivid in everyone's memory, and he told himself not to repeat this mistake. Yet when Ku opened his mouth, somehow that's what came out. There is now no way that Ku can stop. He can only continue, sentence after sentence.

In the slowly brightening daylight, Ku is taken back to the dawn when the Pisha army ambushed Aoba, only this time Ku is the one chanting Tian scripture, looking down at the dark mass of people spreading from the foot of the tower, filling the square and spilling into the desert beyond. Everyone is looking up at him, and he alone gazes out at the sandy waste.

He holds up his palms, face tilted up, staring out the corners of his eyes at what lies beyond the worshippers: the borderless desert. Early one morning a few years ago, as the sky rained dirt, the Pisha troops crept closer and closer from behind the sand dunes, not making a sound, approaching the Heile soldiers as they prayed.

Tomb Road

Once again, Ku sees himself heading towards Aoba Cemetery from Guma, from Siya. He was with Hsieh when this happened before, among the throngs of mourners, but now he is riding HeiChiu the mule, part of the eastward expeditionary force of King Karhan. Each time they pass a village, farmers wielding scythes and hoes join them. There are tombs to make offerings at along the way, sometimes four or five in a single day, and whenever they break their journey for meals or to set up camp, it is always at a cemetery. Their expeditionary route takes them through one burial place after another, passing villages tucked among the oases and sandy wastes. All the roads from before have been transformed, and the eastward route to Pisha now winds between these graves, every one of them a remnant of a previous battle, for every battle resulted in new burial sites.

As they trace this twisty tomb road, they experience once again every moment of the war that has spanned decades. Every grave broadcasts a story once more: the date of the battle, the names of the martyred, their location and any miraculous events that took place. Every hidden tomb has been uncovered, every fallen warrior found, and every buried grudge unearthed.

With each grave they pay reverence at, the army's hatred for Pisha increases a little more.

When they set forth, their destination was the kingdom of Pisha. After passing Aoba Cemetery, though, their goal became simply the next gravesite, and their route of travel began changing to take in more tombs. Sometimes they go several days out of their way, but these detours still point them towards Pisha, and this army of a hundred thousand men pass one burial place after another, absorbing new recruits from every village along the way, the troop of mourners expanding day by day. No road could accommodate such an army. The entire Gobi Desert is now their road, and so is every field or valley in their way. The Heile army surges along, so vast that neither its beginning nor end can be seen. They strip every village bare of anything edible, picking unripe fruit and melons, slaughtering every cow and goat and chicken, devouring every family's store of grain. The wheat isn't ready to harvest but they eat it anyway, and roasted green wheat soon becomes their staple food. The soldiers camp by fields of wheat and start a roaring fire, tossing fistfuls of unripe stalks into the flames. It crackles fragrantly away, until they can rub the husks loose with their hands, blow them off, and pop the blackened kernels into their mouths. The sound of a hundred thousand men chewing drives field mice from their burrows. When the soldiers get impatient, they simply light a field on fire, and after the conflagration has burnt itself out, they squat among the ashes and pick out the scorched grains. A mou of land can feed three hundred people. Anything that remains is packed onto donkeyback, for the next grave is in the desert, and the one after that in the middle of the Gobi. Although they don't encounter farmland every day, they will eventually reach yet another field of almost ripe wheat as they wind back and forth. When they've eaten a village out of house and home, its inhabitants have no choice but to follow the troops. The ever-growing Heile army is a swarm of locusts, filling the sky and covering the earth.

The plan had initially been to invade Pisha in six months. This would have been after the Heile harvest, and the army could have set forth laden with flatbreads. The soldiers are very fond of the freshly picked wheat of their homeland, and a bite of these flatbreads would ensure no regrets even if they were to die in foreign parts.

Karhan thinks differently. He proclaimed, "We will eat the new wheat of Pisha," and that was their signal to begin moving. Now this is their goal. The aroma of Pisha wheat permeates the air— the crop ripens sooner in Pisha, and the farmers there are already sharpening their scythes in preparation for the harvest. Before this happens, however, the Heile intend to lay claim to it.

Steep

They arrive at the dry river gully that marks the division between the two kingdoms, and it is here that the Heile and Pisha armies meet. The drop is dozens of yards, with steep cliffs on either side. One night a few years ago, Ku led Hsieh down into the gully, thick with thorny salt trees, and up the other side into Heile territory. Now the Pisha army holds their position, while Heile locusts pour into the gully and up the opposite side. The Pisha army cannot withstand them—they soon run out of arrows and spears, hurl all the rocks they have piled up in readiness, and still wave after wave of Heile soldiers sweep over them, not holding back, roaring like a flood with the enmity and hatred built up over a thousand graveyards. The frontline thrust their heads out to be decapitated, present their chests to be stabbed. The Pisha soldiers' arms soften and their blades blunt. Fear sprouts in their hearts.

Ku stands next to Karhan, watching the battle from the far side of the cliff. Across the deep, narrow valley, they can clearly see the flood of Heile warriors pouring over the side, not stopping until the Pisha army has been completely submerged.

15

Fence Village

White Poplars

THE ROAD WINDS THROUGH wheat fields, and the white poplars on either side have been beheaded. Same with the trees in the villages. All the way from the outskirts of Heile city through Aoba to Qusha and Guma in the Pisha kingdom, the truncated poplar trees signify that these villages have been converted.

All the villagers and their donkeys have been forced onto the road, and the humans are tied up two to each poplar, hands bound back to back with reins. The donkeys aren't tied up but stand docilely to one side, watching through narrowed eyes.

Accompanied by a dozen Tian devotees, Maisheng questions the captives one by one. Those willing to change their religion are released, those who refuse are decapitated on the spot. Following behind the devotees are butchers with black cloth across their faces, knives jagged from use.

Maisheng knows Pishanese but refuses to use it. Instead he speaks Heilenese, which the inhabitants of Fence Village do not understand. There aren't enough interpreters or Tianmen among the soldiers, and soon they realise there are too many villagers to be converted one by one.

"Cut off half their heads, and ask the other half what they think," orders Karhan.

Ku hastily tells the king he would be more than happy to interpret for Maisheng, and will persuade as many people as possible.

"No," Karhan says firmly, "I have more important business for you."

"These are your subjects now," Ku replies. "One less head chopped off is one person more to plant your crops and guide your donkeys."

Ku rides over on his mule, but by the time he arrives, half their heads are on the ground and the poplar trees are stained red. Those who still have their heads are tied to the beheaded.

Great Tianmen Maisheng is splattered with blood, and the axe wielders on either side of him look as if they have just surfaced from vats of gore.

"Let me speak to these people first," says Ku. "They'll listen to me."

Maisheng says there are still a few hundred people waiting in the next village—there are simply too many Kun devotees to be subjugated or beheaded. The Tian devotees and butchers are overwhelmed.

Each tree has two people tied to it: one decapitated, the other still alive and drenched in blood. The white poplars are beheaded too. Ku dares not look at the bleeding neck stumps.

Ku goes over to a middle-aged man, who has stretched his neck out and is waiting for the axe to fall. In Pishanese he says, "You can keep your head as long as you change your religion."

The man shakes his head. "There is nothing in my brain but Kun."

"Keep your head and reason with the Kun inside it. As long as you have your head, you can deal with your brain later."

The man bows his head in surrender.

The severed neck next to him is still bleeding, and the head that lolls on the ground faces up, ears pricked, but these words have come too late.

The captives tied to the neighbouring trees turn to look. Ku loudly repeats what he just said. His words are effective, and most people surrender. The few who hold out are still chanting Kun scripture as they present their necks to the blade.

Hoes

Half the village is on fire. These houses are made of braided willow strips, like piles of timber. Whenever someone refuses to convert, his dwelling is set alight, but the flames soon spread to the neighbours too. In a short while, all of Fence Village has gone up. Both humans and donkeys flee.

A good many people have gathered in the temple courtyard at the front of the village. Four people stand on the next building's roof; Ku recognises them as the family he stayed with on his last visit. The granny holds a scythe, her face very calm. The daughter-in-law clutches a sobbing baby girl, and the two teenage sons wield hoes, fearlessly staring down the Heile. Most of the soldiers have already left the village, leaving only a few donkeyback troops to surround the house, also armed with farm tools.

The people on the ground scream and hurl clods of earth, which those on the roof block with their hoes.

Ku had intended to persuade this family to give in, or at least to offer the old granny a few words of comfort, but he feels too ashamed to say anything, and doesn't even have the courage to appear before them.

Three years ago, when he stayed at her house with Hsieh, the old woman smiled faintly before her face lapsed into blankness. This moment has stayed with Ku. He feels unspeakable guilt at having deceived her about her son's death. Deep in his heart, he wasn't willing to bear this news to the family, who might believe to this day that their eldest son is still leading his troops on the Pisha frontline, that he's on his way home now. Two of the old woman's sons were dead, and her husband never returned after setting out in search of their heads. He'd tied their decapitated corpses to his donkey's back, handed the reins to a neighbour, and wandered off into the wilderness. The old woman imagines she still has two sons alive who will return to rescue her.

As Ku lowers his head, thinking of these things, a man arrives with a ladder. One of the donkeyback soldiers hands his reins to another, and climbs the ladder with a scythe in his hand.

"It's just some women and children," he says, "I can deal with them myself."

He glances up at the roof as he ascends, then back down at the ground. He has to make sure his feet are planted firmly on each rung, while watching out for an attack from above. No sooner has his head poked above the eaves when the old woman grabs hold of his hair with her left hand, while the blade in the right comes slicing in as if harvesting a melon, lopping his head off with a *tchhaa*. The headless body rolls down the ladder, which tumbles to the ground as well.

The old woman holds up the severed head and flings it down hard. It smashes onto a donkey's back, startling the beast so it screeches and runs, causing the others to *ahnng-jee* as well.

HeiChiu cries out *ahnng-jee* too, her donkey half joining in the chorus of braying. Her horse half watches the mounted troops passing by, while her donkey half sees the ghost TuoJue sitting on Ku's back. Through Tuo's eyes, Jue gazes at his knife-wielding mother on the roof, his wife and three children. His children would not recognise him now. He only ever returned to the village late at night, groping his way into the house as the village dogs barked, touching his sleeping children's faces, wiping the tears from his wife's cheeks. His mother would be sitting in the dark, but even in the blackest night, she'd sense that her son was home. After her four sons went off to war, her ears grew attuned to the village road, and night after night, she listened for their footsteps amid the sounds of wind and dirt.

Jue sees all this through Tuo's eyes, which hold all the desolation of his body, yet he feels no sorrow, but watches with icy calm, just as when he was a child and stood by the road, waiting for his family to return, knowing they'd soon be back where he was. Now, though, he is left with nothing. On his shoulders is a head they would not recognise.

Upright

A man approaches from the bald Gobi Desert, and Ku recognises him at once: the blind Kunmen, walking perfectly upright, not seeing the hundred thousand soldiers before him.

The King sees him too, coming towards them without a hint of fear, as if he alone will confront the army.

A guard sets off on his horse to kill the Kunmen, but Karhan calls him back.

"This blind man is a Kunmen, a holy man," Ku murmurs to the king.

Karhan glances at Maisheng. When the army burst into Peach Blossom Temple and found Maisheng nonchalantly cross-legged on donkeyback, eyes shut, someone said he was a holy man too.

The blind Kunmen comes closer and closer. His ears must be filling with the thunderous racket of horse and donkey hoofbeats, but he does not appear to hear a thing.

Karhan's war horse slows down.

"How should we deal with this person?" Karhan asks Maisheng and the Tian devotees.

Maisheng says nothing, but shoots Ku a look.

"However you deal with him, he won't see it."

Out of habit, Ku extends his neck and turns his eyes up to the sky.

"Leave him alone," says Karhan, waving a hand.

The blind Kunmen walks up to the King, unconcerned, all but brushing against Ku and the mule. As he walks past with his back so straight, the horses and donkeys naturally open up a pathway, the donkeys in particular shying away in fear of him.

Ku watches as the Kunmen passes through the narrow corridor to the village entrance, where the temple is still in flames, though the house next door has been extinguished. All the smoke in the village circulates above the headless white poplars, silently forming a village of smog in the sky, in the same place where the donkey cries gather, along with the human screams that have now stopped.

The Kunmen will walk on and enter the burning temple, Ku knows, just like normal, and seat himself on the dais. He won't see the blaze around him.

16

The Goatman's Grave

Preparation

DARKNESS ARRIVES from the west as the sun is swallowed by yellow sand. Fires are lit around the goatman's grave, and the Heile soldiers sit in vigil around them. There are no wild celebrations at their victory, only silence. Ku and HeiChiu stand by Karhan's tent, where a guard has summoned them—Karhan wants Ku to tell everyone the story of this tomb. Ku says that he has heard part of it, but doesn't know the full story.

"If you aren't willing to say, then I'll tell it," the king says in response.

Actually, there's no need—everyone in Heile knows this story. Countless word bearers have brought it to Heile, and therefore there are countless versions of it. The tales that word bearers bring are fully grown, having gotten bigger and bigger during the long journey. Small matters must expand to be consequential. A sesame seed incident from far away will have become as large as a watermelon by the time it reaches Heile.

All afternoon, Ku has stared uneasily in the direction of the Pisha army's retreat, and just as he expected, a disturbance has abruptly stirred up there. Amid the flames, a horde of Pisha horseback troops show up brandishing their swords, trampling out the fires. The press-ganged farmers, so murderous with their scythes and hoes by day, are terrified by the Pisha night army and scurry in all directions. Turning back into timid little peasants, their daytime bravado is completely gone, replaced by chaos and screaming.

The Heile soldiers guarding the Han King's tent are prepared for this, and their horseback squad quickly assembles to charge the Pisha army. The shadows of the mounted troops flicker in the firelight, and their hoofbeats stamp out more of the bonfires. By the time the two forces meet, all the flames have been put out and the land is pitch dark. The only sound now is blades clashing— no murderous screams, no shrieks from the injured, just the cold collision of steel on steel.

Karhan is already on his horse, and Ku likewise on HeiChiu, facing the direction in which they can see nothing. A moment ago, by the light of the flames, Ku saw the same Pisha army who'd been defeated by the Heile during the day, the same uniforms, the same faces, as if they'd simply climbed up from where they lay on the ground, retrieved their severed heads, arms and legs, found their scimitars, their blood drenched horses, their battle flags, their commanders.

The massacre continues late into the night. Ku falls asleep on his mule, and the sound of blades clashing finds its way into his dreams, where another night battle rages: he is riding Hsieh, and feels the sensation of her gleaming pelt beneath him. He was still young then. It's only been three years, but he has aged so much. These days he feels nothing at all.

Sacrifice

The following morning, they begin the sacrificial rite at the goatman's tomb. The cemetery has acquired a swathe of new graves, proving that the night's fighting was no dream.

More than a hundred Pisha soldiers, prisoners of war, have been tied up and made to kneel by the grave. With a blade to their throats, they are asked one by one if any of them have ever met the goatman who is buried here. Each time a man says no, the knife rises and falls. In a short while, a few dozen bloody heads are rolling across the ground.

Finally, they find one who says yes, and he is brought before Karhan.

"Tell us how the goatman was killed," says Karhan, pointing his sword at the man.

Trembling, the Pisha soldier is too frightened to speak.

Karhan glances at Ku, who hurries over and says in Pishanese, "Don't be afraid, just say what happened and no harm will come to you."

The soldier stutters as he relates what happened: the battle in Siya decades ago, the capture of the goatherd Mazaghan, his interrogation tied upside down to a tree, his severed fingers. The man's words are tumbling left and right, barely coherent as sentences. As he translates into Heilenese, Ku reshapes this tale according to his own recollections.

When the soldier reaches the bit about the goatman's skin being torn off with a knife, he abruptly stops.

"Continue."

Several sharp knives bite into the man's chest.

Steady now, the soldier doesn't seem to see the blades, but stares calmly at Ku.

Ku indicates that he should go on.

The man straightens up, half-closing his eyes, and his dry lips part. He describes in detail how the goatman was caught, how his skin was ripped off, how he died in agony. When he reaches the flaying, Ku feels his own skin being peeled. He translates into Heilenese and feels the words skinning him alive once again.

Karhan points at the other Pisha soldiers and says, "These people must suffer what the goatman did."

As soon as he has spoken, the men are brought over one by one, their clothes torn off, and then their skin. Ku turns his head aside, unable to watch.

Having given his orders, Karhan walks away. Ku follows.

A fair distance away, their screams of pain still fill Ku's ears. A couple of years ago, when he heard the goatman's shrieks, they contained both human and goat suffering. The cries of the Pisha soldiers are purely human.

Return

The sacrificial rite at the goatman's grave fills the soldiers with vigour. As for the peasants who accompanied the troops from Heile's Aoba Cemetery to Siya's Pigeon Graveyard, worshipping at every tomb en route, by the time they reached the goatman's grave, they'd come too far to return, nor did they want to. They were all part of Karhan's courageous army now. It was a shot in the arm for them to see a mere goatherd's grave receiving the reverence of the Han King and all his men. Now they all longed to be martyred, so their final resting place could be here in Pisha, where they would be worshipped forever.

"In the past, we navigated by the river, by sand dunes, by the wind, by the shadows cast by the high walls of West Kun Temple. And now, we will be guided by one grave after another. The dead have claimed this land on our behalf. From this time, it will not matter if the river changes course, the sand dunes are flattened, or the wind shifts direction. These burial places are eternal, and we will never get lost again. I hope all your graves will cover the Pisha land too, and I will be buried alongside you, so we may enjoy the veneration of ten thousand generations to come."

Karhan's words travel across the scorching sand, and the men respond with a hurricane of applause.

17

Guma

Pigeon

TUO, I HEAR THE PIGEONS *gogg gogg* and I know we're here again. The same cooing we heard three years ago. I listen through your ears, but I don't look through your eyes, which you are busy gawking with. We are in Guma.

Three years ago, flocks of pigeons circled overhead as the two armies collided. Blades clashed, startling the birds from the trees. The battle continued late into the night, leaving the field strewn with corpses.

That was the evening I died. Something whacked the back of my head. I swung around and saw a white-bearded goatherd, his crooked wooden club smeared with goat dung. I'd passed him a moment ago, but thinking he was just an innocuous peasant, I hadn't thrust my sword into him. And now he'd hit me. Ashamed to be killed by a goatherd's stick, I quickly glanced around, like a child caught doing something naughty.

Then something ice-cold plunged into my back, and I knew I'd been stabbed, yet I felt no pain. The clubbing had dazed me, and my mind was gone. I no longer knew who I was, nor was I sure what was happening around me. I opened my eyes wide, but couldn't understand what I was looking at. My body didn't know its brain had gone, nor did the brain itself. The battle went on till dusk. After it got dark, the dancing swords no longer recognised me as a foe, and both sides began to pull back. Lacking a brain, I didn't know where I should retreat to, and so I lay there in confusion, waiting for nightfall. The pigeons began to *gogg gogg*, and now that the slaughter had stopped, they swooped down to earth. I heard one coo by my ear, but didn't dare open my eyes in case the flash of white startled her away. I couldn't move my legs either. There was *gogg gogg* all around me, pigeons cooing by the ears of other fallen soldiers, who must have been deliberately keeping as still as I was, not wanting to scare the birds away.

Then the pigeons took flight with a *hwaah* of wings, and someone was chanting scripture. I opened my eyes and there, in the moonlight spilling over the sand, was a kneeling man. The fallen soldiers crawled towards him, some with broken legs, some missing an arm, some half-paralysed. Even the headless bodies frantically clawed their way towards him, and I couldn't stop myself doing the same. I was almost there when I realised that it wasn't Kun scripture being chanted, it was a language I didn't understand, and all around me were Heile soldiers. I buried my head in the sand so they wouldn't see me, but no one was looking, every one of them had both arms raised and their eyes turned to the western sky. Those without hands held up their stumps, those without eyes stared anyway with their bloody sockets. I could tell they were all Tian devotees.

When I looked behind me, I heard Kun scripture being chanted. I crawled in the other direction and came upon a Kun devotee sitting on a sand dune not far away, moonlight reflecting off his head, many others dragging themselves towards him. Ring after ring of people gathered around him at the foot of the dune. As I got closer, I collided head first into a Heile soldier, hauling his injured leg behind him as he tried to get to the Tian chanting. We stared darkly at each other for a long moment. He sized me up—he was smaller than me, and I didn't think he was a threat at all. Yet his eyes were powerful as they fixed me in a deadly stare. I couldn't face him down, so instead I raised my head to the night sky.

Then I heard the familiar sound of horse hoofbeats in the distance. The retreating Pisha troops had quietly turned around, and the rear was now the vanguard. Beneath the moonlight and skyful of stars, they were coming *dok dok dok* in my direction. Like a dream I climbed up from the blood-soaked sand and rejoined the formation, my missing brain returning from very far away, the strength roaring back into my body, my courage and fearlessness too, and from that instant I was transformed into a night soldier who knew neither weariness nor fear. No matter whether General Chokanurkan was victorious or defeated during the day, no matter how far we had retreated, as soon as the handle of the North Dipper pointed at our heads, we didn't need a single order to turn around quietly in the night and go *dok dok dok* back towards the location we had fled by daylight.

Dawn

The Heile man you crashed into must have been me. I was dragging my wounded leg behind me, trying to join the other Tian devotees when you appeared in my path. We were both so badly injured that all we could do was glare at each other. You were stronger, but my stare was more powerful.

Jue, I came back to life that dawn. All night long I'd heard the pigeons *gogg gogg*, my entire body dead except for my ears—knotholes in a withered tree, hollow spaces with the wind whistling through them. Then at sunrise I felt a pigeon flying in my heart. I sat up, and all around me were the sounds of people rising. My eyes came back to life, and I saw fallen horses struggle to their feet, and everyone who'd died the night before started getting up, kneeling there like blocks of wood, as if their lower halves had yet to be resuscitated. On the dunes not far away, Tian devotees were praying, and there was only one sound in my ears, bright and resonant.

Later, I understood. That morning, a pigeon was flying in each person's heart. In the stories of Pigeon Cemetery that spread to Heile, on this dawn, it was the *gogg gogg* of the pigeons that roused the fallen Heile soldiers. They lay looking up at the sky, while the Pisha army had their faces buried in the blood-soaked sand. In the Pisha version of the tale, the *gogg gogg* caused the injured to stop bleeding. When every soldier's wounds had healed, the pigeons took flight again, and the battle was at an end.

*

When I heard the *gogg gogg*, my neck stopped bleeding. Cooing staunches wounds, that's what I heard my mother say when I was a child. She was talking to my father, who was going off to fight in Osh, where he returned after each battle with a new injury on his back, invariably sustained on his way home—the trampled wheat fields, grasslands, white poplar groves, fruit orchards, all the axes and scythes, mallets and rocks landing on his back. And all the way back, he longed for one battle after another to lead him back to his hometown.

Flying

Jue, I remember now. I saw you in the chaos that evening, your bowed legs and powerful body—nothing like mine. I'd ridden a donkey since I was young, and my legs curved in the shape of a donkey's sides, while you grew up on horseback. A horse's ribs stick out much further than a donkey's, so we only had to look at a person's legs to know if they were a warrior or a farmer. You were a strapping man with the chest of a tiger and the back of a bear, lashing out left and right on the battlefield. Anyone who saw you would duck out of the way. No one thought they could defeat you. Blades clashed amid the flying dirt of the vast battlefield, man to man. Experienced soldiers seek out weaker opponents, and weak ones look for even more feeble foes. Bad luck to anyone who encountered you—everyone tried to stay as far away as possible. All but me, who wanted to match swords with you.

Look at us now—after all my admiration of you, your body is now mine. I've swapped my body for a better one. You must be secretly pleased too, to have acquired a cleverer brain. If your head is still around, I'd definitely recognise it. I'm your head now. Your features have changed—you've become me. But what has become of my discarded body?

I remember the instant my head was cut off, and my body fell too. My head rolled past my hand, which twitched as if to grab hold of it, but then lay frozen.

Next, I saw myself flying into the air, soaring skyward over and over only to fall again. Each time I rose, I saw that the ground was littered with headless bodies, and as I came back down, I watched decapitated heads fill the sky. That's how it's been with every battle I've lived through. All swords snap in two and all the knives bend. The ultimate weapon is human heads. Severed Pisha heads flung back at the Pisha army, held up by the hair, swung vigorously and hurled hard. We lobbed Pisha heads and Heile heads came flying back at us. The air was full of heads I recognised, the heads of our brothers-in-arms raining down on us, eyes staring, mouths wide open, and we didn't duck, we met them with our chests, with our own heads.

I can't remember how many times my head flew back and forth. It finally landed next to a Pisha man whose face was smeared with blood and dirt, whose beard was matted with gore. I knew at once he was playing dead—it takes a corpse to know a corpse. I stared at him with my unmoving eyes, and he looked back with his living ones, but he couldn't understand what my still gaze was telling him. Next to him was a headless Pisha soldier whose foot was still twitching, pawing at the blood soaked sand as if it hadn't realised its head was gone. I stared at him for a very long time. I knew that body, solid as a mountain ridge. Had we met in battle? I couldn't remember why we'd been trying to slaughter each other. Perhaps the answer was in my body, perhaps my body had been at odds with him. But now my body was gone, and so was his head. A very long time passed, maybe several lifetimes. Finally the Pisha man who still had his head stood up and ran away, then later still a stinking tanner sewed my head to the bloody neck stump of the burly body next to me. I glared hard at him, trying to explain that this wasn't my body, that I was Tuo, a Heile man. Unfortunately, a dead man's words can't reach the living.

Groove

Now we're here, Jue, I remember everything—my head soaring through the sky, hitting the sand while my eyes still held a last glimpse of the human world. My eyeballs had stopped moving but the light in them hadn't quite died, and in those final moments I saw a man slumped next to me, one eye buried in dirt and blood, breathing and blinking, eyes gleaming with life, not slowly turning grey like mine. I tried hard to wink at him but couldn't summon the will, my body that would have told my eyelids to move was gone, leaving nothing but this final gaze in my eyes, which had suddenly popped open and didn't have the strength to shut again, so the entirety of the sky, the desert, the people, donkeys and horses passed before them. But there was nothing in my open eyes, just what was left from that final vision. Holding on to these final moments made me, now a ghost, remember that instant, and the last person I ever saw. Guess who? Obviously you have no idea, you don't have eyes. The person lying beside you stared at you with his one unburied eye. He watched as your head was cut off, and your eyes must have looked back at him, but the eyes that saw this are lost along with your head. Before my head landed next to your body, he'd been watching your twitching foot dig a groove in the sand—your unruly leg that hadn't had its fill of walking, its muscles hard as steel; your sturdy sole, your toes spreading like a splintering tree trunk, they knew they could walk down all the roads in the entire world, arriving wherever they wanted to go. And now, all of a sudden, the head that had wanted to walk across the world was gone, and with it all the energy in your body evaporated, so it crashed to the ground, and your right leg obediently stiffened, but the left refused and pushed away, pawing at the earth.

All that strength in your left leg, which refused to die, must have been taken over by another person, and he'll never be still, for even when his right leg is exhausted and needs to rest, his left will keep going, unable to stop.

Host

Tuo, I've known for a while who this man is, this Ku. I recognised him with your eyes. He was lying across from me—he smeared my blood over his whole body, and his face too, then he imitated my death and lay there with one half-open eye, and as I lay teetering on the brink of death, he saw I was half alive and copied my dead half, so the Heile soldiers would think he'd departed and he could be spared from their swords.

As he watched me, my body slowly hardened.

"I'm not going anywhere."

But the mouth that would have said those words was petrified, and my brain was abruptly crammed full of roads near and far. I was walking along all of them, facing back the way I'd come, returning. As I walked, the road behind me vanished, and with each step the ground turned back into wilderness, snatching the road away behind me. After leaving on so many occasions, I was coming back from all these different places and times, a battalion of me walking to my own stiffened corpse, like water flowing back to its arid source.

"Everyone's back, all back now."

Before my stationary eyeballs were countless moving eyes like stars filling the sky, eyes like open doors, and their missing vision came flooding back, bringing back all it had seen of the world, all the tears and joy, the silence and terror, the light and shadow, the opening and closing, the completion of one person's world, with nothing but darkness beyond. But in my innermost self, all I could see was this brightness.

The only unexpected thing was my left leg wouldn't stop moving, walking alone through a dark world in which I no longer existed, all roads laid to waste, all doors shut, and still my one leg walked on.

All of a sudden, the brain where all this took place was gone, flown away, surely gliding through the air looking down at the world, at its body that could no longer think of life and death, but just lay there inert as a plank.

If he had shed a tear, my upturned palm would have caught it. If he had shouted, my twitching toes would have heard it.

But in no time, a body without a brain knows nothing at all.

Then your head was fastened onto my neck, and using your brain, I slowly found my way back to my memories.

And now, with your brain, I think of the last person I saw, the one currently walking in front of us. When he passed by here with the little donkey Hsieh, he saw our deaths, but he didn't know that another kind of life happens after that, and when the tanner sewed your head onto my body, I saw through your eyes the body tied to the donkey's back, the ghost sliding out of that body to take up residence in the donkey. We quarrelled all the way, head resenting body, body wishing it could wrench the head off, but even a fool would have known we couldn't be separated. Then the donkey we possessed was killed and skinned, and her ghost joined ours as we moved into this man's body.

Guma

The sky rains dirt, and soil spews up from the ground. Everyone is covered in the stuff, making it hard to tell friend from foe. There is shouting to guide you, but these voices are filled with dirt too, so many languages buried in the soil. The airborne dirt has blocked out the sun and moon, blurring the difference between day and night, so when the armies grapple with each other it feels like daylight, yet in the grey haze nothing can be seen.

Ku's mind fills with the battle three years ago, the one he and Hsieh blundered into. Now he is Karhan's interpreter and aide, and must walk with the Han King through the choking dirt.

An endless stream of commanders comes up to report that this battle cannot be fought, because they cannot locate the enemy.

"If you can't see with your eyes, feel with your hands. I can hear the Pisha men shouting—why can't you find them?" roars Karhan.

"We truly cannot, your highness. My troops run towards the shouting, but they find nothing there, not even hoofprints on the ground. The men say what they're hearing is sounds from the past—a great battle took place here three years ago, and many people died. Our hoofbeats have awakened them."

Not believing them, Karhan leads the men himself in the direction of the Pisha shouting. Ku follows behind on HeiChiu the mule. Not far away, lost in the grey murk, are so many Pisha voices that you'd think there must be more than a thousand men there.

Karhan raises his sword, setting off a string of battle cries in Heile and Tian as they charge, engulfing themselves in the dirt they kick up behind them. Just like that, the Pisha voices are gone. The Heile and Tian ones stop abruptly too, leaving only the *schwaah schwaah* of dirt drifting down and rising again.

"What's happening?" says Karhan, perplexed.

"These are sounds from the past, majesty. Listen closely—the voices hang in mid-air, without a hint of hoofbeats beneath them. No footsteps either."

Ku feels a cold gust of air on his back as he says these words.

See

Out of her donkey eye, HeiChiu sees many severed heads hovering in the air, dirt swirling through their empty mouths, open and shouting their cries from three years ago. Ku sees and hears this, as well as the mismatched ghost that has possessed him. Three years ago, he saw the tanner fusing these two together and making Hsieh carry them. When they fled and abandoned the corpse, he had no idea their spirit had taken possession of the donkey. Then when

Hsieh was flayed at Peach Blossom Temple, and when Ku heard the donkeys crying out in Heile's alleyways, he finally understood that both Hsieh and this hybrid ghost were now in his own body.

The mismatched head and body often appear bickering in Ku's dreams, the head commanding the body to walk west, the body insisting on going east.

"You donkeyfucker," the head says. The body wrenches off the head and kicks it far away, then falls to the ground, unable to function without a head.

Ku even recalls what they call themselves: the head is Tuo, and the body is Jue. Sometimes he sees them as a single body, riding backwards on a donkey that he recognises as Hsieh, and Hsieh turns her head to watch them quarrelling. Hsieh can see them, because donkeys' eyes are full of ghosts. Ku dreams of them at night, and during the day he can sense their presence too. Sometimes he turns around, wanting to say a few words to them. Ku may know dozens of languages, but not one of them allows him to communicate with ghosts.

Finally, Ku has reached the age when he can see ghosts, but unlike Master, he still cannot talk to them.

Master

Ku recollects Master beginning to see ghosts at the age of seventy. By that time, he could neither walk nor leave the house. People's legs get old before their mouths do. Even immobile on the heated kang platform, Master's mouth never stopped moving. He addressed every corner of the room, now in Kun, now in Tai, now in Huang, followed by languages Ku had never heard. He spoke to long-departed friends: "Wang, so you're here too, old man. I thought you went back to the Central Plains?" "Ah, here's Tuya the carpenter. Look, the bench you made is falling apart. Have a seat."

Ku recognised some of the names, but not others. It was as if many people were coming from near and far to see Master, crammed into this tiny space, filling every window sill and roof beam. Sometimes Master looked up at the rafters as he spoke.

Ku sat outside beneath the window, listening to Master chatting to the people inside. He coughed when he wasn't talking, and when this got bad, Ku would go inside and help him sit up with his back against the heated surface, while Ku sat on the edge of the kang. Master would cough, speak for a while, then start coughing again. He looked to Ku's right and spoke with someone named Haihai. Ku turned his face to stare at the emptiness there. Then Master began talking to someone named Goo on Ku's left, and Ku didn't dare look the other way, but he felt people breathing on either side, sandwiching him. He knew both these men, they were old friends of Master's who'd died at the same time a good many years ago, during the invasion of Heile City. Of their circle, it seemed only Master had lived to an old age.

After he began talking to ghosts, Master no longer recognised Ku. Ku brought him food and water, took care of him waking and sleeping, squeezing his way between the ghosts that crowded the house, ghosts he could feel if not see. When a ghost walked into him, Ku felt an assault of cold air, and every hair on his body stood on end.

Similarly, when Ku mentioned ghosts a moment ago, an icy blast went down his spine—the frosty breath of ghosts.

People sweat from the scalp when they encounter ghosts. And when ghosts realise they have been spotted, they fearfully let out cold air. When Ku feels a freezing breath on his back, he knows the ghost is on his spine, along with Hsieh. He looks back, a gesture that reminds him of Hsieh. Whenever she did that, he assumed she was looking at him, her rider, but now he knows it was TuoJue. This confused creature was sitting on Hsieh's back along with him, all the way to Heile. He had sometimes felt chills during that journey, but never knew it was from leaning against a ghost.

Donkey Years

Ku thinks of walking through the wilderness with Hsieh, of the night he spent huddled against her. Her warmth is still within him, the parts of his body that were pressed against her fur still throb with heat.

When Ku thinks of Hsieh, he senses a donkey within him thinking of herself. Using Ku's heart, she misses herself, over and over. It is sometimes unclear whether these thoughts are coming from Ku or Hsieh.

He remembers what Maisheng told him: "You have a donkey within you. Make sure you keep it tied up."

As many Heile folk know, Maisheng can see ghosts. He usually looks at people with his head lowered and eyes narrowed, and no one wants to be seen by him anyway. But Maisheng's eyes were on Ku when he said these words, and Ku's body convulsed violently. At the time, Ku had no idea what he meant, but now he feels the donkey Maisheng was referring to—she is indeed inside him, placid most of the time, but when she gets stubborn, Ku cannot control himself.

Ku has seen people being possessed by ghosts. With each movement of the ghost, the human goes into a fit and talks gibberish. When this happens, you need to summon a Kun devotee—they can see ghosts, but don't want to offend them. Instead, they'll tell the family to break off a length of peachwood and bring it into their house. Ghosts fear peachwood, though they don't know why. They've heard humans saying that peachwood repels ghosts, and that's made them frightened of the very sight. The Kun devotee will also write a charm to stick to the door of the afflicted household. Charms are drawings of ghosts. Ghosts have no form, so fixing them in a single image is scary to them. When a ghost sees one of these charms, they'll get sucked into it, and after that there's no escape—they will have to behave themselves.

Ku knows Maisheng can carry out exorcisms. Ever since he

realised he's housing ghosts, he's avoided Maisheng. He has embraced these things he is carrying within himself.

18

Sleepless

High Bank

"I'M KU, the Pisha translator, bearing word for General Chokanurkan."

Ku stands in the loose shale of the river gully and shouts upwards. His voice climbs the cliff face but falls short of the top. He tries again, but there is no response. His throat is suddenly hoarse, as if the donkey inside him is expanding to fill his whole body.

Ahhnng-jee ahhnng-jee.

Ku's braying ricochets around the gully, and soon a donkey chorus answers him from the north bank: the donkey squad that follows the Heile army, all of them black donkeys, their cries raising a second cliff atop the real one.

The south bank is quiet. Disordered rows of Pisha soldiers stand there. Someone shouts for him to come up, a voice like a falling clod of earth. Ku tries to guide his mule there, but the sides are too steep for her. She turns to look at him.

Anxious, Ku lets out another bray, which causes HeiChiu to turn again. She takes a few steps forward, body twisting. Ku has awakened her donkey half, though her horse half isn't listening.

Virtually all the Pisha troops are by the lip of the gully, a ragged troop of men on horses, no reserves and no supply team behind them. Unlike the Heile, who are amassed five deep with countless donkeyback soldiers bringing up the rear.

Chokanurkan receives Ku atop a vast slab of rock. From here they can see the mass of the Heile army on the opposite bank. Ku knows this spot must be the general's point of command. Their meeting in the general's opulent tent three years ago feels as if it were just yesterday. Back then, Chokanurkan's winning streak was already beginning to wane, but he could never have expected this awful defeat. Even so, there is not a trace of despair on the general's face.

"We've heard that the king has decided to surrender. Will you keep fighting, general?"

"The king decides when the kingdom's war ends, but I'll decide about my own war."

"You're leading the Pisha army, general."

"My troops are only the day and the night."

On top of the face that is speaking to him, Ku sees a second, silent face. One pair of eyes stares at Ku, the other looks elsewhere.

"Did Karhan send you to urge my surrender? I don't have time for this nonsense. I do have a message for you to bring back, though. Listen carefully."

Ku looks wearily at General Chokanurkan. His voice feels scraped by the braying, and he can't say anything at the moment.

Chokanurkan is calm, apparently indifferent to the battle that is about to begin. A couple of commanders sprint over, panting hard, but he waves them away and they wait anxiously to one side.

Ku is anxious too, glancing at the two sweating commanders, then back at the general. He had planned to tell Chokanurkan that a hundred thousand mounted Heile troops were about to invade, and rather than wait like an egg to be struck by a stone, the general ought to either surrender or retreat. Then he thinks there's no need to say any of this. A quick look across the gully shows how vast the Heile force is, yet the general is sitting serenely there. Who could change his mind?

Ku had expected Chokanurkan to send him off with an important report, but no. Instead, the general tells him a very long story.

Chokan and Nurkan

Chokanurkan is actually two different names, for two different people. The person who led the attack last night was Nurkan, my twin brother, and I'm Chokan. We were one person, but then we became two bodies. He sleeps while I lead the troops by day, and dreams of me in battle. While I sleep at night, he takes over the command, and I watch in my dreams.

No one knows we're two people, except our father. He separated us as soon as we were born, so even our mother didn't know she'd given birth to twins. By day she hugged and fed me, at night she held my brother as she slept. We were both named Chokanurkan, born while our father was between battles. When the Pisha-Heile War began, my father led every battle, big or small. This quickly grew exhausting, so the moment we were born, he was certain the person who would share his command had arrived.

He ordered us to divide our time. I was born first, so the day would be mine, and the night would belong to my brother Nurkan. He never allowed us to meet.

"A different you will appear at night," is what he said to me.

"A different you will appear during the day," he said to Nurkan in the night, while I was dreaming of everything he did.

I'd often thought about Nurkan when I was a child, as if he were another me, but he never visited, and I didn't dare venture into the night. Eventually, he sought me out during the day, and I led him down every street under the sun, stopping at every corner to enjoy a fragrant grilled bun. We grew up back to back. Women I seduced by day would sleep with him at night, and when he was done, they remained by my side during the day.

Our father recruited children our age for us to command. This was an era of no sleep. During the day I dressed in black and led my army, charging alongside my father or retreating pursued by the enemy. At night, Nurkan did the same in white on a white horse, fighting the day's battles all over again.

He raised us amid one violent battle after another.

He'd been fighting for three decades, and all his soldiers were old.

Just as his generation was about to die of old age, his sons began to take command. His twin sons became Pisha's young, fearless general who needed no sleep. He fooled everyone. Even the king had no idea.

We were unstoppable. If I was defeated by day, Nurkan would be victorious that night. As soon as the sun set, all authority fell into his hands. He didn't care whether I'd won or lost—I disappeared as soon as it got dark. I knew what happened by night: he set off dressed in white, sitting tall in his saddle, and when he pointed ahead with his sword, the weary, wounded soldiers would rise to their feet, and so would the horses who'd been lying in puddles of blood. Even the corpses would stand. Silently, they all returned to the site of the day's battle. The more people we sacrificed during the day, the larger his contingent. He fought my battles all over again, killed the enemies I'd already slaughtered, and our men who'd died would lose their lives once more. Every battle became two.

Our soldiers fought day and night, and soon became unable to tell waking from sleeping. When the enemy killed them at night, they'd believe they were dreaming, and still woke at dawn. When charging during the day, they'd think they could do it all over again in that night's dreams. Night lessened the burden of day, for everything felt as if it were a dream, whether their eyes were open or shut.

In the whole of our army, only Nurkan and I remained lucid. Or perhaps our minds were less clear than anyone else's. We took turns sleeping, but we were waging war all the time, whether awake or in our dreams. I could lead my men into battle with no qualms during the day, because whatever the outcome, my brother would take the reins at night.

The Heile army was unable to adapt to this manner of war. They fought all day till humans and horses were completely spent, then just as they were tumbling into sleep, wounded and weary, the Pisha night army in white uniforms on white horses came hurtling in, many of them hacked to death while still in dreamland.

They feared Pisha's sleepless general. After each skirmish, they retreated to what they thought was a safe distance away. They slumbered, but we did not. No matter how far they went, we caught up and brought the war to their dreams.

We almost reached Heile City.

After just a few decades, though, everything has changed. The circumstances in which we laid siege to Heile are now gone forever. At the time, the route was strewn with villages whose Kun towers stood tall. Those farmhouses, goat pens, fruit orchards and wheat fields sheltered us. Now virtually all the peasants have converted, and there are no longer crop fields, animal pens, haystacks or vineyards that offer us refuge. Scythe-wielding farmers are liable to cut off our heads at any moment.

I'm telling you all this because I won't live till nightfall. Bear these words to the donkey drovers, and the donkeys will spread them across the land. Anywhere there are donkeys in the future, people will pass on the legend of Chokanurkan. I'd intended to have you bear these words to my family in the city, but they will soon be slaughtered by the enemy. I've killed too many Heile people, and they surely won't let off a single one of my relatives.

Today is my final battle. At our back is Pisha City—we have nowhere left to retreat. I want to finish this before sunset. This will be the easiest fight, because we are destined to lose. All I need to do is lead the remaining men forward, to meet our appointment with death.

As for my little brother, I don't need to say anything to him. Whatever I do by day, he will find out at night. When he wakes up tonight, he will realise he doesn't have a single soldier left to command. I've ended his night battle too.

*

Ku listens without a word until Chokanurkan falls silent as a stone. His soldiers are marching ahead, staunch as rock, gathered around him. Ku has no idea what to say, so he nods and turns to go, but cannot stop himself blurting out, "May I see General Nurkan?"

"You can only see him at night."

Chokan glances at the setting sun, as if he can already see the approaching night sky, where his brother Nurkan lives, where he himself can never go.

As Ku rides away on HeiChiu, Chokan's remaining troops are lined up on the bank impassive as a stone wall, crippled horses and injured men preparing to charge. A vicious, suicidal battle is about to begin. Ku urges his mule into a trot. She goes down into the gully then up the other side, panting with exertion.

Karhan doesn't wait for Ku to arrive before giving the order. A deluge of murderous shouts in Heilenese and Tian flood forth like a bursting dam. Pishanese battle cries from the far bank pour out too. Both torrents of sound gush into the river gully, where they collide on the loose shale.

Nurkan

General Nurkan, dressed all in white, appears before the Heile army on his white horse, and the jubilant Heile troops are stunned into silence. They chopped off General Chokanurkan's head that evening—there it is, hanging in the middle of their camp, mounted on the trunk of a white poplar tree, just as the Pisha did to Lanshihan years ago, holding it up high as they marched into Heile City. On this occasion, the Pisha general's bleeding head stays put, watching the Heile men celebrate.

Bonfires dot the land, and the Heile men dance wildly around them. By firelight, they can see the general's head is still dripping blood, and his staring eyes remain wide open. His body was trampled to pulp by a hundred thousand horses. This evening, after the general's head was cut off in the river gully, one war horse after another galloped over him. Next was the turn of the donkey squad, but though the peasants drove their donkeys towards the body, not one of them would step on him—they all jumped over the corpse. His carcass was pissed on a hundred thousand times, shat on a hundred thousand times. Then the merriment of a hundred thousand men began, thousands of bonfires turning the night bright as day. With General Chokanurkan and his army exterminated, the Pisha troops who terrorised the Heile night and day for several decades are finally gone once and for all. Their daytime foes vanquished, and they can now carouse the night away—it doesn't cross their minds that there is still the night battle to think of.

All of a sudden, here is the dead general come back to life. They do not know that Chokanurkan is two people, and though Chokan is dead, his younger brother Nurkan is still alive.

General Nurkan stands dashingly before a hundred thousand Heile soldiers, waiting for his night army to appear—the weary, battle-scarred men coming to him revived, ready to fight again on the ground they lost by day, the severed heads and decapitated bodies littering the wilderness hurtling back together and assembling before him, just as they have for countless nights before this, when he has summoned the sleeping and the dead.

On this night, however, not a single person stands behind him. All these years, his men have fought with General Chokan by day, and alongside him at night. Thinking the twins were a single person, they fought relentlessly under the leadership of a general who never tired, and so learnt to do without rest. They advanced from Pisha to Heile, then got pushed back. Along the way, many died in battle, others of old age. These war heroes came back to life over and over, ready to fight again, but now not a single one is here. They can no longer fight day and night like this ghostly general. The spirits who accompanied him for decades have gone off in search of home, headless bodies wandering astray, unable to see where they need to go, and bodiless heads cast asunder, who can see the chimney smoke from their hometowns but lack the legs to get there.

General Nurkan knows the night army is not going to show up. All alone, he raises his sword and shouts a battle cry, and charges through the firelit chaos of the Heile camp. No one dares get in his way. They all believe there must be thousands of soldiers on horseback right behind him.

Barely drawing breath, the general blazes through five battalions, and arrives at Karhan's tent.

The king waits in full regalia, armed and on his horse. All these nights of being pursued have taught him how to deal with Pisha's night army. His guards are in battle dress, standing on either side, and Ku waits behind on HeiChiu. In the ferocious firelight and beneath the alluring moon, General Nurkan appears, his lone battle cry as piercing as a sword. He gallops up on his white horse, dressed all in white, melting into the silvery moonlight. Only when he draws close can they make out his direct gaze and thrusting sword, and see that the thousands of mounted soldiers behind him are actually Heile troops in hot pursuit.

The guards standing next to Karhan begin to tremble—they are certain they're seeing a ghost. How can General Chokanurkan, whom they trampled to paste, be appearing before them? Just as in the countless hellish night battles before this, those killed by day are showing up as apparitions.

Karhan raises his sword and his guards charge *hwoo lahh lahh* alongside him.

General Nurkan doesn't see the enemy. His horse gallops right past Karhan, emerging from the tangle of soldiers, not even glancing at the donkeyback Ku as he goes by. Looking right ahead, straight as his sword, in an instant he is through the camp and in the wilderness.

Karhan and his guards gather their wits, swing their horses around, and give chase. Behind them are all five battalions, a vast army roaring into the wild.

Ku whips HeiChiu to make her catch up with the Han King.

General Nurkan's silhouette sways before them, neither near nor far, along with his lone battle cry, eerie and faraway like a spirit's. He is taking Karhan's hundred thousand men on a merry chase, and the scene is indistinguishable from him leading them into battle.

Ku realises they are getting farther and farther from Pisha.

General Nurkan is heading Heile-ward, probably aiming for Heile City, thousands of miles away. With that in mind, he sees nothing of what is around him.

In the latter part of the night, the moon is no longer as bright. Ku worries that if they keep going, dawn will break, and there will be no escape for General Nurkan. The daytime is not his. He must know that his elder brother is dead, and no one will take over come sunrise. Chokan's war is over, and Nurkan's is the only battle left. Night after night, he will lead the enemy towards distant Heile City.

Ku's mule falls farther and farther behind as one battalion after another gallops past. Even the donkey squad charges ahead. General Nurkan's lone battle cry fades in the distance. Hoofbeats tear apart the dark earth.

Waking

Karhan's men fail to capture General Nurkan—he vanishes at the first cockcrow. Abruptly woken by the roosters, the Heile army stops like a large chunk of solidified night, making the wilderness appear even darker. All that can be made out are the vague outlines of humans on horses and donkeys, distinguishable because the donkeys are shorter and their riders lower down.

In the murky morning light, Ku arrives on a heavily perspiring HeiChiu, who looks like she is ready to fall apart after galloping through the night. Her legs splaying every which way, she passes among the other animals, who are standing still as wooden blocks, brays mingling with neighs. The mule suddenly feels both halves of herself. The donkey in her goes *ahnng-jee ahnng-jee* and the horse lets out a nasal whinny. The result is a most peculiar sound belonging to neither species.

Ku greets the Han King and begs forgiveness for falling behind.

"Can the mule really not keep up with these donkeys? His highness sent men to look for you twice, and the whole donkey squad was calling for you, but you were nowhere to be seen. We thought you'd gone back home," scolds Tianmen Ben, standing by the Han King.

Tianmen Ben arrived from outside the city with thirty thousand soldiers for the war effort, so naturally he sounds more overbearing than the other Tian devotees. He can't be too harsh, though, because Ku is his second tongue. Every word he says has to pass through Ku's interpretation before it can reach the Han King. Whenever Ku translates his words into Heilenese, Ben eyes him with suspicion, wondering if he is changing the meaning.

Amid the dozen languages of this rabble, only Ku can accurately bring the meanings of these many tongues to Karhan, then transmit back to them the king's commands and plans. A Heilenese instruction must be translated directly into all these languages, rather than a relay from Tai to Chiu and so forth, turning one command into countless ones which, if you translated them back, would be incomprehensible even to the Han King himself. The difference between languages is so great, translating between them is like herding out a flock of goats in the morning and finding they'd turned into dogs by afternoon.

Ku is in charge of all the languages for the entire army, while also serving as Karhan's guide and navigator through Pisha territory, telling them the names of tiny hamlets of just two households, pointing out paths that hardly anyone knows about. No wonder Karhan can't lose him, and even sent two teams out in the middle of the night to track him down—first in the latter part of the night, when the army had reached the Gobi and the Han King was growing a little drowsy, while his soldiers were finding their vision blurry after being on the move for most of the night. They could no longer tell if the figure up ahead was a man in white on a white horse, or a ghost. If it were a man, why couldn't they catch up? Feeling his heart waver, the Han King turned to Ku, only for an aide to tell him Ku's mule was slow, and they'd left him behind some time ago. The second occasion was when General Chokanurkan disappeared in a burst of cockcrow just as they were about to draw level. Without the protective shield of their quarry, Karhan was stricken with terror, not knowing where he'd led his hundred thousand men. All night long they'd been on a march led by Chokanurkan, passing vast wheat fields, abandoned villages, rivers and dry gullies, through the borderless Gobi. He hadn't paid attention to where they were going, his eyes focused only on the faint motion of the white horse in front, his ears attuned only to the battle cries of the general galloping ahead. Then Chokanurkan disappeared. Just like that, the Han King and his men lost their direction. Again the king sent men in search of Ku. Only Ku could lead them out of this dark night. The search party never returned, but Ku showed up.

"What the hell is this place?" says Karhan, breathing hard.

"It must be Guma, majesty," replies Ku, looking up at the stars.

Saying the word reminds Ku of what he saw here not long ago: men being skinned alive. His own skin throbs with pain all over.

Even Ku can't say where exactly they are—it is pitch dark. Still, he watched the North dipper all the way and knows they were moving west. Hence, he deduces, this must be Guma.

"You mean in a single night, we've undone the last three days' travel."

"Yes, majesty. We'll soon be back in Heile territory."

"My hundred thousand men, led by the nose by a Pisha general. If I didn't know better, I'd think he was bringing my army back to attack Heile," Karhan mumbles to himself.

Cockcrow

Cockcrow passes westward over their heads. Day brightens above the scrubby, yellowing land. The sun is glowing beneath the horizon, but won't rise for quite a while.

The soldiers look around them, seeking out the vanished Chokanurkan, but Ku knows they won't find him. The general has slipped into dreamland. The awakened Heile soldiers won't be able to hunt him down—he is barricaded in dreams.

Karhan turns to the east, where another barrage of cockcrow is sounding. To the donkeys this looks like colourful strands of satin weaving across the sky. Karhan can't see these hues, nor can the Tian devotees, but still they stand next to the Han King, staring alongside him. Ku is watching too. He can't leave Karhan's side, for Karhan might want to speak, and then Ku will have to interpret for the Tian devotees.

Ku has never listened this closely to roosters crowing. They start in Pisha City, then the chorus spreads to one village after another, a dense net of sound cast over the heads of the Heile troops, taken up by chickens in the farther villages, patch after patch of crowing moving towards Heile. Karhan too seems to be intensely experiencing the cries passing over his army.

"I've always heard that Pisha roosters crow before Heile ones, so people in Pisha wake up earlier than in Heile. The Pisha in the east are already eating breakfast, while the Heile in the west go hungry in dreamland. I used to think Pisha people got out of bed two full hours before the Heile each day, and all that time added up, giving the Pisha many extra years over the centuries, more time to deal with their affairs, more time to think things through, and Heile would never catch up. I don't think that any more, because now us Heile can sleep soundly in our beds, while the Pisha must rise early to flee for their lives. They quickly expend their energy, and now is the time when we at our full strength can exterminate them."

Ku conveys Karhan's meaning to Tianmen Ben, the military leader.

Tianmen Ben tells the Han King, "The villages around here have all been taken by us. These roosters are yours."

Ku translates this to Heile, and a rare smile graces Karhan's visage. It's unclear if he realises that even though the land has changed its religion, the roosters are crowing just the same as always without the slightest alteration.

Snoring

The Heile army is exhausted, men and horses both, and so they rest. As the sky brightens, Ku sees that they are between three villages, all quite far away. In the wilderness between these settlements, a hundred thousand Heile troops dream as they snore, a thunderous sound that has scared away all the villagers. These three villages are half a day's journey from Guma. One is called, in the Huang language, Water Village. Three days earlier, when Ku passed through it with the Han King, the inhabitants had already converted to Tian—Tianmen Ben's advance troops chopped off half their heads and held blades to the necks of the other half. Now these newly-converted villagers have fled too. Before dawn, peasant soldiers on donkeyback charged into the village. Guided by the crowing, they sought out every coop, captured every chicken, and while it was still dark, roasted and ate them. The jennies who didn't manage to get away were unlucky too. Randy Heile jacks, riven with appetite, took turns mounting them. It could have been worse—having changed religion, the Heile no longer eat donkeys. The goats and cows were set aside for the horseback troops who would be arriving later. Like locusts, they devoured everything that could be eaten, drank the village's only well dry, and left nothing but snoring in the wasteland outside.

Fight

After half a day's sleep in the open, the Heile army sets off for Pisha. The paths they trod through the wilderness last night are clearly visible, stretching into the distance. Tianmen Ben's men are still at the vanguard, followed by the Heile forces, with Karhan among his own guard, and finally the jumble of other Tian devotees and donkeyback peasant soldiers. This last group keeps getting into disputes with the battalions of Tian devotees and bring their grievances to the Han King. Because of the language barrier, Ku steps in to resolve their differences. Tian devotees from outside the city are mostly farmers press-ganged into service: chaotic in their actions, undisciplined in battle. Good at quarrelling, though. On this occasion, there's an argument over a jenny. A soldier says he found her in the night, so she belongs to him, a spoil of war. The Heile farmer says she belongs to his household, that they've reared her for many years, and she's like a member of the family.

Many Heile peasant soldiers huddle round as this soldier keeps explaining, over and over, how in the middle of the night he found a jenny that nobody wanted and led her along till morning, a journey as arduous as getting from Heile to Pisha. Now he's spent a night with this jenny, he won't give her up to anyone else. He speaks passionately, and the Heile peasant soldiers listen with respect, because he's speaking in the language of Tian scripture and they don't dare display irreverence to these sounds. Instead, they ask Ku to pass on their questions.

Ku asks, "Have you used her?"

The soldier says, "I rode her—she refused to move when I tugged her reins, so I got off my horse and got on her back, and led the horse behind us, all the way till dawn."

Ku translates this into Heilenese, which causes a burst of laughter. The soldier doesn't know what's so funny, and looks at Ku.

"You've had the use of someone else's donkey for a night, but for the sake of Tian, they won't charge you for that. You still have to return the jenny to them, though," Ku says.

Urgent

They keep moving till evening, when an urgent report arrives on a swift horse: General Chokanurkan's night army breached Qusha last night. He was on a white horse, dressed in white, with a sword in his hand. No one dared to stop him—who knew how many men and horses lurked in the gloom behind him?

Karhan listens to this intelligence with an expressionless face, and the army continues moving towards Pisha.

The next morning, another swift horse arrives. General Chokanurkan has advanced past Siya.

The third day's report is even more urgent: Chokanurkan has reached Aoba raising a battle cry in the cavernous ruins of the palace before charging towards Heile City wielding his sword. His war horse galloped down the wide avenues of Heile beneath a starlit sky. People in neighbouring villages heard the *dok dok* of his hoofbeats, and the dogs chased after him, snapping wildly at his horse's hooves, their tangled barking amplifying his lone steps into the galloping of thousands. Through the night, donkeys passed the word from one village to the next, all the way to Heile: Heile City is in imminent danger, and the city's commander begs Karhan's army to return.

By the time they get the news, Karhan's army has reached a temple half a day from West Kun Temple. For days now, they've been walking in its shadow. No matter where they are on the battlefield, they can see its high wall thrusting high above into the clouds. And now Karhan's army is about to set eyes upon the legendary sun-blocking wall of West Kun Temple.

Ku rides HeiChiu, making sure to stay in the Han King's peripheral vision.

"Are we really not turning back to save Heile City?" Ku asks anxiously.

"Let General Chokanurkan invade if he likes. I'm going to take Pisha City and become its ruler."

19

West Kun Temple

Escape

THE SEVEN VILLAGES west of West Kun Temple are an ocean of flames.

Five days ago, half the villagers fled on donkeyback. The clouds of dust raised by the advancing troops had reached these settlements, and so had the murderous yells from the Heile and Pisha armies clashing in the dry river gully. Dogs barked wildly all night, and donkeys passed on brayed messages to ever more distant villages. These animal cries warned the humans to flee. Cockcrow was earlier too, urging them to wake early and escape.

There were two refuges: the city and the hills. The people and donkeys who chose the hills had to run fully exposed across the bare Gobi Desert and up the treeless hillside, until they finally reached the rocky peaks and could take shelter in the crevices. When they looked down, they saw soldiers investigating the depths of the hills. Where could humans and donkeys hide? The beasts were muzzled, to prevent them from calling out. As for the cities, only humans were allowed to enter—donkeys had to be abandoned outside the walls, gates in all four directions shut tight to them. Their braying vaulted the walls, causing the donkeys already inside to cry back. These volleys of sound crashed atop the walls like dry percussive explosions, deafening the sentries.

When they had brayed enough, the donkeys stranded outside the walls turned back and returned to their villages. Donkeys are homing animals—no matter how far they go, they can always find their way back. In twos and threes, they trickled back into the villages, making their homes in the courtyards left empty by the humans. The people who hadn't fled, seeing the donkeys grazing away, assumed their owners must have been killed—how else could the creatures have returned alone? But the donkeys didn't look the least bit mournful.

Just as the remaining villagers were wondering whether to flee, the Heile army retreated. All of Pisha had been thrown into shock when the Heile defeated the Pisha army and slaughtered General Chokanurkan. Backstreet gossip even said King Luo had surrendered, and the Pisha must now convert to Tian. Unexpectedly, the Heile pulled back overnight. Word was that General Chokanurkan had been resurrected and led his ever-victorious night army in an utter rout of the Heile. The villagers witnessed a hundred thousand Heile soldiers fleeing in panic, and heard a hundred thousand hoofbeats leaving Pisha. Some of the villages even put together donkey squads to pick off the Heile rearguard.

In the span of a single night, the enemy had utterly vanished. The villagers who had fled into the hills made a cautious reappearance, only for the Heile army to abruptly show up once more.

The returning troops swept through all the villages. The inhabitants who hadn't escaped were surrounded, and Tianmen Ben's men ordered them to convert. Those who refused had their entire families wiped out and their houses burnt to the ground. Some villagers, stubborn as donkeys, would rather have served as beasts of burden—converting was unthinkable. Many stretched out their necks for the butcher's knife. Others gave in and stuck their heads out in supplication instead, hoping for mercy.

Tianmen Ben's soldiers lopped off all disobedient heads and hung them atop truncated white poplar trunks. It was Karhan's men who decapitated these trees first—they had been ordered not to leave a single one with its branches intact.

And now the houses of those who refused to convert are in flames, which quickly spread to their neighbours. Soon all the villages are up in smoke, and the blaze dyes red the high wall of West Kun Temple.

Donkey Yard

The donkeys run from the conflagration, hair scorched off, fleeing to West Kun Temple. On the hillside north of the temple is a donkey yard, where many of them have carried Kun devotees. Every donkey has spent some time here, a sought-after honour in the donkey community. They believe any donkey who has borne a Kun statue will bring its owner good fortune, and for those who haven't had the opportunity, being ridden by a Kun devotee brings enough reflected glory to keep away any ghost seeking to possess it.

There are more donkeys than Kun devotees in Pisha, so owners rotate between animals. Many donkeys spend their entire lives waiting for their turn to get ridden. The Kun devotees are picky and get all the best donkeys, especially young virgin jennies. Secular households often send jennies to this yard for the use of the faithful.

In the courtyard, white-bellied Pisha jennies stand in small groups, completely unafraid of the *dok dok* of the arriving soldiers.

Seeing the jennies is a shot in the arm for the Heile donkey squad, and the peasant soldiers find themselves charging ahead of the horseback troops—the donkeys have put on speed, and no tugging on the reins will deter them. The stiff rods of these randy Heile jacks poke out beneath them, pointing the way to the donkey yard, so hard that neither donkeys nor humans can gainsay them.

Ku's mule trots along until he pulls her back. Her donkey half wants to follow the rest of her species, but her horse half revolts, and she gives up after a few steps.

The gate to the donkey yard stands open, and the donkeyback troops rush straight in, the jacks ignoring the wishes of their riders and mounting the jennies. Three layers, from top to bottom: humans, jacks, jennies. In the confusion, someone stealthily pushes the gate shut, and steel arrows rain down like locusts from the haystacks, the rooftops, the surrounding walls.

By the time the horseback troops catch up, the yard is full of frantically rutting donkeys, while the corpses of more than three hundred Heile peasant soldiers lie on the ground.

The Pisha Kun devotees who set this ambush take refuge in West Kun Temple, entering through the back door.

Jenny Cemetery

The three hundred donkeyback soldiers are buried on the hillside by the western wall of the temple. The donkey yard is cleared out, and the Han King's great tent set up in the middle, with his guards encamped in the four corners of the courtyard. Not far away is a little temple whose Kun devotees didn't escape, so they were all eliminated. Tianmen Maisheng advises the Han King to stay there instead. The temple walls are high and easy to defend. Besides, this donkey yard is too close to West Kun Temple, making it vulnerable to further attacks.

Karhan says Kun temples are unclean. He'd rather stay in the donkey yard.

Ku and Maisheng take up residence in the feed store by the Han King's tent. Tianmen Ben has his own tent. The Tian devotees from outside the city speak to Karhan, with Ku's interpretation. The Tian devotees say their piece, then look suspiciously at Ku with yellowing eyes, uncertain what he is translating their words into.

A report arrives on donkeyback: an advance scout was ambushed at a hamlet to the east, and thirty-seven people have been sacrificed, their corpses eaten by dogs. Tianmen Ben asks if he may lead his own men in a mission of vengeance, and the Han King orders him to slaughter the entire village, not letting so much as a single dog escape. Ku interprets: kill the guilty, including the dogs, but Tian is merciful, and forgives those who convert.

As a result, half the village survives.

West Kun Temple

Finding the front door of West Kun Temple bricked up, the Heile soldiers tear down the brightly-painted totem in the courtyard, and with fifty men holding it from either side, they ram it again and again at the door, sending a hollow *hoonng loonng* reverberating through the temple. The high walls begin to wobble. Terrified, the soldiers drop their battering ram and try to flee, but the mass of troops behind them blocks their way.

Ku looks up at the walls of West Kun Temple, and his throat throbs so suddenly he must work hard to hold down the braying that would otherwise burst out. He can't, though. The donkey within him is showing its power. The donkey eyes behind his human ones open wide and see the towers of sound above the temple crumble and collapse, then swiftly form again. The scripture chanting from inside the temple is more powerful, reinforcing the courtyard walls and constructing a Kun world in its higher reaches. The Heile horses and donkeys all look up. The donkeys can see the layers of temples and towers taking shape in the air above, just as at Peach Blossom Temple. To a donkey's ears, there is no difference between Pisha's Kun devotees and Heile's Tian devotees chanting scripture. All their voices rise into the sky and call into being these mid-air structures.

Conditions

Ku finds the doorway that Kunmen Virtue once led him and Hsieh through, now also bricked up. When he tries to peep through the cracks, he senses a pair of donkey eyes within him looking too, and braying gurgles in his throat, but he keeps a tight hold on it, not allowing the beast out. On an autumn day three years ago, Ku led Hsieh out of this doorway, with no idea that this jenny he was taking to Heile had scripture carved on her skin. Kunmen Virtue told him to guard this young virgin, and not to let any jacks mount her. He'd actually thought she was being sent as a special gift to win the favour of Tianmen Maisheng at Peach Blosson Temple.

Ku shouts at the door and his voice bounces back at him, smacking him *pakk pakk* on the face.

Returning to the front entrance, he raises his head and cries at the high wall: "I am Ku, I bear word for Kunmen Virtue."

His voice only gets halfway up before falling back down to earth. He tries again a few more times, when his throat suddenly explodes into *ahhnng-jee ahhnng-jee ahhnng-jee*.

He cannot stop the braying that escapes him, and it soars up the wall, almost reaching the top before pouring back down *hwaah laah hwaah laah*, and Ku himself falls backwards onto his bum. HeiChiu the mule glares, lips flapping. The donkey part of her wants to call out too, but no sound issues from her twisted mouth.

The soldiers stare astonished at Ku, uncertain what strange language he is screaming. They know him as the famous chanter of Tian scripture at Peach Blossom Temple, as well as the most important translator by the Han King's side. His brain is stuffed full of dozens of languages from all over the world. The noise he just made sounds familiar, but they can't put their finger on which country it comes from.

Ku yells again, this time in Pishanese. As if roused by the sound, the bricks loosen and a few are removed from within, leaving a hole.

"Quick, crawl in."

Ku stares into the gap, and several pairs of eyes look back at him. After a moment's hesitation, he tentatively reaches in. Someone grabs hold of his arm and drags him bodily through the hole.

From broad daylight, Ku is plunged into night. It is still the middle of the afternoon outside, but within the temple, the sun has fallen below the western high wall, and the sky is thick with crows.

The temple is crammed full of humans and donkeys, refugees from the nearby villages. The Kun devotee standing there recognises Ku, addressing him as "master". Years ago, he says, he often heard Ku in this very place, expounding on various languages.

The Kun devotee opens a narrow channel through the throng of people, and Ku realises he is walking down the same paved path Kunmen Virtue led him along. A crowd has formed around the base of the Kun tower, everyone perfectly silent. The crows are quiet too, except for their flapping wings.

Kunmen Virtue receives Ku in the rear courtyard. Three years ago, this is where he placed Hsieh's reins in Ku's hand.

"I delivered your jenny safe and sound to Maisheng at Peach Blossom Temple."

Kunmen Virtue nods.

"Only thing is, Maisheng is now the Tianmen of that temple."

Kunmen Virtue nods again.

"You didn't tell me Kun scripture was carved into her skin. If you had, I'd have died sooner than leading her through Tian-occupied territory."

Kunmen Virtue nods once more.

"They smothered the donkey to death, scalded off her hair, and removed her skin in one piece. The scripture was even clearer than if it were written on paper, like living words. They bowed to the scripture and Maisheng buried it in the desert. It's good scripture, he said, and though he no longer believes and doesn't chant it any more, people surely will in the future, and so he would leave it for those who come after us."

Kunmen Virtue nods emphatically and gestures for someone to bring Ku two silver ingots. Ku hesitates, but accepts them.

"I know Karhan sent you to convert me. That's what you've been doing all the way from Heile to Pisha. We heard all about it. Some of the villagers you encountered fled and came here. They said you were a good person, that you got them to give in so they kept their heads. Because they remained alive, they were able to convert back to Kun. However, please don't urge us to do whatever it takes to keep our heads."

Ku nods.

He'd had words for Kunmen Virtue, but all of a sudden he feels there is nothing to say. All he can do is stare. He wants to hear the

Kunmen speak—this will be their last conversation, he knows.

"I have three questions, please bear them to Karhan."

Kunmen Virtue looks up at sky and the many towers thrusting into it. Ku follows his gaze. Hsieh's braying from years ago resonates in his mind.

Every one of the Kunmen's words is like a tile falling from a tower's point.

"First, the Pisha people have spent a thousand years building Kun temples and towers. If we convert to Tian, can these structures be spared?

"Second, we have worshipped Kun for a thousand years. If we convert, can the virtue we've accumulated be transferred to the Tian side?

"Third, may we continue speaking Pishanese?

"If Karhan agrees, we will all convert. If not, we will immolate ourselves. I'll wait till sunlight has left the tallest tower for a response, but no longer."

With that, he bows to Ku in a Kun salute.

Ku returns the bow.

"No"

Ku exits the way he entered: head and arms through the hole, and a shove from behind. It's a tight squeeze—the gap seems smaller than it did before, and he gets stuck. Someone grabs his hands and collar, and yanks till he emerges, covered in dirt from head to foot.

Ku hurries to see Karhan, turning back to look over the wall every few paces. He is almost at the tent in the middle of the donkey yard when the tallest tower finally appears, the crimson setting sun lingering on its point, already beginning to sink beneath the tent. The long shadows of soldiers and their horses stretch across the ground. West Kun Temple doesn't have much time left.

The Han King and Tianmen Ben are negotiating something inside the tent. Ku bows to the king, then to Ben.

In Heile, Ku tells Karhan the Kunmen's three conditions. Karhan's reply is the one he expected.

"No," he says, without even thinking about it. "No. No."

In Flames

By the time Ku emerges from the tent, the sun has set, and twilit clouds in all kinds of peculiar shapes fill the western sky. The high walls of West Kun Temple darken, though the spires that reach above them still glisten. The lingering light can't help caressing the golden points. Ku watches as they get brighter and brighter, dazzling him, and then realises this isn't sunlight but the glow of flames from below.

"Look out! The temple's on fire!"

A cry goes up. Men, horses, donkeys and mules gape.

Collapse

Like an enormous chimney, West Kun Temple spurts smoke into the air. Against the darkening sky, the scarlet billows form a gargantuan Kun statue, its head lost amid invisible nebulae, its body sitting atop the high walls. Countless other Kun statues appear around it, smoke from the carved pillars and painted door frames forming pillars and doors in mid-air, while the immolating Kun devotees turn into smoke in their own images. Kun scriptures in various languages produce different scenes, for scrolls of scripture describe the likeness of Kun, and as they go up in flames the smoke describes the likeness of scripture, every language is nothing but smoke, something that has burnt deep within and turned into language smoke, a smoke that tells of what has been burnt, and meanwhile these Kun statues constantly transform and come together and are engulfed.

Points of light fill the sky. Stars and moon ornament this fantastical Kun world of smoke.

*

A rumbling *hooong looong looong* comes from within the walls. The towers and temple building are collapsing, the crashes echoing in the night air, as if the clouds themselves have been scorched and are roiling in agony.

"I want everyone in Pisha to see West Kun Temple burn, to watch as the Kun in their heart falls to pieces."

As Karhan says these words, a series of dull thuds comes from behind the walls: the scripture lofts above the roof pillars are falling to the ground, one after another, each boom causing the flames to jump higher. The churning dark smoke must have blackened the celestial court itself by now.

The fire burns through the night till the next morning. Karhan's army surrounds the blaze. The donkeys and horses crane their necks to see. Ku and HeiChiu watch too. Her donkey eye sees the celestial court crumbling.

The Heile army is shrouded by the twin shadows of high walls and smoke. With the huge conflagration behind it, the wall is like an enormous stove, the soldiers' faces red from its heat.

Something is wrong. Ku thinks of warning Karhan to pull his men back, but says nothing.

In the afternoon, there is a sudden crack, and Ku watches as the high wall shatters from the top and falls outward. The ground is a swathe of screams. The soldiers scramble to get out of the way, but a shadow the size of the sky presses down on them.

"The wall is falling. Run!"

With his guards shielding him, Karhan turns his horse around and breaks into a gallop. Ku jumps onto HeiChiu and follows, looking back to watch the west wall break apart and fall like a piece of sky, followed by the other three walls, a lotus blossom with four unfurling petals. Ku isn't going to make it. His mule is slower than the horses, and the footsoldiers behind him are as frenzied as a nest of ants.

Ku yanks on the reins, and HeiChiu turns onto a goat trail heading north. The falling wall has turned the sky black, and all Ku can see is the darkness swiftly pressing down on him. Stricken with fear, the mule breaks into a sprint.

There is a crack behind them, and a wave of sound tumbles Ku from the mule's back. Just like that, his world turns dark.

After what feels like an entire lifetime, Ku opens his eyes with some effort. A thick layer of dirt covers his eyelids, and in fact his entire head and body. Dirt is still falling. Not far away are other clay figures, standing or squatting or flat on the ground, some squirming out from the dirt, others clutching their heads and moaning. Ku recognises Karhan on his large grey horse, an attendant brushing dirt off his garments so he may quickly emerge from this besmirchment with the dignity expected of the Han King.

Ku sways as he walks over. All of a sudden, a hand thrusts through the soil and catches hold of his arm. Turning, he sees a half-buried head, and quickly claws aside more dirt to reveal a face he does not know.

Soldiers come running over and scrabble to free their buried comrades. Half the Heile army is now beneath the collapsed wall. All around is screaming and groaning.

As the air clears, Ku sees HeiChiu standing not far away, looking back with the same expression Hsieh had on the battlefield at Guma.

Now Ku can see that the four fallen walls have made four wide roads, stretching out towards the north, south, east and west. At their junction are the Kun towers of West Kun Temple, a whole swathe of blackened edifices.

The tallest tower is right in the centre, its gold spire still gleaming—the smoke and flames couldn't reach it.

The scattered soldiers who regroup seem to have lost half their height—a good many men have lost limbs or are bent double, slumping to the ground. Karhan and his men are in a state of shock, and the guards are still covered with dirt as they bustle around their king, scrubbing his face and clothing clean of grime.

Stepping over the bricks that litter the ground, Heile soldiers go towards the temple. Ku stands alongside Karhan on the broad road formed by the fallen walls.

"This was the high wall that blocked our sun each morning. Now it is beneath my feet," says Karhan in Heilenese.

Ku's brain immediately translates this into all kinds of languages. The high wall of West Kun Temple takes many mighty falls, one for every tongue he knows.

A Donkey

A report comes from up ahead: not a single living person was found in West Kun Temple, and not a single corpse either, just a female donkey standing in the middle of the space, a set of Kun scripture in Heilenese strapped to her back, wrapped in linen on which is written that these are the writings translated at West Kun Temple, paid for at vast expense by the Heile imperial court, completed ten years ago but left here because the two countries were at war, not to mention the Heile people no longer worship Kun, so although the plan had originally been for the Pisha troops to bring these translated scriptures with them when they advanced into Heile, what happened instead was the Heile forces invaded Pisha and made this donkey hand the scrolls to the Han King.

"And the scrolls?" asks Karhan.

"We burnt them."

"What about the donkey?" asks Ku.

"She was flung into the fire too."

Kun Scripture

Ku follows the Han King into the scorched air of West Kun Temple, where sure enough there are no signs of neither humans nor donkeys. When Ku worked here as a translator, he heard they were digging beneath the temple, preparing three escape routes for the devotees: one leading to the celestial court, one out into the city, and one going deeper. This latter tunnel reached Kun mountain, from where one branch led up to the surface, and another down to the Bod with its unceasing voice of Kun.

Ku passes through one translation chamber after another, now just a maze of blackened walls. The main structure still stands, though the roof has fallen in and rubble covers the enormous gilded Kun statue, the gold melted and trickling down its face. The scripture loft to one side is still smouldering—thousands of holy scrolls in there are burning, and thick black smoke pours out, roiling and rising into the air, chanting these words a final time in language smoke.

All Ku can think of is the Kun scriptures on the donkey's back. There would have been eighty-seven scrolls—Ku was involved with proofreading seven of them. He lived in this temple for many years, editing scripture translations by Kun devotees. The low-ceilinged rooms of West Kun Temple were once full of translators from all over the world, sitting back to back. Each pair would work on the same section of text, then compare the two versions when they were done.

Bringing scriptures into Heilenese was a big project the temple took on several years before this, back when the Heile still worshipped Kun. The Heile court sent a substantial amount of gold, accompanied by a request to translate eighty-seven sets of scripture from Pishanese.

The job took eighty-seven years. In the twenty-third year, the new king of Heile led his people in converting to Tian, but when the news reached West Kun Temple, the translation didn't stop. Many Kun believers fled from Heile to Pisha, doubling the number of devotees at West Kun Temple. The newcomers bore word from the Heile folk who'd been forced to convert, hoping Pisha would send its army to rescue them.

Around this time, the high wall around the temple was almost finished. Stories about how Heile's sunlight was being blocked, and how the Heile had sworn to topple the wall, had already been arriving with these refugees. The translation work continued, but construction halted—firstly because it had already reached the sky. They'd only intended to block out donkey cries, but now the far reaches of the desert were finding their sunlight blocked. Secondly, the country was going to war, and the king had banned all manual labour unconnected to the war effort. The kingdom's resources couldn't be wasted on a soundproofing wall. The first troops advancing into Heile set off from the lea by this wall, the magnificent Pisha army marching off into the long shadow that stretched west from the temple.

Wall

After so many years, many have forgotten why this endless war is being fought. Only Ku still remembers the original reason: the Heile people heard that Pisha in the east had built a wall that touched the heavens, so as to block the sun and condemn Heile to spend each morning in the shade. This shadowy wall was mentioned by the king in the imperial court, by Tian devotees in their temples, by regular folk in the streets and alleyways. The donkeys' braying was also full of this wall. At the time, Master had to travel to Heile several times a year, and the news he brought back to Pisha was risible, unbelievable. The Heile spent every moment steeped in hatred for Pisha. Rumour was they planned to construct an even taller wall, so as to block Pisha City's afternoon sun.

"The Pisha won't let us see the dawn, so we'll make sure they go dark in the afternoon. The sun will set so early for them, they won't have time to accomplish a single thing."

The Heile king wasn't actually foolish enough to do this—he knew it would take far more energy to build a wall than to tear one down. And so, toppling the high wall of West Kun Temple became the Heile casus belli.

That's how it started. Pisha struck the first blow because the Heile kept proclaiming they were going to attack, but never actually did. This made the Pisha so anxious that they took the initiative, and actually managed to capture Heile City.

Now the first battle had been fought, the second was inevitable. So many people had died that their kingdom wanted national vengeance, and their families wanted personal revenge. Anyway, the war after had nothing to do with the wall, and no one could have said why they were fighting in the first place.

20

Wheat Field

Dust

THE DEFEATED PISHA SOLDIERS are scattered in the wilderness, running helter-skelter back to Pisha City, the Heile army close on their tail. The entire wilderness and all the fields become a vast road. Men, horses and donkeys trample up dust that rises towards the sky. From a distance, it looks as if one great cloud of dust is chasing another. Hsieh sees this from her perch within Ku's body. Three years ago, with Ku on her back, she witnessed the chaos of battle, scenes still engraved on her heart. That was her first time seeing the air fill with heads being flung, terrifying the ghosts on the ground. And now Ku is on a mule, and Hsieh's spirit is on his back. From this height, she can see more. People say you see different things on donkeyback than on horseback. You think differently too. What about on humanback? That's where Hsieh is now, riding Ku.

Startled awake, the wilderness ghosts flee into the air, trailing dirt behind them, escaping to the white poplar trees, where the dirt drifts too. The trees have no crowns, their bald tops are covered in dirt. The floating ghosts each perch atop a grain of dirt, looking at the men and horses below.

Through Tuo's eyes, Jue sees Pisha in the distance, and the hordes of fleeing Pisha people. One battle after another, they have been beaten all the way back home. Jue is home too; he is from Fence Village. But that isn't really his home now. In this village where the white poplar trees have all been beheaded, his mother, wife and children have been burnt to ashes. Their spirits are still in the dirt, amid barking and braying, gusts of wind like mothers calling for their children. When Jue thinks of these things, he feels all he has lost blowing in the full, empty wind, heading in the direction of home, and he too is on the road of return.

Wheat

It is the season of ripening wheat, but no one is in the vast golden fields. Horseback soldiers trample boldly over the crop. Those on donkeyback go around—donkey hooves do not tread on wheat. Ku's mule refuses too, and trots behind the donkey squad.

The fleeing Pisha troops stare in shock. Flinging down their weapons, they run into the fields. Meaning, *I'm not fighting anymore, and don't you attack me either, I'm off to the harvest.*

How could this do? Your war may be over, and you're back home, but mine isn't done yet.

The Heile soldiers run into the fields in pursuit. Meanwhile, the Pisha troops have pulled out scythes and started harvesting the wheat, ignoring the battle. The war isn't done with them, though. The Heile see their target nonchalantly cutting down wheat stalks, as if the hoofbeats and murderous cries have nothing to do with them. The first harvester is cut down, but the ones ahead of him don't even look up, they just keep swinging their scythes. Their heads are bent over their work as they fall to the ground, drenched in blood. A scene reminiscent of a few years ago in Aoba, when the praying Heile didn't let the slaughter interrupt them. A row of men massacred, while the ones in front didn't move; a man slashed down, while his neighbours next to him didn't flinch. They were like crops, planted firmly in the ground with no fear of being plucked, so the Pisha soldiers, who had been hacking away, did not dare to go any further. Now, too, the Heile abruptly stop. They shiver at the sight of Pisha heads hanging low like wheat tassels, allowing themselves to be severed. These Heile peasant soldiers have gone years without touching farming implements. The wheat is ripe and golden, its fragrance softening their hearts and rousing them. They clamber off their horses and try to snatch the scythes from the Pisha soldiers' hands, so they too can scratch the itch to harvest. The Pisha men won't give way, and soon they are tussling amid the crop.

More and more Pisha soldiers dash into the fields, with Heile forces after them. Men, horses and donkeys involuntarily come to a halt. Karhan reins in his horse too, and so does Ku, on his mule just behind.

*

Ku thinks the Han King will ask him to point out a way through the wheat. But no. He glances at Ku, then points towards Pisha City, faintly visible beyond the golden expanse.

"How high are the walls of Pisha City?"

"High as three donkeys atop each other," Ku replies.

"Do you Pisha people need to drag donkeys into everything?" The Han King gives him a sidelong look.

Ku lowers his head a little, but does not reply. The Han King's words almost summoned a bray from within Ku's chest.

"We've toppled the high wall of West Kun Temple. No wall in the kingdom of Pisha will stand in the way of my great army," says Karhan.

Sidelong

The cut wheat stalks splay to form a wide avenue, leading directly to Pisha City. Apart from the infinite yellow expanse, Karhan's army meets no resistance.

The gates to the city are shut tight, and the city wall is thick with a grey coating of dust. At the foot of the wall are rows of donkeys, the ones from the countryside who were barred from entry. Refugees from Pisha's thirty-six towns have crammed themselves into the city, and with so many humans, there's no room for donkeys.

Watching the approaching Heile troops, the donkeys do not get flustered, but merely stare sidelong at them. The horseback troops go by, then the donkeyback ones. The Heile drovers each grab several reins, but the Pisha donkeys dig in their heels and refuse to go with them.

Ku's mule HeiChiu looks at the donkeys with her left eye and the horses with her right. Her donkey half wishes to join the donkeys, but her horse half holds her back. Ku feels the same impulse. His throat itches, and his neck arches back. Before he can bray, the donkeys by the wall begin to cry out, and amid the flying dust, Ku sees would-be donkey thieves tumbling to the ground. Arrows rain down from the ramparts, and mixed in with the donkeys' voices are screams of human agony.

The donkeyback soldiers retreat a hundred yards in utter confusion, mingling with the horse regiments.

Only now does Ku notice the ranks of warriors atop the battlements, their presence increasing the height of the city wall, brandishing swords to make it taller still. Ku is now able to see sounds, and above these soldiers and their weapons, he can see an even greater, more resplendent wall, formed of donkey cries, stretching up into the heavens.

Cutting the Throats

Having retreated to a safe distance, the Heile troops begin shouting at the ramparts, a hundred thousand voices raised in battle cries. Before beginning their invasion, they hope to stupefy the enemy by lobbing their death threats into the city.

The Pisha troops atop the wall are silent and motionless. Ku clearly hears another sound arresting the Heile screams on the other side of the wall—the *ding ding* of metal being beaten and knives being sharpened.

Blacksmith Alley is by the city's western gate. Two regiments stand guard, with a knife-wielding soldier stationed by each forge, supervising the making of more weapons.

At this moment, even with a hundred thousand Heile men

screaming outside, the Pisha troops remain quiet, and all that emerges from the city is the noise of metalwork, which rises into an enormous scimitar that hovers in mid-air, blade slicing towards the west, cutting the throats of all other sounds.

Bearing Word

Beyond the city, all the temples, large and small, stand empty. The Heile army has occupied the Kun pilgrimage pathway, along which Ku used to frequently ride his donkey in his younger days, his mind filled with Kun scripture in all kinds of languages, feeling like a profiteer, selling the Pisha language into Huang and Heile. Or perhaps he was like someone bearing word, passing messages between several different tongues. Now he rides a mule, neither donkey nor horse. It feels as if the Kun within these words has scattered to the winds like ash. This is the greatest change he's experienced in all his life.

Ku accompanies Karhan along the pilgrimage path, making a round of the city as Karhan decides where to attack from. In the end, he settles on the west gate. True, the east gate doesn't look as sturdy, and the wall is lower there—but charging at the western gate, his troops will have the great Heile empire behind them, its imperial force lending them strength. If they were to storm the east gate, behind them would be the Kun-worshipping desert lands, a dangerous prospect no matter how far in the distance these lands may be.

Tongues

Two Pisha men are captured and made to kneel on the ground. They say they wish to offer the Han King their lands and herds of goats.

"What language are they speaking?" asks Karhan, not waiting for Ku to interpret.

"Pishanese," Ku replies.

Karhan's face darkens.

"Cut off their tongues."

Glancing at the Tian devotees and generals beside him, Karhan asks, "What's the first thing we're going to do after we've conquered Pisha?"

"Convert them all," says Tianmen Ben.

"We'll do that the very day we take Pisha," says the Han King.

"Turn them into our slaves, make them work for us like donkeys."

Karhan smiles, a rare event. His lips have only half parted before they snap shut again, leaving him stern once more.

"I want all Pishanese-speaking tongues rotting on the ground. The only words spoken by Pisha mouths from now on shall be Heilenese."

These words cause Ku a spasm of pain, once more slicing off his Pishanese-speaking tongue.

Ku opens his mouth wide, though he is uncertain what to say or how to say it, as if his tongues in all other languages have been cut off, leaving only the Heile one, but no matter how he scours his mouth, he can't find his Heilenese tongue. In a frenzy, he stretches out his neck, a burst of stubbornness deep in his throat.

Tianmen Maisheng notices something is wrong with Ku, and realising he is about to erupt, quickly tugs at his sleeve. Ku abruptly tilts his head back, suppressing the cry rushing into his throat, so the sounds become a roar churning around his belly.

Ahnng-jee ahnng-jee swirls inside him, a wild bellow burying every other language, leaving nothing but a donkey's bray.

Donkeyman

A donkey expands inside Ku, filling his body and brain. He knew all along she was within him, and so he smiles, not refusing her, allowing her head to stretch into his, his ears to obey her commands, moving a little, then a little again, both gestures unmistakably donkeylike. He sees her watching through his eyes. Her hooves slide into his feet, her ribs replace his, the *dupp dupp* of her heart takes over from his.

All of this happens in an instant. His skin splits apart, and he sees again her bald body covered in scripture, completely contained within himself. The goatman springs into his mind, the human who lived inside a goat's body. Now he has a little donkey within him. He has become a donkeyman.

21

Taking Pisha

Vanish

THE SKY REMAINS MURKY on the ninth day of the Heile siege, obscured by clouds of swirling dirt churned up by tens of thousands of humans, horses and donkeys, refusing to disperse. In the midst of this choking dust, the army attacks, while Ku stands beside the Han King on the high platform in front of his great tent. Each time the soldiers get within a li of the gates, Pisha City abruptly vanishes, leaving nothing but dark roiling clouds, startling the Heile troops into retreat. When they get three li back, the city reappears, at which point the Han King commands another charge, only for it to vanish again. From their vantage point, Ku and the Han King can see the city right there, but to the advancing soldiers, it is gone. Flying into a rage, Karhan declares he will lead the charge himself, but when they are a li away, he and Ku both see Pisha City disappear, leaving the soldiers frozen in shock, cries stilled in their throats.

"What is happening?" says Karhan, glancing at Ku.

Ku knows this invisibility is Kun magic, though it's his first time witnessing it.

"This must surely be the city's Kun devotees casting a spell," says Tianmen Ben before Ku can speak. "Your Highness must gather the Tian devotees to counter them."

Having spent decades battling Kun devotees, the Tianmen has learnt of this tactic.

*

Tianmen Ben leads a thousand Tian devotees in white robes to gather outside the city. In neat rows, they kneel and recite Tian scripture in one voice. Ku stands alongside Karhan on the high ground behind, and all they can hear is cries of "Ah Tian, ah Tian," rolling rhythmically towards them, a low and rumbling sound like the voice of the land itself. The entire Heile army takes up the chant, "Ah Tian, ah Tian." Ku feels the ground trembling, the heavens shaking. Dirt rains down on them and the vanished city walls are called back into being: first the ramparts with their sword-wielding soldiers float above the fog, then the foundations and the moat below them are revealed.

Seeing the city reappear, the army launch their attack, and the praying Tian devotees stand too, holding up their knives and charging at the gates.

At this moment, the city vanishes again.

Chanting

Karhan glances sidelong at Ku. The Han King seldom addresses Ku directly, but these sidelong looks are Ku's cue to speak.

"Tianmen Ben is correct, the Kun devotees' chanting protects the city. We have a thousand Tian devotees here chanting scripture, but there are ten thousand Kun devotees within the city doing the same, and the Tian chanting doesn't even cross the walls before getting sent back. We may not be able to defeat the Kun devotees this way. Our chanting casts an enormous net over them, but theirs is the tall peak of a Kun tower thrusting through it. We can't keep them under cover."

"You mean our Tian can't subdue their Kun?"

Karhan gazes at the spot where Pisha City disappeared.

"Tian above all. Tian undefeated," says Ku hastily.

"Then why can't we take the city?"

"Kun scripture has been chanted in Pisha for a thousand years. The soil itself is Kun now, and so is the wind," Ku mumbles.

"Our Tian scripture will be spoken here a thousand years too," says Karhan.

Tianmen Ben, who has been standing behind them, bows to the Han King.

"If your highness grants me ten thousand Heile donkeys, I will take the city."

"Are you saying my hundred thousand soldiers are not as good as donkeys?"

"The donkeys are your subjects too, Majesty."

Karhan looks at Maisheng, sitting cross-legged on his horse, looking just as he did ten years ago when the Han King led his men into Peach Blossom Temple, eyes shut tight and still as a celestial amid the hubbub, the black jenny he was on with her eyes closed too. At this sight, Karhan's men stopped their massacre.

"Give him ten thousand donkeys," says Karhan to the official behind him.

Bray

The white-clad Tian devotees are shunted to the rear, and the troops clear a path for the donkeyback soldiers to herd ten thousand donkeys toward the city walls.

Tianmen Maisheng orders them to allow the hundreds of Pisha donkeys they've captured to mingle with the Heile herd, and immediately there is chaos: the jacks chase the jennies, then begin kicking each other. No sooner has one of them mounted a jenny when another jack will hoof him off. It is bedlam.

Ahnng-jee ahnng-jee.

Ku hears Maisheng braying as he wades into the herd. He's a good mimic, letting out one cry after another, his voice the same as when he used to chant Kun scripture back in the day.

An itch in Ku's throat, and blood surges from his thigh tendons to his neck.

Ahnng-jee ahnng-jee!

Ku cries out, the sound pulsing through his body, awakening his mule's donkey nature so she charges ahead into the herd. Attracting by his braying, the assembled donkeys turn to stare at Ku. He leaps off HeiChiu's back and screams as he sprints along, legs pumping like a donkey's, hands pawing the air like hooves. The donkeys scatter from him.

Maisheng waves at the men behind him, and a gaggle dash into the herd, all shouting *ahnng-jee*, though Ku's voice is the loudest and most resonant. Many have heard him chanting scripture at Peach Blossom Temple, and they know his voice. Ku understands that this is Hsieh braying within him, he recognises Hsieh's cry. She is running with his limbs, calling out with his voice.

Ku knows what Maisheng is trying to do. He can't mimic a bray as well as Ku can, because he doesn't have within him a little jenny named Hsieh. So Ku will play along. He is grateful that Maisheng ordered Hsieh's scripture-inscribed skin to be buried in the sand— even a dead donkey leaves behind a good hide. This was a great gesture of respect for Ku and also for Hsieh, and Ku wants to return the favour. With Hsieh's passionate cries, Ku encourages all the donkeys and humans to let their voices soar, and each of them calls out now, all the humans and all the donkeys, just like that, ten thousand donkeys braying with one voice. For Ku and the donkeys, who see sounds as shapes and colours, ten thousand bray rainbows spring from the ground, reaching over the vanished city.

Soon a chorus of braying starts up from within the city. Stirred up, the Pisha donkeys are retaliating. Now the two volleys of donkey cries clash in mid-air with a tremendous rumble, filling the sky with colours. From outside the walls, the Heile donkeys see a Tian temple connecting heaven and earth, its domed roof covering Pisha city. As for the Pisha donkeys, they see the seven hues of Kun radiance filling the heavens, and a vast Kun statue of sound sitting above the ground.

"Charge towards the braying," Karhan commands.

The ear-splitting donkey cries reveal Pisha City. The soldiers atop its battlements are visible once more, and so are their sharp arrows, flying through the air like locusts.

Whooping wildly, the Heile troops reach the city walls, their battle cries soaring above the braying. The donkeys see mud-brown human voices riding atop their own red *ahnng-jee*'s, streaking towards the city walls together, getting halfway up before falling away, leaving the brays to ascend alone, over the high walls, over the trembling clouds, into the city itself.

In an instant, the city vanishes again. The soldiers who have clambered to the top of the walls fall back down to earth, and the mounted troops halt.

"Towards the braying!"

Waving his sword, Karhan points to where the donkey cries have outlined the city, a low structure, flickering into sight like a single shoe.

The Pisha donkeys see the Heile troops attacking the city of sound they have spoken into being. In a frenzy, they cry out more, raising the buildings higher and higher, and so these foolish creatures reveal their position to the enemy.

Wife

Ku hears his own household's donkeys from the donkey-filled courtyard in the city, every one of them braying towards the city walls. His little wife Sha must be standing beneath their soaring voices. Does she imagine he might be just beyond the walls? He's been gone three years and hasn't sent her a single word in all this time. Perhaps she thinks he's dead.

Ku's heart goes soft when he thinks of his wife, and his body becomes limp, as if his flesh might melt off its bones.

An abrupt realisation: he doesn't even have the energy to miss her. Sha's face, living in his memory just a moment ago, crumbles into a patch of earth. He tries to make out her features in the dirt, but the strength to see is gone, and all he can do is stare at the grime in his heart, the large swathe of dust that has accompanied him all his life. Just as it is about to bury him, he sees it began to rise, and amid the swirling dirt, a blurry figure emerges, coming closer and closer.

Emptying

"Hsieh."

Among the tens of thousands of donkey cries, Ku can clearly hear Hsieh's voice, not a single grain of dirt in it, pure and clean. He knows the sound is coming from within his own body. He died a long time ago, but this little jenny possessed him, extending his life, her innocent gaze propping up his sagging eyelids, her stubborn temper stiffening his neck, her whole being holding up his crumbling body from within. Ku is happy to let her run and shout, to let out a cry from his throat that will drive thousands of people into a frenzy. No one will know that in the last days of his existence, a donkey lived within him, and it was her strength that allowed him to walk this final journey.

"Hsieh."

Ku doesn't actually say her name, but his lips part a little, like a smile frozen before it has fully spread. His body goes slack and falls over. The soldier next to him reaches out an arm and lifts him off the mule like cradling a child, laying him out on the ground.

"He doesn't want to see his hometown destroyed," Karhan says coldly.

As he lies on the ground, Ku feels himself emptying out. A moment ago, when he ran out sweating heavily from the donkey horde, he felt himself lighten, as if the donkey within him had left never to return. He feels himself swiftly deteriorating, the Ku who was sprinting and screaming now far away. His eyes helplessly open, he stares at the colourful brays filling the sky, and for the first time he can make out the shapes that these sounds make. Eyes wide, he wishes he could observe how resplendent his earlier braying must have been, then he thinks he sees it, and his gaze fixes on that point.

Having left Ku's body, Hsieh turns back to look sadly at her former host, slumped on the ground. She nuzzles his face, his shoulder, just as she did back in Aoba, in Guma, those many dawns on the way to Heile when she awoke after sleeping in the open and gently touched her face to Ku's as he lay dreaming.

Ku's soul opens his eyes, as if awakening from a very long sleep, and he sees himself running through a desert covered in donkey hoofprints, pursued by dark figures. He realises he has four legs that end in donkey hooves, and breaks into a full gallop.

Bearing Word

Ku dies in the same moment that Pisha City is taken, passing away from old age in the midst of this very long war. He has enjoyed seventy-one years on earth, the same as Master. Hsieh sees her death once again in his. Previously, in the rear courtyard of Peach Blossom Temple, she was smothered to death with hot wet rags and skinned afterwards. This time, her passing is in a man's heart, more silent than any temple.

In the foggy time before Ku's death, his lips stiffen and there is a gurgling in his throat, words no one can understand. None of Karhan's other interpreters can make out what he is trying to say. Karhan orders them to make a note of these sounds. He wants to know the last words of the man who spoke every language in the world.

Only Ku knows he is speaking the dead language of his hometown, the one he spoke before he was three years old. As they lay him out, his memories from that time come surging back: the peddler wrapping him in goatskin and bringing him to Heile in a cart, being sold to a donkey merchant, Master buying him along with a donkey, the journey to Pisha. He and Master spoke this dead language, known only to the inhabitants of a remote village. Then Master buried this language among so many others and Ku lost it, allowing his hometown to die through his forgetfulness. And now, these long-gone words revive in his mind, and in the gloom he hears someone say, "Speak the story of your life in your mother tongue," as if he has to make an account of himself, his final task before quitting this journey on earth. He speaks sentence after sentence, paragraph after paragraph, recounting how he was sold to a place with an unfamiliar tongue, how he learnt the languages of all these other places, hoping to someday rediscover the one from his hometown. But he never met another person who knew it. His first words to anyone from another place were in this language, but they all just shook their heads.

To start with, he still remembered the faces of his parents and siblings, but their features eventually grew blurry, and then he remembered only their names. When no one was around, he would talk to himself in the language of his village, reminding himself how he came to Pisha. But as time went on, he grew unable to understand himself as he talked over and over about his hometown's wheat and goats, repeating the names of these objects for his own memory. Then even that slipped away. When he said the word for "goat" he would hesitate. Was there really a place on earth where goats were known by this name? Recollections of his village slipped away like dreams. And now they have all come back to him. It is as if his hometown asked him to bear word to a strange place, and he's spent his entire lifetime wandering fruitlessly, never finding anywhere that could receive a message in this language, never meeting another person who could understand these words, travelling for such a long time that he lost them by the wayside. But now he has found them again, and he can speak them all for himself.

"Maybe he made up his own language," an interpreter says helplessly.

"That *gruu lruu* in his throat sounds like a donkey," says the soldier who helped him down.

"It sounds familiar to me too," the interpreter replies, "but I didn't dare think of that."

Ku's voice rises from deep within his throat to his now rigid tongue, escaping in bursts, and indeed it sounds like a faint braying.

"Perhaps he won't deign to speak to us with human language," Tianmen Ben says haughtily. "This false Tianmen. Nothing on his lips but a donkey's cries, even on the brink of death. Not even an 'Ah, Tian.' He's destined to end up in hell."

Tian Celestial Court

Even as the people surrounding his body talk about him, Ku's soul has already departed.

TuoJue realises that Ku has left behind his earthly husk, which is still producing sounds, while his spirit is gone. Riding on these faint brays, TuoJue is able to ascend. Ku's spirit has risen on his own voice, but stops in mid-air. The braying is too short, and won't reach the gates of the celestial court. Ku recalls climbing a ladder when he was a child, only to find it didn't reach the roof. As an adult, he often dreamt of ascending a tall, wobbly ladder rung after rung, reaching the top and still being short of the roof, suspended there in terror. And now he's living the dream. He sways, about to fall back to earth, when the vast land below him produces a chorus of braying, and Ku's soul sees these cries rising into the heavens like a thicket of white poplar trees, their trunks reaching up to the gates of the celestial court. All the decapitated trees are sprouting new heads, with many ghosts scaling them. Ku, too, is lofted by this dense outpouring.

TuoJue sees Ku's spirit arrive at the celestial court first, and barges ahead to stand next to him. This unfortunate man has forgotten everything about his life and doesn't recognise the double ghost who clung to Hsieh all the way to Heile, then possessed him after Hsieh's death on the way back to Pisha. They reach the gates at the same time.

Hsieh's soul is nowhere to be seen. Donkeys may not enter this place, every ghost knows this. Paradise for donkeys is down on earth.

TuoJue longs for Ku's spirit to turn and look at them, for he will finally be able to see this head and body sewn together with a strip of leather. Alas, Ku's eyes are fixed on the celestial court.

And so TuoJue looks in the same direction.

This reminds TuoJue of several years ago—the many victims of war promenading along the terraces of the celestial court, hand in hand like brothers and sisters, strolling among the luxuriant clouds. The recently deceased General Chokan is here too, and he waves at Ku. When an arrow smeared red with poison shot towards him, his soul leapt away in fright, and the soul watched as the arrow darted towards the point between the general's eyebrows. The general saw it too, but remained motionless, lips parting in a smile, as if greeting a visitor from a great distance away, horrifying the soul. In all these decades of battle, among all these waves of blades and showers of arrows, not one ever hit him, and even this fatal blow seemed slightly off centre. But the general could see it might merely graze his eyebrow, so he shifted a little, allowing it to land squarely in the middle of his forehead. In shock, the soul watched as the arrow hit its mark, the general still smiling as his huge black horse realised its owner was dead and let out a scream, and the general's soul ascended into the heavens on this cry.

Even as the general's soul is here chatting and laughing, his body back on earth has been decapitated, his head hung on a donkey hitching post by the west gate of Pisha City, where the Pisha soldiers on the city walls weep to see it, while the rest of his carcass is trampled into paste by ten thousand horses on the dry river bank. Free of his body in the celestial court, the general is as dashing as ever, and the seven or eight Heile soldiers whom he slaughtered smile as they gather around him, while General Chokan is beaming just as broadly as the moment the arrow hit him. The self who died on the shore has been flung into the river of forgetfulness, for in the celestial court, life on earth rolls away like an easily forgotten dream. He pats a Heile soldier on the back and catches a glimpse of a knife wound on his neck, a wound left by the general's blade, a decisive blow, which now he finds slightly familiar, enough to cause a tickle in his brain.

Ku looks at them with envy. Only he knows this is General Chokan, whose other half General Nurkan is at this very moment on his way to fight the Heile, wielding his sword alone, advancing on the enemy night after night. Or perhaps he's already arrived at Heile City, already charged into the dark emptiness, waving his blade through a cityful of dreams, for in that place, everyone is hiding in their own distant dreamscape and he can't find anyone he can bury his sword in. They have all forgotten his war, and now they are asleep.

General Chokan has died for him, and is now in the celestial court instead of him.

Bearing Word

Ku tries to slip through the gate to join the others, but the sentry stops him.

"Aren't you Ku, the translator with a hundred tongues?"

"I have chanted scriptures in a hundred languages praising the Tian celestial court, did you not hear me?"

"All I hear from the mortal realm are donkey cries. Human voices reach no higher than a sparrow's wings. How could your chanting make its way up here?"

"Then how did you know I was Ku the translator?"

"When you were in the world, the gate you passed through each day was the gate of the celestial court, and I was the sentry there too. You are more familiar with this place than the mortal realm. The celestial court is the hometown you forgot."

"I can't remember my hometown on earth. I want to be a translator in the celestial court."

The notion arose suddenly in Ku, the sentry can see it too.

"In the celestial court, all souls are transparent, and need no translation."

All of a sudden, Ku does not know what language to continue in, as if he has reached the end of all his languages. He opens his mouth, but only wind comes out.

The sentry appears to forget Ku, then abruptly swings around to address him.

"Go back to the world. Interpret donkey cries for humans."

"If I return, I'll still be a ghost. The tongue that spoke human words will have rotted."

"The heavens order you to bear word to humankind in the form of a bray. You've been a word bearer all your life, carrying messages from one human to another. This errand is different. You will bear the words spoken by the heavens to donkeykind, and deliver them to the humans."

"Why can't the heavens speak directly to people?"

"When the heavens pass true words to humans, people distort them. Only donkey cries keep their shape."

Ku has travelled to lands where a hundred different languages were spoken, and in all of them, the braying of donkeys needed no translation.

"Go anywhere in the world where there are humans and donkeys. Whatever the heavens needs to convey, the donkeys in that place will tell you, and you will bear their words to the people. This will be an arduous journey, even farther than bearing a donkey from Pisha to Heile."

Ku recalls how, at West Kun Temple, he asked the Great Kunmen why he was bearing a donkey to Heile, not words. The Kunmen squinted at him and said, "Treat the donkey like you would a message."

Ku didn't understand at the time, but now it is piercingly clear.

"West Kun Temple carved Kun scripture into a living donkey's hide and had you bring her to Heile. Long before that, the heavens inscribed words into her heart. Return and listen carefully to what the donkeys say—you will understand. You have a donkey within you, a young and vigorous one. She will make you run and cry out. Bring donkey words to people. The humans born in the donkey year will understand, and so will those of the mouse, rabbit, snake, pig, horse, ox, rooster, dog and tiger."

In Ku's mind, every single donkey's bray turns into words, sentence after sentence, paragraph after paragraph, entire sheaves of text piling up. As a child, he went with Master to West Kun Temple and looked up at the scrolls of Kun scripture stacked so high they reached the roof. Now, he can see donkey's voices, filling all the space between heaven and earth.

TuoJue

The great gates begin to move and creak shut, all the ghosts crammed outside disappear. Now Ku alone is left.

Through a crack between the closed gates, he glimpses the head and body who were wrongly sewn together on the battlefield at Guma, and though he didn't know that this ghost was riding on Hsieh's back to Heile, he often felt a blast of chilly air as he mounted Hsieh, and noticed how she often turned to stare at her own back, eyes dark, but he kept himself ignorant and refused to think of spirits. Then Hsieh died, and they possessed Ku instead. All these things which happened while he was alive feel as distant as a dream. He stares closely at this man's neck, but there is no trace of a scar where the strip of leather bound them together. The man stares back and waves. A pair of Heile eyes and a Pisha hand, but now they have united and are a single person.

Pisha Has Fallen

Out of nowhere, a burst of braying reaches Ku, and he realises one ear was facing Pisha. The cries of ten thousand donkeys sketch an image in his ear: Pisha City, the shape of a shoe. The sentry's ear, too, has witnessed this image countless times, and on lonely summer nights, when the moon screams high above with its round, flat mouth, moonlight spilling everywhere, donkeys hear the voice of the moon and they also cry out, so braying rises from every corner of Pisha City. They stretch their necks so their cries go straight to the heavens and don't awaken so much as a single human, a single dog, here on earth. A thicket of donkey cries, filling the sky like a flock of startled birds.

Ku turns and sees braying rising up from the ground, every single voice speaking of matters of heaven and earth.

His body is not yet cold and stiff, lying on the battlefield outside the city, and that last shred of warmth tugs at his soul. He wants to wait a moment, until his corpse is ice cold, when his spirit will be cold too, without sorrow or joy.

He knows Pisha has fallen. There is no more desolate a sound than a city being taken. Yet he hears nothing. Neither Heile nor Pisha voices, rising and falling like the dirt. All Pisha sounds have been suppressed. Human voices are nowhere to be heard. Instead, the Pisha donkeys are braying, and the Heile donkeys bray alongside them. Ten thousand Heile jacks surge into the city. They made a great effort at the crucial moment. Now the city has fallen, the donkeys enter alongside the soldiers. Humans slaughter other humans by the side of the road, they break into houses to steal valuables and women. Donkeys seek other donkeys, jacks seek jennies. Every jack on earth wishes to mount a white-bellied Pisha jenny. Heile jacks call out towards Pisha whenever they're in heat, and now they're finally here.

The Pisha jennies do not run and hide, but allow the Heile jacks to do as they wish. They know the Pisha humans have been defeated. As soon as they heard the Heile braying from outside the city walls, they understood the crucial moment was here.

The donkeys whisper to each other.

"Our offspring will be grey."

"A grey donkey is still a donkey."

"Yes, Heile people are people too, and humans can't do without donkeys."

This has been a war between humans, and the donkeys didn't play much of a part. But they were roped into the taking of Pisha. Or rather, tricked. People lured the donkeys within the city into calling out. This braying sketched the outline of the city. The donkeys had no idea. Humans may not be able to see sounds as shapes, but they can hear where a sound comes from, and the cityful of braying drew the outline of the shoe-shaped city wall for the Heile troops.

Only Heile donkeys roam the streets now. The humans are either dead or in hiding, perfectly still. Donkeys trip over the corpses in the streets. Afraid of being possessed by human ghosts, they dart around, ducking here and there. The walls, the tree trunks, the Kun towers are all full of ghosts, just waiting for a donkey to pass by. Every spirit on earth sees donkeys as a stepping stone to the heavens. A donkey's bray is more forceful than any other sound, and can serve as a ladder right up to the celestial gates. The growth of a white poplar can do the same thing, as can the smoke of cooking fires by twilight, the sudden blooming of flowers by moonlight, whirlwinds and rainbows. The chanting of Kun devotees will do the job too. Not that any Kun scripture will be chanted from now on.

Ghosts prefer not to possess humans. Their shouting and running around doesn't help anyone get to paradise. Spirits can only rely on their dreams. Humans dream of flying. In their dreams, humans can see ghosts. When they dream, people are simultaneously in heaven and in hell.

Descent

At this moment, Ku's carcass lies outside Pisha City. The shouting in the distance fades away, and as his breath stops, it is taken up by a Heile jack whose neck stretches out in a bellow. Just like that, the donkey's voice changes. Now he sounds more like Ku's impassioned scripture chanting. Ku's soul is mounted backwards on this young, strapping jack, who seems to feel something—he stops dead, and while the other humans and donkeys charge into the city, this one turns and runs the other way. Ku's spirit faces backwards, so he sees people and donkeys roaring as they charge through Pisha's city gates. The ground outside the walls empties out.

The donkey runs to the slope where Ku's body lies. Here stands a young black jenny, whom Ku recognises at once.

"Hsieh," breathes Ku's spirit.

Her eyes narrow as she gazes at the donkey's back.

The young jenny named Hsieh has been reborn. Will she remember her feelings for Ku from her past life?

The small black jenny tosses her head and gives the jack a flirtatious look, then with a wiggle of her round little rump, she begins to gallop. The jack jogs after her, until they reach a courtyard by a river in the woods, where a child is being born in the donkey pen.

"He's born in the year of the donkey. Let's call him Ku."

Ku hears someone speaking, and at the sound of his own name, he abruptly knows nothing at all, as if he is watching himself vanish, but at the same time, he understands that another life on earth is beginning.

What happens next, only the small black jenny sees and hears.

"You disappeared as soon as I turned my back, you little minx. Don't you know there's a war on? And to think you even lured a great big jack home with you," says the woman.

"Hsieh, come see, your new master's being born."

The small black jenny named Hsieh obediently trots over and sticks her head into the donkey pen. A glistening wet baby is howling in his mother's bosom.

Nnnggg wahh nnnggg wahh.

His wailing makes the jack cry out.

Ahnng-jee ahnng-jee.

Hsieh brays too.

The donkeys see their cries as a rainbow rising into the air. Hsieh squints as she stares upward. The little boy named Ku stops crying too. Rapt, he gazes up at the heavens.